Connie Monk grew up in Reading and, following her marriage, lived in the Thames Valley area until 1974, when she moved to Ringwood in Hampshire. After she and her husband retired to Shaldon in Devon she began to write and her first novel *Season of Change* was published in 1984. She has since written over fifteen novels including *The Sands of Time*, *The Running Tide*, *Beyond Downing Wood*, *Tomorrow's Memories*, *The Apple Orchards* and *Family Reunions*. Two of her books, *Jessica* and *A Field of Bright Laughter*, were nominated for the Romantic Novel of the Year Award.

Water's Edge

Connie Monk

PIATKUS

For more information on
other books published by
Piatkus, visit our website
at www.piatkus.co.uk

First published in Great Britain in 1998 by
Judy Piatkus (Publishers) Ltd of
5 Windmill Street, London W1T 2JA
email: info@piatkus.co.uk

First paperback edition 1998
Reprinted 2000

*A catalogue record for this book is available
from the British Library*

ISBN 0 7499 3064 0

Set in Times by
Action Typesetting Ltd, Gloucester

Printed and bound in Great Britain by
Cox & Wyman Ltd, Reading, Berkshire

Chapter One

'Here, Horace! Fetch!' Polly hurled the length of stick into the water. With a bark of excitement her black and white terrier was after it, following the well-trod path made by the cattle, one or two of whom ambled slowly across the meadow towards the river as if they had a duty to oversee what went on at their drinking point.

The stick retrieved, Horace shook himself then barked for more, his tail aquiver with excitement. This time Polly threw it in the other direction; a run across the grass would help dry him before they went home. Or would it? She had taken care to keep the hem of her skirt raised from the wet ground, but there was no way of avoiding her boots getting caked with mud. Oh well, mud never hurt anyone. After the violent thunderstorm that had heralded the day the world smelt fresh and pure, it was far too lovely an afternoon to worry about trifles like dirty boots. Horace hared back to her, stick in mouth, ears cocked in hopeful anticipation. His mind was fixed on the game; hers not entirely. How could it be when at home there was a buzz of preparation for the evening ahead? The furniture had been shifted from the large square hall and put into her father's study so that there would be enough room for dancing, the rugs had been taken away and the flagstone floor cleaned and covered with old newspapers so that nothing should mar it. The pages of the papers told of Disraeli being toppled and Gladstone put in his place – as if any of that mattered when all hands were busy getting ready for the party. The musicians were coming out from Reading – a pianist, a cellist and a violinist. Often her parents had dinner parties, but tonight was something different; tonight was a celebration of her father's fiftieth birthday.

Polly looked at her fob watch then took the stick Horace offered, a stick by now the worse for wear, chewed, river soaked and mud coated.

'Oh, all right, just once more then,' she answered his silent message, 'but this is the last. Understand?'

If Horace understood he was determined not to give up hope. His eyes first on the stick, then on the river, then back to the stick, a woof that refused to be held back. Polly laughed and held the stick high, ready to fling it. 'Just this once. Then, home. Ready? Swim for it!'

Even before the stick landed halfway across the width of the Thames, Horace had raced into the water and struck out after it. A barge was approaching, travelling from further upstream; nothing unusual in the sight, Polly paid no attention to it. Only as it drew closer was she conscious that the bargee was watching her intently. Normally she would have watched the boat pass down the river, idly noticing its cargo, perhaps wondering whether it was going all the way to London. The man's stare put her at a disadvantage, she wouldn't look his way. The boat drew level with her in the same moment that Horace reached the cattle-drinking bay, the stick firmly in his mouth, then bounded back to where she waited.

That was to have been the final throw. Yet before she could stop herself she picked up the stick and hurled it in the direction of the passing barge. Pretending to watch Horace, she was able to steal a glance at the man who stood in the bow of the boat. Apparently he was handling the craft alone, aiding the single sail with his easy and powerful use of a pole. His actions had a perfect rhythm, he moved as though he were tireless. But it was more than that that attracted Polly. She turned away, stooped in the pretence of adjusting the lacing on her boot, suddenly sure that he'd not been fooled into thinking she was watching the dog.

There was a limit to how long the pretence of retying a lace could take. 'Come on, boy. Home, boy,' she shouted as she stood up.

One hand gripping the pole, the bargee gave her an exaggerated bow, his eyes never leaving her, eyes that she was sure were twinkling with laughter. Ignoring him she started back along the towpath towards home, leaving Horace and stick to catch up with her. The barge moved ahead of them. Again holding the pole just with his right hand, the man raised his left to her in silent salute. The action brought her firmly back to earth. How dare he, a common bargee!

A few minutes later Elvira Seagrove watched from her bedroom window as her daughter climbed the stile that led from the towpath into the far end of their garden while Horace wriggled under it, then together they ran up the sloping lawn towards the house.

'Just look at you!' she called, 'I don't know who's in a worse state, you or that dog.'

'It's only top dirt,' Polly laughed. 'I thought you were resting Mother, ready for this evening.'

'I am. Come up and talk to me, Polly.'

'Give me two minutes to shed my boots and rub Horace down.'

A minute ago Elvira had been annoyed by the sight of her dishevelled daughter, but her irritation melted at Polly's quick smile and cheerful reply.

'I'm so pleased the Vaughans are coming this evening. When Matilda told me they were to spend upwards of a month at their place in Dorset I was afraid they would be away. I dare say Christopher persuaded them not to go so soon.' Even though Elvira divided her attention between admiring her reflection in the full-length mirror on her wardrobe and furtively watching Polly's reaction to her remark, her tone made the hidden meaning obvious. The girl ought to be looking for a husband, and who more suitable than Christopher Vaughan? 'And we know why they were so eager to accept the invitation, don't we?' she added archly.

'To celebrate Pappy's half century, I imagine, the same as everyone else. I just looked into the kitchen after I'd dried Horace off. There's a feast fit for a king underway.'

'Never mind the feast, you're just running away from the point I made. I can't think what's the matter with you, Polly. There isn't a prettier girl in the district.' She said it with a

3

certain pride for, apart from the colour of her hair, to look at Polly was like seeing herself at that age. 'And there isn't another amongst them with the money spent on her wardrobe that goes on yours. You could grace any circle of society.' She spoke no more than the truth. Even after an hour playing with Horace in the waterside meadow the picture Polly made was enchanting in a poplin day dress of apple green, the wide brim of her straw hat trimmed with flowers.

'Mother, I know how generous you and Pappy are. I love clothes. You do too, so you can understand that. But I don't love them just as bait so that I can hook a man to give me a comfortable and useless life.'

'Victor Maidment was keen enough to pay court to you – and a good catch he would be for any girl. All right, he may not be anything to look at, but he's well meaning – and well heeled – he's the eldest son, you would have found yourself mistress of a fine household one of these days. But you brushed him off with no more thought than if he'd been – oh, I don't know who – that simpleton who calls to sharpen the knives. And now you've lost him to Violet Gregory, a young woman who will never grace his home as you would.'

'I'm not needing a home. And anyway you're a fine one to talk.' Polly's laugh held genuine affection as she looked at the worried pucker on her mother's pretty face. 'You were years older than I am when you met Pappy.'

'I do wish you wouldn't give your father that silly name. I was twenty-six when I met him and we were wed within a few months. You forget, my life had been very different from yours. Until poor Mama died, what chance had I to go to parties, meet eligible young men? I was marooned in the house, in poor health myself and with an invalid and widowed mother.'

'Look upon it as fate. If you'd rushed off and married some so-called suitable swain – perhaps with boils on his neck like poor scraggy Victor – you wouldn't have been free for Pappy.'

Elvira Seagrove sank gracefully onto the stool in front of her dressing table, her delicate white hand to her brow as she bent forward.

'Mother? Are you all right?'

'Pass me my smelling salts. Oh dear, these arguments always

upset me so.' She sniffed at the small bottle Polly had uncapped and put into her hand. 'I'll lie down for a few moments, I mustn't fail your father this evening by having one of my heads. Oh Polly, how I envy you your vigour. It's something I've never known. You get it from your father. And I'm thankful you do.'

'I'll pull down the blind for a while, you'll rest better without the sunlight. And Mother, I'll be agreeable to the Vaughans. I'll dance with spotty Victor Maidment if he invites me to. You'll see, the evening will be wonderful, a birthday to remember.'

'If we could look in at Burtonfield Court at this moment I'm sure Christopher Vaughan is preparing himself for the evening with such hope. Be kind to him Polly.'

'Try and take a nap, Mother. I'm going to see if there's anything I can do to help them downstairs – poor Emmie was getting in a state about all the flowers still to be arranged. I do love a party, don't you?' She knew it would please her mother to hear her say it. It was true, she'd always loved the excitement of parties; but they weren't nearly the fun now that they used to be when she was a child. It was the same for all her unmarried contemporaries, mothers looking on, silently scheming.

She was determined not to let anything spoil the evening. She'd dance every dance – sometimes with Victor, sometimes with Christopher, sometimes with Hugh Davies who managed her father's boat-building business and was therefore not on her mother's list of eligibles, she'd dance with young and old alike.

Elvira watched the door close behind her only child, not for the first time frustrated by her own inability to coerce her along the lines she was sure she should be going. Nearly twenty years old, surely the prettiest girl in the county social set but with no more interest in finding a husband than she had in going to the moon. Marriage ... why was it she was so keen to wish it onto Polly? The girl was old enough to be mistress of her own home. Yes, but was a wife really mistress of anything? She was a hostess, on show to their acquaintances; but she was a possession – though in her own case she could never honestly complain that Stanley hadn't treated her as his most treasured possession. But there was the other side to marriage, the times when she had no way of avoiding his attention. Polly was forgotten, and the smelling salts too. She had looked forward so much to this birthday celebration, there would be eighteen of them at the dinner table and Elvira was determined that not one – no, not even Polly who was less than half her age – would be able to hold a candle to her. She imagined herself in the pale violet gown designed at the House of Duprés especially for this evening, the belle of the ball as they waltzed and military two-stepped to the strains of the hired trio. Elvira loved to dance, she loved to be warmed by admiring glances – but the inevitable end to the evening would be the departure of the guests, leaving them exhilarated by the excitement. She shrunk from the intimate side of marriage. In the beginning she hadn't complained, she'd seen it as her duty to give Stanley a child – 'a son' was what she'd told herself. But fate had decreed it should be a daughter, Polly. The doctor had warned Stanley that she needed time to build her strength, a loophole that she had clung to. Stanley had been careful with her and when she detected that he'd looked outside marriage for his fun she had been thankful.

Lying on the satin counterpane she thought back to the conversation she'd just had with Polly. Why was she trying to push her towards marriage? The girl had a good home here, one day everything they had would be hers, so why should she give up her individuality to become the chattel and bedmate of some young admirer? For herself all Elvira asked of life was a comfortable home, money enough occasionally to take a trip to London to the House of Duprés so that she could see Madame Doretta's latest materials and be guided into clothes to flatter her natural good looks; that and a smattering of women friends with whom she could while away her hours as they chatted or perhaps stitched together. Household affairs interested her, she enjoyed organizing the smooth running of a home. She loved Stanley dearly, of course she did, he was her husband and she saw herself always as a good wife; even to herself she wouldn't admit her irritation at his noisy voice and hearty laugh, his beastly cigars, his often whisky-laden breath. More than those things – and here there was no running away from the truth – she cringed from his physical demands that were sometimes unavoidable, intruding on the private knowledge of her body. Was it to ensure that Polly's life should be no better that she was intent on pushing her along the welltrod path?

Small chance of pushing Polly in any direction she didn't want to go!

There was no hitch to mar the evening. Elvira knew there wasn't another woman to equal her – unless she took Polly into the equation, which she didn't. She felt nothing but satisfaction as she watched the sons of the county vying with each other to put their names on her daughter's programme: Victor Maidment, Christopher Vaughan, Henry Pottinger whose family owned the brick kiln, there wasn't one who wasn't drawn to her. All of them were families to be reckoned with but neither breeding nor wealth gave a woman that natural flair. Natural? Or did she and Polly owe it to Madame Doretta? Of all the assembly, only *they* favoured gowns where the material of the skirt was raised high to the bustle then draped to the ground in cascading layers, the side exposing an accordion pleated underskirt. No flounces in the front, nothing to hide behind if one's figure wasn't perfect. Elvira smiled at the image of portly Muriel Maidment in such a style. Not that she would be, not for a few years yet. If the Seagrove women were ahead of fashion, the rest of the county were slow in following.

With satisfaction Elvira watched Henry Pottinger lead Polly onto the flagstone floor as the trio struck up a Viennese waltz. But she gave no hint where her thoughts were straying; Elvira was the perfect hostess.

The musicians seemed tireless, and the dancer too. Stanley's second half-century was starting well. He danced with every one of the visiting ladies before he allowed himself to claim Elvira as his partner.

'I must be the proudest man living,' he whispered to her as at last, duty done, he led her into the hall to the opening strains of a gavotte. She felt even more beautiful, her fingers gripped his to tell him that she understood. She was having such a lovely time. Enjoy the moment, she told herself, see what a handsome couple we make. But it doesn't seem fair that Stanley's hair is still that rich auburn, no hint of it changing, yet mine that used to be so blond has faded. He's the proudest man here, her pretty face wore a smile as she stored his words away, she tripped lightly into the dance.

Polly hung her gown in her closet, then took off her numerous layers of petticoat, her bustle and the tightly laced corset that pushed her bust high and made her naturally slim waist appear even tinier. After an evening of music and dancing she was wide awake. Wearing only chemise and drawers she leant far out of the window, the mysterious summery scent of the garden adding to her restlessness. How still everything was … imagine the feeling of the cool water … imagine the special nighttime smell of the river … Imagination got the better of her.

She exchanged her drawers for the calf-length trousers of her dark-blue bathing costume, covered by a matching short skirt; then off came the chemise and in its place the costume top. Lastly she pushed her long hair under a frilly rubber hat. If she went barefoot no one would hear her. Then she remembered Horace; he'd love to come too. But his barks of excitement and thanks would wake everyone and, in any case, she'd have to turn up the gaslight to see to dry him afterwards. No, she'd go out of the front door and leave it open, that way he wouldn't hear her.

Five minutes later, immersed in the cool water of the Thames, she thought back to the evening with a feeling of relief that she was free. She had tried to laugh off her mother's outspoken hope that she might encourage Christopher Vaughan – but laughing about it had become increasingly difficult recently as his friendship had subtly changed. With smooth, even strokes Polly swam, letting herself indulge in a heady sense of freedom.

Tonight Christopher had proposed marriage, he'd wanted her consent that he should speak to her father asking for her hand, he'd even started to set out to her his prospects for his future – until she'd stopped him! She'd been firm, she had to be sure he was left with no loophole of hope. The Vaughans had been family friends for years, she wished she hadn't had to hurt him. Or had she really hurt him? Without realising it, was he being pushed by his family just as she was by hers, or at any rate by her mother? He'd said he loved her – but that was nonsense. With all the faith of youth she was sure that love, when it happened, would come with a shattering certainty, it would push everything else into insignificance. Christopher had had no more experience of it than she had herself. She rolled onto her back, gazing up into the starless night sky as she gently propelled herself through the water, thankful that she had escaped.

Swimming came as naturally to Polly as walking; the time her father had taught her was beyond recall; and familiar as she was with the river, she knew even in the dark where there grew patches of weed that were to be avoided. By nature she wasn't given to depression, but no life runs completely smoothly and it had always been here that she'd come to lick her wounds in solitude when anything had gone wrong. Tonight, though, nothing had. She'd probably done Christopher as big a favour as she had herself.

The last echo of the evening was overtaken by another. A barge, the strong steady motion as the bargee raised the pole then plunged it into the water pushing the boat forward, the rhythm of his movements never faltering even when he'd made her that exaggerated bow. She turned from her back and struck out in the direction of the familiar river bank, silently laughing as she pictured him. What cheek! On the social scale, a bargee came very near the bottom. The man had been as handsome as a gypsy king, he'd been outside the constrictions of behaviour demanded by refined society. It didn't matter that she would never see him again, he belonged to the passing river traffic; the image he left was clear and bright, to see him again could only spoil it.

Polly couldn't pinpoint exactly when the atmosphere changed at Water's Edge. Not for the first time she felt a tension between her parents but she expected it would soon clear just as it always had in the past. This time, though, things were different. When she learnt that on the evening of the party, before speaking to her, Christopher had hinted at his intention to her parents, she believed she was the cause of her mother's ill-used attitude. She'd been brought up to look on Elvira as delicate, often needing to spend a day or two in bed with the blind pulled down, although if Polly had suggested they ought to send for Dr Wright the idea had been pooh-poohed.

'It's nothing a doctor can cure,' Elvira answered bravely. 'You don't know how lucky you are, Polly, you sail through without so much as a headache. I never did. I've looked forward to the change of life, escape from the pains. But I'm dizzy, I can't look at food ... Men! If only they could have a taste of what some of we poor women have to suffer.'

After that Polly accepted her mother's occasional indispositions. In truth she felt sorrier for her ever cheerful father who seemed to be looked on as the villain of the piece.

It was a few weeks after the party and the fifth morning that Elvira hadn't appeared at the breakfast table.

'Pappy, I've been thinking,' there was something in Polly's tone that made Stanley look up from his assumed interest in the morning paper and give her his full attention.

'About your mother?'

'No. About me.' Polly had long given up worrying about her mother's health. It was her secret opinion – and one that she never entirely let herself face up to – that Elvira would have been a good deal fitter if she'd made more effort. 'About me and about Seagrove's. Pappy I don't do anything useful, at the end of each day I feel I've accomplished nothing. No, don't stop me, let me tell you what I want.'

Willingly Stanley let himself be beguiled by his pretty daughter's earnestness.

'Accomplished nothing! That's nonsense,' he smiled affectionately. 'You're never short of invitations —'

'To go out and play! That's all any of them do, Pappy. I want to be useful. I want to help you at the boatyard.'

At that Stanley laughed outright. What a dear child she still was, so much energy and enthusiasm and nowhere to channel it!

'Building boats is man's work, Poppet.' He saw the way Polly reacted to the old childhood name. He spoke to her with loving tolerance but she could see that he wasn't seriously considering her suggestion.

'I'm not stupid, you know. There's more to running the business than actually building the boats. When did *you* ever plug the seams of a new boat with oakum?' She watched him carefully to see the effect of her words. 'When did you ever coat the sides of the hull with tar or fit the gunwales of a barge with cloths so that it could protect its cargo or steam the wood of —'

'Hey, hey,' Stanley's disbelief turned to a hoot of laughter, 'and where, young lady, did you get all your knowledge?'

'I can read. There are dozens of books in your study. Pappy, I've taught myself a lot – well, I've tried to, but book learning is only a start. Anyway, you're throwing me off course. What I was saying – about you – *you've* never worked with the men in the boatyard and you've always found plenty to do. So could I. Let's give it a try. Wouldn't you like it if I were to go off with you in the mornings? I bet you would.' She had been able to work Stanley round her little finger since she'd first held up her arms for him to pick her up.

'It would upset your mother, you realize that? Young ladies don't dabble in the world of business. They only work at all out of necessity and then their work is domestic.'

But Polly knew he was only voicing her mother's views, he was almost won over.

'And this is a necessity, for *me* it truly is. I'm not cut out for crocheting edgings for my petticoats or joining in the empty chatter when visitors call for tea.'

He didn't answer immediately, the conversation hung between them as she waited.

'Call me a coward if you like,' he said at last, and she knew she'd won by the twinkle in his light-brown eyes, 'but you can be the one to tell your mother'.

'Now? Can I come with you today?'

'Get your hat on. But promise me one thing – tell your mother that you're riding in with me. Just that, no more. When you've had a day of it you may have had enough.'

She stood up with all the spring of a Jack-in-the-Box.

'You won't regret it, Pappy. Anyway, it's right that I learn the business. I'm so glad you do what you do, I love boats. Imagine if you had a pie factory or made shoes! But building boats is something really worthwhile.'

'If you were a hungry vagrant you'd have more interest in a pie factory,' he laughed as she swooped down and kissed the crown of his fiery auburn hair as she passed behind his chair. 'Off you go and tell your mother you're having a day in town

11

or somewhere she won't worry about. Promise me, nothing about the yard.'

When Polly presented herself in her mother's bedroom to say goodbye Elvira showed no interest in where she was going, it seemed a waste of a lie but she'd given her father her word. If she'd been less wrapped up in her own affairs she might have noticed the tear-reddened eyes but the blind was pulled down against the light and her thoughts rushing ahead to meet the day.

For Polly it was a day that opened the door to a wider world. Nature had been generous to her, she had inherited Elvira's delicate good looks and Stanley's *joie de vivre* (and his dark auburn hair). Small wonder that her parents had always delighted in indulging her, she was a living symbol of the happy marriage they presented to their friends. As a child there had been music lessons, dancing lessons, her own pony to ride, her own skates the winter when the Thames had frozen from bank to bank, and as she'd grown up a wardrobe of House of Duprés garments designed especially for her. She had lacked for nothing – nothing that could fit into the narrow, sheltered existence of young women of her station in a generation when the one aim in life was expected to be the making of a good matrimonial match, so perpetuating the system.

That summer morning, sitting by her father's side as he drove the pony and trap the two miles that divided Water's Edge from Seagrove's Boatyard, she felt like a young butterfly that had burst free from its chrysalis case. And, like it, for her there could be no turning back. Arriving at the yard the pony and trap were handed over to a lad so young he looked as though he should still have been in the classroom.

Hugh Davies was in the outer office as she and her father passed through on their way to Stanley's private sanctum.

'See who I've brought with me, Hugh. She assures me the old firm will be the better for her presence.'

'Not yet it won't,' Polly cut in, 'I hardly know a thing. But I mean to learn. You'll help me won't you Mr Davies?' She'd known him since childhood. A man about her father's age, to her he had always been 'Mr Davies'.

'My dealings are all with the yard, Miss Polly. It's Mr Seagrove who can teach you the things you want to know –

ordering the timber and such, seeing folk pay their bills. The workshop's a dusty place, wood dust, steam, pitch —'

'The workshop's what I want to understand. I've read lots, but I want to see.'

'A real Seagrove,' boomed Stanley, pride in his daughter in his words and expression. 'Eh, what do you say, Hugh?'

Hugh Davies smiled his agreement, keeping his thoughts to himself. Richard Seagrove, Stanley's elder brother, had been a boat builder through and through, it was he who had drawn up the plans they still worked to in the yard. This one, Stanley, was a generous easy-going master, but give him a blank sheet and a slide rule and he'd be lost. In Hugh's opinion, that the old firm kept going owed precious little to Stanley Seagrove; more likely it was still coasting along on the reputation made for it in his brother's day. We were asked to believe the Lord knew what he was up to, but what could He have been thinking about to take Richard off so suddenly in the prime of life and let everything he'd worked for be passed to 'young Mr Stanley'? Not so young now, but eighteen years ago when Richard had died that's the way the men had all thought of him. And what about Miss Polly here? Pretty as a picture and always with a smile, but whoever heard of a young lady, all dressed up so fancy, wanting to poke her nose into the hard graft in the yard?

Like Hugh, the men expected her interest to be a nine-day wonder – nine days or less! But they soon realized they were wrong.

Prepared for her mother to present fierce opposition, Polly was ready for a battle that never materialized. Elvira was preoccupied with troubles that left no room for anything beyond.

'I've some business to see to in town,' Stanley told Polly a week or so later. 'You can take the trap home. I'll find a hire cab to bring me when I'm ready.'

'Can't I come with you?' Already she saw herself as part of the firm, if he had an order to secure or a debt to collect there was no reason why she couldn't be there.

'No, no, you just take yourself home. Your mother will be anxious if we're both late.' He hesitated, looked as if he were about to say something then changed his mind.

'Pappy, she isn't a bit well is she?' That should be his cue, if what he'd almost confided had been about her mother.

'Why don't you surprise her, get home early, spend a while with her. See if you can lead her to talk.' Still he seemed on the verge of saying more but, instead, ended with a lame 'Try and cheer her up'.

Elvira had been pale and tight-lipped for days. Days? Weeks more likely. She'd refused to see a doctor, just as she'd refused to discuss what Polly assumed she, like most women of her time, considered private.

Polly forced a smile and promised to do her best, even though her heart sank at the prospect. When her mother assumed this withdrawn air of martyrdom, what chance would there be of cheering her?

'I'll write to Merchant & Dill before I go, shall I? Then Mr Davies will put it in the pillar box on his way home.'

'Merchant & Dill?,' Stanley repeated vaguely, his mind somewhere else. 'The millers?' He looked at her blankly, then, 'Ah yes, I remember, we're repairing a barge for them.'

That was Polly's first stab of disappointment in her father. During the week she had been surprised that he never went into the workshop overseeing what went on; then she'd told herself it was because he liked the men to know he had complete trust in them. But that was no excuse for not remembering what jobs had been taken in.

'It went back on the water yesterday. Mr Davies says he's satisfied with the replacement elm they've put in the bottom and Merchant & Dill can send someone to take it. So I'll write and tell them, shall I?'

'Good idea, Poppet.'

'Did you quote them a price? Shall I enclose a bill?'

'Good idea. You'd better have a word with Davies, he'll give you the quantity of elm used and the men's time.' He took out his pocket watch and checked the time. 'I think I'll be off, one or two things I have to do. Nice to have such an efficient helper,' he beamed his pride in her. 'Don't hang around here long, there's nothing the men can't see to.'

She did as he said, finding Hugh Davies able to tell her straight away all she needed to know. Although she tried not to let herself acknowledge it, there was no hiding from the truth that he knew far more about what work was going on than her father did. Of course he does, she told herself, he's the manager ... but the feeling of disappointment in her lifelong hero remained.

Arriving home she found Elvira lying in the hammock, despite the heat of the day a light rug over her legs.

'Pappy's going to be late home, he had a business visit to make this evening,' Polly called as she hurried across the lawn to join her. She heard her voice as strident, too full of rude good health.

'I'm sure he didn't tell you where?'

'Well, no, he didn't.' Then with a broad smile as she remembered her promise to cheer her mother up, 'But then I didn't think to ask him. It's been a gorgeous afternoon for you out here in the garden. Are you feeling better?'

She wasn't prepared for Elvira's blue eyes to fill with tears.

'How can I be better? Polly, I sent Emmie to Dr Wright with a note asking him to call.'

'I'm glad. But, Mother, if you'd said he was coming I would have stayed here with you. What did he tell you? Has he given you some medicine?'

'What did he tell me? What I knew in my heart already. There's no medicine for what ails *me*.'

Polly stood close to the hammock, she gripped one of Elvira's thin, pale hands in her own that was tanned from hours of summer sunshine, the contrast sending a surge of affection through her.

'But there must be something. We'll get another doctor.'

'I tell you, *no*. I'll be the hub of gossip all over the county. A laughing stock. And what does he care?'

'Dr Wright? Mother, I don't understand —'

'Not the doctor, silly. Stanley! Never get married, Polly. Keep your freedom and your independence.' She was crying now, her face towards Polly as though she rejoiced in her tears. 'Once you marry all your rights have gone – your right to refuse him even though —' Anger and self-pity drove her on, in a more rational moment she would never have spoken like it to her closest contemporary let alone to her daughter. 'He's always known I find it repugnant – hateful – submitting myself

15

to him as if I were one of the loose women he takes such pleasure in.'

'Don't, Mother. You're not feeling well, that's why you're upset.'

It was a wonder the hammock didn't throw Elvira to the grass, she sat up with such sudden force.

'I do mean it. And it's time you knew and understood. Instead you put him on a pedestal, he can do no wrong. Why couldn't he have been content with his lady friends? That's where he is now, you know. Business in town! He must take me for a fool.'

'He loves you Mother, you know he does.'

Polly was surprised to realise that what her mother said didn't come as a shock. How long had she suspected that her father's frequent evenings out had nothing to do with business? Perhaps she hadn't actually imagined him with another woman, but she understood him so well that she recognised his need for action, fun and, she saw now, his need for a love he couldn't find in his marriage. She was being unjust, she told herself, her sympathy ought to be with her mother; but sympathy has a will of its own, it had nothing to do with rights and wrongs.

'Love!' Elvira scoffed as she mopped her face with a lacy handkerchief. 'He's proud to show me off, he's proud that I grace his home when our friends come. If he loved me he'd give me space.'

Polly was out of her depth.

'Let's go indoors Mother, wash you face and make yourself pretty again. And of course he loves you and worries about you too. Why do you think I'm home so early? Because he said you were depressed. I'm here as a cheerer-upper,' she hoped her smile didn't look as forced as it felt. 'You'll feel better once you've cried. Isn't that what you always used to tell me when I hurt myself, remember?'

'Crying can't help me, if it could I would have been well weeks ago. Don't you understand even now what's the matter with me? He's made me pregnant. You'll be twenty years old when I'm brought to bed with my second child. Now try telling me I shan't be a laughing stock. Forty-eight years old. I'd thought I was in the change of life and I rejoiced for it, I thought at least that fear would be taken from me. But it wasn't that at all. I'll be the butt of all our friends' private jokes. Me but not *him*, oh no, he'll preen himself, be looked on as a fine fellow. It'll kill me. I've warned him all these years that another child would finish me. I just wish I could end it all now.'

'Mother, don't say that. Please don't let it be a sad thing.' A wave of tenderness filled Polly, and stooping over the hammock she gathered Elvira's frail body into her arms. 'Of course Pappy will be proud, proud of you, proud of himself, proud of the new baby – even of me because we are all part of the family. Laugh at you? Of course no one will. More likely they'll look at you and Pappy and envy you that you still have proper love.' She knew she was going way beyond the bounds her mother would have allowed in normal circumstances, but the two of them were wrapped in a moment of closeness that had nothing to do with age or time. 'That night at his birthday party, it was as if you were a different generation from all the others, so beautiful. That's true and you know it. Poor plain Mrs Vaughan, plump matronly Mrs Maidment – and all the rest of them. They won't find themselves pregnant again you may be sure, not because their husbands love them more than yours does you, but because – well, if you were a man you'd take ''no'' for an answer from any of that lot – probably be glad to —' This time her laugh bubbled up from the depth, it wouldn't be suppressed.

'Oh Polly, you shouldn't say such things.' But Elvira laughed through her tears. It was an angle she hadn't considered. In that moment they were close.

Polly's feelings were a confusion of compassion for her mother, compassion too for the baby who so patently wasn't planned or wanted, and excitement at the thought of the unknown addition to the household. Then her father, how did he fit into the equation? Listening to Elvira's unusually honest outburst she had felt angry with him, not because of the coming child but because she had suddenly understood how for years he had had another life away from their home. Anger at his selfishness was immediately swamped by disappointment as he toppled from the pedestal in her heart, then almost immediately a rush of something akin to protective tenderness for him. From as far back as her memory stretched he had never

17

altered in his love for *her*, he wasn't a fickle man. But how could she blame him if he'd looked outside for a love he was denied in his marriage. At nineteen, Polly felt wiser than her parents, that mixed with sadness for both of them. Hope pushed to the fore, it seldom failed her for long. During the months they waited for the baby surely her father would show pride and tenderness.

With the passing of the weeks it seemed she was right. Her only disappointment was that when Elvira said how long and lonely her days were, Stanley readily – almost eagerly – decreed that Polly would be better occupied staying at home with her than accompanying him each day.

Again Polly's feelings were torn: relief that her parents appeared to be pulling in the same direction and disappointment at the prospect of her own future. She was beginning to feel useful at the boatyard; she sent out orders for timber, oakum, sailcloth, she checked deliveries, she spent hours in the yard where the men were always friendly and helped her understand their craft. Now all that had to finish.

Disappointment was tinged with resentment. With the first chill of autumn Elvira decided to have the fire in her bedroom lit each morning, her room became for her a haven of peace. She rose late and retreated back to it to rest each afternoon.

'I'm no company for Polly,' she said to Stanley one evening. 'I'm too tired for a lot of chatter. She might just as well go off with you each morning, I'm sure she'd rather do that than waste her time here.'

'I'll not hear of it,' Stanley answered almost before she finished speaking, cutting off Polly's escape.

'I'm no company,' Elvira repeated, her eyes swimming with sudden tears. 'I can't expect you to understand, not either of you. So tired ... and it'll get worse. Just look at me!' She gave up the battle and let the tears roll down her pale cheeks.

'My dear, you look lovely,' he answered, but if it was clear to Polly that his mind was far away, Elvira must have realized it too.

'Run upstairs and see if my fire needs mending, Polly. Bed is the only place to find any comfort. Comfort, did I say? I've forgotten what it means.'

18

'That's right, you get an early night. I have work to attend to. I'll try not to wake you.'

Elvira held her face for his kiss.

'I'll say goodnight then. I'm sorry I'm so feeble. Come to bed quietly won't you.'

'Of course.' His answer appeared to satisfy Elvira. So eager to get back to the warmth and privacy of her room, she was in no mood to look for undercurrents. Polly supposed it was anxiety for her mother that had made him so quiet lately, all the old happy-go-lucky sparkle dimmed.

She chose small lumps of coal from the brass scuttle in the bedroom, they would soon burn into bright flames. Then, the spark guard in place, she kissed her mother good night and ran back down the stairs. The suggestion that she should start going to the boatyard again couldn't be allowed to pass, she had always been able to wheedle her father into giving her what she wanted. And so she would over this.

He'd said he had work to do so she made straight for his study. Wasn't this an ideal opportunity for her to show how much more useful she would be at the yard than she was at home with nothing better to do than take Horace for walks?

'I've come to help you, Pappy. You know, Mother's right in what she says. I never sit and talk to her, she always sends me away and says she rests better on her own. If I were with you in the office I could save you lots of the paper work.'

'No, no. I'm not allowing it.' He frowned, he was agitated, something about him was different. A cold finger of fear touched Polly, even though it held no reason.

'Well, at least I can help you this evening. I'd like to, truly.'

He refilled his glass from the whisky decanter he'd brought through and put on his desk. She saw his hand was unsteady.

'She'll be all right, Pappy. You'll see, a few more months and the baby will be here. We'll all have forgotten how difficult she found the waiting.'

'What?' He looked at her as though she'd spoken in a foreign language. 'Oh yes, yes, of course.' He gulped his whisky. She'd never seen him drink it like that.

'Is there something else? Let me help, Pappy. Is it something wrong with you? I know you don't want to worry Mother, not just now, but surely you can talk to me.' She moved round the desk to stand beside him, her arm round his shoulder. In that moment he was right back on his high pedestal, the person she'd always loved above all else.

But she was unprepared.

Chapter Two

'Has something gone wrong at the yard? Is there trouble with one of the men?'

'No, no.' He brushed the suggestion aside.

'If it's not Mother and it's not the yard – Pappy, it's not *you*?' This time there was reason behind the cold stab of fear. She was a child again; he mustn't guess how frightened she was.

Her attempt to sound strong and ready to share his burden, whatever it might be, didn't fool Stanley and her anxiety was his undoing. With elbows on the desk he leant forward, shielding his face with his hands. He felt the hand on his shoulder tighten its grip.

'Don't you trust me enough to tell me?'

'You know I trust you. Oh Poll, Poll, I'm in a hell of a mess. Your mother mustn't know – promise me you'll keep it from your mother.'

'Of course I will. If we share it, it won't seem so bad.'

But she knew by the way he shook his head this was the kind of trouble that couldn't be halved by sharing. He was quiet for so long, not a sound except for his breathing, each breath taken in a gasp and expelled in something bordering on a sigh. Then he slumped back in his chair reaching to hold her hand as it rested on his shoulder.

'Draw up a chair, over there where I can see you. Need to see you, mustn't hide behind me. Want to look at you when I tell you.'

He spoke with a slur, whether from emotion or whisky. Either way she didn't want to cross him, it would take so little to make him retreat into silence. Nothing could possibly be so bad that between them they couldn't think of a way through. If only he wouldn't tip the decanter like that, slopping the amber liquid into his glass in that liberal way.

'Shall I go and fetch the water?' Probably in his present state he didn't notice how much he was drinking.

'Sit over there.' Ignoring the question he shifted his position again, this time to lean forward, staring at her across the desk.

'What sort of a mess, Pappy? What's happened?'

'I never meant it to end like this, it was a good business. Still is a good business. It's me, I'm the rotten apple in the barrel. Don't look down, straight in the eyes I want you to look at me.'

But it was hard to raise her eyes and see the way his mouth was working, his eyes suddenly bloodshot and full of tears.

'Don't Pappy!' To protect him or herself? She couldn't bear it that he should let her see him cry. Damn the whisky, that's what was making him maudlin.

'Can't help it,' his face crumpled. He was lost, all hope and all pride gone.

'Then I'll help you help it.' She was relieved to hear the determination she managed to force into her words. Whatever was wrong, of course she'd help him and for a start she pushed the glass away as he reached for it. It was a bad move on her part, a sign that while he floundered she had control of the situation.

'Think I've drunk too much? Is that it?'

She didn't *think* it, she *knew* it. He sounded like someone spoiling for a fight, he who loved fun and laughter. Her hands crept across the desk and took hold of his.

'I'll look at you if you'll look at me. Now, tell me. You got as far as Seagrove's being a good business. But I knew that already.' She hoped her smile would help him regain control.

'You know there's plenty of work. Work that's well done too —'

'None better on the Thames. Go on, Pappy.'

'Not sure just when it started. A few guineas, that's all it was – and dammit whose business is it anyway? I was entitled to the money. The men got their wages. That's how it began. Don't remember when.' He freed one hand to wipe his face

Then, instead of letting her take it again, put his elbow on the desk and shielded his face from her.

'Go on. How bad is everything? I've seen the order books but I've never seen the cash ledgers.'

'You know why? Because I made sure you didn't. Frightened, see? Fear makes you cunning. You're a bright girl, you might have twigged what I've been doing. Too late to care now.'

'Rubbish! Nothing's so bad it can't be saved. It's true what I said just now, there's no better boatyard on the Thames than Seagrove's. And orders enough to keep the men busy until the punts are back on the water for summer. Isn't that a fact?' She was determined to pull him out of his drunken misery. He must be exaggerating, things couldn't be as bad as he said. It wasn't as if they'd suddenly started to live differently or spend more.

'I've thought all ways round it.' From the way he caught his breath she knew it would have been easier for him to give way to tears than try to muster his thoughts coherently. 'When you and your mother were in bed the other night, you know what I did?'

She waited. He appeared not to notice her silence.

'There were pills upstairs, Dr Wright gives them to Elvira for her headaches. Pills and whisky, that was what I would have, I'd heard somewhere that that would finish a man. Insurance then, you see. Enough to pay off my debtor and leave you and Elvira safe.'

'No. No. You couldn't --'

'I thought I could. See,' he fumbled in the drawer and brought out a small empty box, 'they were in here. But even with that I failed. Couldn't do it, not sober. Tried to find my courage in drink. I drank, I drank ... You know what Hades is like? I can tell you. I was there. I swear I saw it, felt the hell fire burning my entrails. So hot ... I went outside to the air ... if I was going to die I wanted to be by the river. Took the box and a bottle of whisky ... walked down across the lawn ... quite dark it was, you know, but I didn't need a light, I knew every inch. Strange how clear all that is ... the garden, the smell of the wet earth – it had rained, remember? – the sound of the water lapping gently by the boathouse, it was like a benediction, a promise that paradise was waiting. Even for a man as rotten as me the promise was there.'

23

He might have been talking to himself, recalling each changing sensation and, she hoped, laying the ghost of the evening
as he spoke. 'It was joy beyond belief ... all I had to do was
take the tablets and more whisky and nothing would ever come
between me and ...' As if he had just become aware of Polly's
presence he looked directly at her. 'Serenity, that's what it
was. I tipped the tablets into my hand, all of them, and stuffed
the whole lot into my mouth. I started to chew them, the taste
took away all my peace, brought reality back to me. When I
tried to swallow I felt I was choking. I drank from the bottle,
gulped the fiery liquid. Poll, Poll, no, I can't bear to tell you –
foul, degrading – I could feel the tablets blocking my throat, as
if I was being throttled. Couldn't think clearly, just knew I had
to end it. The promise of serenity had gone and my courage
with it. If I couldn't swallow the pills I'd have to go in the
river ... mustn't look like suicide ... insurance wouldn't pay
out for suicide ... that's what I kept thinking ... it had to look
like an accident ... yet when I tried to walk towards the
boathouse I couldn't. Then I was sick, never been so ill.'
Again he turned his head from her. 'Like any common drunk
staggering home from the alehouse. I'd had the best part of a
bottle of whisky while I tried to find the courage to do what I
had to do, it forced the tablets out of me before they'd had a
chance to go down. If I were a man, a real man, I'd have had
the courage to take them one at a time, sure to swallow each
one with a gulp of the drink. But no, even at that I failed, I had
to numb myself with alcohol first.'

'Look at me Pappy, say with me "Thank God it didn't
work".'

He looked at her, his face crumpling as again he wept.

'Say it ...'

Like an obedient child he repeated the words. This time she
didn't try and jolly him out of his tears. What a moment to
remember that afternoon a few months ago when her mother
had wept as she'd faced up to Dr Wright's confirmation of her
fears. 'You'll feel better when you've cried,' she'd told her
mother and now, silently, that's what she said to the broken
man in front of her. It was only after he'd found his composure
that she prompted him with a question.

'You started to tell me ...? Let's talk about it together, we'll find a way to put things right.' If only she could feel as confident as she sounded!

All her life she'd looked on him as without fault, yet through all those years behind his happy, carefree manner, his generous spending, he must surely have seen he was moving steadily towards financial ruin. Once he started to unfold his tale of misery nothing could stop him. It was as if he were freeing himself in the telling. Halving his trouble by sharing it?

Without interrupting, Polly listened. Her attention was on what he told her, her shoulders ready to carry the burden with him. With him? For him? Even as she listened, pictures chased each other through her memory: she was a child again, hearing his praise as she raced him to the other side of the river and back again; then later, she must have been about fourteen that summer when he taught her to use the pole, demonstrating with such exaggerated movements that he had found himself still clinging to it as the punt moved on without him, their uncontrolled laughter as she had hauled him back aboard; fishing together as they watched the sun come up; skating one wonderful winter weekend when the Thames had become an ice rink; playing tennis together; he'd never been like any of her friends' fathers, with him every shared outing had taken on the thrill of adventure. What he was telling her might well have cast a shadow over her memories. But it didn't.

In broken tone he tried to make her understand: he'd not set out to cripple the business, when he put the first few sovereigns in his pocket it had seemed harmless – and easy. That was the point – easy. He recalled to her the business trips that had kept him away sometimes for two or three days at a time; in the flat-racing season his business had been at Ascot or Newbury, the occasional win encouraging him to gamble more. Or else he'd been in London at the gaming tables. Each time he'd gone with hope and faith – Lady Luck would help him. But Lady Luck had laughed, egged him on, stripped him of . . .

'How bad is it, Pappy?' Again she had to prompt him.

'Bad enough to make me try to take my life.' His manner had changed. The weight of his burden had been lifted, no longer was it just his own. Polly knew that by the way he said

25

that one sentence, as if in relating his attempt at suicide ('Thank God it failed, thank God it failed') he had absolved himself of responsibility. 'There's this man, Carpenter is his name, Harry Carpenter. How he knew the hole I was digging for myself I shall never be certain, but I found later that we had a mutual – er, a mutual – friend. He came to me, he offered to lend me money, his terms were clear. I wasn't accepting charity, you understand? This was a business arrangement. I signed a contract to repay the debt within twelve months; that was at the beginning of summer last year. I was desperate, Poll, I'd never have done such a thing if I hadn't been in such a hole. It was either that or sell up, I was getting deeper week by week just trying to keep afloat.'

'But why didn't you say? Mother had no idea, I'm sure she hadn't.'

He didn't need to answer. His open-handed generosity had always been taken for granted.

'Your mother was so keen for you to accept young Maidment, you know. You'd have been well set up for life, they're a wealthy family. I'm not telling you anything you don't know when I say he was yours for the taking, eh?'

A shifting of his burden and now – no, she must be imagining it – a shifting of blame too. If she'd tied the Seagroves to the Maidments she might have been able to help him, saved him from the grip of this moneylender. There was a new cunning in his expression.

'I'm not selling myself to Victor Maidment or anyone else. How long have you been given to repay this – this – Shylock? You say it was for twelve months – that's well passed. You've amended the agreement? How long have you now?'

'No time. He's been pressing me for months – it's been as much as I could do to send him his monthly interest. A big win, just one good win, one that would get me out of this hole. You don't know, Poll, how hard I prayed for that. Now he writes that he isn't prepared to wait any longer. I'm hemmed in at every angle. If only I could have another throw of the dice, Lady Luck might —'

'Then it's a good job you can't. We're in it deep enough without getting worse.'

'If I'd had time I wouldn't have tried to take the way out I did. I tell you Poll, we've no hope. It'll be the end of Seagrove's, the men will lose their work. The shame it will bring on your mother ... I never meant ...' But upset though he was, he'd not missed that Polly said *we're* in it deep enough, not *you're* in it deep enough. 'I had a final letter from Carpenter on Monday, a letter that gave me no hope. This time he wrote that he wasn't prepared to give me any more grace. The debt should have been cleared around the time your mother was so enjoying making plans for my half century. And you say why didn't I tell her! Carpenter is in Reading for a few days this week and writes that he's coming to the yard tomorrow. Tomorrow!'

Polly's mind was working fast. Her pride rebelled at what she had to suggest, but she could see no other way.

'D'you know where he's staying in Reading? With your mutual friend?'

'Gracious no. He may visit her but not take lodging there.' His answer confirmed what Polly had imagined, the so-called friend must be one the paramours her mother had talked of.

'Can you contact him?'

'He always stays at the George. I can send a message. Why? What have you thought of?' Something of his usual confidence was returning: hadn't't Polly told him that together they would find a way?

'We need more time. What sort of a man is he? I mean is he mannered enough to invite to Mother's table?'

'Indeed.'

'Then send a messenger to the George inviting him to come here tomorrow evening. Surely, Pappy, when he sees how poorly Mother is he'll have the human decency not to press for settlement at least until after the baby's born. He'll let you carry on paying interest until —'

'What chance have I repaying the loan when there's a noose like that round my neck?'

'When he meets Mother you'll find he'll not be so hard. She can soften the hardest heart. Imagine how you'd feel if you were in his place and were faced with someone as pretty as she is, delicate, brave – oh, you know, I don't have to spell it out. Only a monster would want to make life harder for her at the moment than it already is. Talk to her Pappy, tell her how 'important it is to get this Carpenter man's sympathy.'

'We'll find a way, eh, Polly? You and me, we won't be beaten.'

She was torn between anger and love. Love won.

'Promise me one thing, hand on your heart,' she said earnestly. 'Promise me that you won't keep things to yourself, you'll confide in me, not shut me out?'

'Hand on heart. Now may I have a sip of my drink? Like going to confession and then taking the communion cup – I feel purged, ready to look forward again.'

How much of his story he told Elvira was *his* secret, but it couldn't have been enough to make her understand the necessity of her playing on their visitor's better nature. In the late afternoon dusk Polly arrived home from Horace's half-hour of chasing sticks to find Emmie waiting for her in the lobby.

'Would you believe, Emmie, he doesn't need drying. The ground's hard as iron and even this crazy dog didn't attempt to go in the water.'

'Real winter day Miss Polly. I've hunted high and low, but there's not a flower, not so much as a sprig of forsythia daring to burst a bud. The mistress does like a few flowers on the table when there's company.'

'Never mind, don't look so worried,' she laughed. 'We can't use what we haven't got.' (If only Pappy had remembered that!) 'Men don't notice flowers anyway. Light the candles in the candelabrum instead, that's much more cheery this time of year.'

'You tell the mistress, will you Miss Polly? She's upstairs lying down. Poor soul.' If Elvira needed sympathy she need look no further than the kitchen.

Polly found her mother in her room, the fire burning brightly in the grate, the blind down and the curtain drawn against the wintry scene outside.

'You needn't dress for a couple of hours, Mother,' Polly reassured her. 'I'll come in to help you and do your hair for you if you like.'

'Wouldn't you think your father might have more consideration than invite a stranger to our table at a time like this. Look at me! Why, it's indecent to flaunt myself in front of even people I know, but a stranger – and a man at that! All very well for the lower classes! But to expect *me* to parade my ugly form ... Some men have no conception of what's seemly.'

'You look very pretty Mother. That you make an effort to be a good hostess in spite of feeling wretched, don't you see that can only give you Mr Carpenter's respect.'

'I don't give a fig for Mr Whatever-his-name-is's respect! In any case, even if your father hadn't been so thoughtless as to invite him, I still couldn't face a table laden with food this evening. I forget what it's like to take pleasure in a good meal.' How pathetic she looked standing at her bedside, one thin hand on the small of her back and one supporting her swollen stomach. Her eyes swam with tears. 'This child will be the death of me. With you I never felt so burdened by discomfort, but then, of course, I was young. It's because I'm too old for breeding, it's unnatural. I shouldn't wonder there's something wrong with it, it's not growing right. Too old did I say? I feel a hundred. And your father expects me to act hostess to some business associate, tells me it's important the man's welcomed. Well, I won't do it. Polly, you'll have to take my place.'

'Lie down for an hour or so, you'll feel better. You always love company, Pappy is proud of the way you are, he doesn't want to hide you away.'

'Proud he's done this to me, wants this newfound friend he seems to set such store in to see what a fine stud he is. Oh, hark at me. A few months ago I would never have talked in that coarse way.' She bit her lip. 'No one understands. I've never been so alone, so miserable.'

'Mother, that's not true —'

'Don't tell me what's true and what isn't. You know nothing about any of it. Well, you can know *this*: I hate, yes *hate*, this child. Why couldn't he have given it to one of his fancy women? Anyway, leave me to rest, bed's the only place I can get relief from the discomfort.'

'I'll come back later Mother.'

'No, don't. I shall try and sleep.'

What sort of a man would Mr Carpenter be? A humourless, tight-lipped moneylender? A coarse, mannerless rogue? One thing was certain, he was a hard businessman, and a cruel one too. It was his fault that Seagrove's had been brought to this state. No, be fair, she told herself, her father had been already in a corner when this self-appointed Shylock had tempted him with an offer. No use wondering now how different today would have been if he'd used the money to pay off his gambling debts, then strived to settle the loan in the twelve months he'd agreed. Instead of that, and after all he had already lost, he had thrown good money after bad! How much Seagrove money had Harry Carpenter already extracted by way of interest?

She was getting away from the point. Tonight it had to be up to *her* to work a miracle, she had to use every scrap of charm she could muster no matter how she abhorred the idea. So what sort of a man would she be facing? Ought she to look innocent and helpless? (Perish the thought!) Ought she to play the coquette? (She shied from where her imagination led her. Hadn't her father inadvertently told her that Mr Carpenter was in the habit of visiting one of his own lady friends in Reading?) In her mind she built an image of the stranger: probably about fifty, florid complexion, a mouth that was thick lipped and sensuous, eyes that leered. Hateful! But no matter how revolting he might be, it had to be up to her to give him the motive for allowing her father more time to settle the debt (How much had he borrowed?); bad enough that her mother had let poor Pappy down just when he needed her, *she* would do whatever it took to help him.

Full of determination, from her wardrobe she took her most daring evening gown, the very latest Madame Doretta had designed and made for her. It was right that she should wear it this evening, a dress that had cost her father money that hadn't been his own to spend. It would be a constant reminder to her; like a lamb to slaughter she would face the man whose money had paid for it. Only when she met him would she decide the role she had to play. But play it she would.

Evening wear demanded a change of petticoats, and her most pronounced bustle. Layer by layer she prepared herself, feeling ever more like a warrior putting on his armour. At last came the gown, a soft green satin creation, the flounced outer hem raised to drape from the bustle so that the matching accordion-pleated hem of her underskirt showed provocatively. The front of both bodice and overskirt were bottlegreen velvet, the same material covered with coffee-coloured lace edging a very lowcut square neck. Only then did she attend to her hair. Tonight she piled it high on her head, setting off the coiffured coils with a band of the same green velvet ornamented with pearls. At last she was satisfied – indeed she was more than satisfied, no wonder the girl who looked back at her from the mirror smiled. She turned up the gaslight and peered closely at the looking glass, her palms pressed hard together as if to stem a surge of excitement as she imagined circumstances so different, saw herself being swept into a dance. She twirled, viewing the effect on her mirrored partner. Reality pushed to the fore, she acknowledged that all she was doing was putting off the evening that waited.

Her mother had said she refused to come down, but perhaps she'd changed her mind. The sight of Polly's new gown might tempt her.

'Oh good, Mother,' was Polly's cheery greeting as she went into the dimly lit bedroom 'you didn't go to bed after all. You were starting to get dressed?' Strewn on the bed were Elvira's petticoats, corset and the day dress she had been wearing earlier, while she slumped in a low boudoir chair by the fire, a negligee covering any remaining underwear. 'Look, see my gown. Isn't it splendid? Shall I get yours out for you and help you?'

'I was undressing to get to bed. Had to stop and rest, my back feels as though it's been kicked by a carthorse and who would believe how just taking off a few garments would be enough to make a person so swimmy?'

Elvira dabbed her brow with a wispy lavender-scented handkerchief. Even if she'd felt well she had no intention of parading her disgusting, misshapen body for some strange man to see – she couldn't think where Stanley's decorum had gone to allow him to imagine that she might.

But if there was one thing designed to catch her interest it was fashion.

'You look lovely,' she told Polly, 'Quite beautiful. Time was when I would have given you worthwhile competition.'

'So you will again before long, Mother. A few more months

and you'll have me back where I belong, playing second fiddle when it comes to looks.'

'Silly girl,' but she could see Elvira was well pleased. 'I've told you until you must be tired of hearing it, there isn't a girl in the county to hold a candle to you. Madame Doretta must so enjoy dressing you – yes, and me too if only I weren't in this miserable plight.'

Silently Polly rephrased it to 'Madame Doretta must have so enjoyed ...' For, even if Pappy's Shylock agreed to give them grace or let them pay off the debt gradually, it would be a long time before they could afford luxuries like the House of Duprés.

'Don't look so glum, child.' Then Elvira showed a rare spark of fun, 'Tonight you're safe, I shan't be trying to marry you off to someone who can give you a life of comfort.'

'That's as well Mother. Mr Carpenter is probably old enough to be my grandfather.'

'Hark! I hear the carriage on the drive. Your father must be home. Go downstairs, be ready to see him when he comes in, tell him what a bad day I'm having. Make him realize I can't face a table laden with food, just to talk of it makes me queasy, tell him I've had to retire to bed.'

'He'll understand. If you like I'll come back and help you into your nightgown.'

'No. I'll manage.' Then, when Polly was almost out of the room. 'But Polly, make him believe I'm sleeping. Suggest he changes in his dressing room. The truth is, I'm always so weak when he needs anything, I can't stand up against him. He said this Carpenter man was an important client, he'll be disappointed and he knows I hate letting him down. Don't let him try to argue me into agreeing to come down.'

'Don't worry, Mother, I'll talk to him.'

After the door had closed behind Polly, Elvira took off her remaining garments, chemise, drawers, garters and stockings. The warmth of the fire was comforting on her naked body. But as if to deprive her even of that moment of simple pleasure the unborn child squirmed. She gritted her teeth, trying to ignore it. Thankfully she slipped her loose, long-sleeved nightgown over her head, climbed into bed and pulled the covers around her shoulder. As if that way she could still its squirming, she pressed her hands firmly against the mound of her stomach. Under her palms she could feel the movement of life, a movement over which she had no control. Before Polly had been born she had loved to lie like that ... but not now, not this time. Clenching her fists she beat hard against her own moving flesh, she tasted the salt of her tears.

Waiting in the drawing room, Polly could hear her father greeting his guest. She strained her ears and tried to imagine from his voice what sort of man the stranger would be, but it told her nothing, it was no more than the low-toned hum of conversation. For some eighteen months he had had contact with the boatyard, first he'd put temptation in her father's way and then brought pressure for repayment. That was the sort of man he was; young or old, coarse or cultured, none of that could alter the facts. She knew her father must have tried desperately to extend the terms of the loan only to be met with stony refusal. So now there was no way of escaping what she had to do: it had to be up to *her* to hide her resentment of the hold he had on them and to persuade him – charm him? – coerce him? – into being ready to ease the pressure, allowing them more grace.

It wasn't often that Polly felt unequal to any task she set herself. Standing in front of the fire, she turned her back on the voices in the hall and looked at Elvira's portrait as if to find inspiration. If only her mother had been here to receive him. No matter how harsh a businessman he might be, he would never have been able to bring himself to refuse her pleading.

Probably Shylock expected to receive full repayment of the loan that very evening, probably he'd brought the contract expecting that he and Pappy would both sign that the transaction was completed. What was the best way to approach him? Should she throw herself on his mercy, a wide-eyed innocent girl – and upstairs an invalid mother? Or should she flirt with him, act the coquette? Whichever way she played her hand, she knew her appearance had to be her trump card.

The drawing-room door opened and, still gazing at the portrait, she heard the visitor being ushered in.

'It's so unfortunate my wife is indisposed, but let me introduce you to my daughter, Polly.'

Polly had positioned herself with extreme care, standing beneath the portrait of the beautiful woman she so resembled. Turning slowly she had a second to size up her opponent – as she thought of him – before she spoke. A tall, gaunt-looking man was her first impression; a hard man was her second, hard and cold too. Younger than she'd expected, but that didn't make her task any easier.

The formalities of introduction did nothing to make her change her mind. Harry Carpenter bowed over her hand, his manners were faultless, yet there was no smile in his eyes of a piercingly pale blue, a colour so light it was hardly blue at all. With every second her antagonism to him increased. Polly wasn't used to being looked on with such aloof disinterest; he presented more of a challenge than she'd expected. His manner put steel into her determination, although there was nothing to suggest it as she seated herself in the centre of the chaise-longue. Aware of the picture she made, she spread her skirt and raised childishly innocent eyes to the tall stranger, her demeanour giving no hint that she was aware of the view he had of the pale skin of her breasts, exposed by her low-cut neckline – more than usually exposed too, she had made sure they were pushed high as she'd laced herself into her corset.

'Time for a drink before we go in to eat. What may I pour for you Mr Carpenter?' Stanley offered.

'A whisky please. No water.'

Stanley busied himself at a side table while Harry Carpenter's attention blatantly remained on Polly. Under his scrutiny she lowered her gaze, feeling her cheeks burn. If she'd disliked him before she met him, she disliked him even more now. His look seemed to scorch her; she who'd dressed with such care felt that his piercing gaze stripped her. Instinct rather than thought brought her onto her feet, taking away his bird's-eye view she'd created with such care.

'Papa,' she said, praying that her use of the unfamiliar title would alert him to the fact that she was playing a part she meant him to fall in with, 'don't forget you promised to go and say good night to Mama. She was so weary by the time I'd helped her into bed, but I know she'll try to fight against sleep until you've kissed her good night.'

Harry had turned to take his glass from Stanley, so she was

34

able to close one eye in an exaggerated wink at her father and flick her hand in the direction of the door, emphasizing the silent message that she wanted him gone. He knew the last thing Elvira would welcome was to be disturbed, but if Polly needed him out of the room he was more than glad to go. He depended on her to bring about the miracle he hoped for and didn't question how she meant to do it. Harry Carpenter was a tough-minded man, as he had learned to his cost. But he could trust Polly to come up with a scheme. In thankfulness he took a quick gulp of his whisky, put down his glass and left them.

'I was just about to go up to my wife when you arrived,' he told Harry, finding that he quite enjoyed entering into Polly's charade. 'My poor Elvira. I'll look in on her very quietly. If she's already asleep I'll be careful not to waken her. You'll excuse me for a brief moment. Polly will look after you.'

'Indeed,' Harry complied. 'You mustn't hurry, I shall be very happy with your charming daughter.'

Polly's cheeks grew even hotter. She was used to compliments, but she wasn't taken in by his smooth words. If a minute ago she'd felt he stripped her of her clothes, now it was as if he knew exactly the game she was playing with him. She met his eyes squarely. There was too much at stake to allow herself to be thrown off her goal.

'It's more than "poor Mama",' she murmured as the door closed behind Stanley. A brief glance in the mirror on the far wall encouraged her, it would take a hard heart not to melt at the sight of her anxious expression. 'To be truthful Mr Carpenter it's poor Papa too. Poor all of us. I can't tell you the strain the past months have been. I just marvel how Papa has been able to carry on, giving so much attention to the business when he has had this constant anxiety.'

'I had no idea Mrs Seagrove was in poor health.'

Ah! Was he softening? Did that mean she had scored the first point? Her even, white teeth held her bottom lip as if to steady it, her eyes beseeched him.

'It upsets Papa to talk of it. Perhaps he feels that to put his fears into words would be a sign of losing faith.'

'I begin to understand.' Harry Carpenter didn't look at her as he answered.

His words encouraged her.

Then her confidence was jolted and worse, the last of her veils was torn from her as she realized why he had turned from her to look in the direction of the mirror on the end wall. In the expression of his reflection she saw mockery – saw it, or imagined it? She understood why his back was to her, why it was that he was watching her from the mirror: he must have seen her silent message to her father! On the face of the girl who looked at him from the gilt-framed mirror Harry Carpenter saw embarrassment – but not for long. It took only seconds for her to recover the mantle of innocent youth, vulnerable to hurt.

'I didn't think you would notice. You see, I was afraid Papa would feel he couldn't leave you when you'd only just arrived. I had to shoo him off.'

Taking a sip of whisky he watched her intently over the rim of the glass. She felt uncomfortably aware of those eyes. But never mind *him*, don't let him throw you off the part you have to play. If he makes it difficult you just have to try twice as hard.

'Anyway I wanted a chance to make you understand about Mama, I was sure he wouldn't have told you. She was so keyed up about you coming this evening, so determined to be here at the table. Mr Carpenter, there is something going on that I don't know about. They treat me like a child, whatever it is that has upset Mama so much today, to me she pretended it was nothing. I could tell this morning that your coming here this evening was important, not casually important but, far more than that, yet she denied it... I don't know what I'm trying to say. That's the trouble, there's something they're hugging to themselves. I've felt it for weeks and – Mr Carpenter, do *you* know what it is? They tell me you're a client of the yard. But you're not, are you? There's something they are hiding.'

A moment ago she had read mockery in his pale blue eyes, now the concern she saw made it harder to deceive him. But she'd never expected the task would be easy and, with determination, she threw herself into her role. 'It has to do with you, with your coming here this evening. I'm sure it has. They tell me you're a client of Papa's, but even the way they say it makes me know they're not telling me the truth.' She'd never realised she was such an actress! As her eyes stung with tears she felt a fresh rush of adrenaline and carried along by it rushed on. 'Is it about Mama? That's it, isn't it? That's why she was in such a state. She was determined to keep going all day, as if that would prove to you that they have nothing to be frightened of. When she had to give in and let me help her to bed, it was almost worse. She blames herself, as if it's *her* fault she's ill. And Papa has been worried half to death lately. I suppose he feels responsible – and it's awful to see her so poorly. I'm not a child, I know it's about Mama you've come. *Please* tell me, how can I help if I don't understand?'

'Miss Seagrove, you mustn't distress yourself. I'm a business acquaintance of your father's, nothing more. You must have imagined your mother's interest.'

'Now you're fobbing me off with half truths, too! If you'd seen my mother earlier when I had to help her to bed, if you'd seen how she wept or heard what she was saying through her tears... sobbing that she mustn't fail Papa, she had to talk to you... That's why I know how important it must be that you've come here. Mama has kept herself hidden away ever since her condition started to become apparent and yet *now*, with only a few more weeks to wait, she was so determined to come to the table.' Then suddenly, as inspiration hit her, 'I know what you are, you're a doctor, you deal with difficult births—'

'Births? You mean your mother is expecting a child?'

Polly nodded, the movement sending a solitary tear to roll down her cheek.

'They are both sick with worry. Even though she has never been strong, it can't be right for her to be as she has been these last months. It's hard enough for *her*, bearing all the wretchedness; but I believe it's worse for Papa, I know he'd do anything to help her. If only they wouldn't always pretend when I'm there ... I'm not a child ...'

Carried away by her tale, she managed to blink another tear, in fact two tears, one from each eye. They rolled down her cheek, one to be wiped away as she bent her head and the other to fall on the curve of her exposed bosom. 'Forgive me,' she looked up at him again, 'I'm behaving badly. No wonder they can't see that I've grown up. If you're not here because of

Mama, then Mr Carpenter you must be a very important client for her to be so upset that she couldn't be downstairs to welcome you.' Her face broke into an eager smile. 'You're placing an important order – or Papa hopes you are. Is that it? Well, you'll never find a better boatbuilder, not the whole length of the Thames. Hush!' She brought a finger to her lips in warning, 'I hear Papa. Let's talk of something else.' Then, as if he were a trusted friend: 'Are my eyes all right? Will he guess I—'

'I think you know your eyes are more than all right, they are quite beautiful.'

She ought to have been pleased by his words, have heard them as proof that he was taking the bait she offered. Instead, for the second time in one evening and completely out of character, she felt her cheeks grow hot.

'She was asleep,' Stanley said as he rejoined them, 'but I have told Mrs Hume we're ready to go into the dining room. Mr Carpenter is returning to London on the last train, I expect he told you, Polly? So the sooner we have our meal the less anxious he will be.'

During the meal Polly made sure there was no opportunity for the conversation to turn to business; better for Harry Carpenter to cling to the illusion that she welcomed him as a potential client. So she kept the conversation moving along on a safer track. London! How she loved to visit London, not that she had ever stayed there but sometimes, until these recent months, she and Mama used to take the railway train from Reading ... it was so exciting, she loved the noise and bustle in the streets, the clatter of the carriages, the cries of the street vendors (better not to mention that their reason for being there was to visit Madame Doretta!) ... for a country girl like she was it was heartbreaking to see the beggars, some of them poor children with no shoes to their feet.

'But poverty isn't restricted to the city,' Harry Carpenter pointed out.

'No, it's everywhere if men have no work. But there isn't the same loneliness in the country or even in the provinces.'

'You've had a sheltered life, my dear. Poverty isn't far away,' Stanley said, his words reminding her of their own troubles.

'Yes, I know you're right Papa, as you say, my own life has been sheltered from hardships. I didn't mean that everyone was as comfortable as we are, nor as lucky. I've seen poor children in the streets in Reading, playing outside those mean little cottages by the Kennet wharf. But there's a feeling of community between them and between the women too, they loll by their open doors talking to each other with as much friendship as Mama and her friends when Emmie brings them their tea in the comfort of the drawing room.'

'The norm is what you are used to,' Harry said. 'If you were born into high society, anything less would bring you face to face with what you might see as poverty. If your roots were in one of those wharfside cottages then, no matter how ambitious you might be or how far you might climb, you would always understand those standards, they wouldn't shock you or make you uncomfortable. Believe me, Miss Seagrove, I speak from experience.'

She looked at him afresh, seeing him as so obviously proud of being self-made. From his confident manner, his clear diction, no-one would guess that in childhood he'd probably run barefoot and learnt not to take the next meal for granted.

'I think that's splendid!' So it may be, but how must it make him feel towards Pappy and the mess he is in? Does he know the history of Seagrove's, does he realise that it was built up by Uncle Fred and that when Pappy inherited it had already earned its reputation? 'Really splendid!' She turned to Harry, her wide eyes shining with admiration. What was the best way to hold his interest and make him their ally? 'I'm sure what you say is true – where, and how, you spend your childhood, your formative years, will always be your yardstick. If my own circumstances were changed *this* would always remain my yardstick. If some really wealthy and handsome knight ever sweeps me into marriage I should always feel conscious of my riches because they would be a higher standard than we have here.' She sat quite upright, her eyes wide with youthful innocence – and again she was delighting in throwing herself wholeheartedly into the role she acted. Only one thing marred her enjoyment and that was her inability to read Harry Carpenter's expression. Did that enigmatic smile mean that he was humouring her as he might a child? Was he laughing at

39

her? Or did he see her as an attractive woman? Somehow it was the last she ducked away from. She'd set out to bend his will to hers, she'd created a character to suit her purpose and bearing no likeness to herself. And the game wasn't won yet. 'If you grew up like those poor children in the wharf I was telling you about, then you must know if what I say is true. Is it? Are you always conscious that you are wealthy?'

'Polly!' Stanley cut in. 'Whatever's come over you? I do beg your pardon, Mr Carpenter.'

But he needn't have worried. Harry laughed outright at her question.

'Am I conscious of wealth? I suppose I must be, Miss Seagrove. Money is power.'

'I'm sorry Papa. Forgive me Mr Carpenter, I can't think what came over me to be so impertinent. Let's talk of something else. I look forward to going back and helping Papa as soon as I can. I was telling you before there isn't a better boat-yard on the Thames – well, you must know that, you told me you are a client. You know what's so special about it? It's the atmosphere, the sense of everyone belonging, being part of a team, almost like part of a family. From Papa down to the young apprentice. And I felt I was part of it too.'

'Work gives a man pride,' Harry said, 'and shared work gives them a sense of unity. That's where the strength of the working man lies – in banding together in unity.'

Sensing the topic was moving off course, Polly smiled across the table at him as she answered.

'Then the men at Seagrove's have nothing to fear. I was starting to learn about the business, you know. Had Papa told you? Not for long, because it was just as Mama – well, some months ago. Since then she's needed me at home. But soon now, by springtime, I shall be there again. I have so much to learn, the short time I was there I didn't even start to go into the book work, but I came to understand the jobs the men were doing, their pride in its perfection. Already I was looking ahead, ordering the timber, making sure the supply of oakum didn't run low ... isn't that right, Papa?'

Stanley looked at her with all the pride she intended, before his face took on a mask of sadness. Genuine? Or was he aware of the role needed of him?

40

'Don't look ahead, Polly child. We can never take tomorrow for granted.'

'Oh Papa, you mustn't worry so. Mother will be herself again in no time. Then you just watch me! *You* can understand how I feel, can't you Mr Carpenter, I know you can. Ambition must have been your guiding star. And so it is mine. You keep your eye on Seagrove's, I'll wager you it'll be known along the Thames from Lechlade to London.'

'Mr Carpenter hasn't come here to hear your plans for the yard, Polly.'

'I'm sorry, Mr Carpenter. I let my tongue run away with me when I picture how things are going to be.'

'Don't apologise, I'm interested in what you say. But you mustn't overlook the fact that the barge trade is declining fast, you know as well as I do how the railways are emptying the waterways of commercial craft.'

'We're boat builders not barge owners. The future for river trade is for pleasure craft. They give a sure and certain future for yards like Seagrove's.'

Harry was watching her closely, uncomfortably closely. Briefly, she met his look with defiance before she remembered to wave her banner of innocent and trusting faith in the yard and her father's place in it.

'Mr Carpenter has come to discuss a business deal, my dear,' Stanley reminded her. 'The minutes are ticking by and he has a train to catch.'

'Yes, of course. When I ride my hobby horse I lose track of time. I'll leave you,' she got to her feet. 'Will you discuss your business over your port at the table, or would you rather I brought a tray to the study. Or brandy?'

'I'll see to it, my dear.' She heard the sadness and resignation in his answer. Was it as obvious to the odious Shylock as it was to her? Had she said enough to loosen his clutch on Pappy? Instinctively she rested her hands on her father's shoulders as she passed behind his chair. In that moment she was herself, honest and loving, there was no play acting in the light kiss she dropped on the crown of his head.

'Close the door as you go out, dear,' he told her. 'Mr Carpenter and I will deal with our business at the table.'

Polly did as he said, tempted to stand just outside straining her ears. But there was a limit to how low she could fall, and eavesdropping was beneath it. Back in the drawing room on her own she tried desperately to think of *some* way, even excluded as she was, that she could let her presence be felt. Inspiration came in the form of the grand piano. That was it! No expense had been spared on Polly's training, she'd learnt to master the keyboard with the same determination that she'd brought to riding a pony, handling a boat or applying oil paint to canvas; in the first three she had been successful, in the fourth she had shown a complete lack of talent. Most girls of the day were trained to make music, even if only well enough to play the hymns for the family to sing on Sunday evenings or to 'entertain' long-suffering guests. Polly came under a quite different category but then she had been instructed by Dr Pilbeam D.Mus. who came under an equally different category from the many teachers who welcomed pupils to their parlours for half an hour each week and were paid sixpence at the end of the session. Her sight-reading was quick, her fingers were nimble, but she would never play with sensitivity – that was a deficiency no teacher could improve. This evening it wasn't sensitivity that was needed, it was noise, something that would make it impossible for Shylock to forget her innocently sensual appearance and her faith in Seagrove's Boatyard. So she opened the drawing-room door wide, put her right foot firmly on the loud pedal and crashed into her most ambitious and fiery offering: Chopin's Revolutionary Polonaise.

For good measure, when the carriage arrived to take Harry Carpenter back to Reading for his train, Polly stood at her father's side to bid him farewell. Only when the door was shut on him did she ask the question.

'Well? How did we do?'

'Come in by the fire.' If his tone was anything to go by, her efforts hadn't been wasted. 'I'll tell—'

Emmie's heavy tread running down the uncarpeted back stairs stopped him mid-sentence.

'Someone come quick,' she called to anyone within earshot. 'I got to get the master.'

Chapter Three

All thought of Harry Carpenter vanished, cleared from Polly's mind as thoroughly as was the charade she'd played, the innocently trusting coquette who had set out to mould him to her will. Her father took the carpeted main stairs two at a time without waiting to hear Emmie's story.

'Is it Mother?' Polly asked urgently, hurrying along the gloomy passage that led to the kitchen quarters and the back stairs where Emmie stood, looking as though she'd been frightened by a ghost. 'Isn't she well?'

'Oh, miss, just you go and see, see what you make of it. In such a mess she is, miss, and stares at you yet I don't reckon she even saw who I was. Hark, can you hear her? Moaning like I never heard – sort of groaning and crying all at once – and I didn't know what to do. Never been as thankful as when I heard the gentleman going – you know, the one who'd come to see the master.'

'Tell Hume to get the trap ready, tell him to go as fast as he can and collect Dr Wright.'

Without waiting for a reply Polly ran up the linoleum-covered back stairs and along the landing to where she could see her parents' bedroom door was open. By now the sound was clear. In those few seconds a great wave of love for her mother flooded through her. Theirs hadn't always been an easy relationship, not as it had between Polly and her fun-loving father, but the irritations melted as she came to the bedside.

'It's all right, Mother, Dr Wright's coming, he'll take the pain away.'

Elvira's glassy stare encompassed everything and yet

nothing. She whimpered like a beaten animal.

'Can't be the child, nowhere near due,' Stanley bit his lip, looking helplessly from wife to daughter. 'I've never seen her like this, why Pol, she doesn't seem to hear us even.' He knelt by the side of the bed, but even his nearness didn't penetrate the veil of pain.

Polly dipped a face flannel in the jug of cold water on the washstand, rang it out then wiped Elvira's face; perhaps the sudden chill would make her aware. But no, she was aware of nothing but pain.

It was a relief to hear Ida Hume's firm tread on the back stairs. She came straight in without knocking, the only sign that she was more agitated than her stern expression showed.

'Arthur's gone for the doctor.' But they knew it must be an hour or more before he could arrive.

'It can't be the baby, Mrs Hume?' Polly's statement was a question. 'It's much too soon.'

'Can't be anything else, not from what Emmie tells me. Poor soul, all her months of suffering and then to end in losing it like this. I've sent young Emmie for Nurse Carey, told her to run all the way.' Ida was careful to sound calm and capable. It wasn't right for a man to watch what a woman had to suffer, for even losing a child two months and more before it was ready for the world wasn't going to be easy. No, this was no place for a man. Dr Wright, now he was different. Come on Arthur, hurry up, do, or the missus'll have got rid of her load of trouble before you get him here. '*You* would be better waiting downstairs, sir. No place for a gentleman up here. Miss Polly and me, we'll try to see to things if – but the nurse will be here in not many minutes. Go down with the master, Miss Polly, find something we can put under the legs at the foot of the bedstead, even a few good thick books. That'll stem the haemorrhaging.' She was proud of how efficient she sounded, no one would guess at the way her heart was hammering.

As soon as they were out of the room she started busying herself. Rubber sheeting, towels, sheets ...

'Like shutting the stable door when the horse has bolted,' she muttered as Polly returned bearing the family bible and a thick encyclopaedia, 'but it'll make the poor soul more comfortable.'

44

'Mama, you'll be all right, Mama.' Bending over Elvira Polly heard herself revert to the name she hadn't used for years – except this evening. What a mockery the evening had been, and while she had been putting on a performance to call on Shylock's better nature, whatever had her mother been going through all alone. 'Mama ...'

The moaning hadn't varied in tone or volume, but now quite suddenly it gave way to sharp gasps, then like a dummy brought to life, Elvira's body writhed as she let out a long, piercing scream, the first of many that followed in the time they waited for the lying-in nurse.

Emmie's fright was giving way to a feeling of self-importance. It had been *she* who had heard that spine-chilling moan from the mistress's bedroom and, now that the responsibility had been taken from her, she related her part in the drama to Ida Hume for the third time.

'I keep telling myself what a mercy it was I went up to get my knitting. Nearly didn't bother to fetch it, it being so near bedtime.'

'Bedtime! No chance of that for any of us.'

'Honest, Mrs Hume, if I hadn't been passing her door it's likely no one would have heard her. Do you reckon she'd been calling out for long? And talk of mercy – good job you were on hand or I don't know what the master and Miss Polly would have done.' Emmie hoped that the past hour would have put Ida Hume in a talkative frame of mind.

But clearly she was wrong. A tall, angular woman, her hair pinned securely and unflatteringly on the top of her head, Ida looked down her long nose at the girl's eagerness to gossip.

'Miss Polly had been hammering the keys of that piano enough to snap its strings,' was the nearest she got. 'Small chance there was of anyone hearing, even if the poor soul had been calling out with all her strength. I shan't be easy until Mr Hume gets back and brings the doctor with him.' (It wouldn't do to refer to her husband as Arthur, not to young Emmie.)

'Yes, but Mrs Hume, I got that Nurse Cox here quick as lightning, you can't say I didn't. Puffing and blowing she was, trying to keep up with me. Well, like I told her, there was not time to dilly-dally. But she'll be all right, won't she – the missus? The little one isn't due for weeks – months. If it gets itself born now is it going to be made proper? I don't know about babies coming – I mean, I know how they come, but I ain't never been about when one was born if you see what I mean, me being the youngest of our lot at home. Moaning and crying the missus was, seemed like she didn't know I'd heard her and come to help, she looked sort of wild. That hot she was, her face was wet with sweat. I thought the best was to pull back the covers and try and smooth her out, get her a bit more comfy. Never forget it ... well, you saw for yourself.'

Ida Hume tried to be tolerant, the girl was very young. Poor little lass, she'd looked as though she'd seen a ghost when she'd come rattling down those stairs to fetch help. But Ida was determined not to let her austere and efficient expression slip; it had helped her put up a show of competence she'd certainly not felt as she and Polly had waited for Nurse Cox.

''S'truth,' Emmie appeared not to have noticed that she'd just been "put in her place", 'if we're expected to go through all that then I tell you what, you'll not catch me having no babies.'

'When there's something we should know, then the master or Miss Polly will tell us. Meantime, it's no use picking up your knitting, girl, you've got better things to do tonight than knit. Fill that spare kettle and put it to heat, if we want to be useful then the best thing we can do is be ready in case we're called for.' Then, her anxiety getting the better of her: 'Oh come along Arthur Hume, do. What can be keeping you and that doctor?'

Emmie knew better than to show that she noticed.

On hearing the doctor's tread, Stanley and Polly hurried to the foot of the stairs to hear his news.

'Well? How is she?'

'I think you'd better come. She's very weak. The delivery is over, but – I'm afraid the child has no chance.'

'I can see her?'

'She's very weak ... I've done all I can for her ... never been strong ... at her age there's always far more risk ... no strength in her for the fight ...' The only thing the doctor didn't say was 'She's dying.'

When they came to the bedroom he told the nurse, 'Wrap something around the child and leave it. Time enough to see to that later.'

Doing as he said, Nurse Cox wrapped a large towel around the unwashed, minute form and dumped it on the chair where only hours before Elvira had been sitting.

'And you, Polly,' using her Christian name as he had since her childhood, Dr Wright signalled for Polly to follow.

But how could they do this? The tiny, helpless creature was alive. He was theirs to protect and care for.

'We'll leave her with your father.'

Ignoring him she moved to the fireside chair, bending over the newborn infant, unprepared for the surge of tenderness that flooded through her. Bloody from birth, it was as it had entered the world – as the doctor and nurse expected it to leave the world too. But not Polly. She gathered the bundle into her arms, discounting the stains on her gown she cradled it close against her as if the warmth and health of her own body would will it to keep a grasp on its slim hold on life. For months her mother had suffered, the agony of the past few hours had taken every remaining ounce of her strength. But now it was over and she would start to get strong again. Until then, Polly silently vowed, *she* would care for her tiny brother? ... sister? It. That's what Dr Wright had called the baby. It! *She*'d show them! *She*'d not let the baby die and her mother have gone through all that for nothing.

Looking back on it years later she believed that nothing of those moments had faded from her memory, but of course that wasn't so.

'Elvira! It's all over. Can you hear me? Elvira.' In the background was the frightened tone of her father's voice; it was that that would stay with her, imagination would give it the reality of words. And what a moment for her gaze to be drawn to the walnut wardrobe on the far side of the room, beyond the bed where Elvira lay silent now and still, her eyes staring at Stanley, at him and through him. The wardrobe, the image of the gowns hanging in it, that more than anything brought Polly face to face with the truth. 'Mama —' Yes, she'd never forget the way she cried out to Elvira, the hot sting of unshed tears that diffused her vision.

'You'd better come,' Stanley opened the bedroom to shout.

Silence as the doctor put his stethoscope to Elvira's still chest.

'Gone ... poor soul ... she was in no state to bear this child. I'm sorry, Seagrove my friend, more sorry than I can say. The child – a boy – he would have been a son for you.'

'Never mind the child—'

'A seven-month baby has barely a slim chance even with a healthy mother to suckle it. A sad end.' He had an arm around Stanley's shoulder, they had been friends a good many years.

Polly was to believe none of it dimmed in her memory, but of one thing she was certain: a rush of love for the tiny, helpless form in her arms. Her father didn't so much as look at his son; the doctor discounted him as a lost cause. Her brother, no one to love him except *her*. *She'd* take care of him, *she'd* find a way to make him grow strong.

In hushed whispers her father and Dr Wright were talking, she heard something about asking the Rector to come so that the baby could be baptised straight away, morning might be too late. That must be so that he could be buried in the churchyard with his mother. Buried ... Polly cupped his head in her warm hand ... buried ... he hadn't even started to live ...

Picking up two clean towels from the pile Mrs Hume had put on the ottoman, Polly wrapped one around the baby for extra warmth then carried him downstairs to the kitchen where Nurse Cox was waiting to be called back upstairs.

'It's all over for her, is it? Poor soul.'

Polly nodded. How could she feel so removed from what was happening upstairs? It was as if this new and fragile life left no room in her heart or head for anything but the will to protect him. He started to cry, not a lusty yell but a cry for all that, her first sound of him. He was telling her he needed her.

'Nurse Cox, what do we do first? He hasn't been cleaned. Can he be washed in a large bowl? You tell me what's right and *I'll* do it.'

'Tis no use, Miss Seagrove. Many a full-term babe is lost, I've seen it times enough, but one as premature as this hasn't a chance. No good building your hopes. If it's God's will there isn't a thing we can do to alter it.'

'*If* it had been God's will, then he wouldn't be alive at all.

So why don't you turn it around and say it's God's will he lives.' Her look defied anyone to argue.

'Oh dear, oh dear,' Ida Hume muttered to Arthur, 'and the poor missus wasted her dear life on giving birth to a poor miserable creature not ready for the world.'

'Ah,' her husband agreed. 'You'd buy a bigger rabbit for threepence in Reading market any Saturday night. Did ever you see such a miserable scrap?'

'We'll go into the drawing room to see to him Nurse Cox. You can teach me the right way to bathe him.' Even though Polly asked to be taught, there was no doubt that she meant to take control. 'And Emmie, go up to the nursery and get him some clothes. You'll find what we need in the top drawer of the chest, that's where Mother put the things she had collected together. Bring a vest and gown and napkin —'

'There should be a binder too. And pins,' Nurse Cox called after Emmie's fleeting figure, 'shawl, bonnet, anything to keep the air off him.' Then, pouring water into the bowl Mrs Hume fetched for her, she added her final word to let it be known that dressing him for life was only adding to their misery. 'Got to get him cleaned up, come what may. But no good can come of it, it's no use letting yourself think different. The doctor said it and I say it too. Nature knows best. If babies came into the world the same say as chicken do, then this one wouldn't have had the strength to crack the shell. Nature knows best, Miss Seagrove.' She supposed the poor girl was running away from facing up to losing her mother, finding it easier to concentrate on the child. Oh well, if it helped her over the shock, then so much the better.

In the drawing room where only an hour or so before Polly had pounded the piano keys, under Nurse Cox's guidance she gave her brother his first bath. It was she who wound a binder around his middle, pinned on his first napkin ('Good job he can't wriggle about too much, or he'd soon get out of it' was Nurse Cox's silent opinion of her clumsy effort), pulled his tiny arms through the sleeves of his flannelette gown, then swathed him into a shawl leaving only his face showing.

'We can't get him a bottle until tomorrow. I'll have to try him with a spoon?' Polly meant it for a statement but, uncertain as she was, it came out like a question.

Looking at him, Gussie Cox didn't think he'd last until Polly could send to town for a feeding bottle.

'God's will,' she muttered, 'I tell you one thing Miss Seagrove, it's not always easy to follow His reasoning. Only yesterday I brought a baby into the world not a couple of miles from here, I doubt you'd know the Warwicks, they keep a farm – not worth calling it a farm, enough ground to graze three or four cows, a few chicken, a pig for the table – a real rosy, healthy woman is Blanche Warwick, breeds as easy as a rabbit you might say. Her eldest must be all of your age, and they go down in step, with just a few gaps where they've been taken in their early years. Her eldest has helped enough to be able to deliver a child on her own, I half expected they'd not run into the expense of sending for me. But I got called yesterday morning. It wasn't anyone's fault, it would have been just the same if I'd been there all the time, the cord was caught around his little neck. All the shaking and smacking couldn't get a breath out of him.'

Polly's mind was working fast.

'She lost her baby . . .'

'Like I say, sometimes it's hard to see His reasoning.'

'Oh, but it isn't! Not with this! Don't you see, Nurse Cox? You say she's a strong, healthy woman. If Arthur Hume took you there in the trap, would you tell her what's happened here, tell her we have a newborn baby with no mother. Would she be able to travel so soon?'

'Get her to wet-nurse him, you mean? Oh but Miss Seagrove, duckie, nature's milk or no, you'll never rear this child. Look at him, poor wee mite, hardly the power in his lungs to cry out.'

'Will you go with Arthur? Or tell me where to find her and let me try to persuade her.'

'Hark, there's your father coming down with the doctor. Your Arthur Hume's next job will be to take Dr Wright home and, as for me, mine is to do what's necessary with your poor mother upstairs.'

'But first answer what I asked: would Mrs Warwick be fit enough to come here so soon?'

'She's had too many babies to expect to linger weeks in bed after each one – and this time, poor soul, with nothing to show for her labour ... It wouldn't surprise me she'll be defying them all and being up and about already.' She considered the proposition. If Blanche Warwick would make the journey, living here with nothing to do but wetnurse this scrap of a child would be a real rest for her, would set her up far better than slaving away her days like she did at home. 'You'd pay her, of course?'

'Of course we would, we'd pay her well.' What a moment for Polly to remember their fallen fortunes and Harry Carpenter's visit.

'Clara, that's Mrs Warwick's eldest, she can look after the family as easy as her mother can. But that doesn't mean Mrs Warwick will take up your suggestion, perhaps she will, perhaps she won't. Nursing a child of your own's one thing, taking on an outsider's is another. I must go and tidy your poor mother up. Your father may not agree to what you're suggesting. Even with a wet nurse you're not going to rear this child, you're only building up to disappointment, duckie. And that's what your father may think, he may just want the whole thing over and done. Not forgotten, he won't find this night easy to forget, poor man. And your dear mother such a lovely lady.'

'He won't want to be bothered, not tonight. He'll leave it to me. You didn't tell me, can I give him water or something with a spoon?'

'First thing he needs to learn is how to suck. Give him the tip of your little finger on his mouth, instinct will soon tell him what to do with it. There's no goodness in the milk for the first day or two. Soon as I've done the necessary upstairs I'll slip off home. But I'll be back first thing in the morning. *If* he's still hanging on – and I'd be surprised, just look at him, no more meat on him than on the pen'orth of scrag I get from the butcher to feed my dog – I boil it up first, mind you, makes a nice drop of soup. So first thing in the morning I'll look in and check whether he needs Mrs Warwick. Even if Mr Hume hadn't to take the doctor, I couldn't knock the Warwicks up at this time of night and expect her to get up from her bed and come. Keep the lad warm, and even if he isn't eating he'll need changing. Are you going to be all right or ought I to slip home and see to my animals then take a nap back here?'

'No, I can manage. But thank you for offering, Nurse Cox.'

The nurse bent over the baby, her sniff speaking as clearly as any words that she expected this to be the last she'd see of him. As she went to fetch a kettle of hot water from the kitchen, the front door closed on Dr Wright.

'Pappy ...?' Polly spoke as her father came into the room, one word spoken like a question, yet Stanley could hear in it anguish, disbelief, uncertainty.

'Poll, what have I done to her?' The foundation of his life had been kicked from under him. He was filled with guilt. 'She told me, all these years she's told me another baby would kill her.' He looked drained of emotion, tired and grey.

What could Polly say? Her mind leapt back to the afternoon last summer when her mother had wept when she told her of the coming baby.

'I swear to God I never believed her.' Stanley lay back in the armchair, his eyes closed, and when he talked it wasn't so much to Polly as to himself. 'No wonder she was frightened ... aches and pains, headaches ... any excuse. I behaved like a sulky child, spiteful when I couldn't have what I wanted!' His eyes shot open, he stared hard at Polly. 'I forced that on her,' he nodded his head towards the bundle she cradled close against her, 'she's lying upstairs dead and it's my fault. Beautiful Elvira. You know what I did?' His stare defied Polly to look away from him. 'My own wife and I raped her. She wept. Tears of pain or tears of fear? God forgive me, I killed her. "Haven't you women enough without forcing yourself on *me*?" I can hear her saying it. The perfect couple, the perfect family, that's how our friends see us – saw us. Remember my birthday, there wasn't one there to touch her. I wouldn't listen ... God forgive me ...'

'Pappy,' Polly brought the infant to Stanley, 'look Pappy. See who she's left for us to care for.'

Stanley's expression didn't alter as he surveyed the tiny bundle Polly held towards him.

'Reverend Carter will be here soon. Wright promised to stop at the Rectory on his way home and tell him what's happened. The child must be baptized if it's to be interred in consecrated ground, morning may be too late. Although I doubt Elvira would want it with her.'

'Not *it*, Pappy. *Him*. Your son, my brother. What name shall we give him?'

'What? Oh, a name ... You think of something, anything you like. Silly rigmarole anyway, but Carter won't agree to it any other way.'

They were wrong, Polly vowed. She'd make him keep his hold on life. She had to keep him warm, she had to hold him close as if he were still in his mother's womb. Arthur Hume had likened him to a threepenny rabbit in Reading market, Nurse Cox had said he was no better than the pennyworth of scrag she cooked for her animals.

'*I'll* show them!' Polly vowed silently. Then aloud. 'He'll be baptised Robert – then he'll be Bob, Bobby.' Her mouth twitched into a hint of a smile as she considered how she'd raised his value.

A few minutes later the Rector arrived. Even then Bobby was pushed into second place, for first of all Reverend Carter went to Elvira. What prayers and incantations he went through with her lifeless body Polly had no idea, she just wanted the baptism over and Bobby back into her care. Supposing the shock of cold water on his head was too much for him. No, it mustn't be. Please, please don't let it hurt him. 'Suffer little children to come unto me', she remembered the words under a picture in the bible. As if Bobby wouldn't get through the gates of Heaven without Reverend Carter's help. But he wasn't going to die, she'd keep him warm, she'd force her own strength into him. Face to face with reality, she knew she was helpless: her mother was dead, no one except her gave Bobby any hope of living through the night.

Into her mind sprang something else, something that had been forgotten in the trauma of the last hours: the boatyard, the debt to Harry Carpenter.

Her prayers must have been heard, for Bobby's reaction to the cold water of baptism was the same as it would have been had he waited his turn to be born. His cry might not have had as much power, but it was enough to prove that his lungs were in working order.

Then, at last, the Rector had gone, Stanley retired to spend the night in a spare room, and except for those in the drawing room the lamps had been turned out. Water's Edge slept, only Polly kept vigil through the long hours of night. She built up the fire, warmed cushions and put them on the hearth rug, then she loosened Bobby's tight wrapping and laid him on them, plumped the feathers around him and pulled the footstool so that she could sit on it protecting him from any draught.

How could they say the baby wouldn't live? Just look at him, he moves his arms, he draws up his knees then stretches his thin and wrinkled legs. She dropped to her knees and bent over him, surprised by the physical ache in her own limbs. Aching with love, she thought. It really happens, I ache with love. Help me to help him, just look at him, not enough flesh on him to fit his skin ... Please see to it that that Mrs Warwick comes, let her give him nourishment, make him fill out so that he fits himself. What a moment to look at the elegant skirt of her gown spread like a curtain to protect him from the cold. It was stained and creased. Only a few hours ago she had twirled in front of the mirror admiring the image. Remember going to show yourself to Mother ...

'You look lovely,' recalling her mother's words she could almost hear her voice. 'Time was when I would have given you worthwhile competition.'

'So you will again before long, Mother,' her reply came back to mock her now, 'a few more months and you'll have me back where I belong, playing second fiddle.'

Her eyes filled with tears, through them she looked at the baby, thrust into the cold world before his time.

'Poor little boy,' she held her finger to his mouth, 'poor little boy.' She felt alone and inadequate.

Mid morning the next day Blanche Warwick arrived. No more than fifty hours since her stillborn son's delivery yet, as Nurse Cox had promised, there was nothing of the invalid about the rosy-faced woman.

'Dear me,' she muttered on making Bobby's acquaintance. 'Seen many a newborn, helped to bring some of them into the world even, but 'pon my soul I've never set eyes on one as wee as this little man. Come on my lovey,' she lifted him into the security of her experienced hold, 'time you and me got to know one another. See, see how he turns his head to me.' She thrust him back to Polly, sat herself in the nursing chair which hadn't been used for nearly two decades, unbuttoned her blouse and dug amongst layers of loose-fitting undergarments finally to bring forth one bulging breast. 'Now I'll have him. Reckon I need him as much as he needs me.'

'I'll wait outside ...'

'Don't you want to see how he goes with his first drop of food?' She seemed surprised. 'Come on now my lovey, you show your big sister what a clever man you are.' A rough, hard-working country woman, yet to the baby her voice was gentle, she almost cooed.

'Don't you mind me staying?' Polly's only experience of young babies had been when she'd gone with her mother to visit a friend whose married daughter had come to stay, bringing her two-month-old son. Breast-feeding had been carried out in privacy, no mention made of why the baby had been taken upstairs; when the young mother had returned to the gathering after an absence of about half an hour by common consent neither Elvira nor her friend referred to where she had been. It seemed that anything so intimate was a taboo subject in refined society. To expose a full breast with Blanche Warwick's abandon was unheard of!

'Why should I mind, Miss Seagrove dearie? See, see he's getting the hang. Oh m' dear Lord,' Blanche held her jaw stiff, but she couldn't stop the tears that burned her eyes and rolled down her cheek. 'Don't take no notice,' she sniffed, her mouth contorted. Wiping the sleeve of her flannelette blouse across her face she made an effort to regain control. 'Not like me to get weepy,' another sniff, another wipe, 'just the feel of his tug on me. Haven't shed a tear, even when they told me about losing my own, not till now. Sorry Miss Seagrove, whatever must you think. I'm all right ... all right now ...' nodding her head to emphasise her words.

'I'm so sorry,' Polly dropped to her knees by the side of the low nursing chair. 'For you I mean. But I'm thankful too, thankful and grateful to you that you're prepared to do this.'

Blanche was winning her battle.

'Reckon he's doing me as big a favour as I am him,' Blanche made an effort to laugh. 'Just look at me,' and Polly knew she meant look at her ample breast, not her tear-stained face, 'I tell you, the more often he's hungry the more he'll be doing me a favour. Always the same, I am, I wonder the good Lord never sees fit to give me twins! Your little man's come to the right shop here.' She made an attempt to joke. 'They've had me bound up that tight round my chest, that's what they do you know when there's no babe to suckle. 'Struth but the pain was ten times worse than the labour. Sultanas, eat plenty of sultanas, fill yourself up on them, that'll stop the milk coming in. That's what Nurse Cox said. My Bert, he sent the kids to get a great load of sultanas and I did as she said. Ate so many I don't care if I never see another 'tana as long as I live. Huh! Old wives' tale if ever I heard one. Just look at me. You wait all that time for a babe to get born ... your mind might know it didn't live, but there's no telling your body, it just rushes on to the next stage. I know I had a little blub just now that it wasn't my own flesh and blood at my breast, but I'm thankful your little man needs the nurturing, bless his heart. Sultanas! Lot of nonsense some of these clever people talk.'

Blanche Warwick's eldest daughter, Clara, arrived later in the morning with a change of clothes for her mother, two night-gowns, a thick and well-worn dressing gown and toilet things. Answering Nurse Cox's call as quickly as she had, Blanche had brought nothing but the clothes she stood up in.

Just as Polly had inherited Elvira's beauty, so Clara showed every sign that as the years went by she would grow ever more like Blanche. At twenty her stolid build spoke of rude good health, her round face of good humour. One didn't need riches to be tidy, Polly scoffed silently as she watched the visitor plod upstairs to the room given to her mother: her boots looked as though they didn't know what it was to shine, the hem was unstitched at the back of her calico skirt, and surely she could-n't have looked in the mirror when she'd pinned her hair loosely to the top of her head (so loosely that a straight strand had come unanchored and was hanging down her back).

Polly retreated to the morning room, her glance going immediately to the gilt-framed mirror as if for reassurance even while her thoughts leapt ahead to her father. She knew he hadn't gone to the yard this morning. Instead Hume had been sent with a note telling Hugh Davies what had happened. This was where she'd expected to find him, but when he wasn't there she went across the hall to his study.

'Pappy?' Again there was a question in the word. 'That was Mrs Warwick's daughter, she's brought her mother's things.'

'Um ...? Warwick? That's the woman's name is it?' Clearly his mind was elsewhere. 'I've too much else to think about, I'm not getting involved with arrangements of that sort, I leave all that to you.' Then, almost visibly pulling his thoughts together, he stretched out his hand and rested it on her shoulder. 'Pol, don't expect a miracle. You know Dr Wright's opinion: the kindest thing for a child so premature would be for it to be over quickly. Don't fight the inevitable, Pol, you'll be the one to get hurt.'

She didn't answer. At any other time she would have argued but, this morning, how could she?

'Come in and close the door, I want to talk to you about last night, about my talk with Carpenter.'

Her instant reaction was hurt disappointment, then coming immediately after was resentment on her mother's account. His words conjured up a picture: she saw herself coming out of the drawing room as the cabby drove their visitor away, she remembered the mixture of eagerness and dread as she looked enquiringly at her father. Now none of that was important, she didn't want to talk about it, she just wanted the comfort of being with him, sharing their wretchedness, sharing the will to make Bobby live.

'You did well with him, Pol.' Stanley's thoughts hadn't kept pace with hers, he was still with last night's visitor. 'I could see he was taken with you.' And he actually chuckled at the memory.

Polly couldn't look at him, she turned away. With her back to him she made herself ask, 'So he's taken off the pressure? Given us time?'

'That's the idea,' his answer was too eager. 'Yes, I could tell he was taken with you. I fancy we'll be seeing a good deal more of him. He'll find himself a welcome visitor here, eh?' Not so much a question as a statement. 'He means to keep an eye on the business – but it wasn't the business he had an eye on last evening.'

Polly ignored the inference.

'You mean control the finances?'

'Nonsense, nonsense,' he blustered. 'Nothing for you to worry your head about. And with my dear Elvira gone, you'll have your hands full here at home.'

She felt ill at ease with his over-confident tone, his forced optimism. How could he say '... with my dear Elvira gone ...' in the same voice as a minute before he'd told her 'I could see he was taken with you'? Sure that he was holding something back from her, her instinct was to probe. But she couldn't, not this morning.

Moving her head a fraction she caught a glimpse of his reflection in the mirror. His face was a mask of misery.

'Oh Pappy,' in an instant her arms were around him, 'we'll prop each other up, we'll have to.'

'Yes, yes, that's the way.' Yet her words hadn't made him lower his defences, even in the looking glass he didn't let his eyes meet hers. 'Leave the business side of things to me, eh? Look after the home, that's what your mother would want. And be nice to Mr Carpenter – let him see what an effort you're making to keep the wheels turning.'

'Of course I'll see the wheels keep turning – not that what we do is any business of Shylock's!'

A new order was born at Water's Edge. Over the previous few months Elvira had had very little to do with the running of the household, with the exception of checking the tradesmen's accounts and paying the bills promptly, she'd been glad to leave Mrs Hume in charge. Polly saw no reason to interfere. Fourteen-year-old Daisy Dawkins, distantly related to Emmie, was given a job and half Emmie's bed; officially she was employed to take over the additional work made by having a baby in the house. As she boiled and scrubbed the nappies, ironed his gowns, made sure everything he used was aired and warm, Daisy liked to think of herself as Bobby's nursemaid even though Mrs Hume preferred to use her as an extra pair of hands.

Polly threw herself wholeheartedly into caring for her infant brother as, only a few months before, she had into the trade at the boatyard. She'd always thrived on challenge although until now she'd never been faced with one that had tugged at her heartstrings as this tiny brother. She bought a feeding bottle, diluted the rich farm milk with boiled water and sugar, so that he could gradually be weaned away from Blanche. To start with it was during the nights that she persuaded him to accept the rubber teat as a substitute. So small, so helpless, the innocent stare of his blue eyes as he watched her, Polly had never known she could feel such tenderness as she did holding him close against her. When he went to sleep in her arms, more often than not she would wriggle to lie down still holding him. In a minute she'd put him back in his crib, she'd think, only to drift back into contented slumber.

It was easy to grow fond of Blanche. A woman so different from anyone Polly had known, yet there was a down-to-earth honesty in her that struck a chord and formed an easy, almost mother-and-daughter relationship if the idea hadn't been so incongruous. Blanche never laid down rules in the care of a baby, in her opinion that was the way to build trouble.

'Never a child born who lives by a rule book and if we're fool enough to expect it then we'll end up a bag of nerves, getting fidgety for nothing. Be happy with the lad, that's the best way, Miss Polly my duckie. He'll get the message right enough.' Even when Blanche was serious, Polly felt a smile was only just beneath the surface. And under the good-natured woman's guidance her own confidence in dealing with Bobby developed without her realizing.

The Warwicks were a large household, Blanche's children ranged down the years from Clara to Sammy who was barely two, nine of them living and three in the churchyard. The reason for the feeding bottle was because she was keen to get home to them and the only alternative would be to let her take Bobby with her to Little Roost, the Warwicks' small farm, something Polly wouldn't let happen. So, when he was eight weeks old Blanche packed her few possessions in her straw basket and moved back home, walking the distance – nearly two miles – back to Water's Edge each morning and being taken home in the trap each evening.

'How's our little man, then,' she'd coo to be rewarded with a gummy beam of delight. 'Here's ol' Blanche come with your breakfast.'

Listening to her, Polly would remember Elvira, always so

elegant, fastidious, beautiful right to the last. What would she have made of the hearty, earthy Blanche? The answer was plain, but it did nothing to dim the fondness Polly felt for the jolly countrywoman.

'Clara's sweetheart came by yesterday,' she said one morning as she tucked one breast away and eased the other from its mysterious folds of underwear. 'Over you come then, lovey, here's your afters. Doing well isn't he, Miss Polly, cheeks filling out lovely. We're winning, gal, never you fear. Just listen to him slurping away ... oh, love 'im.' No wonder Polly looked on her with such affection. 'I was telling you, Chaw came by yesterday. I missed him, of course, he'd gone on his way before I got home. Not often he gets Clara to himself, what with me being about the place and her Pa too. Yesterday when Chaw bowled up there was just Clara,' she chuckled, imagining the scene, 'well, that's to say there was Clara and young Sammy, but he's too little to tell tales. Bet that made their eyes sparkle! My Bert had gone to the Cattle Market and taken the eldest three boys with him, the rest of 'em weren't back from school. Not often they get a chance for a kiss and a cuddle, not with all us lot about the place. They must have had long enough to give them the urge to get on with things. Clara was talking last night of a wedding before this year's gone.'

By then it was April. To talk of 'before this year's gone' didn't sound to Polly as though there was much strength in the urge yesterday's unexpected solitude had given them.

'Will – Chaw, did you say? – will he take Clara far away? Where does he come from?'

'Good few miles from here. But once they get themselves wed he means to settle in with us. Clara was saying he was talking about trying to rent a bit more land from Home Farm. Me and Bert, we've known Chaw's people for years, I remember the first time Bert took me to see them. Just before we were married, and there was Chaw no bigger than this little treasure. It's ten years since we made a move to Little Roost, but we never lost touch and the two of them, Chaw and our Clara, they've been thick as thieves all their days. He's a bare twelve-month older than her, you see. Right from when they were toddlers they've been thick. When he started journeying

for his Pa he always broke off to come in on us for an hour –
not to see Bert and me,' she laughed, 'oh no, our Clara's the
attraction.'

'And now they're engaged to be married?'

'Been promised to each other – properly spoken for
promised I mean – this two years. But before that we all knew
the way they were heading. Clara's been getting her bottom
drawer together, it surprised me how well she turned her hand
to a bit of lacework to go around her petticoats. She's a good
girl is Clara – well, you've seen her, you can tell can't you? –
but I'm jiggered if I ever thought I'd see her with a crochet
hook in her hand. Can turn her hand to anything in the way of
dairy work, mucking out the cowshed, making a good meal,
but lace ... Just goes to show what love can do to a girl. You
wait till it hits you, Miss Polly my duckie, you'll get struck one
of these days like the rest of us.'

Recalling her reaction to Victor Maidment, Christopher
Vaughan and others who made shy advances from the side-
lines, Polly made no reply. Clara and her Chaw had played
together as children, just as she'd played with the sons of her
parents' friends. But surely love, real love, couldn't have its
roots in games of 'hunt the thimble' and 'hide and seek'? No,
it must hit you with blinding intensity, it must change your life.
With the trust of youth that's what Polly believed. In her
mind's eye she saw her dream lover, someone tall, dark hair,
dark eyes that knew about laughter and passion too ... her
imagination carried her further, she was again on the towpath.
A bargee with all the grace and beauty of a gypsy king was
waving farewell to her as he moved the boat downstream and
away. Even in her imagination she didn't raise him to the rank
of lover, he was no more than the template she used to create
the man of her dreams.

With Elvira's death and Bobby's birth the easy companionship
between Polly and her father was knocked off course. She
could sense his withdrawal but felt inadequate to try to help
him. Of course he was lonely, she told herself, and no one, *no
one*, not even she could share his loss. Her sympathy for him
was clouded by disappointment – and anger too if she were
honest enough to admit to it. Couldn't he see that he wasn't

the only one to be sad about her mother? And none of it was Bobby's fault, poor little boy. No mother and a father who never looked at him, never asked about him ... that was something for which Polly couldn't forgive.

'Tell Mrs Hume I shan't be home this evening.' Increasingly often he'd say it as he left for the yard in the mornings.

Polly was worried. That's the way he used to carry on – only not quite so frequently – and look at the mess that made of the finances of the business. Was he working late into the evenings or was he playing cards? Winning? More likely losing.

There was one night of each week when she knew he was bound to be at home, that was the evening when Harry Carpenter regularly dined at Water's Edge. Her father had told her he wasn't being pressed to clear his debt but she'd sized Shylock up well enough to know why each week, the meal over, the two men retired to the study. She ought to be affronted that a moneylender had the presumption to interfere with the running of Seagrove's. Instead what she felt was relief – and shame, both for what she told herself was disloyalty to her father and for the act of welcome she always played out for the visitor.

It was spring, and she dressed for the evening as usual and with an eye to entrancing Harry (always Mr Carpenter on her lips, but when had he lost the name of Shylock in her mind and become Harry?), anything to ensure that he didn't change his mind and demand payment they couldn't make. Her father was late that evening, perhaps purposely meaning to be dressing still when Harry arrived. '... very taken with you ...', 'has an eye for you ...' That he might be pushing them into a tête-à-tête annoyed her, she'd played the role of innocent young daughter long enough – too long. Ah! Hark! Yes that was Hume with the carriage, Pappy must be home. Hurrying down the stairs she opened the wide front door just in time to see Hume rounding the bend to the stables.

'What's happened?' She caught up with him as he clambered down, 'is my father meeting Mr Carpenter in Reading instead?'

'I've a note to give you, Miss Polly. I took the master to the station – but the note will explain to you.'

It did. Business had taken him to London, he'd not be home

for a day or two but was sure she could explain his absence to Mr Carpenter. Business trip. Did he think she was a fool? Had he forgotten his whisky-fed confessions the evening he'd told her of his financial ruin?

She'd never felt more resentful of playing the unconsciously attractive naïve young daughter than she did a few minutes later when Emmie ushered Harry into the drawing room.

'Mr Carpenter, good evening. I'm so sorry Papa can't be here. See, he had this note passed to me.' Wide-eyed, timid and eager to please, she looked at him.

Surely he couldn't be laughing at her! His light-blue eyes held an expression she couldn't fathom.

'I was with him when he wrote it.'

Chapter Four

Polly wasn't used to being out of control of a situation. The note had asked her to explain her father's absence – yet Harry Carpenter said he had been there when it had been written. He couldn't be telling the truth! He must have called at the yard, been told of the necessity of an unexpected trip to London on business (and here she put a rein on her thoughts, with Harry watching her she wouldn't let herself imagine the 'business'). Pappy would have given him credit for being more of a gentleman than he was, and taken it for granted that, their weekly talk dealt with at the yard, Shylock naturally wouldn't have come to the house this evening. Anyway, why should he have wanted to, knowing that their meal would be a tête-à-tête? Her silent question received a silent answer – a silent answer that made her pulses quicken as she clutched at a composure she didn't feel. She had never known what it was to be gauche or shy, and had Harry Carpenter come here in the mistaken belief that her father would be waiting for him she would have carried the situation – be honest, she told herself, you would have revelled in it. Think of the care you took dressing for the evening, making sure the picture you made was appealing – yes, and enticing too, the laces of your corsets pulled so tight you could hardly breathe. All these weeks you've enjoyed the game you've played with him, the 'innocent' encouragement you've given him, the challenge of having such an influence on his hard-bitten nature that he took the pressure off Seagrove's.

His one sentence, 'I was with him when he wrote it,' the teasing light in his pale eyes, they alone would have been enough to destroy her composure; but there was something else, something far more complex. She'd disliked him even before she'd met him and when he'd first come to the house she'd fitted him straight into the slot she'd had ready – a hard-hearted, middle-aged moneylender. She refused to admit (or, more accurately she wouldn't let herself see) that, had the circumstances of his visit been different, so too would have been her view of him. Physically he bore no resemblance to the man she'd been prepared to face. Her father's age, she'd expected; Harry Carpenter must have been quite fifteen years younger. Hard, arrogant, she'd told herself; yet had the circumstances been different she would have been excited by his air of confidence. Her experience of men went no further than the sons of family friends, none of them any more worldly than she was herself. They were drawn to her like moths to light, if she bestowed a favour on any one of them he was her slave. Where was the sport in that? Or the danger? No wonder she thrived on the challenge of the game of tantalising a man practised in the ways of life far beyond her ken, tantalising him from a safe distance and behind a façade of innocence. Excitement was something she'd craved more than ever over these last weeks. Her life had been turned upside down: her mother was gone, Bobby her precious responsibility, her father completely disinterested in his son and, despite passing the burden of his care onto her the night before Bobby was born, now he wouldn't be drawn into telling her how long he'd been given to pay off the debt or what Shylock's interest was in the yard's trade.

Her dislike of Harry was as strong as it had been that first evening. Yes, of course it was. Yet in the intervening two months she'd found herself giving him grudging respect for his business acumen. And when had she stopped thinking of him as middle aged? She told herself – repeatedly she told herself – she didn't think of him at all, but deep in her subconscious she recognised an animal virility in him. Wasn't that what made the game she played such sport? Pappy had said, 'he's very taken with you' and in her naïveté she'd let that encourage her to play her role to the full, half siren and half child unaware of her power to allure.

Now she was to spend an evening alone with the man whose hold over her father had driven him to the brink of suicide.

Through all these weeks, sometimes even more vivid in her mind than the tragedy of losing her mother or the love she felt for Bobby, was the memory of her father's tears and her own realisation that in confessing his failings he was moving the burden from his shoulders to hers. It was the echo of those tears that helped her now. Like an actress moving from the wings onto the stage she smiled shyly at Harry, clamping her bottom lip uncertainly between her teeth.

He was watching her, watching her in a way that made her uncomfortable. It was as if through his narrowed eyes he could see below the surface and read her mind.

'You're asking yourself why I came here, knowing your father would be away? You want me to believe you don't know.'

'Mr Carpenter,' came the childlike reply, 'I'll do my best to help you if I can, but I don't understand business. Is it that Papa left something behind he wanted you to see? Something in his study perhaps? I know you talk business with him ... I don't understand any of it—'

His laugh cut her short.

'I don't understand any of it ...' he mimicked, one eyebrow raised in quizzical mockery. 'Oh but Polly there's little *you* don't understand. You know as well as I do that's not why I'm here.'

Like a non-swimmer out of her depth she floundered, fighting to get the conversation on stable ground.

'Is something wrong with the work they're doing for you at the yard?' Her tawny eyes were wide with concern. 'But it can't be! In any case, you say you were there this afternoon, you say you saw Papa ...'

He slowly shook his head, his teasing eyes making it impossible for her to turn away.

'You know exactly why I'm here and your father somewhere else. Just as you know exactly why I didn't dissuade him from taking a trip to London, in fact a hint or two from me was enough to put temptation in his way.'

'He's gone to meet someone on business, his note told me so. I expect he knows that by going personally he will ensure Seagrove's wins a good order of work.'

As she spoke he'd moved across the room to stand in front of her, near enough that his hands gripped her shoulders. With

66

Christopher, Victor, any of the youths she'd mildly flirted with, it had always been she who had set the pace, she who had decided when enough was enough. With Harry Carpenter she was struggling in deep water – it had never been part of her plan that her heart should race like this or that she should find the faint violet perfume of his brilliantine so exhilarating. Shylock! That's what he is! She clung to reason while she could. How dare he – how dare he what —? His hold on her was like a vice. His mouth was inches from hers, moving closer, she felt hypnotised by his nearness. In a moment of panic she ducked her head; against her will her excitement mounted when he changed his hold on her, his left arm anchoring her while his right hand forced her chin up. He was mocking her, teasing her, punishing her for the game she'd played with him, yet every instinct in her wanted to cling to him, move her mouth on his.

Whether she'd followed her impulse or struggled for freedom would have made no difference, when his mouth covered hers he held her in a grip like steel. Then without easing his hold, he moved his head an inch or two back so that he could look at her, her eyes closed, lips parted. Her hands drew his head close, she was driven by a strange, wild feeling that blotted out reason. Only seconds ago Polly had panicked, been out of her depth; now she drowned in the deep water, she was lost.

But not for long. Her feet back on *terra firma*, in her anger she despised herself and him too. How dare he use her as if she were no different from that 'lady' in Reading, the one visited by him and by her father!

'Let go of me,' she struggled, raising a hand either to strike him or to tug at his hair, as she kicked his shin with the pointed toe of her elegant evening shoe. She might as well have vent her anger on the table leg for all the sign he gave of having noticed. Instead he gripped her wrists, his expression inscrutable.

'You're a remarkable woman, Polly Seagrove. Sought after by every promising buck in the county, or so I've heard say.' There was no kindly humour in his laugh. 'No fresh-faced youth is ever going to satisfy you. You and I are two of a kind, half measures aren't for us.'

The memory of her moment of abandonment mocked her as surely as the light in his eyes. Two of a kind ... neither prepared to accept half measures ... how did he know what she was like?

'I won't listen to you. You don't know anything about me.' Pride stopped her struggling, she knew she couldn't shake off his hold on her wrists until he was ready. 'When Papa hears that you've been here, knowing he wouldn't be at home, he'll not be pleased.' How hard it was to sound cold and dignified when his expression stripped her of all pretence. Her tightly corseted figure, breasts pushed high, neck of her gown pulled low ... and she'd believed she held him in the palm of her hand ... all the time had he been laughing at her? She vent her hatred on him, but her contempt was for herself.

'On the contrary,' his answer mocked her, 'your father was delighted that I should come.' He raised his brow, making a question of what he told her. 'He assured me you would be alone and disappointed if I added my message of regret to his note.'

The ghost of her father's weeping confession cast its shadow. With an effort she forced herself to look Harry in the eye and reply coldly.

'Papa depends on me to welcome his visitors, but Mr Carpenter that's what you have always been – *his* guest. I try to fill Mama's place.'

The smile left his face. Was it anger she saw? Or, even worse, was it contempt?

'That's unworthy even of you,' his quiet voice only served to emphasise the words. 'I never met your mother, but I'm sure you do her an injustice if you tell me she would have behaved to your father's business acquaintances as you have on my visits. Nor, I vouch, do you entice the youthful swains who vie for your favours as blatantly as you see fit to behave for my benefit. All right, my dear,' there was scorn not affection in the endearment, 'play your game if it amuses you, but play it by the rules.'

She'd never felt such anger, such humiliation.

Hark, wasn't that Bobby? Yes, his screams were getting louder, coming closer. Something was wrong! In an instant, as she raised her head as if to hear him better, Harry's opinion of her was knocked off course. He released his hold on her wrists and they moved apart as Daisy's knock came on the door.

'Come in,' then even before the door was fully opened, 'What's wrong with him?'

'Oh Miss Polly, I'm that sorry to come disturbing you when you've got a visitor. But I can't do nothing with him. See what he's like.' And to prove her point Bobby held himself stiff in her arms, yelling with all the power he could muster, his face nearer purple than pink. 'Nearly took him to Mrs Hume,' Daisy shouted above the noise, 'but she ain't no better than what I am with him.'

'Come on now, hinney,' Polly took the little tornado into her arms, lifting him against her shoulder. 'Has he finished his bottle, Daisy?'

'No, Miss, kept on trying to get it in 'is mouth, I did. If he'd had the strength I reckon he'd have chucked it at me.'

'See it's warm enough then bring it to me in here. Perhaps he'll be different with a fresh start. Leave him with me while you see to it.'

'Been putting off bringing him. Thought you'd be wild, being disturbed like.'

'Silly.' Could this be the same woman who'd lashed out with hands and feet only minutes before? Harry found this more fascinating than the crudely brazen performance he was accustomed to.

It seemed he was forgotten as she sat down and laid her little brother on his stomach across her knees. Her wrists still bore the red wheals left by his fingers, her hand was gentle as she rubbed Bobby's back. Even at two months old the baby must have recognised a familiar and secure resting place for, even though he still cried, his choking frenzy had gone.

'I told my cabby to wait,' Harry spoke with his natural assurance, nothing to hint at the atmosphere between them when Daisy had interrupted. 'Hume took him to the kitchen. When the maid comes back I shall send a message that I'm ready to leave.'

Polly couldn't put the last few minutes behind her so easily. Gladly she hid behind the screen of Bobby's need of her.

'As you wish, Mr Carpenter. I'm prepared to overlook your behaviour, I shan't mention it to my father.'

'Fancy that!' Behind his words she detected teasing laughter.

'I prefer we both forget the incident,' she said coldly as she lifted Bobby to lay him across her shoulder and in the momentary silence he gave a belch that might have come from an ale-filled customer in the 'spit and sawdust' bar of The Plough. Polly felt a trickle of warmth on her neck and in the same instant Harry pulled the silk handkerchief from his breast pocket and handed it to her. This couldn't be Shylock! Keeping her eyes lowered to avoid meeting his gaze, she murmured her thanks. This was a side to his nature she wasn't ready for.

A minute later she held the lukewarm bottle firmly while a much happier Bobby slurped his way into his supper. It seemed to Harry that she hardly noticed his departure.

Two days later Stanley returned home in better spirits than Polly had known him for weeks. She told him nothing of Harry's visit, neither did he ask, anymore than she enquired of him about his absence. If he'd been at the gaming tables (and where else was he likely to have been?) then Lady Luck must have favoured him.

Turning away from the window, Ida Hume went in search of her husband.

'I don't know what her poor dear mother must make of her, if she can look down and see how she goes on. Did you see them?' When she'd watched Polly set off towards the towpath she had bitten her tongue; no one would catch her gossiping with those bits of girls in the kitchen, nor yet with those of her own generation: Mavis Simmons, who came each Monday to deal with the household laundry and each Wednesday for ironing and mending; George Baker, the gardener, a nice enough body but she'd no more think of chattering with him than she would with young Algie who climbed the ladder to see to the upstairs windows, cleaned boots, knives, drains, in fact being the bottom of the domestic pile, landed up with any job no one else wanted. Indeed no! Ida Hume kept them all firmly in their place. Even so, it was no good, she'd had to let off steam to someone! That's why she'd gone in search of Arthur.

'Who's that, my dear? I've been busying myself here in my coachhouse. What is it I missed, eh?'

'Young Miss Polly. Just like that didicoy woman who comes to our door selling her clothes pegs and ribbons and bits of rubbish we can do without.'

'Our Miss Polly,' he chuckled, 'smart as paint. Nowt o' the didicoy about her.'

'Just listen and stop interrupting. If you didn't see her, you don't know. She'd tied that baby onto her, right tight up against her front. I tell you it's just the way that gypsy woman carried hers when she called here the other day. I suppose Polly must have seen her and thought what's good for one is good for another. There they've gone off down to the river, striding out free as air she is, the dog jumping all round them.'

'Lovely spring day, Ida love, the lad won't come to any harm. She fair dotes on that boy, she'll take good care of him, never you fret.'

'It's not right. He has a fine new bassinet, a nice walk around the lanes would have done him good. Any other woman would have been proud to push their young brother, perhaps meet one or two to show him off to. But not *her*, oh dear me no. Once she gets out there with Horace she's no better than a hoodlum.' She sighed. 'Well, agree or not as you please. I've got it off my chest.' She had no control over the way Polly behaved, but as long as she voiced her views she felt she was doing her bit to keep the standards at Water's Edge on the right path.

Meanwhile Polly was introducing wide-awake Bobby to the joys to be found by the riverside. Unlike Ida, he clearly approved of his new mode of travel. At three months old in size he still had some catching up to do, but in intelligence he was as forward as any other child; slung in his hammock-type carrier he gazed up at Polly, beaming in delight. When she stooped to pick up the sticks Horace brought to her feet, he crowed with excitement as if he were part of the game. Although the sling held his weight, still she kept her left arm around him, not only as a precaution in case the knot behind her neck came loose, but because she loved to hug him to her.

It would soon be a year since she'd first seen her Gypsy King as she had privately named the handsome young bargee. Since then she had twice caught sight of him, each time when she'd been in this same field, along the riverside path from her garden. Neither time had he changed the steady pace as he'd propelled the barge along, punting to aid the single sail. The first occasion had been a very hot evening last August, the barge had been unladen and he'd been travelling homeward – wherever home might be. With the front of his collarless shirt unbuttoned, his sleeves rolled up, he had been a perfect figure, enough to arouse even the most sluggish imagination – and Polly's was certainly not that. Fearful that he might guess where it was carrying her, she had ignored what she had believed was an invitation in his wave. Invitation to what? Head in air, she had looked deliberately ahead. As he had disappeared upstream she'd felt she had made herself look a fool. A friendly wave in reply would have disguised the excitement she felt at the sight of him better than ignoring him with her nose in the air. So on the second occasion, a foggy winter day, scarcely glancing at him, she raised her hand in casual acknowledgement of his salute. That had been in December, five months ago. Since Bobby's birth Horace's exercise had had to be compressed into a shorter space of time each day. She never failed to bring him to the field, throwing sticks for him to chase as if his life depended on it and making sure he had as much exercise in half an hour as, in the days of their leisurely freedom, he would have had in half a morning.

But from now on things would be different. With Bobby tied securely to her, time was her own again. This was better than a bassinet; now there was nowhere she couldn't take him.

'What do you think then?' she hugged him. 'You, me and Horace. And I'll take you somewhere else, too. Yes, I will,' in answer to his gummy chuckle, 'somewhere even better. You'll like it on the water.'

With his mouth open, Bobby's tongue trembled with happiness. For the moment he was content with the discovery of white clouds scudding across a blue sky, Polly's soft voice and the warmth of her body rocking him gently as she walked. His lids grew pleasantly heavy, he drifted into sleep.

Harry's weekly visits had continued as if the evening when her father had been away hadn't left any shadow. Polly supposed that if he thought of it at all it would be with amusement, amusement at *her* expense. She continued to take the same pains over her appearance: laced her stays as tightly, coloured her cheeks and lips with a hint of rouge, brushed her hair and piled it high, entwined it with velvet ribbon or pearls. But since that evening, she'd dressed with decorum, no hint of what she'd supposed was a tantalising cleavage nor yet of the wide-eyed innocence that had been part of her creation. Despite her new (assumed? Or natural? How could Harry know?) reserved demeanour, one thing remained: her championship of her father, her faith in Seagrove's. She showed Harry the politeness and grace society demanded of a hostess, and he responded in the same vein. Yet she could no more erase the memory of that other evening than she could keep her imagination in check. No one could describe him as a handsome man, taller than average, slim – nearer the truth to call him thin, she corrected herself, for there seemed to be not an ounce of spare flesh on his body. But, for all that, his strength was apparent, strength that came as much from character as physique. Time and again she found herself watching him.

Only afterwards, looking back to those months, did she wonder how it was she let her father evade telling her how much grace Seagrove's had before the loan had to be repaid. She worried that by summer he seemed to be following his old pattern, many an evening not coming home until the early hours, occasionally kept away 'on business' for a day or two at a time. To dig deeper into her troubled mind would have been openly to admit to herself something she preferred to keep under wraps: Harry Carpenter was an astute businessman, they owed him money and as long as he came each week to keep a watchful eye on the figure then Seagrove's Boatyard must be prospering.

Summer was full of promise, by June the roses were in the first glorious flush of colour, the Thames Valley was enjoying – or not, according to personal taste – a spell of unseasonal heat.

Fashion decreed that for beauty a woman's skin should be pale and in this nature favoured Polly, she had the fair, delicate skin that so often goes with auburn hair. But pale skin isn't without its drawbacks and, for her, sunshine brought the peppering of freckles she detested. Whether she was paddling along on the water, throwing sticks in the meadow for Horace or driving further afield in the trap, her bright hair was always topped by a wide-brimmed straw hat in the hope of shielding her nose from the sun's rays.

With Bobby's comfort to be considered it took longer to get her canoe ready than it had in previous years. Specially built for her at the yard, it was made of strips of hard-grained wood. First she laid him in his bassinet, then she went back indoors for two spare pillows and lodged them across the foot and wheeled her load down the sloping garden. In the past she'd usually left her canoe moored to the bank at the end of the garden, even the paddle would have been in there waiting for her. Now there was Bobby to consider, rather than leave the boat in the open in all weathers she always saw that it was safely in the boathouse each evening. On the floor planking she put the cushion intended to fit across the back of one of the seats, and on top of that she made a nest with the pillows. Next came an old sunshade of her mother's, one that she'd found in the summerhouse; with its handle wedged carefully between the planks it gave him protection from the overhead glare. Then, and carefully, in he went, delighting in the gentle motion of the boat. Sometimes he kicked and gurgled as if he understood that this was no ordinary rest time, this was adventure.

Using a single paddle she propelled them out of the boathouse, turning the boat to face downstream. Today Bobby had played about with his afternoon bottle, not eaten properly despite all her efforts. Blanche Warwick came in twice a day, about ten o'clock in the morning and six in the evening, but early afternoon and nighttime Polly gave him a bottle. Strangely, he took the nighttime offering without protest, but made no attempt to hide his feelings that he was being fobbed off with second best during the day. Usually Polly finally managed to coax him into it, but today he'd been the winner. He'd played about, gazing about him fascinated by the paper on his nursery walls, sucking hard at the teat then blowing the milk out in a shower of bubbles. He hadn't been cross, he hadn't been in pain – and neither had he been interested in his dinner. So she'd conceded victory.

Settled on the nest of pillows he was engrossed contemplating his latest discovery – his hands. With arms outstretched he gazed at them, fascinated. He talked to them in his own inimitable way, wriggling his fingers, touching one hand against the other.

Facing in a forward direction Polly used her paddle with the expertise of experience, her hands effortlessly changing their hold as the punt cut through the water, four strokes to one side, four strokes to the other, keeping well over to the right-hand side of the river and her course straight. She hoped the motion of the boat would send him to sleep for *she* knew, even if he didn't, that he must be hungry. Instead he lay on his back talking to his fingers, kicking his legs with delight.

Unaware that a barge was closing in on her from behind, the first she knew of it was when it came alongside her. Not just any barge, but *the* barge.

At close quarters her Gypsy King was even more handsome than her dreams had let her imagine. Eyes of the darkest brown she'd ever seen, a cleft in his chin (an angel's thumb print, that's what her mother used to call a cleft, she remembered as she looked up at him), there was no redness in his sunburn, his deeply tanned skin gave the impression of someone from far-off places. And when he smiled, his teeth were white and even, just as she'd known they would be.

This time there was no way of ignoring him, he measured his pace to hers.

'How was it I knew it was you?' His pleasure at seeing her was apparent. Did he really recognise her? She had a suspicion that this might have been no more than an opening gambit to any promising-looking stranger. His next words banished the thought. 'This time you can't scurry away from me back over your stile.'

'Indeed, you must have imagined it. Why should I do that? I've grown up so used to the passing barges that I hardly notice them.' That's true, she told herself. Most of them I don't notice. Most of them ...

His answer was in the twinkle of his dark eyes.

'A baby – not your own? No, of course it can't be, I see you wear no rings. Could it be you're the nursemaid?'

'Of course not. He's my brother, I look after him.' Then, thawing to his easy manner, she chuckled. 'Whoever saw a nursemaid taking her charge out this way? If I were that I'd have to be pushing him around the lanes. He likes the river, I'm training him young.'

'Where's the dog?'

'I don't bring Horace on the water, not now. He has a habit of suddenly jumping in, almost capsizing me. I have to be careful with Bobby on board.'

He was looking at her in an odd way. She tried to read what was in his mind and when she couldn't she felt at a disadvantage. But that only lasted the few seconds until he spoke again.

'What I said just now – about how was it I knew it was you. How do you think? Was it because I was disappointed you weren't in your field? Don't know why I go on looking out for you there, I haven't seen you for months.'

'You've hardly seen me at all,' she laughed. 'Three times! Hardly enough to encourage you to believe I spend my days exercising Horace in the field.'

She knew he was laughing at her, his eyes made no secret of it. But it was his raised eyebrows that made her consider what she had said. She'd admitted the impression those three occasions had made on her. But what did it matter? He'd remembered them as clearly as she had herself. What a moment for her to think of Christopher Vaughan and his timid proposal. Raising her glance to meet the bargee's, she laughed aloud. It was one of those special moments, she was only aware of the good things: she was young, she was free, life was beckoning.

Bobby couldn't have chosen a worse moment to start to scream, not the cries of a baby fighting sleep and about to give up the battle, but of one who needs attention. (In truth, one who should have eaten his dinner and was only just aware of the empty feeling inside him.)

'He wins,' the bargee laughed, nodding towards the baby. 'Lungs like his will drown us out.'

'I must get him home.'

'Pray the weather holds, then I'll see you again on my way home. That'll be Thursday or Friday.' He plunged his pole into the water, quickening the pace of the barge while she started deftly to turn her boat. His cocksure certainty that she'd be watching for him annoyed her – if it was too near the truth she wasn't going to admit to it.

'I may not be on the river then ...' she called after him. Above Bobby's yells perhaps he didn't hear what she said for his only reply was that familiar exaggerated salute of farewell, then his attention was back on his journey.

She wouldn't take the boat out on Thursday. And just as she had the first time she'd seen him, she pushed him firmly down the social strata to the bottom of the pile. No, she wouldn't be on the river. Thursday *or* Friday. The cheek!

Stanley liked her to have breakfast with him on her own. When she'd carried an almost newborn Bobby down, meaning to lay him on cushions by the breakfast room fire, it hadn't been a welcome move. Sympathy for her father decided her that it should be a meal just for the two of them together; having the baby there rubbed salt in his wound.

'I suppose Mr Carpenter will be here this evening, Pappy?' she said the morning after her encounter with her Gypsy King.

'You look forward to his visits, Polly? That's good. I've told you before, one man can read another's mind you know, Harry Carpenter is very – very, er, *aware* of you. No, no,' he raised his hand as she opened her mouth to interrupt, 'I know how you always shied away from your mother's attempts at match-making for you. But this is no fresh-faced boy'. (She remembered being in Harry's arms, she heard the echo '... no fresh-faced youth will ever satisfy you ...'), 'he is a real man, a strong character, the sort you can respect.'

'I'm always polite to your friends Pappy, even to him.'

'Don't brush him aside hastily, Pol. Perhaps he hasn't appeared to show any interest in you, you probably think I'm imagining things. But I can sense it.'

'If you can read people's minds, why don't you read mine too. I'll welcome him for your sake, but, Pappy, how long before we can be free of the hold he has on us? Are you paying him off slowly, is that why he comes each week? Or is he keeping an eye on the accounts to make sure his money is going to be ready at whatever date you've agreed?' There! She actually asked!

He pushed his plate away from him, the kedgeree half eaten.

'It's not like that.'

'How do you mean – not like that? How else can it be?'

77

'Don't be hard on me, Pol. I've had such a bad time, losing your dear mother. It's not for myself that I worried – you can never say I've been a selfish man, I wanted Elvira to have the best, yes and you too, when have I ever grudged you anything.'

Mrs Hume's kedgeree was as good as usual but suddenly it was as hard to swallow as a mouthful of sawdust. Polly fixed her gaze on her father, compelling him to look at her. Just for a second he did, then he lowered his eyes concentrating on the cruet as if he'd never seen it before.

'That was *then* Pappy. It's now I want to hear about.'

'You're saying you think I'm mean with you because there isn't the money for you to gallivant off to that French woman for more gowns?'

'You know I'm not! I just want to know the truth, how we stand with Harry Carpenter.'

Stanley made a supreme effort, he even managed to twist his face into what he supposed was a smile.

'We stand well enough with Carpenter. As I told you, he's a fine man, a natural businessman.'

She knew he wanted that to be the end of the conversation. But he had told her nothing.

'How much more do we have to pay him?' She had to ask it. Partly because she knew too much already to be able to be reassured so easily and, in a way that she wasn't prepared to examine, there was something else. It had to do with Harry: he'd seen through her own play-acting, for the brief moment when he'd stripped her of the veil of illusion there had been honesty between them. Or so she'd believed. She hated him for his arrogance, for understanding her too well and, most of all, for his power over them because of their debt. She clung to the emotion of hatred, but how could she give full vent to it unless she knew the extent of the debt?

'I've settled my account with him.'

'But that's wonderful! And you hadn't even told me!'

'I should never have involved you in any of it. I should have shielded you just as I always tried to shield your dear mother.'

She wished he wouldn't call her that. Why not simply 'your mother' as he used to when she was alive? It was as if he talked about a stranger. Mrs Hume did it too, 'the dear mistress'.

'And all this time in my mind I've been sticking pins in Mr Carpenter's effigy! You must really like him for himself if you invite him here still.'

In her relief she found herself hungry. The kedgeree on her plate was cold and unappetizing, but she spread a slice of crusty bread thickly with butter and topped it with honey. Life was good, life was wonderful. Today was Tuesday (even the thought of Harry's visit this evening didn't matter so much now) and by either Thursday or Friday the bargee would be looking out for her. Her resolution to play cat and mouse with him was forgotten, pushed from her mind by the relief that Seagrove's was free again.

It was Bobby's daily routine that Polly bathed him in the wash-stand basin then handed him over to Blanche Warwick. Usually he was awake before breakfast was over and that was when Daisy was in charge.

Humming softly under her breath, her spirit high, Polly started up the stairs. She could hear him crying, a normal 'I'm ready for someone to pick me up' cry. Then as she came to the first-floor landing the sound changed, he was choking on his screams, making so much noise that Daisy didn't hear her coming. That's how it was that she saw exactly what happened. Daisy was holding him, not cradling him to her but grasping him round his tiny waist, shaking him.

'Stop that bloody row or I'll give you another, an' 'arder this time too! D'you hear me. Shut yer row!' As she spoke she moved her hold on him so that her right hand was free then she brought it sharply across his puckered face. His breath was caught in a gasp, his mouth wide open. Silence.

In that second Polly was across the room to tear him out of Daisy's hold, thankful that the sudden movement started him breathing again.

'I saw what you did. You can pack your things and go. This instant.'

'Go? You mean clear out? You heard the way he was yelling. I can't never do anything with him. He doesn't like me.'

'And you don't like him, that's obvious. I'll give you your money until the end of the month, but I want you gone this morning.'

'Oh no, Miss. Don't pack me off. Who's going to do his washing, iron his gowns? I do all that, Miss Polly. I work hard as anything. It's not my fault I'm no good with babies.'

Holding Bobby closely against her shoulder Polly viewed the thin little fourteen-year-old. What would happen to her if she sent her back to her parents, dismissed from her job?

'What am I goin' to do?' Daisy sniffed, her mouth working. 'Best pack my bag.'

'I'll see you before you leave.'

'Yes, Miss.'

Oh Bobby boy, what are we going to do with her. Your poor little face, I can see where her fingers hit you. She looked so frightened . . .

'Here I am,' Blanche's voice cut across her thoughts a few minutes later as she rinsed the lukewarm water over Bobby's body. He liked his bath, it seemed that even though his face was still red he'd forgotten his recent misery. 'Bit early but my Bert was off to the store down in the Cattle Market for a few things. Don't hurry the lad.'

'He's done, I won't take long to get him dressed.'

'He's filling out a real treat, aren't you my pretty.'

Blanche was like a breath of fresh air coming between Polly and the memory of Daisy. And this morning she was in philosophical mood.

'Funny old world. Nature, we're all part of it. I thought that as I watched the cart go off taking Bert to the store he likes to deal with in the Cattle Market. He's gone to get a new milking pail or two, new heads for the hay forks, new shares for the plough – not for now, won't be ploughing up the field this time of year, but it's good to have things stored away ready.' She'd wasted no time, already she was in the nursing chair, her ample breast exposed. 'Come on then my bonny one, sounds like you're ready for me.'

Polly watched her affectionately, sure there was more to come. And she was right.

'See what I mean? All part of nature. I come her to nurse this wee lamb, you give me money for what nature lets me do. That's my bit towards it and that's how it is my Bert can go on his spend at Reading market, not just getting a pail to replace the one that's sprung a leak. No, this time he's buying in a stock of things he knows we shall want as the months go on. Not just one new share for the plough, dear me, no, not this time. He'll set himself up for a season or two. So he'll be able to plough the field then plant it with mangelwurzels that'll be fed to the cows, then they give milk for the pails ...' she laughed contentedly, happy at her part in nature's scheme of things.

But for all Blanche's contentment in her personal lot in life, she was always sensitive to other people's troubles.

'Something bothering you, Miss Polly duckie?'

Polly was tempted to tell her that Bobby's flushed face hadn't come from tears of hunger. Then she pictured Daisy upstairs pushing her few poor belongings into her straw basket, probably frightened of going home and saying she'd lost her job.

'I've been bothered about Daisy. She works hard, looks after Bobby's washing, and she never gives a speck of dust time to settle in his nursery. But she's not the right person to be looking after him. So I've told her to go.'

Blanche detected defiance in her tone.

'You're right, Miss Polly, Daisy never did fit her job. It was me who asked you to take her on, but I've seen she's not the right one. Oh dear, oh dear. Now what's to happen?' Blanche chewed her lips, her brow puckered. 'Not my business, I've no right to say such dreadful things,' then propping Bobby on her knee and tapping his back with her capable and experienced hand before changing his position to her other breast, 'there's a clever boy. I enjoy our talks while you sit watching him take his food, easy as anything to speak about things that would normally go unsaid. Like I say, it's none of my business. It's wicked to say such things about a man. But then, in a way it *is* my business, if I turn my back on it I'm no better than that Pharisee passing by on the other side of the road.'

'Turn your back on what, Mrs Warwick?' Polly could make no sense of the jumble of sentences.

'Young Daisy Dawkins. Related to Emmie or no, it was *me* brought her to your attention, I did it because I was frightened for the child. No doubt in my mind what was going on.' Blanche looked uneasy, uncertain whether to say more.

'What was going on? I've told her to go, I suppose it's

nothing to do with me. But she looked so distressed ... frightened. That's what's worrying me.'

'I'll make a clean breast of it, tell you all I know. It's what her mother would want me to do. You see, her Ma, Mabel her name was, she and me were best of friends. Mabel never had no more than the one child, something wrong with her insides. Not like me,' she chuckled, 'I told you before Bert only has to hang his trousers over the end of the bed! Yes, I've been lucky, well blessed, we both have, me and Bert. But I tell you one thing, if it'd been my insides that had let me down, I'd never have found him sniffing after our girls, eyeing them, trying to feel them. Mabel told Jo off about it and all the change she got from him was that she was imagining it. Load of lies! More than once she caught him red-handed and Daisy frightened out of her wits. Poor Mabel, took to her bed just before Christmas and was buried before the end of February. Not so long after your own poor Ma. That's why I put Daisy forward to come here. I figured it was the Lord's way of making amends for taking her poor Ma, putting a live-in job her way. Wouldn't have been able to rest easy knowing she was alone in that house with Jo. When she was little he never interested himself, so Mabel told me, not till this last year or so. Slightest chance and he'd be getting her cornered, having a feel. Dirty ol' sod.' Then, her mind back on Bobby, she rocked him gently as he stopped sucking to gaze up at her, his mouth wide open in a milky grin. 'Oh, love 'im. You got a right little treasure here, Miss Polly, and no mistake.'

'I'd better go and see Daisy. I said I would before she left, I have to pay her.'

'What I just told you, mind that's just between you, me and this little fella. Don't you go saying anything to her will you.'

Instead of going up to Daisy's attic room, Polly went down to the semi-basement. What she was going to suggest might find no favour in the kitchen but it was the only way she could think of round the problem. And the more she thought of it the better she liked the idea.

'I've come for the grocery bill, Mrs Hume. I'll pay it when I go out later.' Then, while the housekeeper was getting it from the dresser drawer, 'Emmie, how old were you when you came here?'

'Not quite fourteen.'

'Younger than Dolly?' Then plunging straight in: 'How would you like to help with Bobby?'

'Me help young Dolly! That bit of a kid!'

'No, of course not,' Polly laughed. 'Mrs Hume, I'm taking Bobby out of Daisy's care. She can still be responsible for his laundry, but apart from that I think you can make better use of her than I can. She's a great worker —'

'You don't have to tell me. If you ask my opinion she'll be better occupied down here helping than she is with him. It's having no brothers and sisters I expect, the girl is cackhanded with him. But she won't replace Emmie. If you take Emmie away I'll feel the pinch and I don't mind saying it.'

Emmie coloured with pleasure.

'Oh Mrs Hume, do you mean you'd miss me?'

If it were possible to pull back words that had been spoken, Ida Hume would have pulled hers back. The best she could do was to stand an inch taller, her long bony hands spread across her flat stomach.

'Miss your silly chatter more likely.'

But Emmie wasn't fooled.

Mrs Hume asked no question, but she noted Daisy's red-rimmed eyes. Nothing like work for taking a girl's mind off her troubles, whatever they may be.

'You can give this batter a good hard whipping,' she told Daisy, 'no pussy-footing about with it. Like this – I'll show you just the first time.'

'I used to whip up the batter for Ma, I can do it Mrs Hume. If you can tell me when you think it's got enough bubbles. Then we leave it out of the draught till it's time for it to go in the oven, that's what Ma used to say.'

Funny little slip of a girl, poor lass losing her mother like she had. Well, she seemed willing, might even say she seemed keen. Perhaps the tears hadn't been because she'd been sent to work in the kitchen after all.

'That's the way,' Ida's angular face relaxed into what was almost a smile. Things might not be so bad, hardly more than a child though she was, Daisy showed signs of being eager to please. She'd soon knock her into shape.

That was the first afternoon Polly hadn't been with Bobby. Instead, Emmie pushed him out in his bassinet hoping to meet someone she knew so that she could show him off and boast of the trust that had been shown in her. This was better than being in the kitchen at Mrs Hume's beck and call – not that she hadn't liked her job well enough, but then she'd known no other. This was freedom – better than freedom – with no one watching her she stopped walking and leant over the baby. When Daisy had come near him he'd never opened his mouth in that gummy smile, his protruding tongue aquiver with excitement.

'I'll be back either Thursday or Friday,' the handsome bargee had told Polly. And she'd vowed she wasn't going to paddle up and down the river waiting for him. True to her word she left the canoe in the boathouse on Thursday afternoon while, with Bobby tied to her in the improvised carrying sling, she played with Horace in the meadow. He must have thought it was his birthday; instead of the usual half hour or so, there seemed no end to Polly's patience as she threw sticks for him.

When there was no sign of the barge she pretended she didn't care.

'Come on boy, time to go home.' This afternoon Horace didn't plead to stay. The word 'home' conjured up a picture of his bowl of water by the side of his basket. He set off towards the stile, his tail swinging.

Friday morning was a repetition of Thursday afternoon. Friday afternoon Emmie took Bobby out and Polly sank her pride. She and Horace – carrying the piece of broken branch he'd left by the stile on his way home in the morning – boarded the canoe. She paddled downstream, with Horace standing sentinel, eyes fixed firmly ahead as if he were as anxious as she was to be the first to see the barge approaching.

Thursday or Friday ... hope was fading ... yes, but perhaps unloading had taken longer than he'd expected ... perhaps he had to pick up a load to take up the river ... not that it's important, I just happened to be out here ... ships that pass in the night, a barge and a canoe that pass in the afternoon ... probably he's miles away by now, upstream somewhere, wherever it is he comes from. Well, it's nothing to me ... ships that pass ...

This time when she paddled home she moored at the end of the garden, stepping deftly onto the wooden landing stage with Horace bounding ahead then dropping his branch at her feet.

'Sorry boy. Home, boy.' Another half hour and Blanche would be here, but before that she'd let Emmie help get Bobby ready for bed. Later on she'd come back and put the canoe under cover.

Hume went as usual to collect Stanley from the yard, to return with the message that he had things to do and wouldn't be home until late. So Polly had a solitary meal. It was illogical that she'd never resented his frequent absences when her mother had been alive, not as she did now. Whereabouts in Reading did he go? Would he be playing cards (yes, that must have been what worried her, that he would be playing and losing) or would he be visiting a woman? She imagined him later in the evening walking to Station Square to find a hansom to bring him home.

Dusk fell late, they were almost at the longest day of the year. Restless, Polly went upstairs to check Bobby. Lately he'd hardly woken for his late evening bottle. When he'd cried out she had given it to him, but he'd soon lost interest and gone back to sleep.

'He hasn't stirred yet, Miss Polly,' Emily looked up as Polly came into the nursery, her fingers not altering their steady movement as she knitted. This was her domain, the nursery and the small adjoining room where, when Polly had been young, her own nursemaid had slept. From being a young and, in Ida's opinion, irritatingly chatty housemaid, Emmie had taken on the role of nanny and, seeing how keen she was, Polly had agreed that she should move down from her attic room to the far smaller one that adjoined the nursery. 'I've got everything to hand for when he does. But Mrs Warwick, she thinks he may be changing his habits. You know how he likes to hold a finger of hard toast to chew on, helping his teeth through. Well, you'd be surprised how much of it he manages to eat. Goes to sleep satisfied, enough in him to last him. She reckons he's ready to start sleeping through. Not always, he won't change of a sudden like that. But why don't you leave his crib where it is in here. I'll have my door open, I'll hear every sound.'

'If he cries in the night, promise you'll bring him to me.'

'Cross my heart, Miss, if he don't settle himself for me then I'll come to you.'

Despite the relief of knowing Bobby was in loving hands, Polly had a sense of loss as she wandered out into the summer-scented garden. It was already nearly dark, a moonless night. She went down the sloping lawn, her intention being to put the canoe into the boathouse. At the water's edge she stood, breathing in the evocative nighttime smell of the river, welcoming the memories that crowded in on her. She was a child again, like a pair of conspirators she and her father had stolen down here dressed in their swimming costumes. The first time they'd swum at night there had been a full moon, magic had been abroad. When had he stopped accompanying her? How long ago was it that he'd started borrowing money from the business? But now his debt was cleared, he'd told her so himself. So where was he when he went out so often, trips to London, nights away? There was no need now to depend on Lady Luck. Or hadn't he learnt his lesson, was he starting again on the slippery slope that had made them beholden to Harry Carpenter? Harry Carpenter ... if he talked about the business to Pappy as she'd always imagined, then surely they couldn't be heading for trouble again.

She climbed into the boat, slipped it from its mooring, then sat still, comforted by the gentle movement of the water, letting the craft drift. She trusted Pappy, of course she did ... trust ... yes, she trusted Emmie too. So what if, say, two days a week she went into the yard. She had been useful before, she could be useful again, and she could keep an eye on the books. She pulled her thoughts up short. That sounds beastly, as if I don't trust him. I do, I do – anyway Harry would know if anything was wrong ... and again she pulled her thoughts away from the way they wanted to go. Hardly realizing it she'd taken up the paddle. Gently, almost soundlessly, she turned the canoe and this time moved slowly, idly, upstream. The air was warm, as soft as a caress, the only sound the movement of the water under her paddle. As if to still the sound she let herself drift, her fingers trailing in the water. She was level with Rat Island – although why people called it that she didn't know, for it had no more resident water rats than any other bank of the river. Even on a night as dark as this she knew just where she was, where the willow overhung the water, the place she could secure the boat.

Excitement drove her. The river was a world of empty darkness. A good thing it was, she laughed silently! Climbing onto the island she undressed, making sure – by touch alone – that she laid her clothes in an orderly pile so that she wouldn't have trouble putting them back on. Her petticoats would be a makeshift towel. Then back on the canoe so that she could lower herself into the water. So cold that for a moment it took her breath away. Then she struck out into a strong crawl, moving fast and effortlessly and knowing just where the patches of weeds were that had to be avoided.

Turning onto her back she floated, gazing up at the starless canopy above, listening to the silence.

Silence? What was that? An oar breaking the water? Another swimmer? If she swam back to the island whoever it was would hear her! She'd never been so conscious of her nakedness.

'A water nymph, I do declare!'

On a night as dark as this only familiarity had helped her discern the shapes of the river bank, the trees she'd known all her life. Yet now that he spoke she recognised something that she hadn't noticed: tied up on the far bank she could make out the vague shape of a barge.

Chapter Five

A minute ago she had been revelling in freedom, feeling herself to be as much part of the night as the bat that rushed on its way overhead or the distant call of an owl.

Although she'd never consciously considered it, modesty had been as much part of her upbringing as correct table manners and good deportment. In that she'd been no different from most girls of her generation. No wonder she was aware of her nakedness, unsure of her next move. Silence! No sound now of the other swimmer, only the rise and fall of the water over her floating body warned her of his presence. Where was he? His strokes weren't breaking the surface, he must be moving under water. Was he coming closer?

She must get back to the island, grab her clothes – almost clumsily she rolled onto her front and struck out towards safety.

'Wait. I didn't mean to frighten you.' He emerged so close that her foot contacted his naked body, so close that as he surfaced by her side his hand brushed against her. 'A naiad I declare, risen from her weedy home on the bed of the river.'

He suspected he heard her laugh and, encouraging her not to run away, he rolled onto his back purposely splashing noisily with his feet as he propelled himself out into deeper water. The effect on his unknown naiad was just as he'd hoped. Instead of rushing for the bank she too struck out to the middle of the river, not following him, yet conscious of him, excited that together they shared the freedom of the night.

'When did you get back?' She called softly, instinctively keeping her voice low even though the only living creatures within hearing distance were the four-legged – or two-winged – variety.

Until then she'd been a faceless water nymph, but immediately she spoke he realized who she was. The girl from the canoe! The girl from the house by the river! The sister of the baby who ... he pulled his thoughts quickly away from the direction they were heading and managed to answer in a voice that suggested he'd known who he was speaking to when he'd first called out to her.

'Not when I told you,' he answered. 'Have you been watching for me? I can never be sure how long a trip will take.'

'No, I wasn't watching – I'd forgotten until this afternoon when I happened to be on the river.' She was proud of the cool lie.

'I'll be gone at first light. I looked out for you as I came along – but this is even better. Come back to the barge, I'll lend you my shirt to put on.'

She imagined herself climbing naked aboard the work boat, pulling on a shirt he'd been wearing. If for a second she was tempted, it was the thought of that soiled shirt that made her turn back towards Rat Island.

This time he followed her. The carefully reared daughter of Elvira ought to have been angry, even frightened. Polly surprised herself that she was neither. All her initial panic had gone, she didn't doubt she would be safe with him. She knew exactly the best place to pull herself clear of the water.

'It's deep enough not to be muddy here, you can pull yourself up onto the bank,' which she did with one effortless spring. Then, as he followed, she stepped gingerly over the hard earth to reach her pile of clothes. Looking back over her shoulder she could see her Gypsy King, not clearly, but as a ghostly figure.

'Adam and Eve,' he laughed as though reading her thoughts, 'ashore in a Garden of Paradise.'

'You won't find any apple trees on Rat Island. Here, catch, you can borrow a petticoat to get dry.'

He had more sense than to rush her, he dried himself then knotted the garment around his waist while she hastily rubbed herself half dry with a second then scrambled into her clothes.

'Don't run away,' he said. 'When I wear a lady's petticoat I always make a point of knowing her name.'

Polly laughed. This sort of fun was a new experience.

'I'm Polly Seagrove. And you?'

'Charles, Charles Dunton.' he heard the name fall into the silence. He waited, more than half expecting it to mean something to her. Clearly it didn't.

Now that he was dry there seemed no reason to expect him to swim back across the river to the barge. To her it seemed the most natural thing to offer to paddle him across; and to him, to suggest she should come aboard so that they could brew up a warm drink after their swim.

It was a typical narrow barge, the sleeping accommodation a covered section no more than eight feet in length and some four feet higher than the gunwales, too low for Charles to stand erect inside. Loaded, the vessel would carry about sixty tons, no more than half the capacity of some of the wide barges.

Charles lit the storm lantern that hung in the doorless opening to his sleeping quarters, then taking a billy can filled it with river water ready to boil on the primus stove.

'Let me prove what a perfect host I am. I'll brew us a hot drink.'

Perhaps it was the river water, perhaps it was the billy can or even the view she had of his pile of grey blankets looking much as he'd unrolled himself from them this morning; whatever the reason, Polly found she wasn't thirsty.

'Not for me. I can't stay as long as that.'

He shrugged, and tipped the water back overboard.

'Not every night I have the chance to entertain a naiad,' he told her with a grin, obviously having no idea why she'd not been tempted.

Sitting on the side of the barge she surveyed her surroundings, but most of all she surveyed Charles. Half dry, his hair was an unruly mop of dark curls; in the yellow light of the lamp he was even more handsome than she'd dreamed, his eyes were as black as coals, his torso changed to pale gold.

If he followed her thoughts he gave no indication of it.

'Well? And how does she impress the experienced eye of a boat builder?' he asked, the nod of his head indicating that he referred to the barge.

'How do you know I'm anything to do with boatbuilding?'

90

'Word spreads, Polly. The name Seagrove is known the length of the Thames.'

Pleased by his answer she didn't delve, instead she told him of the weeks she'd spent at the yard and her plans that she'd soon be back there again. With Polly fully dressed and Charles still wearing her petticoat tied around his waist they sat on the side of the barge. It must be a dream, any minute she'd wake up and find it was just another day, another day when she'd keep her eyes alert for a sign of *Maryanne*, the name painted on the side of the barge.

'I thought you had charge of your young brother?'

'Yes, I do, and I wouldn't dream of leaving him if I weren't sure he'd be happy with Emmie. I shan't go to the yard every day, just ...' But her sentence faded into silence, only silently did she finish it '... just often enough that I can keep an eye on the books.' Even unspoken it cast a shadow.

A few minutes later, Charles once again in his trousers and both petticoats rolled up by her side on the seat of the canoe, Polly moved out to the centre of the river. In contrast to the pool of light given by the hurricane lantern the night was black, she knew that she would have disappeared from Charles's vision into the darkness. But looking back over her shoulder she was able to watch him without his knowing. She saw him light a spill from the lamp and hold it to the bowl of his pipe. In years he was probably not much older than she was herself, but there was nothing boyish about him. Charles Dunton was a man, with a man's strength, a man's appetites. She thought of his muscular arms, the breadth of his chest ...

'No fresh-faced youth will ever satisfy you,' Harry's voice echoed. And with it came memories she wanted to forget.

From the way her father beat a tattoo on the leather top of his desk Polly knew her suggestion would be met with opposition. She pulled forward a chair and sat facing him – then wished she hadn't, the scene was too reminiscent of the evening he'd told her about his debt.

But all that was behind them and she spoke with the determination of one who meant to look to the future not the past.

'You don't need to worry about Bobby,' she assured him, 'if I weren't absolutely certain he'd be happy with Emmie I wouldn't dream of starting at the yard again. I shan't go in with you first thing in the mornings, I'll stay until I put him down to sleep after Mrs Warwick has seen to him. By that time Hume will be back with the trap, so I'll bring myself to the yard and we can keep it there and drive home together.'

'No, no, I can't have you do that.'

'But why? Pappy, it's honestly not necessary for me to stay here all day. I never interfere with Mrs Hume, she knows more about running a house than I do. And Bobby has taken such a fancy to Emmie it almost makes me jealous!' But her laugh disproved her words. 'Next you'll be trying to make me believe you didn't enjoy having me at the yard with you.'

'You know I did. But don't push me, Pol. Don't ask me to explain.' His face was a picture of misery. The desk top drumming stopped, he raised his hand to run his fingers around the inside of his stiff wing collar as if it threatened to choke him. 'It's because of the mess I got myself into, you don't trust me, is that it?'

'It's *our* business – well, it's *yours* but I want it to be *ours*. It must stay in the family, first it was Uncle Fred's and now it's yours ... All right, I won't be able to work on the boats with my hands, but I want to learn, I want to understand. Someone said to me the other day that the name of Seagrove is known the length of the Thames. And you expect me to want to idle my hours away at home, living on the proceeds and not doing a hand's turn to help.'

'Once more I'll ask it – Pol, don't push me. Won't you let it rest?'

Something was wrong!

'You trusted me before, can't you trust me now? Why don't you want me there?' She kept her voice low, she mustn't let him see that she'd already guessed why he was frightened that she would delve too deeply into the ledgers. Into her mind flashed the image of Harry and for one crazy moment she wished her father were still in his debt. As long as he kept a check on each week's business, no matter how much she had resented that he had the right, she had felt safe.

'Not want you ... oh, Pol, if only it were as you think.' He forced himself to look her in the eye. 'All right, I'll tell you. The debt to Carpenter – I paid him—'

'Yes, I know. You told me.' So why were a thousand butterflies fluttering in her chest? Why was her tongue stiff and dry, wanting to cleave to the roof of her mouth?

'I paid him with an interest in the yard – No, don't say anything, let me finish. He's a meticulous businessman, there wasn't a plank of wood or a sack of oakum that escaped the valuer. You say Seagrove's is *mine*, *ours*. Half of it perhaps, no not even that.'

A minute ago there had been no reason in Polly's fear; now shock numbed her reason and drove away her fear. All she was left with was a blinding rage at Harry Carpenter, the meticulous businessman, the Shylock who took his pound of flesh and retained his grip on them.

'I see.'

'Don't say it like that, Pol. What else could I do? Your dear mother gone, no one to turn to. Oh yes, I know I had you. But I couldn't burden you. You spared me the responsibility of the boy, I couldn't worry you with this.'

'Did Mr Carpenter refuse to give us any grace?'

'It wasn't like that. To repay him, live at the standard we've been used to, keep the yard fully staffed – and with less men there would be less turnover. You don't know the worry of it.'

'There's one thing I'm sure of. No, two things. One is that I'm glad you've told me, now I know where we stand; the second is that now I'm more determined that ever to work with you. We'll do it, between us we will. It's Seagrove's name that's known all along the Thames, not Carpenter's. And that's the way it's going to stay.'

The next morning Emmie watched the pony and trap set out for the yard. Fully fed, Bobby was contentedly asleep.

'Now then, my duck, you sure about being on your own with him? I'm not meaning I don't think you can look after him as well as any of us, but when he yells you've no one to turn to.'

'Tell you the honest truth, Mrs Warwick, I'm looking forward to it. No,' she laughed, 'I don't mean I want you gone, but I like to feel he's really mine to care for.'

Satisfied, Blanche Warwick tied on her old-fashioned bonnet.

'You remind me of my Clara, a real natural with the little ones she always was. You'd get on well with her. Why don't you push the bassinet along to Little Roost when you're taking him for his airing. I've told Clara how it is you're looking after the little love. Mind you, I never imagined till I heard it this morning that Miss Polly would be off to join her Pa at the boatyard.'

'I might just do that – come to call on you. Miss Polly wouldn't have left him if she hadn't known he takes to me happy enough. He never did to young Daisy, as soon as she picked him up he'd scream. They know, babies do, they know who loves them.'

If that's what Emmie believed, then Blanche wouldn't be the one to cast a doubt. Babies certainly were happier in some people's arms than in others, but that was because they could sense where they were safe. Poor little Daisy, likely as not she'd handled him as if he'd break as easy as the best bone china; no wonder the wee mite hadn't been comfy with her.

'I might just push him along as far as your place later on Mrs Warwick – show him off to your Clara.'

So she did and although she wasn't there long it was the beginning of a friendship between the two of them.

Sitting on the high wooden stool in front of the tall desk, Polly was spending her afternoon bringing the Sales Ledger up to date in her best handwriting and entering up accounts. The bookkeeping system at Seagrove's was a simple one: two books were known as the Bought Ledgers, one noting each order sent to suppliers for goods needed in the yard, then crossed through and dated when delivery was made; the second listing invoices received, then crossed through and dated when payment was made. Of the two Sales Ledgers, the first noted the date each job was accepted and detailed the materials used and the hours worked; the second showed the amount charged to the client, the date the account was posted and finally the date it was paid.

On such an airlessly hot day the timber-built office was hot despite door and window both being open. Before Polly inked in the total on an itemised account she always added the columns of figures twice to make sure she'd not made any mistakes. This time the answers didn't tally, so she started from the top of the page a third time, so engrossed that she didn't hear Harry come into the room.

'I didn't notice your father in the yard,' his voice startled her, 'is he not here?' Already he was in the room, his top hat removed.

'I didn't realise anyone was there, I must have missed your knock,' she said pointedly, knowing full well there hadn't been a knock to miss.

'And I didn't realise you were here, Polly, or I might have come sooner.'

Of course he wasn't serious, she was sure of that. Was he humouring her as he might a child, or was he mocking her as he had on that evening she tried hard to forget? Either way did nothing to put her at her ease.

'Then I'm glad you didn't realize it. I have been much too busy to waste time talking to a visitor.'

He raised his brows, his silence reminding her as clearly as any words of the thing she was finding it so hard to come to terms with – Harry Carpenter was no ordinary visitor, he had every right to walk unannounced into the office.

'My father wasn't expecting you I don't think? I'm sure he would have written it in his appointment book. He had business elsewhere, I'm not expecting him back this afternoon.'

'I had someone to see in Reading and as I was in the vicinity I decided to be brought out here before catching the train back to London.'

She turned again to her column of figures, conscious that she was behaving badly yet not able to act any other way, angry with herself for being gauche and impolite and hating him for – for what? For having the right to be here? For destroying her confidence with his own air of success so apparent in his appearance from the cloth of his well-cut frock coat and silk top hat to the self-assurance of his expression? If she concentrated on the ledger he must surely go outside, look at the work the men were doing ... 'make a nuisance of himself to *them* and leave me alone.'

Moving to stand behind her he looked over her shoulder, saw the account she had written so carefully in ink, in ink except for the final total which she'd put lightly in pencil until she was sure she had it right. A hint of a smile touched the corners of his mouth as he glanced down the neatly written figures, making a mental calculation. What had been a hint established itself – how angry she would have been had she seen it and recognised what to her would have appeared to be kindly tolerance! – as he saw the childish way she'd noted the number of shillings carried forward from the pence, the pounds from the shillings.

'It's in the pounds that you've gone wrong,' he leant over her pointing his finger, 'you must have forgotten to add in the two you had to carry forward.'

'No, I didn't. See, it's pencilled at the top.'

With one hand on her should he bent forward, running his finger down the list of figures as he added aloud. His face was only inches from hers, she could smell the hint of lavender from his brilliantine just as she had that evening. She held herself away from him as if she were giving him a better view of the account.

Slipping the pencil from her fingers he lightly marked in the correct total.

'Your father didn't tell me you had started coming to the yard again.'

'Should he have? I suppose you think he should, I suppose you think I've no right to be working here. Well, you needn't be alarmed Mr Carpenter, I don't intend to draw a wage. Anything I do here is for Seagrove's, *Seagrove's*, you hear me?' She ought not to have started down this road; she felt too strongly about it. She held her clenched fists in her lap.

'And very creditable.' Standing upright again he moved to lean back against the desk by her side.

Polly heard his answer as condescending, it touched her on a raw nerve and fuelled her anger.

'Neither of you have been honest with me, not Pappy,' as soon as she'd given her father that familiar and special name she regretted it, she could see it hadn't passed unnoticed, 'and not you either. You took advantage of my father's circumstances to offer him a loan. You took advantage of his personal circumstances at home instead of agreeing to give him a little longer to repay you. I suppose all the time you were waiting your opportunity to get your foot into the door here, so you seized your chance when you knew he was at his lowest ebb after he'd lost Mother.' She had blown her safety valve, once started not even his changed expression, nor the narrowing of his startlingly light blue eyes, could stop her. 'Because he wanted to keep the home as it always had been he agreed to this – this – this tomfool arrangement. If he'd told me I would never have let it happen. As if a home compares with *this*. There are lots of things we could have sold, we have no need of such a grand house.' But what was the use of railing about how things might have been? 'Yes, I played a game too. And you know very well why I did it, all the time you were laughing at me for how I behaved. You must have known. The yard owed *precious* Mr Carpenter money, for Seagrove's I was prepared to sink my pride, hoping that even a hardened businessman had a soft spot in his heart. And you let me go on playing it, making a fool of myself even after the two of you had carved Seagrove's up so that you got your pound of flesh – Shylock, that's what I called you!'

'Our contract was drawn up perfectly amicably. Yes, I meant to – what was it you said? – get my foot in the door here. Seagrove's is, or rather *was*, a good business. I mean to see that that's what it will be again.'

She jumped to her feet, she needed to be face to face with him.

'Are you criticizing our work? There's real craftsmanship in this yard. What do you know about boats? Nothing!'

'I don't need to be a boat builder, there's an excellent team of those in the yard already and, no, Polly I am not criticizing the men's work.' Again that flicker of a smile touched the corner of his mouth as he told her, 'I mean to see the figures tally and the firm prospers as it should.'

'You interrupted me, that's what made me go wrong. And if you hadn't interfered Mr Carpenter I would have found where the mistake was.' Polly glowered at him, she hadn't been blessed with red hair for nothing!

He laughed. 'Polly, oh Polly, can I do no right for you? We have a common goal, can't we work for it together? And don't you think it's time I was Harry, not Mr Carpenter?'

She ignored both suggestions.

'My father hasn't told me how much he borrowed from you.

So I don't know what I'm up against. But one thing I promise you, however much of this business you like to think is yours one of these days I shall find a way to get you out of it. If I'd been a son not a daughter I would have been here years ago, I wouldn't have let any of this happen.' How dreadful that sounded, it was like saying 'I would have been watching Pappy.'

Why was Harry looking at her so strangely, as if he could see into her mind, as if his thoughts went beyond what she said? It was no use trying to move back from him when he put his hands on her shoulder, she knew that if she tried to step back his grip would tighten. Defiantly she forced her eyes to meet his.

'You'll only hurt yourself if you try to fight me, Polly. We both mean this yard to prosper, it'll succeed more quickly if we pull in the same direction.' Then, with a sudden smile, 'We're two of a kind, you and I, neither of us accept defeat. That being so, the future of Seagrove's is assured.'

It would have been so easy to smile back at him. But she couldn't, *wouldn't*, there were too many ghosts. She'd made a fool of herself once with the crude way she'd flirted with him, as if an inch of pale bosom would go to his head as it might have to one of those 'fresh-faced youths' he'd talked about. He'd not fallen for that any more than he had for her play of dependent innocence. And whatever she answered him now, he would doubt her honesty.

So she said nothing.

Surely she couldn't have been disappointed when he released his hold on her and opened the case of his pocket watch.

'I shall hinder you no longer, it's time I left. Tell me, Polly, what have you done with that young brother of yours? Is the young girl I saw capable of being left so long with him?'

She couldn't know that the memory of her he cherished was of her concern for the baby, the unaffected warmth in her handling of him. And he couldn't know how his question conjured up the memory of a silk handkerchief being pushed into her hand. Now, both of them following their own thoughts they look at each other with honesty.

'No, I wouldn't have come if Daisy had still been looking

after him. But Emmie's different, he's always happy with Emmie. I'm not leaving him every day though, I expect I'll be here about two days a week.'

'Mondays and ...?'

She saw the teasing light in his eyes. Why did he treat her as though she were a child looking for compliments? After the way she'd behaved towards him for months she had no right to expect anything better from him. Her mind took a sideways leap without any prompting. Supposing it had been Charles Dunton who had walked unannounced into the office, suppose it were he who asked that question, so simple yet so full of meaning?

'I have no schedule,' she told Harry coolly. 'Today just happens to be Monday. It depends on Bobby when I'm free to be here. If he's fretful I wouldn't dream of leaving him, after all I can write accounts as easily in father's study as here as long as he brings the ledgers home with him. Now, if you'll excuse me, I really have wasted more than enough of my afternoon.'

'Forgive me.' He picked up his tall silk hat from the bench-like desk. 'I don't think we have wasted anything this afternoon, I prefer to believe we have a truer understanding of each other. Convey my respect to your father. Goodbye Polly.'

'Goodbye Mr Carpenter.'

Half way to the door he turned. Was he coming back?

'Goodbye ... *Polly*.' He waited.

'... Harry.'

'No, we've not wasted the afternoon, Polly.'

Pointedly she turned back to the desk until the door closed behind him. It had been open when he arrived, she told herself, it was because she wanted a through current of air that she opened it again, first giving him time to reach the yard and even then turning the handle quietly. There was no such excuse for moving through it, careful to make no sound, and watching him as he stopped to talk to Hugh Davies. A middle-aged bony-faced moneylender, hadn't that been her first impression? So when had she started to see him differently? Not straight away ... although how could she have found such sport in trying to interest him if that's how she'd thought of him? Or was it when he'd kissed her, was that when she'd seen him anew ... no don't think about that ... he was hateful, right from the beginning he'd meant to get a hold on Seagrove's, he'd just admitted to it ... he's going now, mind he doesn't turn round and see you watching ... he's so erect he ought to be a soldier ... there's something aristocratic, almost regal, in his bearing ... don't be stupid, he told you himself his childhood had been no different from those barefoot urchins from the cottages on the wharf ... no one would ever get the better of him, see the way the cabby has climbed down to open the door for him ... No one would get the better of him, did I say? I'll show him!

Bobby thrived. By the time he was six months old Blanche Warwick's part in his welfare came to an end, he was used to taking milk from a bottle and helping his front teeth through by gnawing on toast crusts. But that wasn't to say Blanche parted company from him.

'Me and Bobby, we went along to the farm this afternoon, to Mrs Warwick's place. Pleased as anything he was to see her, you'd think he knew I wanted him to show off his two new teeth the way he beamed when she spoke to him,' Emmie told Polly one evening towards the end of July. There was nothing she liked better than to chatter, and it was her opinion that the half hour they usually shared as they got the baby ready for bed had a special intimacy. Working downstairs had never been so cosy, as starchy as her apron, that Mrs Hume always was; she'd put a dampener on a nice friendly chat before it had time to get going: 'We've no time to waste gossiping, girl. Other's people's affairs aren't our business and best you remember it.'

'Look at the dimples coming in his knees, Miss Polly. Couldn't you just gobble him all up!' And to demonstrate her point she swooped on Bobby as if she were doing just that, opening and shutting her mouth and smacking her lips. At his peals of laughter her cup of happiness was overflowing.

'Good, I'm glad you take him to see Mrs Warwick.'

'I hoped I'd see Clara, two of a kind that's what Mrs Warwick says we are. But this afternoon she wasn't there, it seems she was on the river with her young man, Chaw.'

In Polly's opinion there was precious little resemblance between the two girls, never had she seen Emmie anything but clean. Mrs Hume's training had instilled in her that each morning she should have a freshly washed apron, her hair should be out of the way under her mob cap and her shoes shining. As for Clara Warwick, Polly had formed a very low opinion the one and only time she'd seen her and nothing she heard from Emmie had any power to change it.

'When is the wedding to be?' Polly had no interest in Clara's wedding plans, but she sensed that Emmie was lonely for someone of her own age to talk to. 'Sometime this year, Mrs Warwick told me. Is it soon?'

'I don't know just when. But Mrs Warwick says that Chaw has been to see Farmer Maidlow to try and rent the two fields across the lane from Little Roost, you know where I mean, the meadows by the river. He might as well get rid of them for all the use he makes of them, whenever I've walked that far along the towpath I've never seen so much as a cow on them. Mind you, old Archie Maidlow's a mucky sort of farmer, reckon rats breed better than cattle in his dirty old barns, that's what my grandad used to say about him. Who's going to give our baby his bottle, Miss Polly? Me or you?'

'You can, Emmie. My father is expecting Mr Carpenter this evening and a lady as well. You go and get the bottle ready.' Polly picked Bobby up as she spoke.

'If you want to be changing your dress, Miss Polly, we can lie him in his crib while I'm downstairs.'

'No, I've plenty of time.' She hadn't, her answer was prompted by her first twinge of jealousy, the second following quickly in its wake as Bobby turned his head to watch Emmie go out of the nursery, his bottom lip as clear an expression of how he felt about being left behind as the words he was too young for.

Lying him on her knee Polly talked to him, secret talk for no ears but his. His lip recovered and so did her spirits. He treated her to a view of his brand-new teeth as she started on her tale of how vital it was that *she* made sure the books were always in order, a written account sent out for every job done so that when payment was made there was no way of it not being recorded. *She* knew how it was that the yard had been in such financial straits when Harry Carpenter had come onto the scene, he must have a good idea of it too. But she'd never let him have the satisfaction of finding fault now. When he checks the books ... 'Oh, Bobby, *our* books, the trade of *our* yard, that's what it was and so it will be again. He's so arrogant and right, we've got to get rid of him, but until we do I can't stop him, he can check everything, watch us, watch the way the men work, probably suspect us of cheating him. We've got to get rid of him, I hate him, everything he touches turns to gold! I'll never let him have the satisfaction of finding we're a farthing out. You know what he's doing? He's bringing some woman with him this evening! Not that I care, he can have all the lady friends he wants, it's nothing to me. But you know why he's bringing her here, don't you? It's to pay me back for the way I used to behave. I've learnt my lesson, I'd have more sense now. What will she be like? Mrs Banks, a widow, that's all Pappy told me. She'll be rich, you can be sure she'll be rich or Harry Carpenter wouldn't waste his time with her.'

Bobby's bottom lip pulled her up short, told her he didn't like her tone and misunderstood where her resentment was aimed. Before she had time to bring back his smile, Emmie returned bearing the bottle.

'Come on then my lovey,' she took him from Polly, 'what's that funny face about then?' He settled contentedly in her arms. Whatever unease Polly's serious confidences had given him was forgotten.

Cool and reserved – at any rate on the surface – Polly played hostess to their guests. Cecily Banks gave the appearance of fitting perfectly into the niche prepared for her, diamond rings glinting in the light from the candelabrum at the centre of the dining table, a gown as elegant as any creation from the House of Duprés. A woman of perhaps the same age as Elvira would have been, dressed with the same impeccable taste but with no helping hand from nature. That she hadn't beauty as well as wealth surprised Polly, she had taken it for granted that Harry would have wanted both. She's not young either, she thought spitefully, not that he'd care about that anymore than he would that she's got front teeth like a buck rabbit and the makings of a double chin! A minute later her unkind thoughts made her feel mean and smallminded when Cecily turned to her with a smile that seemed to bear genuine warmth.

'Whatever would your father do without you? I've heard how you have taken charge of your tiny brother.'

'Naturally.' Polly heard her answer as curt. Cecily's remark had brought back to her 'that' evening, she remembered how she and Harry had been interrupted by Daisy bringing Bobby to her, she remembered the silk handkerchief thrust into her hand. He had no right to talk her over with his lady friends.

'Natural to you, perhaps, but it wouldn't have been to every young woman,' Cecily answered.

'Polly does very well,' Stanley said proudly. 'Not just with the child, but with the business too. Isn't that so, Harry?'

'Indeed,' Harry agreed soberly, his voice seeming to compel her to look at him. How did he mean her to hear that one word? As corroboration of what her father had said or was he mocking her for what he saw as the impossible task of ousting him from Seagrove's?

'Of course I care about Bobby and about the boatyard too. As for the time I spend there, it's what I want to do. Uncle Fred started the business, I was quite young when he died, but I remember being intrigued when he told me the River Thames flowed in his veins. I think it does in mine too.'

'And yours, Stanley?' Cecily turned her toothy smile on him. 'Does river water run through your veins too?'

'Nothing but normal red blood, my dear.'

Polly heard his answer as a betrayal. Just because he wanted to ingratiate himself with Harry Carpenter, how could he brush Seagrove's aside in that flippant way? And 'my dear' too!

'Of course it does, Pappy! Ours is a family business, at least it was until recently. And so it will be again, I'll not rest with anything less.'

'That's enough, Pol. There are more pleasant things to talk to our visitors about than the yard.'

'I beg your pardon, Mrs Banks. Of course you can't be interested in a boatyard, why should you? When I ride my hobby horse there's no stopping me.'

'But you're wrong, I am interested.'

Polly bit back her natural retort, 'Then you've no right to be interested.' She felt rather than saw that Harry was watching her. She concentrated on her meal, knowing that as a hostess she was behaving badly. Not that her father seemed to notice, this evening he was in fine form and giving every appearance of enjoying Mrs Banks's company. It seemed to Polly pathetic that he should be paying more attention to Mrs Banks than Harry did himself, a certain sign of his insecurity in the business.

She knew she was being ill-mannered but she was too cross to care. Her food had no more appeal than sawdust, she just wanted the evening over.

The meal finished, the men didn't sit over their port, instead everyone moved into the drawing room and when Stanley suggested some music Polly expected he would ask her to play.

'Won't you sing for us, Cecily?'

Polly felt trapped. She could gallop through her party pieces with volume and precision but little artistry, her repertoire being no greater now than when, at eighteen, she had persuaded her father to discontinue her lessons. Faced with music she hadn't seen before she knew she wasn't up to playing accompaniment while 'Mrs Rabbit', as she'd found a certain solace in silently naming their guest, warbled.

'I must go and look at Bobby,' she made the first excuse that came into her head.

Once upstairs she went to her own room, checked her appearance, smoothed her hair, dabbed the powder puff over her face, then a little lip rouge. Would they have forgotten about the music? She crept out onto the landing and listened just as the first chords were struck. Safe that she wouldn't be called on to make a fool of herself, she started down the stairs. 'Mrs Rabbit' must play her own accompaniment.

Harry Carpenter never ceased to surprise her. Unlike her own toneless hammering, he was playing Handel with sensitivity, softly, his fingers seeming to caress the keyboard as Cecily started to sing. And here was shock Number Two. Standing by his side, her hands lightly clasped in front of her her notes were as pure as any choirboy.

'I know that my Redeemer liveth . . .' she sang effortlessly, the clear soprano notes having the effect on Polly of making her ashamed of the less than kindly thoughts she had been harbouring. Over the fireplace hung the portrait of her mother . . . what was in Pappy's mind as he stood gazing towards the two at the piano? So sure she knew the answer, just for a second she slipped her hand into his. He turned to her, something in his expression she couldn't read ... it might have been relief. Whatever it was, it was soon gone, overtaken by a smile of appreciation as he listened to the music.

The visitors left together, Mrs Banks having offered that her coachman would make a detour and take Harry to Reading Station.

'Well?' Stanley hardly waited for the front door to be closed on them before he asked her, 'What did you make of Cecily?'

'I don't know either of them well enough to form an opinion.' Then with an honest laugh, 'I was jolly glad I didn't have to play for her singing.'

'A voice like an angel. You would have acquitted yourself very well, Pol, had you not disappeared upstairs. Carpenter offered to play for her. I had no idea he was so accomplished.'

'They're probably used to making music together,' Polly wasn't ready to give him praise. 'I should have just made a fool of myself.'

Stanley looked puzzled.

'Used to making music together? But they can't be. They'd never met until this evening.'

It seemed she had made a fool of herself anyway, even if she was the only one to know it. It was as she pulled herself out of her first confusion that she remembered her father's eager question, 'What did you make of Cecily?' If she hadn't come here as Harry's friend, then she must be his.

The lamps were out, the house shut up for the night.

Polly was restless. Still fully dressed, she opened the window wide and leant out, breathing in the strange scent of the summer night. A country garden would be heady with flowers, but at Water's Edge the air was full of a perfume more subtle, a combination of river and garden.

From downstairs she heard a gruff bark; Horace was restless too. Perhaps he needed a run. Already her mind was rushing ahead, she saw the two of them free of the house, running across the sloping lawn to the stile and the towpath. Carrying her shoes she went down the carpeted stairs, warning Horace of her approach with a whispered, 'Hush, boy,' then when she went into the scullery where he slept and he sniffed and bounced in anticipation, 'Got to be quiet, Horace. Mustn't bark.' So he sneezed instead, a sign that he understood. Stooping down in the darkness she hugged him and his answer to that was to hit her with his swishing tail.

Then, just as she'd imagined moments before, they were down the garden and climbing over – or, in Horace's case, through – the stile to the towpath. In the dark he didn't bring her his stick, he seemed content to rush ahead of her, back to tear around her, then off again. She hardly noticed, her thoughts were on the events of the evening. How important to Pappy was Cecily Banks? Important enough for him to bring her home and be anxious that she was welcomed. A year ago her mother had been ill and miserable, bitter against him that he'd made her pregnant with a child she hadn't wanted. A child she hadn't wanted ... Bobby ... if only she had lived she would have wanted him and loved him. But that was 'if only'. Pappy had been out a good deal lately, coming home late, staying away a day or two at a time. It hadn't made sense in her mind, the ledgers had been correct, every penny spent out or paid in had been recorded. Had Mrs Banks been entertaining him when he was away from home? Hadn't he been playing cards, backing horses, flirting with Lady Luck? Or had his wealthy widow been financing him? Polly pulled her thoughts up short, she even stopped walking, stilled by self disgust that even in her imagination she could harbour such disloyalty. Determined to set her mind on a safer track she pictured the scene at the piano, Harry and Cecily making music in such harmony. It occurred to her that at the time she'd thought of the visitor as 'Mrs Rabbit', bent on seeing her as unattractive. Now she thought of her as Mrs Banks, her projecting teeth had become no more than part of her friendly smile. But why was that? Surely, suspecting that the bejewelled widow was important to her father should have added fuel to her previous dislike?

The sound of Horace barking ahead of her in the darkness set her into a run. What was he doing? Was he aggravating the cows?

'Horace!' she shouted. 'Come here, Horace!' She expected him to come charging back to her out of the darkness, but instead she heard his low and threatening growl. 'Horace leave the cows alone,' she panted.

106

'Do I hear my naiad?' came that unexpected but familiar voice. 'All right, boy, put your teeth away, I'm friend not foe.'

Polly laughed aloud as she ran, the evening pushed out of her mind. In the uncanny way dogs have, Horace sensed her pleasure, stopped growling and stood still, peering through the moonless night for first sight of her then turning back to the man he'd thought it his duty to defend her from. He wasn't ready yet to wag his tail, he held it at the ready, uncertain of the next move; he was still on guard, ready to take his cue from Polly.

'You're a very nocturnal creature,' Charles greeted Polly.

'Horace barked to come out. I expect he thought he'd been short-changed, I only had time to give him a short run this morning. I've been at the boatyard all day. When did you get here? Which way are you going?'

'Downstream. But I didn't want to pass by when it was already dusk, so I decided to tie up here for the night.'

She heard the meaning behind his words: if he passed by their stretch of the river in the dusk he wouldn't have seen her, if he waited for morning she might have been in the meadow with Horace.

He reached to take her hand.

'I'm tied up just round the bend of the river. Come on board and talk to me, let Horace see that I'm harmless and he can come off guard duty.'

'I'd like that.' Her meetings with Charles always gave her a sensation of freedom, cleared her mind of worries about Seagrove's, whether her father was running into debt again, the hold Harry Carpenter had on them ... all of it would be waiting for her later, but as she walked hand in hand with Charles towards his barge daily problems had no hold on her. So Cinderella must have felt as she was ushered into the palace and swept into the dance by Prince Charming.

He leapt aboard, then held out his hand to help her as she followed. With one woof – and only he knew whether it was meant as excitement, a warning or simply a reminder that he was with them – Horace followed. Could Charles have been expecting her, or at least hoping that she would come, Polly wondered? For, as he lit the storm lamp, she noticed how different his sleeping quarters looked: the blankets were spread neatly over the mattress, even the pillow had been plumped up.

But she didn't go into the small sheltered apartment, neither did he suggest that she should. They sat on either side of the flat-bottomed boat, Horace leaning close against her leg, ready to defend if necessary but, gathering from the easy way she talked that the stranger was a friend, letting his tail thump the floor every now and again as a sign that he was enjoying himself.

That evening Polly and Charles learnt a little more about each other. She talked of Seagrove's – not of the financial tightrope they walked but of the craftsmanship, of river craft generally, of the increasing number of steamers that carried passengers for pleasure; he told her of the cargoes he carried, flour from his father's mill some ten miles upstream, either turning onto the Kennet at Reading and making for Theale or Newbury, or continuing down the Thames to Maidenhead and beyond. Sometimes he would return empty, sometimes he would collect a load to bring as far as Reading. Talking, listening, building a picture, without realizing it her Gypsy King, the handsome bargee who had been at the bottom of the social pile, was overtaken by the man of flesh and bone, the man of spirit. She was never sure when she ceased to see Charles Dunton as more than someone to dream about, a dream that could have no place in reality. But that night must have been the start of it.

There were nights when they swam together. Polly wore her dark blue bathing costume and frilly rubber hat; Charles, who in the past had always swum at night, naked and alone, for lack of a costume wore winter combinations. Hardly the apparel to encourage romance, but the excitement of stealing out alone knowing he would be by the water waiting for her was more thrilling than anything she had ever known. Polly was falling in love, willingly, eagerly. She even dreamed that because Charles was a man of the river one day he would be part of Seagrove's. She dreamed that – and so much more. In years he wasn't far ahead of her, but he was nothing of a fresh-faced youth. He was a god amongst men.

It was an evening early in October. Polly dressed with excitement, sure that by now Charles must have come. When he'd set off a fortnight ago he'd told her that this time when his cargo was off-loaded he was to collect a consignment to carry on downstream to Chertsey, then back to Reading to load timber to be taken up the Kennet as far as Hungerford. He took all the extra work he could, he'd said, because although he carried flour for his father any additional jobs meant money for himself, money he was soon to need. Travelling alone he had to operate the locks on the Kennet for himself, everything seemed geared to hinder him. Even allowing for delays he must be back by this evening and he'd promised her that no matter how early in the day he arrived he wouldn't travel on until he'd seen her.

Tonight she made a quiet exit not even rousing Horace. Early in the autumn though it was, by the river the air was damp with fog. Overhead the sky was clear, she could see the crescent of a new moon, yet to look ahead there was nothing except a blanket of thick white mist. As she came through the first meadow and opened the gate into the second she saw a hazy golden light ahead of her. He's there, he's waiting, that's his lamp! She started to run, the light guiding her until she came close and he stepped out of the gloom into her path. She ran straight into his waiting arms.

Tonight they stooped to go into the shelter of his sleeping quarters, the roof so low that they sat on the mattress. The hanging lantern came between them and the fog, between them and everything.

Something about him was different, she felt it in the way he gripped her hand. Briefly he told her about his trip but she knew his mind wasn't on what he was saying. Then turning her face towards him so that the light shone on her, 'I never thought I'd know a woman like you. Polly ... I wanted time ... I wanted ... It's you I want, you're like a beautiful dream, everything about you, your voice, your face, everything ...' One hand moved down her body. 'I didn't mean to wed so soon ...' What was happening to her, such a wild longing possessed her, she looked no further than the moment, than being here with him. Soon they would be wed ... she could feel the pounding of her heart, when with his free hand he unbuttoned her bodice and fondled her breast she pushed his palm against her, she wanted him to hear her heart beat, to

109

know all the things that she didn't understand well enough to put into words.

He needed no words. Firmly he pressed her down so that her head was on his pillow. She knew he pushed her skirt out of the way, she knew he was easing her out of her long drawers. He was neither rough nor timid, she knew what he was doing and had no will to stop him. His voice told her all she wanted to know: 'You are perfect,' 'I never knew I could want to make love to a woman like I do to you. Polly, I'm going to love you. You want me, tell me you want me.'

'Yes,' she breathed, her whole being yearned for him.

With unerring deftness he entered her, if he heard her involuntary gasp of sudden pain it didn't interrupt him. He was hurting her, for her there was no physical pleasure in his pounding body, yet she wanted to shout for joy. She had never felt so alive, so vital ... he loved her ... never thought he could want to make love to a woman as he did her. Then, so quickly, it was over, he rolled from her onto the wooden floor of the boat.

'I remember you the night we swam,' he panted, 'that first night. Have thought of you ever since, knew that night I'd got to have you.' He struggled to sit up, still gasping for breath. 'Always scoffed at people talking of falling in love. But that's what happens, isn't it? You've come between me and what I've been doing, the memory of you, the need —'

'I know. It's been like that for me too.'

She reached her hand to touch his strong arm, glorifying in his manliness.

'I was saying before, I'd never expected to get wed yet awhile, I'm not ready to give up my river work. Things have rushed ahead of me.'

'But there could be work for you at the yard, you could —'

'At your yard? Why would I do that? You know about the meadows, Clara's mother told us she'd talked to you about us trying to get them from Farmer Maidlow.'

'Meadows ...?' Why did she ask when already she knew. Charles Dunton ... Chaw ... Clara's childhood sweetheart.

Chapter Six

'Chaw ... the Chaw Mrs Warwick told me about. You and Clara were going to marry.'

He sat on the floor beside her, his arms around his drawn up knees. A minute before she had reached out to touch him, revelling in his strength, his manliness; now he looked suddenly young, vulnerable and she loved him even more.

'It had to happen Charles. When Mrs Warwick first told me that Chaw and Clara were to marry, I knew even then that it couldn't be right. "Soon" she said, she called it "sometime to the back end of the year". She told me you'd been "promised to each other for two years" – how dull and boring that sounds.'

Polly stretched full length, glorifying in the urgency of their own love. Then catching sight of her drawers lying in a crumpled ball by her side, she spread her wide skirt to hide them, their presence was an intrusion. 'Ours is real love, not the wishy-washy child's sort that can wait on convenience. Poor Charles, it won't be easy for you to tell her.'

'What d'you mean? There's nothing to tell Clara. But I'd wanted to keep things as they are, not to be rushed. Old Man Maidlow is prepared to rent me the meadows and Clara's folk say I can move in there. The twenty-first of November, that's the date fixed, just six weeks away.'

'But you don't love Clara!' Polly knelt up on the mattress – to stand was impossible under the boat's low roof. 'You can't marry her when it's *me* you want.'

'Wanting you's got nothing to do with it. You know I want you – you saw just now – but Polly, nothing need change for

111

us. Listen,' he turned to face her, his dark eyes pleading, 'I've told you Old Man Maidlow is ready to rent me the fields, and I've got money put by to pay the rent. But I put it to the Warwicks that I can't afford to give up the boat work, not just yet. So except that when I'm this way I'll be living at Little Roost instead of up river at the mill, nothing will be changed. You and me can—'

'Do you think I'm no different from a whore you can pick up in town? You don't know what love is! No, don't touch me.' She wanted to stand tall, throw her cloak around her shoulders with a flourish and sweep out with her head high, hiding her wound behind a show of dignity. Instead she crawled to the edge of the horsehair mattress and stretched forward to reach where her cloak lay on the floor then inched it toward her. And what dignity was there in easing it around her shoulders as she crouched on the mattress – and worse, what dignity in pushing her drawers into the pocket in its lining?

'You're not going yet? Don't go, Polly. And what you just said – I don't think of you as a whore, how could you say that to me? I love you, I tell you.'

'Love!' she scoffed. 'What you mean is you wanted me in your bed.'

He was kneeling now, too, his hands on her shoulders.

'Yes, I did. It's what you wanted too. Won't you try and understand? I can't jilt Clara, we've known for years that when we had enough behind us we'd marry. She's never doubted me, she thinks of me as certain as tomorrow's sunrise. She works hard, she'd never hurt anyone. All the things you take for granted, money, fine clothes – Polly, you're different from her—'

'And if I am, I thank God for it.'

He ignored that, perhaps he didn't understand the meaning behind the short retort.

'Don't go yet, Polly. We can't part like this. Would you want me any different? You say I don't know anything about love, but I tell you I think about you all the time. Clara is different – here alone in my bed when I yearn for a woman, it's you, *you* I want. But even if things were different and I was free, what sort of a hope would we have? You're angry. But what did you expect? You don't honestly think you could take me home and introduce me to your father as his future son-in-law?'

'Doesn't matter to you what I think.' With her bottom lip gripped between her teeth she wouldn't trust herself to look directly at him.

'Try and see it my way, Polly. I can't let Clara down, everyone's known for years that one day we'll get married.'

'And you think that's enough. Well, it may be for you, and I expect it is for her too from what I've seen of her. But it wouldn't be enough for me.'

He must have misunderstood what was behind her words.

'Just now when I made love to you it was like – like – like a moment of paradise.'

Her heart longed to believe him, even now to make him realise that no good could come out of marrying a childhood friend rather than let her down; but Polly had learned too many lessons of life over the last year to listen just to her heart. Charles Dunton, her Gypsy King, he may idolise her, he may want to make love to her, but slovenly Clara Warwick's feelings had to be put first.

She stood up, glad that she banged her head on the roof. *That* ought to bring home to him what a hovel he lived in here. Then bending exaggeratedly low she went through the opening to the night air. For a couple of seconds she stood still and erect, conscious of the picture she made in the golden light of the hurricane lamp. Every other time she'd been with him on the barge he'd been the first to leap to the river bank, holding a hand to her as she jumped.

'Wait. Polly, don't let's spoil everything—'

With one spring she was on dry land, the sight of her was lost in the foggy night. She longed to turn back to see him standing in the aura of diffuse light. Instead she looked straight ahead, making herself concentrate on the feeling of ground underfoot, careful not to lose the direction of the towpath. It helped to have to think of *that*, if she hesitated she wasn't sure that either hurt or anger would keep her from running back to him.

At last she reached the stile, climbed onto it, then put one leg across. One more step and she'd be home, in her own garden ... no matter how she stiffened her jaw there was no holding back her tears, she could feel them trembling in her chest, catching the breath in her throat until they found release in a harsh stifled sob. She was home. Home. But she couldn't find the courage to climb down into the garden, walk up the sloping lawn and into the house, its familiarity enveloping her. Lost in the blanket of fog was all the joy, the thrill, the unquestioning abandon of hurtling into first love. Now there was nothing for her but to go back to being the girl she used to be. But that wasn't possible. Not just physically, but in everything that she was. She was drowning in the misery of her own tears, all her yesterdays marching through her mind, crowding one upon another. She needed to find comfort in them, but they brought her none. She was in a No Man's Land of hopelessness, the past was remote, the future empty.

Only yards away from the stile were the posts where in summer they hung the hammock: poor Mother, think how she'd cried about the baby. No, think of when she'd been well and happy, think of the fun it had always been looking at Madame Doretta's sketches together; remember how cocky you were when she and Pappy praised you for doing something well, yes but you were a child then; think of Pappy, you weren't a child when he told you about the mess he'd got the yard into. She shied away from the next image, there was no place in her pageant of memories for Harry Carpenter ... 'no fresh-faced youth will ever satisfy you'. But Charles wasn't a fresh-faced fumbling youth, he was a man. How many times when he'd been moored by the far meadow had he been there because of Clara Warwick? Slovenly, shapeless lump ... how could he put her before *me*? He's fond of her like he is of – what? – a pint of ale on a hot day, a newspaper and a warm fire in the winter. But *me*, he loves me with passion, he'd wanted me ever since the night we climbed out of the water onto Rat Island. Every time he makes love to Clara Warwick – no she won't be that, she'll be Clara Dunton – but that won't chain his thoughts, every time he makes love to her he'll think of *me*, he'll compare her with *me*. But what use is that, to him or to me? I hate her! Plain, dreary, suety—

Lost for an adjective contemptuous enough to describe her, Polly banged her fists on the wooden post at the end of the stile.

I've got to go home, go on as if there is no Charles Dunton, listen to Emmie talking about Clara and her Chaw. Misery and self-pity consumed her – until another thought pushed everything from her mind. Suppose what he'd done tonight had made her pregnant? Could it have? No, it hurt, I hated it. Oh but I didn't, I wanted what he did to hurt me, like the pain of a branding iron on an animal it was making me *his*, I rejoiced in the agony – no, of course I didn't, I only believed I did at the time, no one could like that sort of pain. I'm not going to think about how I felt, sort of exalted, nothing else mattered ... But pregnant? No, to actually start a baby must be quite different, such bliss that you must know ... mustn't you? Yet Mother had been bitter and resentful, there had been no bliss in the way she'd conceived Bobby. Pregnant? Polly rubbed the palms of her hands across her face, and climbed down from the stile; already she was emerging from the depths of her misery. Pregnant? He'd *have* to marry her if he'd made her pregnant. Pictures chased each other across her imagination: her father's jealous indignation, the pointing fingers of the villagers, slovenly Clara's sitting in the back of the church and watching while *she*, Polly Seagrove, walked down the aisle on Charles's arm. None of that would be important, not even her father's disappointment, for she was sure that once he got to know Charles he would see him as the only husband for her.

Her period wasn't due for over a week. Charles wouldn't be back this way for at least a fortnight. Her imagination ran riot. She saw her pregnancy as the way out for both of them, she saw Charles going each morning to the yard where he would be popular with the men, she saw the adoration in his eyes as she told him she was having his child, she saw a future of unending joy.

Nine days later, on time almost to the hour, her period started, putting an end to her dreams.

Polly saw nothing of Charles over the next few weeks. She took sadistic pleasure in listening to Emmie's reports on the wedding preparations at Little Roost, in hearing about Clara's excitement for the future. She played her part well, always careful not to let it show.

It was the second Wednesday in November, only a week and a half before the bells of St Peter's church in the village would peal as the new Mr and Mrs Dunton stepped out of its dim interior. It must have been fate that made Polly look up from penning a quotation she wanted to get into the mid-morning postal collection. There he was! With his usual steady rhythm he was aiding the single sail by punting the barge upstream. He mustn't see her, she kept well back from the window. But what satisfaction it gave her to notice the way he peered towards the yard obviously thinking he might catch a glimpse of her out there talking to one of the men, even turning his head after he'd gone past before hope died.

'Will you need the trap this afternoon, Pappy? If not I'll finish off this quotation to Mr Silver and post it on the way home. It's such a glorious day, look at the autumn colours of those trees across the river.'

'You do that, Pol, I don't like you to spend your days in this gloomy little office.'

'I don't find it gloomy, I enjoy it here.' And so she did, she enjoyed the smell of tar and wood, the sound of hammering and sawing, the men whistling, singing, calling out to each other; never noisy, yet never still, it was a busy sound and working at her books she felt herself to be part of it.

But today was different, today she knew just what she meant to do.

'Why, Miss Polly, could hardly believe my eyes when I saw who it was.' Blanche Warwick came out into the farm yard to meet Polly. 'What a surprise!' From her excitement clearly it was a good one. 'Often enough Emmie brings my little man along here, but fancy you pushing him to see his old Blanche. Mind your lovely clothes in our mucky yard. Push the bassinet indoors, Emmie always does, you don't want the cold air getting to it.'

'I've been meaning to come for weeks, but lately I've spent so much time at the yard. Winter will be on us so soon now, I made up my mind to make the most of today's sunshine.'

'And quite right too. Stuck there over your books every day you'll lose the roses in your cheeks. 'Tis only me here, Chaw turned up late morning. Those two lovebirds, they're off down at his boat, she likes to tidy it up for him,' she chuckled contentedly, 'at any rate, that's what they tell me. Think I was

116

born yesterday! Still, come what may, not much more than a fortnight and the knot will be tied so I'm not going to lose any sleep worrying about how much tidying goes on.'

'On a boat?' Polly was proud of the casual way she laughed. 'Tidying? You mean he's repairing it? I wonder what he's doing?' She sounded genuinely interested, as interested as anyone who knew about repair work to river craft. 'You didn't tell me Chaw kept a boat here.' What could be more innocently said than that? Polly was beginning to enjoy her mission.

'Bless you, no. The idea of Chaw having money enough to have one of your pleasure boats tied up waiting for him! I used to tell you when he'd looked in on Clara on his way by, I suppose I thought you'd know I meant on the river. I wonder you've never noticed the *Maryanne*, that's the name of his barge. His Pa's a miller, it's his boat of course not Chaw's.'

'So Clara is marrying a bargee. I thought he was a farmer.'

'Marrying a bargee, fiddlesticks! One more trip and he's off the water for good. And I'm glad. Something and nothing for a young couple to be parted like they would have been if he'd stuck to his intention.' She talked of Chaw and Clara, but all the time her interest was on Bobby, sitting propped against his pillows and watching her. 'Come along, my luvey, come and tell Blanche all about it.'

Bobby sensed release, he held up his arms hopefully.

'Wasn't he meaning to give up the barge, then? You told me he wanted to rent land from Mr Maidlow?' Polly gave no indication that it was her first question that mattered.

'That's right. He's got the meadows he was after. But – just a flash in the pan of an idea he had – he said he could do with the extra spondulicks he could make by carrying on working the waterways for a few months longer.' She sat down on a wooden chair, Bobby on her knee, indicating to Polly to take the one and only easy chair by the fire. 'You take Bert's seat, Miss Polly. It's good to have a proper talk with you, like we did when I was putting a bit of goodness into this little lamb. Some folk you can open your heart to, some you just say what's expected. You and me, we came close to real understanding. Now, I was saying about Chaw. Like I told you back last spring when they first named the day, he was to get the waterside meadows from Farmer Maidlow, rent the land and pay out for cattle. And he's got money enough saved up for that. Then they'd have shares in Little Roost, we'd work it all in together. Suited Bert and me well, to be honest although our next three after Clara are all boys, none of them have a feeling for the land. Always been set on getting away to town. Clara's a home bird, a real country lass through and through. Oh, look at this little one, won't you, trying to tell me something aren't you, my little precious. Don't you just love to hear him Miss Polly, duckie, the way he tries to shape his mouth. Bet you he thinks he's telling me a fine tale.'

Polly knew better than to steer the conversation straight back to Chaw.

'I expect you and Mr Warwick were disappointed that the boys don't want to farm.'

'Yes and no. If they'd been keen, real keen, then I know Bert would have been pleased as Punch. But there's nothing worse than a half-hearted helper about the place.' She frowned, uncertain whether to say more or turn the conversation. 'That worries me a bit about Chaw. He's been used to the river, out on that barge in all weathers. A strong enough young fellow. But he doesn't know anything about animals, cattle and such.'

'He'll learn, Mrs Warwick. Another trip, didn't you say, and he'll be off the river for good.'

'That's true. Once his Pa takes on this new man, then Chaw will have burnt his bridges, no more river work. But is he ready, really ready? I've got an uneasy feeling, there's something I can't put my finger on. He had some idea that he'd carry on travelling the river even after taking Clara for his wife. She would stay here, just like she was still a maiden, and he'd stop by on his way past. Now what sort of marriage would that be? Not so different from now. They get time enough to themselves down on that barge, married or no. Seems to me the only difference would be that she'd be the one to wash his shirt instead of his Ma. Call that marriage?'

'But you say he's changed his mind after all, he'll be here all the time.'

'Ah, so he will and I say thank God he's come to his senses. It bothers me though, Miss Polly. All through the summer he was dead set that he'd leave her at home along with us and go off free as a bird. Clara was disappointed, not that she complained, she's not the complaining sort, but I could see it wasn't the way she'd wanted things. Then, no warning at all, he turns up here one morning back last month. He'd been here the day before, full of talk about the regular jobs he was getting, fitting them in with what he did for his Pa. We thought he'd set off for home when he left us. It must have been he could see the fog coming up. He changed his mind – not a breath of air to stir his sail. Anyway, in he marched, told Clara he'd had enough of the river, couldn't give up quick enough. Like I say, it bothers me, Miss Polly. Not like Chaw to be impulsive, change his mind quick as that.'

Polly laughed, reaching forward to lay a hand on Blanche's plump arm.

'A foggy night – by himself on a barge. With winter coming and the choice of living here or alone on the river, I don't wonder he changed his mind.'

'Talk of the devil, here they come. Not a word about what I've been telling you.'

'Of course not,' Polly promised as the back door opened.

'Got the boat put to rights again, Clara love?'

'Pretty nearly the last time, Ma. Good afternoon Miss, it's Miss Seagrove isn't it?'

'You've a good memory Clara. I think we only met once.' Polly didn't attempt to stand up from Bert Warwick's fireside seat.

'I've been telling Miss Polly about the wedding. This is him, Clara's Chaw I was telling you is taking on the fields down by the river,' Blanche performed what she supposed was an introduction.

'Chaw, Mrs Warwick calls you. You must really be Charles, surely?' Polly looked up at him with much the same wide-eyed innocence that had been wasted on Harry Carpenter.

'Most people call me Chaw.'

'That's a shame. Charles has a brave ring to it. Chaw sounds like some dreary domestic task no one would do from choice.' She laughed as she said it.

Charles looked sullen.

'Nothing wrong with Emmie is there, Miss?' Clara's round face was full of concern.

'Emmie's very well. I gave her a free afternoon.'

'That's all right then. Got me worried for a moment seeing you looking after young Bobby.'

She and her mother exchanged glances, the silent message understood by both of them. And there it might have rested had Blanche not noticed the quick way Polly looked from one to the other.

'What Clara's thinking about is our Clive. I was telling you, Miss Polly, my eldest boys are all set on working in town. Clive rides his bicycle all the way to Reading each day, he's got himself a proper stiff collar and tie job with the auctioneer. If it's what he wants then I suppose he thinks it's worth while, but it makes a long day when you add the time it takes him to bicycle in and out.'

'No longer than Chaw works on his barge,' came Clara's loyal rejoinder.

'What's Clive to do with Emmie?' Polly asked, feeling the conversation had gone on without her.

'Not for us to gossip about Emmie's affairs,' Clara said.

'That it isn't,' Blanche agreed, 'but I don't mind telling you, Miss Polly, Clive is sweet as anything on her. They're a couple of years behind these two, but I'd stake my best bonnet on it that they'll be the next up the aisle.'

There was no logic in Polly's sudden change of mood. Perhaps she'd been a fool to come to Little Roost knowing she was likely to see Charles there. Chaw and Clara, Clive and Emily, how cosy it all sounded.

'I ought to start for home, I want to get Bobby back there while it's still nice.' She stood up, her spirits reviving when she noticed how, just for a second, Charles looked at her. He must be seeing her against the background of what his future would be. 'Are you going to put him in his bassinet Mrs Warwick or shall I?'

It seemed Blanche wanted the job, carrying on a private conversation with Bobby in a language he appeared to understand.

Standing consciously straight, Polly bestowed a smile on the engaged couple.

'I shall think of you two on the twenty-first when I hear the church bells ringing out. And I'll make sure Emmie is free to be there.'

'That's real kind, Miss Polly. Emmie and me get on ever so well, I shouldn't wonder she's told you. Hearing Chaw and me making our promises might put the idea into our Clive's head – if it's not there already.'

'Goodbye Charles.'

Clara saw the wide-eyed look as guileless, Charles knew Polly better.

'Good afternoon, Miss Polly.'

Outside in the yard Bert was herding his cows into the shed for milking.

'Your Pa'll be waiting, best you cut on over to the shed for milking, Clara love,' Blanche watched as the last stragglers of the Warwick's small herd were ushered across the yard, 'and what about you Chaw, why don't you go along with her, try your hand? There's nowt to it, once you get the feel.' Then, the last cow disappeared from sight, she opened the door to wheel the bassinet into the yard. 'I'll push the lad as far as the gate, you'll need both hands to hold that pretty skirt off the ground. Watch how you tread, Miss Polly, see the mess those animals make, the yards covered with mud and worse.'

Polly looked back for one last glance at Charles before she followed Blanche, her skirt and pleated petticoats held well above her ankles, too far away to hear Clara's comment as she tied her hessian apron around her thick waist.

'D'you see that, Chaw? The way she looked at us? Come swanking down here in all her finery.' Then she laughed at herself. 'Hark at me, won't you! Being a real old tom cat. I ought to be ashamed, poor Miss Seagrove. There's me, with all I've got to look forward to, and there's *her*. For all her fine clothes and pretty ways – and she is pretty, Chaw, you can't say she's not – I know who I'd rather be.'

'Come on, your father's waiting.' Charles knew all too well why Polly had come. He strode across the muddy – and worse – yard determined not to look towards Polly's departing figure.

The visit had been a successful one, for Blanche who had been delighted to welcome Polly, for Clara who saw it as no more than confirmation – if she needed it – of her own happiness, for Bobby for obvious reasons and for Polly herself who felt she had accomplished all she'd intended.

121

I saw the way he looked at me ... what must he feel when he compares me with that lump? That's what she is, she's a lump, she's got no more shape than the Reading gasometer he must see every time he takes his barge up the Kennet. He can't possibly be in love with her – well, he isn't, he's in love with *me*, run away from it as fast as he likes but it can't alter it. If he marries her – if? there isn't an if, he *will* marry her – but it's duty, just duty. Hands like a scullery maid, round shiny face, so fat she's got dimples in her elbows – and her knees too I expect. How can he do it? I'll make him sorry, just see if I don't.

'Emmie's going to a wedding, Pappy. I know she wants to look especially nice and I'd give her something of mine, but she's a bit bigger than I am. I've been looking at Mother's things. Would you mind very much if I found something that I think would fit her? Nothing Mother was especially fond of –'

'I wish you'd sort out your mother's clothes, Polly. She had cupboards full of gowns. Of course try and find something suitable for the girl to wear to the wedding – as for the rest, Elvira's clothes are hardly the sort you could give to the servants. You take responsibility for them, Pol, I can't have them hanging month after month.'

An idea was born in Polly. But she wouldn't waste time thinking about it now. Today she would sort out something for Emmie to wear that would impress Clive Warwick as she walked by his side following the bridal procession out of the church. Poor Emmie's clothes were all workaday, Polly was determined there should be nothing drab in her appearance on 21 November. Whether that was honestly her only reason, whether she took morbid pleasure in hurting herself or whether she simply intended the nursemaid to be a reminder to Charles of what he was turning his back on, she wasn't prepared to consider. Instead she put all her concentration into helping Emmie's dreams to come true.

Polly prided herself on her small waist, she liked to recall how Madame Doretta had enjoyed designing for her; Emmie's figure would have presented more of a challenge. The gown she selected for her to try on had been made for Elvira in the autumn of the previous year, designed to camouflage and flatter. The House of Duprés had created it as an afternoon gown, but everything that came from that establishment was as near perfect as human hands could make. By Elvira's standards the cut was simple, the quality of the pale lilac silk put it in a bracket ahead of Emmie's wildest dreams. Over it she wore a dove grey coat made at the same time, a coat with no less than three layers of cape at the shoulders. The whole outfit was set off by a deep lilac bonnet which had originally belonged to Polly, as had the shoes, gloves and umbrella.

Emmie's outfit was complete.

'Cor ...' she breathed, viewing her reflection, then again, 'cor ... gloves an' all ... Miss Polly, I don't hardly know what to say.' She bit her lip as if that way she'd manage to stop her mouth turning upwards.

'You look really pretty, Emmie. Clive Warwick will fall head over heels in love with you – if he isn't already.'

'You don't think I'm too posh? I mean, Clara won't think I'm trying to outshine her. After all, it's Clara's day, hers and Chaw's. Oh I wish you were going to be there, Miss.'

'You'd outshine Clara Warwick if you went in your mob cap and overall!'

'Oh no, Miss Polly. Clara's got a real nice face, you only got to look at her to know she's good and kind. Like her Ma.'

The day of the wedding was clear and fair. In the afternoon Polly sat Bobby in his bassinet and wheeled him down the lawn, Horace wrongly interpreting her intention and leaping ahead of her towards the stile, not stopping to worry his canine head over why it was she carried a garden rake.

'Here, boy.' She picked up a fallen twig and threw it for him by way of compensation, then started to rake the leaves that had come down from the tall elms by the river. Horace found a new game, as fast as she made a pile of leaves he jumped at it, digging with his front paws and scattering her effort. Bobby seemed to find his antics hilarious and for good measure hurled his ivory teething ring in the direction of the fun.

'You're fighting a losing battle. Will this help?'

Harry Carpenter! Polly had seen him often enough in sombre evening wear or in the formal black dress coat, black striped trousers and silk top hat he invariably wore when he came to the yard. On this autumn Saturday afternoon his less austere appearance made a stranger of him. Trousers, jacket, waistcoat and even the cap with its narrow brim were all made of the same brown small-check tweed. Her first impression was that he might be taken for a country squire, her second that the informal costume made him seem years younger. But it wasn't only his attire that surprised her, it was that he should be trundling the large wooden wheelbarrow towards her.

'Where did you come from? I didn't hear a carriage. My father said he was going out, I don't know whether he has left yet.'

'No, you wouldn't have heard a carriage, I dismissed it at the end of the lane, I preferred to walk. And yes, your father has already left the house, we met each other just as I started to walk. He offered to take me back with him to town – I might have accepted had he not said that you were busy gardening. Temptation overcame me. I told him there was something I wanted to talk to you about. So here I am, a willing pair of hands. You don't mind, Polly?'

It was so unusual for him to sound less than completely sure of himself that she bit back any crushing retort before the words took form in her mind.

'I hope you'll be more useful than Horace,' she told him, 'just look at him!'

Suddenly from the village church a mile or so away came the joyous peal of bells, the sound carried by the water.

'You didn't answer me. Will this help?' he brought the wooden barrow to the side of her latest attempt to pile the leaves.

'I was just going to get it,' she heard herself reply. Mrs Charles Dunton, by now that's who lumpy Clara is. Did I believe deep in my heart that he wouldn't go through with it? If I did, I was wrong. Hear the bells. He wouldn't let her down, that's what he said. What sort of stupid chivalry is that? And what about me? What about *us*? My wife, that's what he'll call her. Will he say it proudly? No, of course he won't, how could he be proud? Charles, how could you do it? People marry for money or for convenience, that's more or less what Mother wanted me to do. But there is no money to be gained from marrying Clara Warwick. Convenience? Easier to marry her than to face the bad feeling it would create in your families if you jilted her. So you sink all that you are into taking the easy way. What can you want with a field of cows, milking, washing down that disgusting yard, cleaning out the cow-sheds ... you belong to the river, the same as I do. You could have worked with me at the yard, together we could have worked to buy Harry out ... Harry! Was there no way of ridding herself of him? Even this afternoon with the sound of Charles's wedding bells clamouring in her head, Harry had to intrude on her solitude.

Busying himself transferring the leaves into the wheelbarrow he stopped to throw a stick for Horace, then back to the leaves. When he came upon Bobby's teething ring he held it enquiringly to Polly while, recognising it, Bobby shouted in a frenzy of impatience at not making himself understood.

Polly pulled her wandering thoughts back into line.

'I ought to have tied it round his neck. Give it to me, I'll go and rinse it in the river.'

For answer Harry took it through the trees and down to the water's edge. Bobby's outstretched hand thrashed the air impatiently as he waited for Harry to dry it in the 'show only' silk handkerchief he took from his breast pocket.

'Wait.' Polly dropped her rake and come over to the bassinet. 'I'll take the ribbon out of his bonnet, it's only there for effect.' In no time Bobby's bonnet was stripped of decoration, the ribbon slipped through the teething ring and tied around his neck. 'There, young man, see what you can do with that.'

The resounding kiss she planted on his forehead was rewarded by gurgles of appreciation, but his good humour was too fragile to be taken for granted. He soon tired of a teething ring that couldn't be thrown to attract attention. He felt neglected – so did Horace who stood waiting with a stick at his feet. Dog and baby exchanged a glance of silent understanding. Grown ups! it seemed to say. But Polly and Harry were too deep in conversation to notice.

'But we always deal with Mannering & Toms. We've built steam launches before, you know.' Polly faced him, ready for battle.

'In the future we shall use Maunders. Their engines are second to none.'

'Rubbish! Whoever heard of a Maunders engine? No one!'

Harry's eyes smiled, the corner of his mouth almost took the message. Neither Polly's eyes nor mouth showed any answering sign.

'*I've* heard of them. Where's your business sense Polly? The men are dedicated and skilled. A small company trying to make a mark will quote good terms.'

'Seagrove's never cut corners just for the sake of what looks like a bargain. Anyway,' her tone was childishly rude, 'who do you think you are, to judge whether they're good engineers? Where would our future orders for motor launches come from once word got round that we fitted some cheap engine instead of a tested and tried Mannering & Toms?'

'I'm sorry you take that attitude. Without change there would never be progress. John & Edwin Maunders are fine engineers, nothing comes out of their workshops that they don't personally approve. When I came upon them I was impressed, *most* impressed. Two young men with a vision but little money to back it.'

'Ah! So that's it. I suppose you took advantage of them, offered a loan.'

'When I have faith in a business I see it as a sound investment.'

She glowered at him. (Hark! The bells have stopped. It's all over. By now they'll be walking back to the farm. Clara and Chaw – home in time for the afternoon milking – he'll hate it, he'll be miserable. Charles, Charles, why did you do it!)

'How can your sort of loan help them to grow? What will you do – take the interest and wait your moment to pounce when you have them on their knees? Isn't that the way you work?'

'Is it? You appear to know me better than I know myself.'

If he'd argued she had been ready to fight, but his answer was calm, polite, almost indifferent. It knocked her off balance.

She pouted, uncertain of the next step.

'I don't know you at all – only the way you treated Seagrove's.'

'Oh yes, you do know me. Just as I know you. We are too much alike not to understand each other.'

Even if he hadn't been holding her shoulders it would have been impossible to turn away from him, impossible not to meet his gaze; his power over her was hypnotic. No matter that she resented the authority he had at the yard, that she despised his ruthlessness, the one thing she couldn't do was ignore him.

Horace nosed his stick forward, his short sharp bark breaking the invisible cord that bound them. Harry threw the stick, Horace chased at such speed and stopped so suddenly that he somersaulted, Bobby forgot that he was feeling neglected and laughed aloud, Polly took up her rake.

'Do these go on a compost heap somewhere?' For Harry too, the moment was over.

'To the left of the house, at the back of the kitchen garden. If Baker hears the wheelbarrow he'll be there like a shot, he's very protective of his compost heap.' Like the sun coming from behind a cloud, Polly's mood was suddenly light.

George Baker was in charge of the garden, there was no need for her to rake leaves. She liked to think she'd been tempted out by the cold, bright autumn day (or could it have been self-inflicted misery to hear the sound of the bells?). There had certainly been no need for Harry to spend his afternoon helping her.

Lying in bed Polly tried to keep her thoughts on the afternoon. But how hard it was. Would the wedding party be over yet? She knew that the guests were going back to Little Roost, Emmie had told her about the cake Blanche had made and Clara had iced, just as Emmie had told her about how industriously the bride-to-be had been working on a patchwork bedspread. Bert Warwick had a barrel of homemade cider on tap for the festivities, the party was expected to last all the evening. But it must be over by now, Emmie would be walking home, her lantern lighting her through the gloom of the autumn mist that had followed the clear day.

Polly's thoughts ran riot. She'd never seen Clara's bedroom, but that didn't stop her imagining it. She's your wife Charles, solid, dull, hard-working Clara. Today she wouldn't have been wearing her usual mob cap, all her hair pushed out of sight. What would her hair be like? Would he take the pins out for her and let it hang loose down her back? More likely she

127

would put it in its nightly plait. And Charles ... Chaw ... no, don't think of Charles. But how can I stop thinking of him? The way he was on the boat with me, remember the urgency, the passion. Tonight will be her first time, will she grit her teeth and bear it as a duty? Or will she glory in the pain of loving? He'll be remembering, he'll be thinking about me. Will she guess that you don't love her, you love me? Even plain, dowdy Clara must feel that something is missing. I feel pity for her, yes I do. To Charles she is a duty.

Polly plumped her pillow, lay down again and closed her eyes as if that way she'd shut out the picture. A duty ... damn her, damn her, even if she is only a duty, it's she who is in Charles's arms ...

Think about something else. Think about what Harry had told her. John and Edwin Maunders, two young brothers, both of them apprenticed in the workings of steam engines, both of them with the sort of ambition that knows no limits. She supposed she had been right in her accusation: a loan to a young and struggling company, a loan they'd been unable to repay. So Shylock had taken his pound of flesh from them just as he had from her father, he was what he called a sleeping partner.

Sleeping partner ... her imagination ran away with her ... a painstakingly stitched patchwork quilt carefully folded ... Harry walking by her side as she pushed Bobby back to the house ... 'what a domesticated picture we make' ... an expression she couldn't fathom and preferred to forget ... and his parting remark, even after she had bid him goodbye, 'I'll take you to Maunder's workshops. Unless I'm mistaken – and I know I'm not – when Seagrove's puts a steam launch on the river you like to understand what drives it.'

As good as his word, keeping the cabby waiting outside the gate to the yard, he collected her to escort her to London, a district of London very different from the elegant establishment where she and her mother had always been welcomed by Madame Doretta – no doubt with an eye to business every bit as sharp as Harry Carpenter's. At Paddington he handed her into a hansom and gave the cabby an address that meant nothing to her.

She loved the bustle of the city, the cries of street vendors, the cacophony of horses' hoofs and the rattle of carriages, the occasional sight of some young urchin darting into the street with his shovel and bucket, surely in his humble way as much an entrepreneur as was Harry.

'It's a long way,' she commented after the first ten minutes or so.

'The further you go from the centre the less you pay for premises.'

By the time they came to journey's end she had decided that the Maunders brothers must pay very little indeed!

As soon as she met them she was aware of their enthusiasm, their certainty that the goal they strove for would be reached.

'This is Miss Seagrove, you remember I told you when you undertook to build the steam engine for the Seagrove launch that I intended to bring her.'

He'd told them, indeed! Such was Polly's contrary nature where he was concerned that she wished she'd refused to come.

'How much do you understand, Miss Seagrove?' John Maunder asked her.

'I'd like to be taught from the beginning,' she hedged, 'to refresh my memory.' She wished she hadn't looked towards Harry at that second and been met with his look of exaggerated surprise, his brows raised, his mouth not quite smiling.

'Good idea. We'll start with the drawings,' John agreed. 'They're on the table in here.' He led the way; gladly she followed, all too aware that Harry was still watching her.

The large sheet of drawing paper was headed 'Double Acting Steam Engine for Seagrove's River Launch'. The words helped enormously to concentrate her mind. She considered she was doing well, nodding her understanding in all the right places, making a mental note of terms like double-acting engine, expansion of steam in the cylinders, compound expansion engine. John Maunders considered he was keeping his briefing to the basic essentials: pistons and cylinders with the necessary force of steam to transmit the motion of the piston to the shaft.

'Does Mr Carpenter know about steam engines?' she asked. 'He and your brother appear to be very engrossed out there in the workshop.'

'That he does! It was our lucky day when he stumbled on one of our engines and took the trouble to look us up. It's hard to get your foot into any trade when you haven't the money behind you.'

'Oh, he knows that right enough.' So she'd been correct in what she'd suspected. Or so she believed until John knocked down her preconceived ideas.

'He was trained for engineering, but he's more than that. He's got vision. Like Edwin and I have, you might say. We know our engines are second to none, aye and better than many. He knows it too. That's why he came to us with his proposition. He put money, real money not just the odd few sovereigns, into our business and bought himself in. So far he's not seen a return for his investment, but he will. He knows it and we know it. He'll never regret the investment.'

'You mean he bought himself a partnership, he didn't lend you money that had to be repaid.'

'No. If it had been that way we could never have got out of debt, interest would have crippled us. But that was a year or more ago and we've had orders, our name is getting known. He's seen to it that work comes our way, many a factory wants engine-driven machines, times are changing. Like I say, Mr Carpenter is a visionary, whereas most folk look at yesterday and today, he has an eye on tomorrow.'

After Christmas, after an engagement so brief that it caught the attention of the local gossip-mongers, Emmie married Clive Warwick. Polly attended the wedding, sitting in the second pew from the front on the left side of the aisle behind Emmie's family. Immediately opposite her was Charles.

How would she have felt if he'd walked in proudly with Clara on his arm, given her a brief nod of recognition then forgotten her presence? But she'd known it couldn't have been like that. He was as aware of her nearness as she was of his and, even though she wouldn't let herself look across the aisle at him, she could feel his gaze was on her. On this dull January day she would have had to be blind not to know how attractive she looked, how she stood out from everyone else in the little church. She was wearing a coat of russet velvet, a hat of the same shade adorned with flowers of cream and gold. No one would have guessed that it had hung in her mother's wardrobe for more than two years and had been altered and updated by a tailoress in Reading.

'Miss Polly, what a happy day.' Blanche spoke to her in the jostle as they left the church. 'Is your Pa keeping an eye on Bobby? I see the Humes are in church, and young Daisy. I thought perhaps you'd be bringing the lad.'

'No, Pappy's not baby-care material,' Polly laughed. 'Nurse Cox is looking after him. He's going to miss Emmie, so am I, she has cared for him as if he belongs.'

'Make a good mother one of these days. I dare say there are those who've come to see the knot tied today thinking that that's what the rush is all about. You say you're going to miss her – and so am I. Most afternoons she and Bobby would walk our way. Have you found anyone to replace her, Miss Polly?'

'No, I don't want to leave him with a stranger. Mrs Warwick – say no if you can't manage it – but I was wondering, if I cut my time at the yard to two days a week could I bring Bobby to you at Little Roost?'

'Bless his heart yes, he's not a bit of trouble. Be good practice for Clara,' with a knowing wink.

'You mean—?'

'August,' she confirmed, nodding. Then she called to Clara and Charles, 'You hear what Miss Polly and I have been arranging? She's going to bring our little Bobby to us of a day while she's helping her Pa.'

Charles was to be a father, his homely wife was beaming her willingness to welcome Bobby to their home. This time Polly met Charles's eyes and what she read there made her pulses race with excitement.

Chapter Seven

One morning in early March as Polly drove the pony and trap towards the gate leading to the yard at Little Roost she was surprised to find Charles wielding a long-handled scythe, cutting back the old straggling nettles and weeds that encroached onto the narrow track. Or was she completely surprised? The meeting wasn't pre-arranged and yet she had been aware for days that he was never far away when she arrived with Bobby.

'Good morning, Charles.' She was pleased with her cool tone. So she would have addressed him had he been of no more importance to her than 'Clara's Chaw'. 'I'm glad you're here, it saves us climbing out to open the gate.'

'Is that the only reason you're glad I'm here? Polly, I never have a chance to talk to you, always there are people—'

'You're part of a large family now, Charles. Of course there are people.' Well done, she congratulated herself.

'It was so different when we had the boat—'

'Of course it was. I'm sure you *must* miss the freedom of the river. I know I would.'

'A bargeman's life isn't one of freedom, Polly. You know, and I know, what it is I miss.' Looking up at her as she sat holding the reins his eyes seemed to devour her. 'The hours I had with you were like a beacon that lighted my life. And it was the same for you, isn't that why you asked Ma to look after the boy? So that we could see each other, find a way of being together.'

'Nonsense!'

But was it nonsense? She knew the true answer, but this

wasn't the moment to dwell on it. 'I must get on, Bobby keeps still as long as the trap is moving.' He was at a difficult age, too old to lie on a pillow by her feet, too young to sit at her side, so she held him on her knee, her arms encircling him. As she said, as long as there was movement he loved this mode of transport, he liked to touch the reins, and kept up an endless conversation of his own peculiar kind to Tubby, the pony, as she trotted over the rutted ground. 'Walk on.' Leaving Charles, yet gloriously conscious that he was still watching her, Polly finished her journey to the ramshackle little farmhouse.

Answering her rap on the back door, Clara called out to her.

'Bring him in, Miss Polly.' Clara never became any more familiar, but her easy-going acceptance was friendly. She stood at the well-scrubbed kitchen table, her reddened hands kneading dough in a large earthenware bowl as she performed her regular morning task, making the day's supply of bread. 'Ma's just finishing the beds, he can busy himself helping me with the bread, he likes a bit of dough to handle. My hands are too messy to touch him. Just pop him in the high seat by the table. There, Bobby,' she plonked a dollop of dough on the wooden surface ready for him, 'that's your bit.'

Polly could see that he was used to having a hand in any cooking that went on, his tiny fingers embedded themselves into the pliant and already kneaded lump he'd been given. Being able to leave him with the Warwicks had come as a Godsend to her and probably to all of them: it brought a few extra shillings a week into Blanche's tight budget, it was good for Bobby to be accepted into an already large family, it meant that she saw Charles and, even more important, that he saw her. Always she had taken pains with her appearance, but never more than now. Partly it was pride that drove her – and that she readily admitted; partly though it was to punish him, daily more clearly to bring it home to him what a fool he'd been.

Just look at Clara this morning, her baby not due for five months or more and already the waist fastener on her well-worn grey skirt was left undone with more care for comfort than appearance. Where was her self-respect?

'Leave him with me, Miss Polly,' the object of her scorn beamed at her, never varying the rhythm of her hands on the dough. 'I expect you saw Chaw on your way in, didn't you?

He's taken it on himself to cut back the growth alongside the track,' she chuckled. 'Chaw likes to be busy.'

'He probably misses the constant change of scene when he worked the waterways.'

'Likely that's it. If he's still out there when you pass by, would you tell him the kettle's singing ready and I'm just going to brew us a hot drink.'

Climbing back into the trap Polly felt a moment's shame. But it didn't last. By the time she brought Tubby almost to a halt where Charles was waiting vanity once more asserted itself. Without quite stopping and with something bordering on a regal air she passed on Clara's message.

The steam launch had been moored on the water for the past two days, the wooden hull was finished, watertight and elegant, furnished with wooden bench seats on both the outer and inner deck areas. All it waited for was the Maunders engine. About this Polly's mind was pulled in two directions: she had liked John and Edwin Maunders; more than that she had respected them with their enthusiasm and certainty of purpose. So, for their sake, she wanted the engine to be every bit as satisfactory as the boat demanded; on the other hand, if there was a hold-up of some sort, or if when it was installed a problem manifested itself, then she would feel she'd scored a point against cocksure Harry.

She called her greeting to the men as she went through the yard. When Hugh Davies told her this was a day they'd looked forward to she didn't question him, in fact she wasn't sure that she'd heard him correctly.

'There you are, Pol'. Her father called as she came toward the office. 'In time for the maiden trip, eh?'

'The launch?' She had already been on board as it floated on its moorings in all its glory.

'Harry's aboard now with the Maunders brothers. Before the morning's out they'll have the engine installed. They're very inexperienced, it wouldn't have been *my* choice to give them the order, but then he who pays the piper calls the tune, it's not for me to make decisions at Seagrove's. It's my opinion we should have gone back to Mannering & Toms, but my opinion doesn't count these days.'

All along that had been her view too, yet hearing her father voice it now put her on the defensive on the Maunders' account – or was it on Harry's.

'He has sufficient faith in them that he has invested – invested a considerable amount so John Maunders told me – in their company.'

'Ah well, if that's the case we know why he was so keen for them to get the work. Money into his own pocket I suppose.'

She felt disappointed and strangely lonely.

'Cheer up, Pappy. The launch was a fine order for our books, the men have made a splendid job and Maunders' price is considerably lower than any quote we should have got from Mannering & Toms.'

Whether her words cheered him was hard to tell, for when he spoke again his mind had moved onto another track.

'Pol, you'll manage without me at home for a few days won't you. One way and another I've had a worrying year, I thought I'd try and take a short holiday, just a week or so. You needn't bother yourself about the yard, I've told Carpenter I'm going away. If he thinks it necessary he'll stay at the George so that he's on hand to keep the wheels turning. Just as long as you can manage at the house.'

'Mrs Hume looks after things at home, you know she does. As for asking Harry Carpenter to stay at the George—'

'You think I should propose he stay at the house? There's nothing I should like better. And I'm sure he'd jump at the invitation.'

'What I meant was – we don't need him at all. I'll come in here each day while you're away, Mrs Warwick will be happy to have Bobby. Tell Harry I can manage without him, Pappy. If you don't, *I* shall.'

'Look!' he cut in, 'see the funnel! They've done it, the engine's in.' Ushering Polly ahead of him he made for the jetty.

At the sight of the Maunders brothers' faces Polly forgot all about her wish to score points off Harry, she shared their pride, she rejoiced with them.

'May I make her whistle?'

This wasn't the first steamer Seagroves had built. Long before Polly worked at the yard her father would bring her to

135

the launching and it had always been her privilege to pull the cord and release steam to blow the whistle. It was part of the ceremony, the equivalent of breaking a bottle of champagne on the keel. 'It's a Seagrove tradition,' she laughed as she reached for the cord.

Two loud whistles pierced the silence and, just as she'd known they would, to a man everyone from the yard came to the jetty.

'Untie her,' Harry called, 'throw me the rope.'

John and Edwin Maunders watched the pressure gauge, released the steam with a sound like the hiss of an angry animal.

'Ready to cast off ...'

And the moment of truth, the throbbing of the engine and with Stanley taking the wheel they moved away from the bank and started downstream. In the centre of the river they stopped, then he manoeuvred the launch, backwards and turning, forwards and turning, and again backwards, again forwards, until finally it had completed a 180-degree turn.

'She handles well,' he told Harry. 'Here, you take over.'

Upstream they went, beyond Water's Edge, beyond Rat Island and the meadows where Charles's cattle weren't sufficiently impressed at the sight to stop munching the sweet grass.

'She has real power,' Harry agreed, 'listen to the sound of that engine, power and plenty in reserve. You take her Polly. You've handled a launch before?'

Without hesitating she moved closer, her hands ready to take over from his.

'No, but everyone has to start.'

There was something in his smile that almost took her mind away from the wonderful feeling of power she had, she, Polly Seagrove at the helm of what was probably the biggest launch on the Thames. Later she'd think about the way he'd looked at her, as if he understood her pride and shared it.

'Before we come to the lock we'll turn and take her back,' Harry said. 'Don't you think so, sir?' to Stanley.

'I think we've seen enough to know she's a fine boat. And I must take my hat off to you two,' he told the Maunders brothers. 'She handles like a race horse ready to be given its head.'

'Right, so start slowing her down,' standing behind Polly Harry covered her hands with his, 'just relax, let me guide your hands.'

The boat was gradually slowed to a standstill, then the same operation as before, backwards turning, forwards turning, backwards again, then forwards, until they were set to start the journey back to the yard.

Once they were on course he released his hold on her. She ought to have been glad, she was once again in sole control, so why was it she felt ... felt ...? She took a quick glance at him to find that he was gazing at her, his expression hard to fathom.

'You're doing well,' he told her, to be answered with a smile that corresponded with the light that shone in her eyes. 'Do you want to take her into her mooring?'

'If you'll help me.'

'Start to lose speed.'

He came to stand behind her again watching over her. She found herself looking forward to the moment when his hands would cover hers. But that's ridiculous, she told herself, you don't even like him. He has no business to be taking control of what I do, a boat out of Seagrove's Boatyard, if I can't handle it alone – and I almost can – then it should be Pappy who directs me in. That's what she told herself, but as he leant forward and covered her hands with his she was filled with a strange sensation: a sense of the rightness of the moment, certainty that he shared her pride.

So they brought the launch to rest alongside Seagrove's landing stage and Harry threw a rope to Hugh Davies. The throb of the engine was stilled.

'Well?' Moving to her side Harry rested his hand on her shoulder. At any other time she might have shrugged it off. But not today.

'Wonderful,' she nodded, her eyes luminous with pleasure as she raised her face towards his. 'I'm so glad, truly I am. And I was wrong, Harry, I'm sorry for the things I said to you about lending them money ... in any case it wasn't my business but I know now that I was wrong.'

He didn't reply, unless the pressure of a hand and a teasing glint in his eyes added up to an answer.

'I'm sure your money will bring you good profit,' she told him, by this time with her excitement well in control.

'And I'm sure of it, too, Polly. I'm not in the habit of backing losers.'

The next day a carriage arrived at Water's Edge to collect Stanley and his trunk. When Cecily Banks had visited it had been evening, Polly had seen neither carriage nor coachman so, unlike Mrs Hume, she didn't recognise the man who helped Hume lift the luggage aboard. When he'd driven his mistress to Water's Edge he had eaten with the staff and Ida Hume was quick to see who it was the master was going off with.

Polly came down the front steps with her father.

'I'm sure there won't be any need,' she said, 'but in case of something dreadful, can you leave an address where I can get a message to you?'

'You'll find a card in the desk drawer. It's Cecily's London house.'

'You're staying with Mrs Banks?' There was no hiding her surprise, but what Stanley didn't guess was her sense of relief. With Mrs Banks accompanying him he wasn't likely to spend his evenings gambling money he could ill afford.

'Not just me, Pol, she has arranged a house party for a few days. She and I are to travel up together by train this afternoon. I'm going to her home now, then her luggage will be lifted onto the carriage with mine.' His smile was better suited to an excited schoolboy than to a no-longer-young widower, 'ready for us to be taken to the station. Once we're in London we shall be well chaperoned, I'd have more care for her reputation than to be her only house guest.' If it were possible his smile deepened. 'I'm really looking forward to it. It's a fine house, well you'll see that from the address. She has such a flair ... I asked you before, you *do* like her, Pol?'

'If she can put that smile on your face, of course I like her. Forget all your worries, Pappy, have a wonderful few days.' She hugged him, then raised her face for his goodbye kiss.

Craning her neck Mrs Hume watched through the kitchen window as the carriage rattled down the gravel drive.

'Now what was he up to?' she asked herself silently. 'I don't know the woman and I can do very nicely without getting to know her. No oil painting, that much I did see. Shouldn't think the men would be queuing up for her. Off you go and enjoy yourself, but don't you bring her back here in the poor dear mistress's place, upsetting the way I like to see the place run. One thing's certain, she's not without a bit of brass. If you were barmy enough to take her on, more than likely she'd want to put some of her own staff in here. Well, if she comes the old soldier with me then I'll sling my hook – and I'll see to it that my Arthur does the same.'

Ida Hume's day had got off to a bad start. It didn't bode well for poor Daisy.

In the study Polly found the card in the desk drawer. Belgravia! No wonder he'd been so keen to escape his responsibilities for a week.

Standing on the landing pier Polly watched the launch move away, starting on its journey down river to the thriving company of pleasure-boat hirers who had commissioned it. The men who had worked on it had all come to watch it set out, but now one by one they were returning to the yard.

'She's a beauty,' Harry's voice surprised her, 'and she represents a good profit too.'

'I didn't know you were here. There's no need, you know. I'm perfectly able to look after things while Pap – while my father's on holiday.'

'You think I doubt you? Polly, if everyone had your enthusiasm and ability there wouldn't be a firm that didn't prosper.' Was it genuine praise? Or was it meant as a reminder of her father's failings? 'That's not the reason I'm here.'

'You have business interests in – oh, I don't know where, all over the place so I believe. It's a waste of valuable time your being here looking over my shoulder at everything I do.' It was unreasonable that she felt threatened by his nearness.

'How long have we known each other, Pol?' It surprised her to hear him shorten her name, no one had ever done that except her father.

'Since the night Bobby was born. You came to collect settlement of the loan. You must know exactly when that was, a year ago last February, the night you pressured Pap – Papa—'

'Why do you still pretend to me that he's Papa to you, not Pappy? Pol, isn't it time we were honest with each other?'

She stood very straight, her hands clasped so tightly that her knuckles were white.

'If Pappy were here I couldn't talk to you like it – because I'd be wanting to spare him, not you. But if it's honesty you want, well then, that's what you shall have. Our whole relationship is based on – on – on a cruel trick. When you knew Pappy was at his wit's end you lent him money, each month he paid you interest on what he owed. How you must have laughed when the year was up and he couldn't pay you any of the capital. But how could he, when you bled him dry with the monthly interest.'

Harry's expression had changed as he listened, he was looking at her through narrowed eyes. But it had to be said, if it was honesty he was asking for, then she'd let him have it.

'The arrangement was that he would repay you in a year. Have you ever thought of how he felt coming to you at the end of the twelve months and asking for longer? No wonder you agreed, like an angler playing a fish you knew you couldn't lose. Extra months simply meant extra payment of interest; however long you waited in the end you would get your capital – in gold or in kind.'

He didn't attempt to interrupt her, neither did he take his gaze off her.

'When the months of grace you'd allowed were over and the day of reckoning came – did you care about the despair you drove him to when all the while he was worried to death about my mother? No, of course you didn't! The first time you came to our home it was to collect money you knew he wouldn't have. I hated you for the way I made myself behave, trying to find your soft spot – as if you had such a thing! I ought to have recognized that I'd be wasting my time. No wonder you rose from the gutter to be what you are, with your sort of business ethics nothing could stop you. Did you listen to Pappy's plea to give us more grace, pay you bit by bit with interest on what we still owed?'

'Don't say "us" and "we", Polly. If you'd been here things would never have got to the state they were.'

'Of course it's "us" and "we", I'm part of Seagrove's. And

of course you didn't listen.'

For a moment they looked at each other in silence. There was nothing defensive in his manner, indeed his expression was impossible to read. But, once started, she was powerless to stop herself.

'You knew you had him cornered, whatever suggestion you chose to come forward with he would have agreed. I expect you were well pleased with your clever business deal. You know what I regret more than anything? It's that Seagrove's, a yard that has a reputation for good craftsmanship and honest dealings, has to be saddled with you. For eighteen months or more you pocketed your interest and after all that you ended up by taking part of the business as repayment. And what was my father left with? A partnership in a business that should be his – *ours* – having paid you for months for the privilege.'

Harry came close to her, too close. Her movement backwards was instinctive just as was his to grab her shoulders and pull her towards him. For a second the scene in the drawing room at Water's Edge was alive in her mind, she thought he was going to draw her into his arms. The veil between the passion of anger and the passion that surprised her at this touch was thin. Then she realised she had been only inches from falling backwards into the river.

'Is that what he told you?' Harry asked her quietly, making no attempt to release her.

'Yes ... no ... I don't know what he told me. Nothing for ages, he wanted to keep it from me that you had any part in the boatyard.' Polly never cried, she'd always scorned women who wept. Perhaps it was temper that made her eyes fill with tears. Yet how could it be when her rage had suddenly gone? 'I was rude. I'm sorry. You had every right to do what you did.'

'You were honest. Isn't that what I wanted of you?'

'I've always promised myself that I'll pay you back, buy you out of the business. We used to spend money like water, we had no idea there were any problems at the yard. I'm trying to watch the bills now. But when the accounts for the yard show that you could be paid out, I suppose it won't be that simple. Not now that the money that's made here is partly yours in any case.'

His expression softened.

'You and I weren't made for quarrelling, Polly. We have too

much in common.'

'I don't know what,' she pouted, feeling uncomfortably aware that in losing her temper she had made herself appear childish, the one thing she wanted to avoid. It was important that he saw her as proficient, then perhaps he would go about his business and leave her to go about hers. 'Anyway, I *was* rude and I shouldn't have been. It all started because I was trying to make you see there's no need for you to keep a watchful eye on what I do. I can be trusted. And I know Seagrove's is small fry to a busy person like you.'

Why was he looking at her like that? Letting go of his hold on her he turned away. She didn't move, a premonition told her that he had something important to say. Perhaps he had a suggestion about the terms he'd agree if he were to be bought out.

'At any time I could have made a deal with your father. Polly, have you *no* idea why I kept coming to your home – waiting for you to grow up perhaps?'

'I don't know what you mean.' But was that the truth? Remember the evening he'd come because she was there alone, remember the moment when he'd kissed her ...

He turned round to face her. There was none of his usual arrogant self-confidence in his manner, almost she believed he was pleading with her.

'I've never felt like this about anyone, Polly. All my life I've fought for what I want, fought until I reached my goal. I've known plenty of women, but – Polly, you're the only one I've loved.'

'No,' she breathed. 'You hardly know me. You said so yourself, I've played games with you, until just now I've not been honest.'

'I'm nearly twenty years your senior, nearer your father's age than yours. Is that what you're thinking?'

'No. The idea – it's impossible —'

'Marry me, Polly. Fight it as much as you like, you can't alter the truth. I want the right to be with you, to cherish you,' then, his mouth twitching into what was almost a smile, 'to argue with you too I dare say, to share my life with you. I shall love you till the day I died.'

'No! I'm not listening to you. Anyway I don't believe you.'

He gripped her hands in his, crushing her fingers together. She felt trapped. Harry Carpenter always fought until he had his own way.

'I don't want to believe you. Harry I can never love you—'

'We understand each other, we value the same things. How can I feel like this about you and yet you say you can never love me? I'll tell you. It's because we belong together. I believe I knew it from the moment I saw you. Remember how you signalled your father to leave us alone.'

A barge was passing along the river, a barge quite twice the capacity of the *Maryanne*, but to Polly its size had no relevance, at the sight of it she was again with Charles. She saw the silent message of his eyes when she brought or collected Bobby at Little Roost, she knew without any doubt that his marriage hadn't touched the way he thought of *her*.

'No, Harry. I can never love you. There's someone else.'

'You're not letting yourself be pushed into accepting some youth for the sake of restoring the family fortunes?'

'If I were prepared to sell myself for that, then why would I be refusing you?' she retorted. 'The man I love is married already. But it's me he loves. Marriage is just duty.'

He let go of her hands and raised her chin so that she looked directly at him.

'Are you telling me the truth? Do you swear it on all that you hold dear at the yard here?'

'I swear it's the truth. I loved him even before I met you.' Then in a moment's sympathy for him, she added, 'Anyway, if I hadn't made such an exhibition of myself in my effort to help Pappy and the yard, you wouldn't have noticed me.'

'I'd have noticed you if you'd been amongst a thousand others. Be my wife, let me teach you what love can mean—'

'For someone who's never known it before, you seem very sure.'

This time he did smile, pulling her close against him.

'Oh yes, I'm sure.'

'Let me go. I told you – no. How can you even want me when you know my heart belongs to someone else?'

She thought he was going to do as she said. His hold on her slackened, then he crushed her against him, his mouth on hers.

Seconds later, without a word, he left her. She looked down at her hands as if she expected to see the impression of his fingers.

'Carpenter suggests we take on a full-time clerk at the yard, Pol,' Stanley told her at breakfast a week or two later. 'I don't mind admitting, the idea suits me very well, yes very well indeed. I should like to have proposed it myself, at one time that's what I would have done, but as things are now I'm in no position. Boat building staff, that's a different matter, there he doesn't interfere.'

'And neither should he with the books. Is he suggesting we cheat him? There can't be any other reason. You're there every day, I'm there at least three times a week. There won't be anything for a clerk to do. Anyway, what's the use of somebody who doesn't know a rowlock from a bulwark?'

Stanley laughed at her outburst.

'Come, come, Pol, why are you so touchy about him? Of course he trusts us – and if he doesn't he's at liberty to have an accountant check our books.'

'Tell him we don't want some outsider interfering – if you won't tell him *I* will.'

'And enjoy doing it I'll be bound,' he teased. Then more seriously, 'It will give me the opportunity for more freedom, perhaps he could see I've lost some of my old fire for work.' Loyalty made her stamp on her retort and on the thought that went with it. 'I've had a worrying year, Pol, a worrying two years – what with fighting a losing battle in the struggle to keep up standards here so that your dear mother wouldn't suspect that things were bad at the yard, that I no longer had money to spend like water; having to stand by powerless to help her through her last months; losing her, losing my hold on the business.'

'I know, Pappy. But I'm there to help you.'

At fifteen months Bobby was too old to be left alone while Polly and her father shared breakfast time; now he was anchored into the long-legged chair that twenty years before had been Polly's, and was being fed spoonfuls of porridge as he looked from one to the other of them. Conscious that it was minutes since he had had the whole of Polly's attention, he let her tip the next spoonful into his mouth, then showed his displeasure at being ignored by blowing it out with all his force.

'Enough of that!' If it was his father's attention he'd been aiming at, there was no doubt he had it now. His bottom lip trembled at the angry tone. 'We can't have this sort of thing at the table, Polly. And look at the mess on the cloth. I had in mind to invite Cecily for a few days, it's a lonely life for a widow. I should know, man or woman, loneliness is the same. But how could we have her here and then inflict that sort of behaviour on her?'

'If she's too good to share the table with the family then she's best to stay away.' Polly answered tartly as she wiped the porridge from the cloth and lifted Bobby onto her knee. 'Come on, open wide, there's my boy.'

Stanley watched her, loving her just as he had all her life and yet helpless to stamp down his irritation. 'We were talking about Carpenter, his reason for appointing a man for the office at the yard.' He tried to ignore the interruption.

'*You* were talking about it. As for me, I think it's an unnecessary waste of money. If he's such an astute business man as you always say, I can't think why he should be so stupid.'

'I was saying just now I wonder if he can sense how much I need the pressure lifted. Perhaps that has something to do with it. But Polly, I think it's *your* well-being he has in mind.'

'If he has, then the best thing he can do is stop meddling.'

Stanley sighed, looking at her keenly, undecided how to answer.

'It's not right for a gently reared woman to spend her days in a boatyard. What sort of a life will that bring you? Things could be so very different, Pol. You hold a hand of trump cards if only you'd see fit to use them. I've told you often enough, if you made yourself more agreeable to him you'd have Harry Carpenter eating out of your hand.'

'I wish you wouldn't talk me over with him, Pappy. I never discuss you.'

'Bless the girl, as if I would. Men understand each other, they don't have to spell things out. That's how it is that I suspect he can see I'm at the stage where I *must* ease up; and that's how it is I'm so sure that his frequent trips down from London have little to do with the yard. Haven't you noticed that if you're not in the office on the day he comes, then he unfailingly accepts my invitation to come home with me in the evening. Oh, Pol, if only you could look on him with an open mind – forget all that Shylock nonsense you used to talk.'

'You mean if only I would sell myself for the price of his share in Seagrove's?'

'No, no, of course I don't. None of it is worth you and me falling out over. We never have, not through all the bad times I was talking about just now. There's no way of putting back the clock, things are as they are. It's to the future we must look. You can't tell me there isn't a girl to be found who'd come here to look after that child. Of course there is. It's not right have a drooling infant at an adult meal table. If you engaged a girl then you and I could go in together in the mornings.'

Polly's answer was lost in the sudden excitement of the door being pushed open and Horace bounding in, a tiny slipper belonging to Bobby in his mouth. Feeling all eyes were on him he did his party piece, threw it up in the air, caught it, threw it up again. By this time porridge was the last thing on Bobby's mind. His peals of mirth were music to Polly's ears – but clearly not to his father's.

Whatever reply she'd made she certainly hadn't admitted her real reason for not wanting a nursery maid living-in and caring for Bobby. Only she knew the importance of her morning and teatime visits to Little Roost; even Charles couldn't guess how aware she was that he watched for her coming, found some excuse to be in the yard or, better still, in the lane where what he said could be heard by no ears but hers.

One question she didn't ask herself: would she have felt the same contempt for Clara had she been married to anyone other than Charles? Even now, contempt was sometimes overshadowed with sympathy. Long before Bobby was delivered, Clara would have been out helping with the morning milking; she helped with the great load of washing and ironing that came from the large Warwick family, she made the daily loaves. The one thing she never seemed to do was complain. 'Like Reading gasometer' Polly had thought of her even before she spread into pregnancy. With three months to wait before her child was due, the opening of her black workaday skirt was fastened by tapes that had been neatly stitched onto the band. She accepted the bearing of a child with the same unquestioning cheerfulness as she'd always accepted the tasks that had come her way, shovelling snow from the yard on winter mornings, mucking out the cowsheds, churning the butter, following behind her father and the horse-drawn plough and dropping potatoes into the furrow so that later in the year she, with the rest of the family, could gather them up as the crop was dug.

On a morning in late May Polly arrived with Bobby to find Charles in the farm kitchen with Clara.

'Morning Miss Polly,' came Clara's cheery greeting while Charles said nothing. 'It's going to be a scorcher today I reckon. Hits you when it comes sudden in May like this.'

'You find it tiring I expect,' Polly answered, taking in the sight of the rosy-faced young woman and at the same time priding herself that Charles was faced with the contrasting sight of the two of them together.

'Never grumble about the sunshine, it's a grand day for Pa and Chaw to be making a start on cutting the hay. Wish I could be out there with you Chaw. Hello then my lovey,' she held out her arms to Bobby.

'He's too heavy for you.' Polly kept her hold on him.

'Stuff and nonsense, I still lug our Sammy about when he plays the old soldier and won't walk properly. He's two years ahead of this one – and a strong great lad. I'm no china doll, eh Chaw?' she laughed.

'I'll be off,' Charles answered. 'We ought to be started on the cutting. Goodbye, Pol – Miss Polly,' and then to Clara, 'You'll bring us our dinner later – unless Ma comes across to get it?'

'Not so fast ... don't I get a kiss?'

Clara's back was turned to Polly as Charles pecked his wife's cheek, so she was innocent of the glance they exchanged, his embarrassed, hers mocking. Then he was gone, just as Bobby caught the sound of Sammy and Liz, eighteen months his senior, coming back from throwing corn to the hens.

'I'll put him an overall over his tidy clothes,' Clara said, 'then he can't come to any harm with the others. Nothing he likes more than to join in, but I'll be keeping a good eye on him, you needn't worry.'

'Where's your mother this morning? Isn't she at home? You've got more than enough to do without an extra child on your hands.'

'Now what difference does one little 'un his size make? There've been youngsters underfoot here as long as I can remember. Reckon the old house likes the noise of them. Honest, you don't need to worry about him Miss Polly. These three, they're best of friends. Even if he crawls out into the yard there's nothing worse than top dirt to hurt him. Didn't you notice how spruce it looked out there this morning? Chaw spent the whole of yesterday evening cleaning up the mess, never known it to have such a spring clean.'

'He must find livestock and all their mess hard to get used to after being on the river.'

'Reckon that must be it.' Clara laughed good-humouredly. 'He's made up his mind it's not going to get in that state again. Gave it another sloosh over this morning while I was putting the cows back in the meadow. A day like today though it dried out in no time, so you needn't have a care about Bobby.' She opened the back door to let in the morning sunshine. 'You were asking about Ma. She's over in the fields this morning. This'll be the first year I've not been out there helping stack the hay, but Ma said me being like I am it's better for me to do the indoor jobs and she'll help in the field.'

It was a rare thing for Polly to consider Clara without her thoughts being clouded by the image of Charles. Now, looking at her, she had a twinge of guilt. Everyone worked hard at Little Roost, leisure and relaxation were unknown to them. But was it right for her to add to Clara's load?

'I'll come back early today,' she voiced her decision even as she made it. In truth her job had been more or less taken from her by Mr Giles, Teddy Giles, the book-keeper Harry had engaged. It was stubbornness rather than necessity that made her continue working three days a week at the yard – that and the fact that her father spent ever less time there and she had no intention of letting Harry Carpenter run away with the impression that Seagrove's Boatyard wasn't in the hands of a Seagrove!

As she drove her trap back along the rutted lane she noticed the verge was getting overgrown again and smile to herself at the certainty that as soon as the hay was cut she would see Charles and his scythe waiting for her. From her high seat on the trap she could look over the hedge to where the three were working in the hayfield. She liked to think it was telepathy that made the object of her thoughts raise his head at that precise moment and, seeing her, wave a greeting with the same flourish that had first drawn her attention to him two years ago. This time she waved back. It was as if in that action, unnoticed by Blanche and Bert, a silent message was given and answered. A few minutes before she had been touched by an unfamiliar concern for Clara; now neither the good-natured, untidy, happily pregnant girl nor the child she carried found a way into her mind.

It wasn't so easy to push thoughts of Harry to one side. If anything he had been coming to the yard even more frequently and, although he had made no attempt to corner her by herself, to re-open the scene on the landing stage, yet she knew that for both of them it was always there between them.

'Is anything wrong, Mr Davies?' Despite her adult status. Polly still used the address to him that she had as a child. 'You're not ill, are you? Something seems to be worrying you?'

'I never thought I let it show, Miss Polly. I promise you, I've not been letting the work suffer.'

'You know that's not what I meant.'

For a minute Hugh hesitated, whatever it was that troubled him he found it hard to talk to her about. She wished, not for the first time and not for the same reason, that her father hadn't gone away: a day or two quietly in the country, he'd told her, as if she would be likely to believe that when this was the beginning of the season as Ascot.

'It's my sister, Miss Polly. A lot younger than me, born when I'd already started earning my living. She married a year or two back. There were others in between me and her, but we were living in Somerset – that's where I come from you know – and the rest of them are all married and settled round about their home ground as you might say. But Millie, that's the one I'm telling you about, she took up with a right bounder. Wouldn't listen to me. Love! I count myself lucky I've never been caught up with it. Wouldn't hear a word against him, she wouldn't. Great burly hunk of a man, worked in the clay pits down in

Devon. Was an unlucky day for Mill when he went travelling and landed up in Somerset. One look at him and she was lost.'

'She married him?' Polly prompted when it looked as though the tale had ground to a halt.

'Ah, that she did. And off she went to Devon with him, never seen a girl as happy. Three years ago that was. I ought to have kept an eye on things better than I did. But when she wrote she never gave me a hint that things were wrong. Was three days ago she turned up on my doorstep. Never forget the sight of her, the change ... she'd gone away a girl, a girl with her head full of dreams I dare say. Nothing of a girl about her now. Thin as a rake she is, gaunt, ay, that's the word for it, gaunt and a worse shiner I've never seen than the eye he'd given her. Wonder he hadn't knocked the sight out of it. If I could get my hands on the bugger – begging your pardon Miss Polly but there ain't no other word. She's come to me and quite right she should, all her life it's been me she's looked to. But this time I'm failing her. I've given her my bed, she's welcome to anything I've got. The place is clean and tidy, but it's not a home for a woman. Nice little cottage they had down in Devon, she wrote and told me all about it when she went there, before she woke up to what he really is.'

'How do you mean – what he really is?'

'Can't think why he ever asked her to marry him. To cook and clean for him most likely. Even now she jibs at telling me, only lets things slip out by mistake as you might say. He's a good bit older than her, had plenty of women before she came along, but that didn't have to mean that marriage wouldn't change his ways. It seems it didn't. She wanted a family, loves little ones does Millie, always has. I suppose she must be one of those who can't have them. She blames herself – says that if she could have given him a son everything would have been different.'

'I'm sorry Mr Davies. There must be something we can do about her.'

'No future for her, keeping house for a brother.'

'Does she still love her husband do you think? Does she regret coming away?'

'Don't ask me about love, Miss. Nor you either I expect at your age, you've not been struck down yet. When you are I just hope it's for a good man, one who will keep his vows of faithfulness, not one who treats you like a skivvy and worse. I tell you, I sent it round and round in my brain, but I can't think of any way to give the girl a future.'

Polly covered his hand with hers.

'It's not just your worry now, it's mine too. Thank you for taking me into your confidence. Between us we'll work something out.' Already the idea had formed, but she wasn't ready yet to face up to it.

She knew Bobby was loved and cared for at Little Roost, she knew the shillings she paid each week were probably a welcome addition to Blanche's budget. But honesty made her face up to the thing she wasn't proud to admit to: the satisfaction she found in seeing the way Charles looked at her, the certainty that his marriage had been a coward's way of doing what was expected of him.

It was out of character for her to be guided by events, she liked to make her own decisions, follow her own instincts. Sitting in the little office, the only sound the scratching of Teddy Giles's pen on the page of the ledger she knew that, even though Fate had pushed Millie across her path, the decision for what she intended was her own.

After that things happened quickly. Two mornings later, Bobby once again safely ensconced with Clara and the preschool Warwicks while Blanche raked the cut hay, as arranged Millie was waiting for her at the yard. For some reason Polly had expected someone younger, probably because Hugh Davies still looked on her as his little sister, a defenceless child. She was some years older than Polly, probably somewhere around thirty, very thin, her eyes sunk into their sockets. Only when she smiled – a pathetic smile, begging to be accepted – and showed perfect white teeth did she drop the mantle of middle-aged hardship. Fancy being so crushed by life – by life or by some brute of a husband who found pleasure with other women and destroyed hope. Because that was what she looked like, Polly decided, as if all hope was gone.

'Let's walk by the river,' she suggested, 'we can talk as we go.'

'It's kind of you to think you might have work for me. I'll do anything.'

151

'You may not want to do what I'm going to suggest. It depends how well you get on with children – well, he's only a baby really. You've got to like him and even more important – although I expect it comes to the same thing – *he* has to like *you*.'

They walked, they talked, Millie came out of her shell and told Polly of how her marriage had started out so well.

'Until death do us part ... that's what we promised,' she sniffed, even without looking at her Polly knew what a battle she was having not to cry. 'Both of us broke our vows, I did as much as Bruce – that's his name – Bruce. He wasn't happy just to have one woman, well anyway he wasn't if that woman was *me*, but I don't think he would have been anyway. He'd been a free man too long, been between the sheets with too many others to be content with what he could find at home. Oh Miss Seagrove, I oughtn't to talk like this to you, you a single lady. I'm sorry, my tongue ran away with me.'

'But you said you both broke your vows?' Polly ignored the flustered apology.

'Well, so I did. I promised to love – and I do, that's the misery of the whole thing, if I can love him now with my eye still purple from his fist then I'm not going to change – I promised to honour – I broke that one, honour hasn't anything to do with loving – and I promised to obey. Fine sort of obedience I showed, running out on him.'

'You have to make a clear decision, Millie, then forget all this sackcloth and ashes talk. In my opinion if Bruce was taking other women, probably whores—'

'Oh Miss Seagrove, I shouldn't lead you on to talk about such things.'

Polly laughed. They stopped walking and turned to look at each other, Millie gripping her bottom lip between her startlingly white teeth. Then even while a single tear overspilled to roll down her thin face, she too laughed. It was like the sun after rain.

Taking her hand in a firm grip Polly told her, 'Ride home with me, we can go together to collect Bobby from the farm where he's looked after. See if you take to each other.'

So Millie Godwin, unknown to her deserted husband, came to Water's Edge. If Polly had wanted it she had all the freedom of her own girlhood back again, for Millie was loving and dependable, a woman who found caring for Bobby salve to her own wounded spirit. At the boatyard Teddy Giles was always at his desk, accounts were sent out on time, stock was ordered and deliveries checked. Stanley was only too happy to fill his days in ways more to his liking, but to Polly it was important that either she or her father were always there. Harry never gave warning of his visits, but it was a strange thing that they always coincided with her presence and her father's absence.

Millie's presence brought a pleasant change to Horace's life. No longer had he to take his exercise either on his own in the garden or, having wriggled under the stile, having to be content chasing after cows who appeared oblivious of his presence. For recently even on the days when Polly hadn't gone to the yard, walks hadn't been the adventures he'd been used to; with Bobby too young to walk, too big for the sling he'd ridden in the previous year and too heavy to carry for what Horace would consider 'real walk' much of the fun had gone. Now, with Polly to himself again, there were days when life was good again, there were sticks to chase across the water meadow or to retrieve from the river. Only for her the familiar walks had lost their zest. She never walked through the fields without picturing the *Maryanne* appearing round the bend in the river.

Polly had always prided herself that she shaped her own destiny. Midsummer's night, Bobby asleep in the nursery, Millie 'keeping an ear open' as she heated the irons on the range to press his day's washing, Stanley out for the evening as he so often was, Horace sensing Polly's restlessness and hinting by an occasional gruff bark and a beating of his long tail on the ground that he could offer her a perfect remedy.

'All right, boy,' she let him know she understood. And within minutes she was over the stile – and he under it – striding along the riverside path. The moon rode high, the night had all the magic of midsummer.

They were in the second meadow, Horace leaping ahead as if to make sure that the further he went the further she would follow. She heard him bark, a bark of excitement not of anger. The next hedge was between her and whoever it was the dog had met. It wasn't fear that made her heart hammer, fear would have driven her back home but instead she started forwards.

153

Chapter Eight

In the pale moonlight she could see him clearly: he was sitting on the ground at the place where he used to moor the barge. Horace was beside himself, dashing a few yards away just for the pleasure of bounding back to him. Then, as if he were trying to tell her about the friend he'd found, he tore towards Polly, skidding to a halt, then back to Charles.

'I hoped you were with him.' As soon as he saw her Charles got to his feet and came to meet her. 'When he appeared on his own I thought he'd escaped. Polly, why did you stop bringing the boy to the farm? And without even telling me, explaining ...?'

'I found someone suitable to live in. I'd been grateful to Mrs Warwick for having him, but I knew it could only be a temporary arrangement. She and Clara have enough to look after without an extra. And in a few weeks there will be another baby.' She was pleased with her answer, the tone casually friendly as she fell into step by his side, no hint that she was holding in check an excitement every bit as wild as Horace's.

'I ought to have kept the barge-work going. Do you ever think of the hours we used to spend there last summer, just us alone? Of course you do and so do I. That was freedom, real freedom. Remember the swimming, remember how we used to talk, about your yard, about my journeying, about the cargoes I carried, about life on the waterways ... and about ourselves, Polly.'

It would have been so gloriously easy to follow his lead, it was like a game – the first move his, the second hers. What stopped her was the memory of her last sight of Clara lumbering

154

from the cowshed to the dairy with a pail of milk, the hessian apron emphasising her girth, her hair hidden under her mob cap. For a second she'd stood the pail on the ground, stretched to ease her back, her cheeks blown out as she puffed, then she'd caught sight of Polly bringing the trap into the year and waved her unfailingly welcoming greeting, 'Morning Miss Polly, you'll find Ma in the kitchen.' Picking up the pail she'd staggered on to the far shed to start the churning or whatever mysteries were performed there.

'What brings you down here at this time of evening? Is something wrong with one of your herd?' Polly let him know that she wasn't the easy prey he anticipated.

'I often walk down to the water late like this. They all go to bed early – it's the way with farming folk.'

'That's what you are now Charles. You needn't have been, it was your own choice.'

'Don't, Polly. Please don't let's bicker, let's just be grateful that we're here together now.'

'Midsummer's night. Can't you feel the magic in the air?'

'There's always magic in the air by the river, breathe it in, Polly. Even blindfold you'd know where you were. There's a special nighttime smell – the meadows, the water weeds, the stillness. The ground's rock hard, even at this time of evening it's dry. Let's sit here.'

'Close your eyes and imagine *Maryanne* tied up like she used to be.'

He reached for her hand and held it against his cheek before he turned it and kissed her palm.

'Oh Charles,' she whispered, 'why? Why did you do it?'

'Why did I kiss you?'

'You know I don't mean that.'

For answer he turned towards her. The next second she was no longer sitting, she was lying on the parched ground, he was bending above her. Did he push her or did she make the first move? She could feel the hunger in him as his mouth covered hers.

'No —' She must fight him off. Longing and temptation were pulling her, but she must hold on to sanity before it was lost.

'Yes, yes,' he breathed, his mouth barely moving away from

hers as he spoke, 'I made you mine, you know you're still mine. Let me love you.' He pressed his body against hers.

He still loved her, it was *her* he wanted. In that instant she surrendered to the joy and triumph that flooded through her. Then the instant became time past, gone beyond recall; her sudden strength took him by surprise as she pushed him off her and scrambled to her feet.

'It's too late Charles. It needn't have been like this ... you let it happen ...' Joy, frustration, passion, even anger, she was consumed by all these things, tangled emotions that instantly filled her mind and threatened to find release in tears. But why should she cry? It was she who had won. He wanted her, he'd pleaded with her, wasn't that even more important than that gold band he wore on his finger or his dowdy wife waiting at home under the patchwork quilt she'd taken dreary years to make? She wouldn't cry. She must get away before he answered, before he realized how slim was her hold on control.

Her salvation came in the form of Horace, bounding towards them out of the night and jumping up to them in a welter of excitement as if he sensed the importance of the moment. Charles changed his position so that he knelt, his arms around her waist, his head moving against her. So when did he loosen his hold, let one hand touch her slender ankle, move tenderly up to her knee?

He still loved her, her heart cried joyously, marriage to poor homely Clara hadn't taken him away from her. But she mustn't listen to her heart, she mustn't listen to the strange longing that possessed her.

'Home, boy,' she told a mystified Horace who stood close, pressing himself heavily against them, making sure that he wasn't left out, his tail flailing wildly.

Charles dropped his hand, then got to his feet.

'I shouldn't have done that. Polly I can't forget ...'

'You think I forget?' She told herself she was thankful to have Horace with them. Alone with Charles could she have found the strength to say what had to be said? 'Go home to Clara, she'll wonder what's become of you.'

'She'll be asleep. As soon as her head touches the pillow she's gone, I could stay out all night and she wouldn't miss me.'

Again she pictured poor hard-working Clara and this time surprised herself at her reaction of loyalty to one of her own sex.

'And no wonder she gets tired, she works as hard as any man. Most women rest when there's a child coming, lie with their feet up so that their ankles don't swell—'

'Most women *you* know might make a meal of it, but Clara has been brought up on a farm, birth is part of nature.'

'Well, stay out here if you want, but Horace and I are going.'

'Tomorrow – come back tomorrow evening. If you feel safer,' she knew he smiled by the way his voice softened, 'bring your friend with you again. Come just to talk, surely we can be friends.'

'I'm not promising.'

'Wait,' he gripped her hands, 'just tell me one thing. Tell me you're glad we've talked again, tell me you want us still to be friends.'

'Oh yes, yes to both those things.'

She felt a twinge of disappointment that he seemed content at that, let go of her hands without carrying one to his mouth. Then she was gone without looking back.

In the early hours of the morning she was woken by a clap of thunder, the forerunner of many over the next hours. The storm abated but left a day of steady rain, so that by evening the ground that had been rock hard had become a quagmire. Polly told herself she was glad: secret meetings with Charles could only have one ending. Ending?

No, there could be no ending, not for them. Clara was the loser, he had married her out of kindness, duty. But what sort of marriage could that be ... and what sort of a marriage did Clara deserve? If she had any wit at all, surely she would know that a man ought to be able to feel pride in his wife. Polly's thoughts ran away with her, her confidence in the ultimate outcome becoming ever more certain. Remember how pretty Mother had been, even though she'd felt so wretched. Not for a single day had she let her standard fall. But then Clara has never had a standard to uphold, being pregnant has given her the excuse to let herself go completely to pot! If ever I'm expecting a child I vow I shall take even more trouble to look my best, even better than my best. What a difference he'll see when he remembers *her* and looks at *me*.

'I made you mine ... you're still mine ...' She could almost hear his voice. Then came another, echoing uninvited and unwanted, 'I shall love you till the day I die.' Harry, his softly spoken words not driven by the demand of momentary passion, the memory of the strange pleading expression in his startlingly light-blue eyes making her uncomfortable. Don't think about Harry Carpenter, think about Charles, Charles her Gypsy King, Charles who had loved her and made her his own.

When an English summer allows a crack wide enough to let in a thunderstorm, it so often happens that the crack becomes a break. Blue skies are lost in a cover of pale grey and the wind teases the surface of the river into uncharitable ripples. So it was for the next four days. Then as if by magic on the fifth day the sun rose in a cloudless sky, the garden was filled with the scent of warm, damp earth and the heady perfume of flowers. The river flowed gently as if the stormy days had never been.

Arriving at the boatyard Polly found herself as irritated as she always had been at the sight of harmless and diligent Teddy Giles, his eyes on the ledgers, his pen scratching its way across the pages as he made the neat entries. She ought to be glad, she ought to take a page out of her father's book. Stanley never hurried himself to the office, instead he lingered in the yard talking to the men. 'Taking an interest in the work' he liked to call it, but in truth his interest was in the people and his satisfaction in the feeling of male camaraderie amongst them. A harder taskmaster would have considered he was wasting his own time and theirs too, but it was because he was as he was – fun-loving, warm-hearted but indolent – that they gave of their best.

When Polly had started coming to the office she wouldn't have thought of opening any letters that waited, but now whichever of them arrived first read the mail.

'If it's an order for work to be done, Pol, you know how we're placed as well as I do,' her father had told her. Then he'd laughed, his expression like that of a mischievous boy, 'better than I do I dare say. If you're not sure when we can take a job on, then speak to Davies.'

That had been some months back, since when he'd been as happy to relinquish authority to her for the everyday running of the yard as later he had been to pass responsibility for keeping the ledgers up-to-date to Teddy Giles.

This morning as she took the paper knife and slit open the two envelopes that waited, she heard the sound of laughter from the yard, her father's as loud as any. Already the corrugated-roofed office was warm, the door propped wide with a heavy weight. She peeped out, her gaze falling on him affectionately. Then she hung up her hat and climbed onto the high stool next to Teddy Giles. The first envelope contained an order for no less than three skiffs for a small firm of hirers; the second, payment for re-flooring a narrow boat. It was the skiffs that set her own wheels of thought in motion, but there was no time for following their course, she'd come back to them later. In the meantime she took the letter out to talk to Hugh Davies about the time he estimated the work would take, then she started to prepare the quotation ... quantities of oak-planking, quantities of elm, of oakum, of tar, of metal for the rudders ...

'Pol, did you wonder what had become of me?' Stanley didn't attempt to disguise the excitement in his voice. Looking down at her fob watch she realized she had been working on the figures for more than an hour and this was her father's first appearance.

'I didn't notice how the time had gone.'

'Good girl. I don't know what I'd do without you – and of course Giles too,' he added, careful not to hurt the book-keeper's feelings. 'Good morning to you Giles, lovely day.'

'Indeed it is, sir.'

'This will bring the boats out on the water, Pappy. See the order we have from Ruddick & Pears, doesn't that show the trade is in hiring?'

'That's what we want. Plenty of work coming in. Pol, I've had this message. Here, you read it, a letter from Cecily. I told her man to wait, he's out there with the trap.'

It seemed that Cecily Banks had received news that her uncle was very ill. She was faced with the journey to his home a few miles from Lake Garda. Naturally she wouldn't travel alone, she would take a manservant to see to the baggage and a maid for herself, but even so she was loath to take responsibility for the journey and to be alone to face what she feared she would find at the end of it. As long as she could remember, her Great-uncle Vincent had held a special place in her affection. She prayed she would be in time to see him once more. Could her very dear friend Stanley find it in his heart to share whatever sadness she had to face? She could give him so little warning, he would understand she wanted to set out without delay.

'Her man's waiting, Pol. First of all I must go and talk to her. We couldn't set out immediately, there would be travel arrangements to make—'

'Garda? Is that in the Lake District?'

'No, no. This would be a long trip, across the channel and then onward overland I suspect. Lake Garda is in northern Italy, in the Dolomites. That's why I'm putting it to you. Pol, I'd be away for weeks, perhaps it would go into months; if she reaches this elderly relative in time, I'm sure she'll not leave him to face the end alone. She's talked of him often, of his villa, of the long visits she's spent there first with her parents and then with her late husband.'

'Italy!' He might as well have told her he was taking a trip to the moon, Polly had never known any of their friends to travel abroad.

'I'd have to make arrangement about the business, make sure you have my authority to act on my behalf in my absence. Just tell me not to go, say you'd not be able to manage, then you know I'd explain to her that I must refuse. It's a sad burden for her, though, I hate to think of her shouldering it alone. I've grown very fond of her.'

Teddy Giles's pen scratched unceasingly as if to assure them that he wasn't listening.

'Of course I can manage. That doesn't mean that I shan't be looking forward to when you get home again.'

He put his arm around her shoulder.

'Good girl, you never let me down. I'll make sure Carpenter knows I'll be away. If you need him he'll gladly come – but I don't need to tell you that.' His tone gave nothing away. Teddy Giles couldn't possibly guess at the secret message his eyes carried.

'Go and talk to Mrs Banks, Pappy. Don't worry about the yard – or home – all the wheels will keep turning I promise.'

'Bless you.'

It was strange to watch him walk back through the yard, climb into the waiting carriage and be bowled away through the gate to the narrow street. It might be many days before the arrangements were finalized and a passage booked for the party to start their long journey, but she knew that as far as the yard was concerned this would be his farewell, he wouldn't be here again until he returned to England. June was nearly over, would he be back by the autumn? By Christmas? She tried to imagine the excitement of his first day back here. She pictured herself boasting about the work the yard had turned out in his absence; but she knew that in truth his heart wasn't involved in what went on here, perhaps it never had been. She was overcome by a sense of loss. When had he ceased to be the centre of her universe, her friend, her mentor, her partner in adventure, her hero? Of course he was still her friend, she told herself, of course she loved him as dearly as she ever had, just as he did her. Only now he didn't belong to her, nor to any of this. If only Mother were still alive ...

The thrill had gone from the calculations that formed the basis of her quotation to Ruddick & Pears, but that didn't prevent her from marshalling her concentration and carrying on from where she'd been when her father had interrupted her with his letter from Mrs Banks. Was he in love with her? Concentration slipped. Of course he couldn't be, men of his age didn't fall in love. He's fifty-two, Polly's thought confirmed the impossibility that being fond of Cecily could bear any relationship to being in love. And remember Mother, there could never be another woman as lovely as she was; just imagine *her*, then think of Cecily Banks with her protruding teeth that always got ahead of the rest of her smile. He's lonely, she told herself, lonely for companionship of his own age – and she's lost her husband, she must be lonely too.

Dipping her pen in the inkwell she made another effort. Three skiffs ... each summer more hire boats were seen on the Thames. Ruddick & Pears must find there was good profit in it even though they had to pay far more for their boats than the cost of material and labour. The wheels of thought that had been set in motion when she'd read their order gained momentum.

When she recognized Harry's voice talking to Hugh Davies, she felt her familiar irritation that Teddy Giles must hear every word she said as she explained her father's extended absence. He would pretend not to listen, but his very presence took away her freedom. Not that their personal affairs were Harry Carpenter's business; he'd get his profit from the yard. Slipping from her stool she went outside, making a show of checking over a punt that was tied at the landing stage, knowing he was bound to see her there.

'Polly, you're enjoying the sunshine. I hate to think of you wasting the summer inside that airless office.'

'You don't need to concern yourself. I'm at the yard from choice, the last thing I intend to do with my life is – is the nothingness of wasting my days. I came out here purposely, it's impossible to talk freely since you've engaged some outsider to do the work that was mine.'

'Let's bury the hatchet Polly, an afternoon like this is a gift. And if you want to talk to me, I too would rather we weren't overheard.'

'It's not about me, it's to explain that my father's about to travel to Italy. He may be away for some time.' He listened as she related the news that had been brought in Cecily's letter. 'But everything here will continue unchanged, he's arranging for me to assume his authority until he comes back. He trusts me, Harry.'

'Are you implying that I don't. You know I do, Polly. You've a natural grasp of the work here and I've always realized that your interest is as genuine as is your ambition for Seagrove's.' So might he have spoken to any business acquaintance, except that the expression in his eyes didn't correspond with his clear-cut words.

'Then listen to what I've been thinking.' Polly chose only to hear the words. 'This morning we had an order for three skiffs from Ruddick & Pears – you may not know them as you're not local, they're on the edge of town. They started in a very small way. Even now they only have small craft to hire out. But don't you see, Harry, they're increasing their stake in the market.

When you found me I was looking at the landing stage here and thinking: we could extend it along the bank this way. Don't you see, we could put hire boats on the water for ourselves so much more cheaply than people like Ruddick & Pears can. Why should we let them take all the trade? There must be money in it.'

'Seagrove's are boat builders, craftsmen. Think how proud you are of their skill. Anyone can hire out a boat for a penny or two an hour.'

'I don't see why we can't do both.'

'It wouldn't be viable, the yard's too far out of town. Where d'you think you'd get your trade? Why should anyone travel out here to hire a boat when they can get one more conveniently?'

How dare he talk down to her as if she were some silly child! She felt crushed, but didn't mean to let it show.

'I'll talk to my father when he comes back from his trip.'

He tipped her chin so that she looked up at him.

'If it would make you happy I'd agree to giving it a trial even though I don't think it would do Seagrove's name any good. But darling Polly,' his gentle use of the endearment startled her, 'it wouldn't bring you happiness. You'd see your boats tied up here while those taken out near town punted past you – and word would get round that Seagrove's couldn't be doing well, they were looking for a second string to their bow. There's no surer way of losing people's confidence than the thought that a business is falling on hard times.'

She pouted. 'You're always so sure you're right! If that's what you say, then there's nothing I can do about it. Seagrove's isn't Seagrove's any more.'

'It will remain Seagrove's. You say I'm always sure, you know the one thing I'm sure of above all others.' He didn't elaborate, he didn't need to. He half expected her to argue but when she didn't answer he went on, 'I didn't realize my life lacked for anything until I met you. Ambition had been my guiding light and that had been sufficient. No one woman had ever meant anything more to me than a temporary plaything. Polly, you tell me you're in love with some married man, and he with you, and I tell you *this* – something else I'm sure about: if he can live with his wife and philander with you, then he's not worthy of you – and probably not worthy of her either, whoever she is. I could make you forget him. Arrogant? Is that how you see me? Perhaps I am too, but not over this.' He took hold of her hands, his grip on them in contrast with the quiet, intense way he spoke as he asked her, 'Do you believe in the power of prayer? If you do, Polly, then you must know you've no chance of standing out against me. Only God knows how I've prayed you'd find it in your heart to care. Now I'm begging you, let me prove I'm right when I tell you we should be together. Marry me, give me the chance to make you care. Pol, I can't look ahead to a life without you.'

She was sure it took all his control to speak in that low, steady tone and when he paused, his jaw held rigid, she knew it was because he was frightened of his own emotion.

'Don't!' She looked down at his hands gripping hers. What good hands they were, she thought, wondering how she could so readily let her mind be diverted. 'I've told you there's someone else. There's nothing special about me, Harry. Can't you just see me as the meddlesome daughter at Seagrove's yard? If we'd met some other way would I have felt different? Or probably in different circumstances you wouldn't have noticed me.'

'Oh yes I would. Nothing has been the same for either of us since that first evening. Am I not right?'

'At any rate for me nothing has been the same, how could it be? That was the evening I lost my mother, I gained a little brother to care for, and you took more than half our livelihood. You can pray as much as you like—'

He released her hands.

'Prayer is nothing without faith, and I have the faith. I know one day our lives must be bound together. Even *you*, my blessed Polly, can't be untouched by what I feel for you.'

'I wish you didn't—'

He cupped her face in his hands. She felt his power was hypnotic, forcing her to raise her eyes to his.

'Sometimes I wish it too,' he murmured, 'wish I could be free of you. Then I think how empty my life would be without the hope, the trust ...'

'Can't we forget everything else and try to be friends, Harry?'

'A beggar is grateful for the crumbs from the rich man's table.' But this time he smiled at her when he said it, his manner seeming to draw a line under what had gone before.

'With my father likely to be away for months,' she forced herself to match what she liked to see as his change of mood, 'one thing I'm sure is that your faith in my actions won't stretch to your leaving me to run the yard on my own.' Confident that he was once more restored to the role she could handle, that of hard-headed businessman, her relief showed in the smile he heard in her voice. 'So you'd better come into the office and I'll show you the quotation I've been preparing for Ruddick & Pears.' Their feet were firmly on the ground – or at least, she liked to think so – as they turned away from the landing stage. She was proud of the work she'd put into her quotation; but she wasn't ready to admit that she was showing it to him in the certain hope of hearing his praise.

A sinking sun painted the sky glorious shades of gold and red, colours that were reluctant to give way to the deep canopy of night; the first bat appeared as if from nowhere, dipping and swooping in its mad flight, circling the garden, then disappearing into the darkness as suddenly as it had come.

This evening Polly had 'used' Millie Godwin, she had even 'used' Bobby. Helping him spoon his supper into his mouth, playing with him while Millie filled his little zinc bath, seeing the way his eyes lighted with pleasure and with love as he looked at her, tonight these things had been even more precious to her than usual. While she was with him it was easier to push the afternoon to the back of her mind and hold away the thought of the evening before her. Would Charles be waiting for her in the meadow? Would he expect that she would come to find him as they had arranged before the storms broke? Ought she to go at all? Wasn't she building up hurt for both of them – and for Clara too?

'. . . I'll tell you this,' came the echo of Harry's warning, 'if he can live with his wife and philander' (oh, but Charles wasn't philandering, he loved her, duty kept him with dull, lumpy Clara, just as duty had made him marry her in the first place), 'then he's not worthy of you, and not worthy of her either.' What arrogant rubbish and anyway what business was it of Harry

Carpenter? '. . . The power of prayer,' she didn't want to remember his changed tones, the painful grip of his hands.

Stanley hadn't returned, he must still be with Cecily Banks. How long had he known her? He'd never brought her to the house until these last months, never even mentioned her. Surely she must have other friends – a woman of her affluence must mix with plenty of moneyed people who would be free to travel with her. But was that all they were to each other, just friends? (Another echo of the afternoon, this time the voice was her own, 'Can't we forget . . . just be friends.' But friendship was a comfortable relationship, at ease with itself.) No wonder she tore her mind away from where it was taking her, and marshalled her thoughts back to her father and Cecily.

'While I think of it, Miss Polly – I'll tell you because I know *he* wouldn't even if he could speak. Your Horace, he came out with Bobby and me this afternoon. I must have pushed Bobby a good three miles or more and, as for Horace, for every mile I walked I reckon he ran more than twice the distance. Hot day or no, he enjoyed himself.'

'You're a saint, Millie. He's had short shrift these last few days, it's been so wet.'

Polly ate a solitary meal then, throwing caution to the winds, let herself imagine Charles seeing her coming by the light of the waning moon, realizing she was alone, hurrying along the riverside path to meet her. '. . . living with his wife . . . not worthy of you . . .' What right had Harry Carpenter to interfere? No right, *no right*. Forget him. Or if you must think about him, then think of how he schemed his way into Seagrove's, think how low Pappy was brought from worry, remember how he waited until Pappy had nothing to fight with and then moved in for the kill.

Getting ready to meet Charles helped her to put the thought of Harry behind her. Always she looked her best, but for Charles she wanted even more than that. The night was far too warm to need a cloak, but she threw one round her shoulders just the same, then ran down the stairs planning to go out through the front door so that Horace wouldn't suspect he was being cheated.

'Pol, is that you?' Her father's voice came from his study, he must have returned while she was upstairs.

'Hello Pappy,' she put her head around the door, 'I didn't know you were home. Have you eaten?'

'Yes, with Cecily. Just off with the dog, were you? Let him wait, you can take him out presently. Come in Pol, there are things I want to talk to you about.'

A good thing Horace hadn't been near enough to hear, or there would be no chance of getting out without him later.

'How's Mrs Banks? Does she know how ill her uncle is?'

Instead of answering, he stood gazing at her, then said, 'You're a dear girl, Pol. My anchor. You always have been.'

Again that sense of loss that had hit her as he'd walked out of the yard that morning. She stamped it down, and made sure her own voice gave him no hint of her feelings.

'How did your day go?' she asked. 'Have you managed to get anything arranged?'

'Cecily had already sent to the shipping agent. She's travelled on the Continent many times, she's *au fait* with what has to be done. A remarkable woman, Pol. The better I come to know her, the more I realize it. But it's not my own arrangements I need to discuss with you, it's yours. Tomorrow morning before we do anything else we have to go together to see Mr Buckeridge.'

'He's your solicitor ... what has he to do with your going to Italy?'

'Nothing. What he has to do with is your own situation here. I want to give you Power of Attorney to act on my behalf in every respect. Legally this is quite possible, you are twenty-one, able to shoulder the burden of responsibility. Twenty-one, a grown woman ... when did you cease to be a child, I wonder ... what a joy you always were to me .... remember the times we used to have together, on the water – and in it too – the games, tennis ... remember?'

'Of course I remember, Pappy. And you mustn't go away worrying, I promise I'll look after everything while you're not here. I'm surprised we need to see Mr Buckeridge though. I thought you would have told Mr Crouch at the bank and that would have been all that was necessary.'

'Power of Attorney gives you authority over anything, then I shall have peace of mind. As a courtesy I've penned a letter to Carpenter, but before I drop it in the post box I want just to confirm your reaction to taking responsibility. You see, I've explained to him that you are to have Power of Attorney, but if you feel you don't want full responsibility, Pol, I'll alter my letter to him. I could discharge the authority to Mr Buckeridge, that's not at all unusual.'

'Of course I don't need Mr Buckeridge or Harry Carpenter either. I'm not a child.' Talking about Harry again brought the scene on the landing stage alive in her memory. She tried not to heed it. These moments with her father were important, for him and for her too, she'd not let other things – not even Charles waiting by the river and certainly not Harry Carpenter – cut across what might be the last real time they'd have together until he came home at some unknown date in the future.

'... let me read it,' he was saying. Who let him read what? 'His writing is weak, spindly, frail even for an elderly man. It was that that so upset Cecily, she said the change was so marked since his last letter. It seems he has a nurse in residence to look after him, but it's not like someone belonging to him. Poor Cecily. She has often spoken to me of him, it seems that even when she was a child – before he went on the Grand Tour and lost his heart to Italy – they had a very close bond. That's why I was moved to see her so upset this morning, I suppose it touched a chord in me when I thought of the closeness there has always been between you and me.' Then again, 'Poor Cecily. You see her as a kindly, practical woman I expect. I've come to know her well. It quite upset me to see her weep for her uncle.'

'Are you in love with Mrs Banks?' A straight question, it deserved a straight answer.

'In love? Polly my dear, I'm into my sixth decade. Falling in love is for the young.'

'Perhaps you don't want to tell me ... I only asked because I want you to be happy.'

'Bless you, Poll. I fell in love with Elvira' (what a joy it was to hear him say her name, to speak of her as Elvira and not 'your poor dear mother'). 'I was twenty-eight when I met her, the loveliest creature that ever lived. Poor Elvira, she suffered a good deal from her health. Cecily,' he smiled as he said her name, contentment in his voice, 'she's of tougher fibre you might say. You know, until this morning I've never thought of her as shedding a tear. A caring woman, warm, generous in her affection.' Then, his smile broadening into that mischievous grin Polly had never been able to resist, 'She accepts my weaknesses. Love – you're the one who should be falling in love. But, there! Now I sound like your poor mother. While I'm away you'll have enough to occupy your mind without looking out for eligible young men. So I'll post my letter to Carpenter in the morning, tell him I'm off on the Grand Tour.'

'Oh, Pappy, you're a rascal,' but she couldn't help laughing at his excitement. 'You're supposed to be there to give comfort and solace. As for Harry, I told him this afternoon, but send your letter by all means. As you say, it's a courtesy that you tell him yourself.'

'Comfort and solace,' he took up the first part of her statement, 'she knows I shall give her those.' He looked directly at Polly, undecided how to express what he wanted to say. 'Life's short, Pol, I realize it more all the time; get frightened by the thought, to tell the truth. We must always make the most of every opportunity of enjoying it. And if you think that sounds frivolous, look at it this way: we're given just one life to live in this beautiful – yes, wonderfully beautiful – world. It's a gift, a heaven-sent gift, and not to live every hour of it to the full is – I was going to say a sin. Yes, that's what it would be to accept the gift and then let yourself get bogged down with worries and grumbles and routine that fills your mind and clouds your vision.' Then, seriousness falling from him, he laughed. 'Just hark at me, won't you. If there's one thing you and I have in common it's that we know how to have fun, eh? And so does Cecily, bless her, so how can it be wrong for me to intend to see there's more to the trip than heartache and despair.' Then, changing the subject, 'You say you told Carpenter I was going away? I didn't know he was coming to the yard today.'

'He only looked in for a few minutes. I brought him up to date with the work on hand and showed him our quotation to Ruddick & Pears. I imagine he had business in Reading, he often gets driven out to us while he's in the district.'

'He's a good man,' he said tentatively, 'straight as a dye.'

'Huh! Not the way I'd describe someone who could do what he did to get his foot in the door at the yard.'

'How d'you mean?'

'For eighteen months, probably more, you paid him his dues. How he must have been laughing, sure that you wouldn't be able to settle the debt. And where did that get him? Eighteen months' profit and to top it all a king-size share in—'

'No, no, no,' Stanley cut her short. 'I never told you he did that. We had a contract. I would pay him back what I owed at the end of twelve months. I couldn't do it, he extended the terms a further six months. I suspect he knew very well that I still couldn't do it, for that first time he came here he had a further contract with him drawn up ready. That was the night we lost your mother—'

'I know.'

'This second contract was quite clear, already written, mind you, none of it as an answer to requests from me. He was to return to me in full all the payments I'd made over the eighteen months, the exact amount without interest for the time he'd held the money, and was to take the value of the initial loan as a partnership in the business.'

'Pay back ... but I said ... I accused him ... Why didn't he tell me that was what had happened? So, Pappy, that must mean we have something in hand towards buying him out, not enough, not anywhere near enough, but we'll build on it.'

'Let it rest, Polly. The business will prosper better with him in it than it would without him. See, for instance, how he brought about the fitting of that Maunders' engine, a good price, a fine engine.'

Polly didn't press the point, she would rather do as he said and 'let it rest' than hear that his unexpected windfall already had a big hole in it. Nothing must be said that would cast a shadow to grow and darken over the time he was away.

'Are you coming into the yard tomorrow after we've seen Mr Buckeridge, Pappy? To check on where the work stands, to leave any instructions?'

'No, I think not. I have things to see to for myself. Tell you what, Pol, draw up a chair next to mine at the desk, we'll go over a few things together.'

She did as he said. She tried not to see him as a rather bored pupil trying hard to make an effort so that teacher would be pleased.

'That's about all the jobs on hand,' he put his pen down and gave her a hopeful smile. 'Poor Horace will think you've deserted him.'

'Actually I intended to creep out without him.'

Stanley raised his brows in surprised enquiry.

'Wherever could you be creeping to at this hour of the evening.'

'I give you three guesses,' she laughed. 'No I won't, you don't need more than one.'

'By yourself in the canoe? What a funny girl you are.'

'It was you who taught me to love the river at night.'

'Off you go, my dear. I'll leave you to bolt the door when you come in. As for me, I shan't be late to bed. But first I want to sort through my clothes, see what I need to pack.' And again that grin that over the years had made her his partner in what she'd seen as such glorious adventures. 'What a holiday, eh, Pol. Italy ... We shall get there as quickly as we can, of course, but coming back I dare say we'll make a detour or two. I've a mind to see Florence, yes and Paris.'

'Oh, Pappy, you're an old rogue.' She hugged him, 'What am I going to do without you?'

The river was as still as a pond. She'd paddled upstream, telling herself there could be no chance that Charles would still be waiting for her – even if he'd expected her. She needed to be with him, the day had been unsettling. Harry had disturbed her more than she would admit, only Charles could lay the ghost.

She passed Rat Island, round the bend in the river she would come to the place where he used to moor his barge. She'd go as far as that – but of course, she told herself again, he wouldn't be there. It was late. The old farmhouse would be in darkness by now, he'd be under that patchwork quilt with his workaday wife.

For one who wasn't expecting him, she was remarkably disappointed when she could discern no figure by the bank. She stopped paddling, let the boat drift at its will; but with the water so still it barely moved. Her eyes were attuned to the night, the moon was lower in the sky than when they'd been together before the storms. Leaning against the wooden backrest she looked up at the summer sky, lit by what looked like thousands of stars. A beautiful, wonderfully beautiful world, that's what her father had called it. Oh but so it was. She yearned to share its loveliness.

She turned sharply as she heard a splash. Nothing ... it must have been a fish jumping. At this time of night? No moths or waterboatmen skimmed the surface to attract them in the dark. Again, and closer. But this time she knew what it was, even before he surfaced for air a couple of yards from her, she knew.

'I'd given you up.'

'I had things to go over with my father. He's leaving for Italy, so I'm looking after the business while he's away.' How grand it sounded!

'Can I come aboard? I don't want to make the cushions wet.'

'You can have my cloak, dry yourself in that.'

He raised himself out of the water, then rolled and tumbled inelegantly into the boat. Unembarrassed by his nakedness, he took her cloak and threw it around him.

'You must have known we'd find a use for this, you certainly didn't need to bring it for warmth.'

'I thought the ground might not be dry to sit on, there's been so much rain,' she answered primly.

'There, I'm dry, move along so that there's room for me next to you.'

The boat drifted idly, they talked fitfully but, she believed, contentedly. He hadn't so much as put an arm around her. Wasn't that proof that he wasn't just a bored husband philandering? As if to spite Harry, she leant towards Charles, wanting him to notice the rosewater she had dabbed on her neck and hair. Clara would never smell of rosewater, more likely sour milk from her work in the dairy or 'even worse' as Mrs Warwick had called it from the farmyard.

'Ten minutes ago I was in the cold water,' he whispered, 'now look at me, look what it does to me to be near you.'

She didn't analyse what it was excited her, whether it was the shock of his words telling her what she'd already known, whether it was love, passion, or even the danger of the situation. When he kissed her he drove away the echo of Harry's warning.

'Don't stop me,' he mumbled, his mouth on her neck, his hand moving on her leg.

'Charles, no.'

His hand reached its goal.

'No use pretending. You want me to love you, yes you do. I've got to. I'm on fire – and you, and you.'

'Yes, I want you to,' she rasped, wanting to hold him closer, wanting to push him away. 'I want you to want me. But we can't, Charles we mustn't.'

'Then let me hold you. Let's just lie close,' already he was throwing the cloak over the battens that covered the floor of the canoe, then he pulled the seat cushion from under her to make the bed complete. 'Down here. Let me hold you.'

He stood before her, pulling her to her feet. In the pale moonlight he was a perfect figure, glorious in his manhood, his passion aroused, strong, vibrant. She saw all that, but she surely saw tenderness too. So she lay on the hard bed and held her arms up to draw him down.

Always strong, tonight the passion that drove him made him doubly strong. Had she been less naïve she would have known where holding her would lead.

'Charles—' she tried to force him off her, but it was useless, he was heavy, there was no stopping him.

'Don't talk,' he panted, 'don't fight it. We must – I must—'

She could barely hear his words. His movements were hard, rough, the rhythm unchanging. Last time she had felt searing pain, this time was ... was ... she pushed against him to try to move him from her ... the planks in the boat were relentlessly hard ... her whole body seemed stretched, he was part of her ... the rhythm quickened ... she heard his cry as one of ecstasy and was filled with humility that it was *she* who gave him a joy that blotted everything else from his mind.

A dead weight he sprawled on her, crushing the air from her lungs.

'Christ, I needed that.'

This time she heard him clearly, but she wouldn't acknowledge her disappointment or the distance his words put between them.

'Get off me,' she panted, pushing his shoulder from her face.

'What? Whew,' he rolled onto the battens on the floor.

'Charles, what are we going to do? We can't go on like this. It's not fair to anyone. You should have been honest and told her before. What would she think tonight if she could know we're here like this?'

'You wouldn't tell her?'

'... live with his wife ... philander with you ...' the night seemed full of Harry's voice.

'I'm not meeting you any more, I shouldn't have come tonight. Either you live with Clara or you tell her you love me and leave her.'

'Women! I told you last time you gave me all that talk – I'm not giving Clara up. I don't see that that means we can't see each other. All your "oh no Charles", you didn't expect me to believe you meant it?'

She sat up. What was she doing here? Drifting in the middle of the Thames with Charles Dunton naked, a one-time bargee treating her as though she were a whore keen for his attention. Polly struggled to her feet with as much dignity as an unstable canoe allows, then picked up the paddle.

'Get out of my boat Charles Dunton. I want to forget you've ever been on it.'

'Take me back to the bank, I left my clothes at our usual place.'

'Then swim for them.' Catching him by surprise she pushed him with the paddle, sending him backwards into the water.

Chapter Nine

It wasn't that she expected Charles to chase her, to follow the boat and try to climb back aboard, yet she paddled down the river towards the shelter of Water's Edge as if all the fiends of hell were after her. Not once did she look back at him.

She felt degraded. Her anger was partly towards him, but mostly it was directed at herself. '... live with his wife ... philander with you.' She'd demeaned herself, played right into his hands. Her self-disgust was tempered with humiliation; for Charles there was no clouding of her contempt. How could she ever have pitied him for having plodding, plain Clara for his wife. Pity *him*? Poor, trusting Clara, he wasn't fit to clean her boots – not that they were often given such a treat.

Despise him though she might, what was the use of pretending he had forced himself on her against her will? Forced himself, yes; against the dictates of her conscience, yes: but against her will? He'd known as clearly as if she'd begged him in words, she'd craved for him to make love to her. How could she? She felt unclean, cheap. He may look like a god, but at heart he was a lout, a guttersnipe. Guttersnipe ... of its own accord her thoughts carried her in another direction. Harry Carpenter, brought up to know poverty, real poverty. Straight as a dye, that's what her father had said. 'Only God knows how I've prayed ...' '... shall love you until the day I die.'

To paddle her canoe, three strokes on one side then three strokes on the other, was an action as automatic to her as walking. She had the crazy thought of carrying on past Water's Edge where by now the lamps would be out and everyone asleep, to follow the river, to Reading and beyond. Instead of flagging with the miles she would be untiring, past Henley, Marlow, Windsor, Richmond. Here imagination failed her, she didn't know the river in its approaches to London. But it wasn't the details of the journey that mattered, it was her ever-increasing energy as she made for her goal, her certainty in the rightness of what she did.

It was no more than a dream. Reality found her level with the open doors of the boathouse but instead of negotiating the turn to go inside she went just beyond it to where she often tied the boat up under the overhanging weeping willow. That's what she did now, the soft lapping of the water comforting and familiar. No moonlight filtered through the curtain of leaves, with the paddle stowed on the floor of the boat she sat very still, the events of the evening pressing in on her again. What a fool she had been, blinded by a beautiful body, a handsome face, by Charles's gypsylike charm. 'I was blind and now I can see,' she whispered not knowing where the words came from, then 'Wash me and I shall be clean,' somewhere she'd heard that too. She'd never longed to be cleansed as she did now, her body scoured and her mind cleared of shame and bitterness. Tearing off her clothes she rolled them in a bundle, then lowered herself from the back of the punt into the cold water. Even now she daren't swim out into the stream lest he had followed her. Here in the dark shelter of the willow she felt safe – and soon she felt cold too. Pulling herself back into the boat she threw the cape around her, groped to check that the punt was safely tied, picked up her bundle of clothes and climbed onto the grassy bank at the end of the garden.

Spiritually the cold water had cleansed her, it must have, or why should she suddenly have this feeling of such joy? She remembered how her mother once told her about a house near where she'd lived as a child, a house said to have been haunted with the spirit of a highwayman who'd once lived there. The local priest had been called in to exorcize it and the occupants had never been troubled again. They'd laughed, she and her mother, they'd said what nonsense it all was. Yet was what she had done so different? She'd needed no priest, no group of believers to offer up prayers. 'Do you believe in the power of prayer?' Yes, Harry, yes I do. If I'd never believed before I would now.

Here where the trees flanked the end of the sloping lawn was where he'd helped her to sweep last year's fallen leaves. If only he were here now so that she could tell him. Tomorrow she'd go to London, his address was in her father's desk drawer, she'd find him and tell him. Patience had never been her strong point, the hours between night and morning stretched ahead like eternity.

'I'm not going into the yard after we leave Mr Buckeridge, Pappy,' she told Stanley next morning. 'I'm going to London. I'm going to see Harry.'

Stanley looked at her searchingly.

'Something you forgot yesterday?'

Only for a second she hesitated. If he hadn't been going away so soon she might have kept her secret, but it was important that he should know.

'Something I couldn't see clearly yesterday. Harry could. But I still went on fighting him—'

'What could he see, Pol? Are you telling me what I hope you're telling me?'

'I think I probably am. He asked me to marry him, I told him I didn't love him, I believed it was true. But I was wrong, Pappy, I was stubborn and stupid, I *wouldn't* see that what he said was right.'

How could she have expected his easy acceptance of her sudden change of heart?

'But how can you be so sure? Has my going away got something to do with rushing you? No, you couldn't make a decision like this to please me – or for the sake of the yard – could you?'

'It's not like that, Pappy. I've never been as sure of anything.'

'You'd never knowingly marry for money – if you would you had opportunity enough and scoffed at it. Power, you've always admired power. Are you certain you're not confusing the power his business successes give him with the man himself.'

'If Harry hadn't a farthing to his name I would marry him. There! That should satisfy you.' Then she laughed. 'We'd soon get rich. We're two of a kind, that's what he says. And we are. Quite suddenly I realized ... Say you're pleased.'

His answer was in the way he covered her hand with his, the pride and affection in his eyes.

'I don't like you rattling around London on your own. I'd come with you—'

'No, you mustn't. I have to go on my own. I'll get a cab at Paddington Station, I can hardly get abducted.'

He'd anticipated his own day with pleasure, he was meeting Cecily, pulling together their own plans. Even so he was disappointed not to be part of Polly's day. They would have made a real celebration of it.

The hansom soon carried her from Paddington Railway Station to the address of Harry's rooms. A hall porter directed her to the first floor. If Harry were out, surely the man would have known and told her. But at this time of day, nearly two o'clock in the afternoon, reason told her he was unlikely to be at home. Imagine if when she knocked at his door he opened it himself, just picture his expression.

She knocked ... footsteps ... he was coming.

Her eagerness died as she came face to face with a stranger, a tall man with a slight stoop, his gilt-framed spectacles clipped to his nose while, with head bent forward, he viewed her over the top of the lenses.

'Good afternoon, Madam. May I be of assistance to you? I don't believe Mr Carpenter was expecting you?' In fact he knew very well Mr Carpenter hadn't been expecting her or anyone else.

'No, he didn't know I was coming. Is he here? Is he out? When will he be back?'

'Not today, Madam, he isn't expected back in London until tomorrow.'

There is no doubt the world is a kinder place to a woman who is beautiful than to one who is plain. Looking at Polly, Cedric Halsey could see her disappointment, he wanted to help her.

'He's not still in Reading, is he? I didn't even enquire at the George. I'm Polly Seagrove, he has business dealings with Seagrove's.'

'Indeed Miss Seagrove, I know something of his business affairs,' then his thin and no-longer-young face creased into a smile, 'I have been with Mr Carpenter a good many years.'

'Then can you help me find him. If he's out of London, shall I find him in Reading?' Perhaps he decided to stay intending to have a final discussion with her father.

'I keep his engagement book up-to-date for him, perhaps I can make you an appointment.'

That Harry should be away was something she'd not considered. Her initial disappointment had sent her spirits plummeting, but already they were bouncing back. An appointment written in Harry's engagement book, the very idea was a joke!

'What I want to see him for is terribly important, Mr ...?'

'Halsey, Miss Seagrove, Cedric Halsey. You're putting me in a most difficult position.' But she could tell by his worried expression that he was tempted to break the rules and disclose his master's whereabouts.

'Mr Halsey, I talked to him yesterday. What I want to see him for today is important, really it is, it's something he'll be glad to see me for. I can't tell you more than that – but honestly it's true. He'd be much more angry if you sent me away than if you let me go and find him.'

In all his sixty-four years Cedric Halsey had never had such a lovely young woman look at him in that beseeching way. To refuse her was impossible.

'Come inside, Miss Seagrove. I'll write the name of the hotel he always uses. But it's a long way, not at all the sort of journey for a young lady to contemplate alone.'

By now Polly's spirits were riding high, even the carefully written address of the hotel in Brighton could do nothing to cast them down.

She'd never been to Brighton before, in fact her only visit to the seaside had been to Hastings when her mother had been convalescing from bronchitis. Add to that that never until today had she travelled alone, and small wonder she was excited. She bought a ticket for a seat in a First Class Ladies Only compartment just as she had from Reading to Paddington – that was something she had promised her father she would do. If she hadn't been so anxious to arrive she would have enjoyed every moment of the journey.

At Brighton Station she hired a waiting hansom and was taken to the address Cedric Halsey had written for her, a hotel on the seafront, where she was received by someone who to judge from his airs and graces must have been the majordomo. Her experience of hotels was slim and of being received by anyone with such an exalted opinion of his importance even slimmer.

In her most dignified voice she told him, 'I've come to see Mr Carpenter, I understand he's staying here.'

She was pleased with her quietly confident manner. But what a moment for her empty stomach to rumble a protest so loud she felt it must be heard all over the reception foyer. Better to ignore it, pretend it was nothing to do with *her*.

Mr Superior snapped his fingers and as if from nowhere a pageboy appeared.

'Take a message to Room 106. A lady ...?' he looked at Polly every bit as disdainfully as he had the young boy, 'your name, Madam?'

'Po – I'm Miss Seagrove.' Then she smiled at the boy who looked no more than nine or ten years old, 'If you'd tell Mr Carpenter I've come I'd be grateful.'

Such friendliness with a mere messenger cast the Maître d'Hôtel's opinion of her even lower than her uncontrolled rumbles of hunger. But Polly didn't waste her thoughts on him, he was her very least favourite type of person. Only seconds now and Harry would come down the stairs ...

It was already evening, if he intended dining at the hotel he would probably be dressing. Perhaps he would send the boy back with a message that she was to be taken to his room. Or would that be frowned on? This was patently a respectable establishment, one where convention would be upheld. She watched the stairs, listening for his step.

But the boy returned alone and made his whispered report to Mr Superior who, in turn, passed it on to Polly.

'I'm sorry Miss Seagrove, it appears he is not in his room. I haven't been informed what time he expects to return.' Sorry indeed, more likely you're glad to be able to play God and tell me I can't see him.

'Then perhaps you'll be kind enough to show me where I may wait for him and, when he arrives, tell him I'm here.'

'Polly!'

She turned at the sound of his voice, everything else forgotten. There was so much she wanted to say to him.

'Miss Seagrove was asking that she might wait for you, sir.'

Again her stomach cried out for sustenance, but this time she felt no embarrassment.

'When did you last eat?' Harry laughed, his arm around her shoulder as he turned towards the wide, shallow stairway.

'At breakfast,' she laughed. 'It's been quite a day. I didn't waste any of it with meals.'

'Miss Seagrove and I will eat in my room. Will you arrange to have a meal sent up straight away.'

Was Harry as aware as she was of the way the majordomo's haughty stare followed them up the stairs. She almost expected him to thunder a command that they come down, may he remind them that this wasn't the standard of hotel where ladies could be entertained in gentlemen's bedrooms!

'Now,' Harry said as he ushered her into his room and closed the door, 'there's something you want to tell me.'

'Harry, don't you know? Can't you guess? It was last night – I was on the river and quite suddenly – Harry I knew, it was as if a fog had cleared ... I wanted to come to you there and then.'

His hands were on her shoulders, she met his gaze. She'd thought this moment would be full of joy, yet her arms ached, her legs ached, her chest ached.

'Tell me what you knew so suddenly. Darling Polly, let me hear you say it,' he whispered.

'That you're right, that we need to be together, that – that – oh Harry that I love you so much that I ache all over.'

Then came the joy she'd longed for, his mouth found hers. Gently, almost reverently he kissed her, and then as thankfulness, passion, love that was akin to worship, flooded over him, he crushed her to him.

It was Horace's custom to sleep in the scullery on a blanket but with the uncanny instinct of his kind that night he sensed unrest. The Humes had gone to bed, Millie had retired to her room next to the nursery, only Daisy was left. Lowest in the scale of importance it was for her to wait up in case the master called for anything.

Horace fidgeted backwards and forwards from kitchen to scullery. He looked at her hopefully and wagged his tail but her only answer to that was to open the back door in case he needed to go outside. Two minutes later he was in again. He went as far as his blanket, changed his mind and came back to her.

'You silly dog, you, you've had your supper, you've been outside. What is it you want now? I'm not taking you anywhere, if your missus isn't here that's your bad luck. Honest, Horace, wouldn't you think he'd get himself off to bed. Nearly midnight it is. Well, I'm buggered if I'm going to sit here like a dummy half the night. Like it or not, I'll go and ask him if he'll be wanting anything else or if I can see to turning the lamps out. That might shift him.'

Horace had no idea what she was talking about but he could tell that she was disgruntled and he had an uneasy feeling that something was wrong in the house. So when the young maid went to the drawing room, opening the door as she knocked, in he slipped.

'Was there anything else you'd be wanting, sir? 'Cos if not, I thought I'd turn the lamps down and get to bed. The others have gone ages back, it's late.'

'Yes, off you go Daisy. Leave the lamp on in the hall, I'll see to it when I'm ready. Miss Polly may have had to stay in London overnight, but I'll give her a little longer.'

A fine life for some people, Daisy grumbled silently. Miss Polly might have to stay in London overnight indeed! Wonder what she's doing in London. Off to some smart supper room probably or a theatre. All very well for her with her fancy clothes and pots of money. Now, where was that silly dog? Oh well, wherever he is, he can find his way to the scullery in the dark.

'Hello old chap,' Stanley addressed Horace, 'where do you think she can be, eh? Would he let her come home alone at this hour? No, no, of course he wouldn't. Perhaps she's staying ... no, no, she wouldn't do that ...' Horace sat close to his side, pressing against his leg and looking at him solefully. 'Ought I to go away like this, leave her when perhaps she needs me. My little Pol – she's going to marry him you know,' and as if he did indeed know, Horace thumped his tail on the ground in reply. 'It's what I wanted for her. But not now, not when everything was looking so good for Cecily and me. Pol, my little Pol, wanting to get married and me gallivanting off. She won't like waiting till I get back to give her away. I'd wanted her to marry Carpenter, now it'll cast a cloud on my holiday. It'll be on my mind that she's anxious for me to get home, it'll take the freedom away. What are we going to do, old chap?' He rested his hand on the dog's head, the action seen as an invitation. In a second two heavy paws were planted on his lap and Horace's reached to try and lick his face.

It was at that moment that there was a heavy knocking on the front door. Horace barked with all the ferocity of a guard dog, all the while wagging his tail.

'Telegram for Seagrove,' the boy who passed Stanley the envelope didn't look old enough to be out alone at night. 'Do you want me to wait for a reply.'

Something had happened to her! Any self-pity vanished as Stanley tore open the envelope and took out the single sheet.

POLLY WITH ME IN BRIGHTON STOP RETURNING TO LONDON NEXT TRAIN STOP WILL REACH YOU AS SOON AS POSSIBLE STOP APPLYING FOR SPECIAL LICENCE TOMORROW STOP TRUST HER TO ME STOP HARRY

'No reply,' he felt in his pocket for a coin for the boy. A copper or two would have been enough to put a smile on the young face; when a florin was put into his hand he was almost too speechless to answer.

'Cor, thanks mister, thank you sir.'

'You've a long way to walk, mind how you go.'

'I got a lantern here, I'm safe enough.' Then, sure that anyone with such generosity could be trusted, he added with a saucy grin: 'Suits me fine when I get sent out of town like this. My girl keeps me company, see.'

That was on Tuesday night. Stanley and Cecily had passages booked to cross the channel from Dover on Saturday evening.

Between bringing Polly home in the early hours of the Wednesday morning and the actual wedding on the Saturday Harry stayed, as he always did when he was in the area, at the

183

George. He had various appointments to keep, where they were or what was involved she had no idea, except that one was to the office of Reading's suffragan bishop for a special licence. On the Thursday he was expected at Water's Edge in the evening and neither he nor Stanley told her how it was that they returned to the house together; perhaps they'd met somewhere by chance, perhaps by arrangement. She knew her father hadn't been to the boatyard, so it didn't enter her head that whatever Harry's business appointment had been on that afternoon it would have repercussions on her future.

In an out-of-town district that liked to think of itself as a village but was, in truth, no more than a hamlet, plenty of eyebrows had been raised, whispers and nudges passed, when Emmie had become Mrs Clive Warwick without a betrothal long enough to trim her best petticoat with a bit of lace, let alone put together a bottom drawer. By the middle of summer it was accepted the speculation had been misplaced; even the leading gossipers' disappointment was tempered with relief, they'd all known and liked Emmie Lovegrove all her days so they couldn't have found unalloyed relish in a tasty morsel of scandal at her expense.

But with Polly Seagrove it was a different matter. She belonged to the 'big house' – not that Water's Edge could be compared with the grander establishments of the county where Elvira had expected her daughter to take her place. The news that Miss Seagrove was to marry some man from 'foreign parts' as they considered anywhere beyond their personal knowledge and to marry him without enough warning to get a cake baked, now that was a bit of news that could only go from good to better as the months went by. What do you make of this then? Fine clothes don't make her a fair lady, that's for sure. Not like her Ma, now *there* was a sweet and gentle soul. Pretty face, that can't be denied, but that girl always was a tearaway. Well, time will tell ... This time they could wait and watch with pleasure.

How word got out that there was to be a hurried and quiet wedding arranged at St Peter's on Saturday morning, so early the vicar would scarcely have time to swallow his breakfast, no one was sure, although Ida Hume had a pretty good idea.

'Not a word of family business ever passes my lips,' she

grumbled to Arthur, 'you know that's the truth. Nor yours either, I'm bound to say. Millie Godwin knows no one so we can rule her out. It's that young Daisy. I've only got to take my eyes off her for two minutes and she's outside hanging round Algie and stopping him getting on with his jobs.'

'It's only natural, Ida love. A young girl needs a lad to talk with and I've got no grumble about Algie any more than George Baker has. House or garden, the boy is always willing. More likely Daisy has slipped out when she's seen someone she knows passing up the lane. Word spreads like wildfire round these parts.'

'Gossip! Can't abide it. Plenty of useful ways of spending the hours without chit-chatting about other people's affairs. Just between ourselves though, Arth, I'm not happy about it. Any other young girl would take pleasure in looking forward, planning a proper wedding when her father's home again, invite all their friends. Remember the lovely "do" they had for the master's half century. But, of course, that was when the poor dear missus was here, she knew how to see things were done right. What must she make of this hole-in-the-corner job? Doesn't do to ask yourself. Our Miss Polly, right from a toddler she's been the same. Thinks of something one minute, has to get on with it the next.'

'She's a good lass though, Ida. Quick she may be, impatient nearer the mark, but no one can say she's fickle.'

Daisy may have been responsible for the first spark that spread like wildfire in the district. How the Maidments heard and ignited another remained a mystery, but one thing was certain, Maidments, Vaughans, and parents of many a young hopeful in the county set breathed a sigh of relief that their sons had escaped.

Their honeymoon was no more than a brief weekend, but joy can't be measured in minutes and hours. Less than a week ago, alone on her canoe paddling through the darkness the truth had come to her: it was Harry she loved, body and soul she wanted to be one with him. She was free of Charles, she felt her eyes had been opened; no longer was he her Gypsy King, she despised herself that she could have been so blind. Why, he wasn't worthy even of Clara, poor plain Clara.

The wedding over, Harry had brought her to London. They'd travelled by train in a reserved compartment, something she'd never done before. In the evening when he'd taken her to dine she had felt his pride in her, it had been for him as much as for herself that she had dressed with such care. Mrs Harry Carpenter, the lovely Mrs Harry Carpenter.

Then the evening was over, they were alone in his bedroom. Her long, wavy hair was brushed; bare-footed and wearing a silk nightgown she stood before him.

'I want to go down on my knees and thank God,' he whispered. 'There are no words ...' he rested a hand gently on her head, moved it to her shoulder. But it was she who tore open the front fastenings of her nightgown and pushed it off her shoulders to fall to the ground; it was she who made the first move to free him of his night shirt.

'I want us to know each other, every inch, all that we are,' her hands caressed him, the sight of his passion adding to her own.

Sweeping her into his arms he carried her to the bed, then knelt at her side. She felt humbled by the expression in his eyes as he whispered so softly that he might have been thinking aloud, 'I never knew I could feel like this ... you're my heart and soul ...' With hands and mouth he caressed her, she was weak with longing.

'I want to be more, I want us to be one.' She pulled him closer. Then she felt the warm weight of his body on hers. Only for a second did the memory of Charles blot out the wonder of what was happening to her, Charles, with his rough, greedy pounding of her flesh. Harry was tender, but every movement was filled with passion and strength. She was his and the wonder of it was beyond anything she'd dreamed. Every nerve in her body was alive as she held him close, moved in unison with him until she grasped the miracle that touched them like a benediction, the miracle that was beyond anything she had known, that held them apart from the world, aware only of each other.

'... I feel ...' she panted, a smile in her voice, 'feel I've been ... to heaven and back.'

'Polly, my blessed Polly,' he held her close. Wherever she'd journeyed, he'd travelled with her.

186

The room was filled with soft yellow light from the gas, but neither of them moved to turn it off.

Sunday morning she was the first to wake. Opening her eyes she looked at him sleeping at her side. She wanted to touch him, to lay the palm of her hand on his chin with its early-morning stubble; she wanted him to open his eyes so that she could see his reaction when consciousness returned and he found her with him. She wanted – oh yes, she wanted it to happen again. Could anything so wonderful happen again? Would it always be like that?

In his sleep he turned onto his back, pushing the covers away. See his hands, beautifully kept hands, long, bony hands; she lay one of hers next to his, comparing them, seeing them as belonging together. Charles's hands – no, don't think of them, don't think of him at all – his hands had been strong, toughened and weathered, you'd seen them as a sign of manhood, you'd not let yourself admit the grime that hadn't been scrubbed away or the badly tended nails. Well, think of them now, be honest and see him as he is, not as the dream hero you made of him. You called his hands manly, but roughness doesn't make a person manly!

Carefully she wriggled out of bed and opened the curtains to let in a stream of morning light. The London street was empty, the day was young and, more important, the day was Sunday. Less than a week ago she had come here to Harry's rooms for the first time; now she was his wife, to live with him, love, honour and obey him as long as they both should live. Turning back to the bed she saw that he was awake, watching her, holding his hand towards her to draw her back. First though she tugged the chain that hung from the light fitting, turning off the gas that had been left burning all night.

The pale daylight of early morning gave the room no atmosphere of warm intimacy as the yellowy gaslight had. Last night had been filled with romance and mystery; with morning came reality.

'Well?' he whispered breathlessly, a laugh not far behind the question.

Polly stretched luxuriantly.

'Well,' she repeated, laughing delightedly, 'very well, very, very well.' She turned on her side to look at him. 'I never knew – well, of course I didn't – but I never expected love could be such fun.'

'Only fun?' he asked unnecessarily.

'Oh no.' She wrapped arms and legs around him, 'no, it's – it's – you're just leading me on, wanting to hear me say how much I love you.'

'Say it, then.'

'What was it you told me last night? There are no words …' For a moment she was serious, solemn even. But not for long. 'Can you believe it, we've got a whole lifetime ahead of us. Do you suppose it will always be – a sort of new miracle? Last night I thought that's what it was, I was afraid that was because it was our first time and it wouldn't be as special again. Just now was different, not so sort of holy, but – I wish I knew the right words to explain what I mean – nothing was secret or private, yet the miracle was just as blinding. Will it always be like that for us? We won't get dull and bored will we?'

He didn't answer unless the teasing laughter in his eyes counted as an answer.

Again she stretched full-length, her hands high above her head. Life was so good.

'I hope Pappy wasn't seasick,' she mused. 'Perhaps one day we'll go to Italy, would you like that? You, me and Bobby. What a good thing Millie's at home to look after him while we're here.'

'It would have been unusual to take a young brother on one's honeymoon, but then you're not made in the usual mould. Which would you rather do, Mrs Carpenter, idle here in bed or be taken out to see the sights of London?'

After a weekend in London they returned to Water's Edge. It hadn't occurred to Polly to query the arrangement; after all, she had promised her father that she would look after everything for him while he was away.

That even a single girl in her position should have immersed herself so wholeheartedly in the boatyard defied convention; that as a married woman she intended to carry on just the same 'beggared belief'. At least, that was Ida's opinion as she watched Polly depart in the trap just as if a ring on her didn't carry with it obligations of domesticity.

'Off she goes again.' As usual, she bent poor Arthur's ear to her grumbles. 'Well, you saw for yourself, it was you who brought the trap round to the door for her. Married woman indeed, the only difference in that girl's life is a man in her bed. No sense of responsibility, hell-bent on doing just as she likes. You know who I blame? I blame the master. He's made a fool of her all her life – and now her husband has to put up with her selfishness.'

'Ida, my dear, what would it benefit Mr Carpenter to have her hanging around the house here. As long as Bobby needed her she never put herself first – and look at her even now, never does she leave the house until she's spent an hour or more with him first.'

'A fat lot of good that does him, too. Plays with him, I've heard his shrieks of laughter, gets him over-excited and then swans off and leaves poor Millie to settle him down again.'

'It won't go on for ever.' No one but Arthur would ever have dared to give her such a knowing wink. 'Not now there's a man in her bed. Look ahead a year Ida, my dear, and I'd stake a baleful of straw to a feather duster that bassinet will have another one using it.'

''Tis to be hoped you're right. Quite time something clipped her wings.'

Polly had never been so happy. Each day she and Harry discovered something else about each other, romantic love was being bolstered by easy, natural friendship. He had his irons in many fires, that much she'd known; now he told her about business projects, she knew she had his respect as well as his love. Or perhaps the two go hand in hand, she amended the thought, neither she nor Harry could ever love what they couldn't respect. Another thing that added to her certainty of his trust was that, despite Stanley being away, he didn't check what went on at the boatyard as he had previously. For the first time she was glad to have Teddy Giles there, the ledgers were kept up to date, the bills sent out on time, while her own role subtly changed: she knew exactly the progress of each job she took in, it was she who quoted terms, it was she who made sure work was completed on time. She felt, as she never had before, that it was *she* who ran Seagrove's Boatyard. Even so she had more freedom of movement than she'd allowed herself in the days when she'd handled the ledgers, sent out the accounts.

If ever she could have heard Ida Hume's opinion of her (spoilt, self-willed, vain, headstrong) she wouldn't have recognized herself. Yet, married on 4 July, before the month was out she couldn't keep herself away from Little Roost. Another heatwave had settled over southern England, the temperatures soared into the eighties on the day she decided to take Bobby to pay Mrs Warwick a visit. Having dealt with the mail at the yard, had a word with Hugh Davies and made sure that the wheels were turning smoothly, she surprised everyone by returning home in time for lunch. ('Why can't the girl tell me she's needing to be fed? Cold meat, that'll have to do her, and I'll have to use a few of the potatoes young Dolly has scraped ready for this evening.' Ida kept her thoughts to herself, but Polly's unexpected return didn't bode well for poor Daisy who inevitably got the sharp edge of the housekeeper's tongue.)

'It's a lovely afternoon, Millie,' Polly burst into the nursery where an already full-up Bobby was delighting in knocking egg custard off the spoon each time it came near his mouth.

'Poh, Poh,' he shouted his delight at the sight of his favourite person.

'Eat up, Bobby, then I'm going to take you out. Lovely afternoon Millie, you deserve a break. Get him ready while I change my gown. About a quarter of an hour.'

So it was that in the sultry heat of the afternoon she wheeled the bassinet through the yard at Little Roost. She trod carefully, making sure that the hem of her gown was hoisted out of harm's way. She had given even more attention than usual to her outfit: satin of a pale gold that belonged to the summer day, the cut emphasizing her slim figure, and the trimming of tawny-brown ribbon on her front-tilting straw hat picking up the colour of her eyes.

Seeing her coming, Blanche Warwick hurried out to take the bassinet from her.

'Take two hands to that pretty frock, Miss Polly, this yard's a disgrace. And how's my little angel then? Pleased to see your old Blanche?' Clearly her little angel was delighted. 'In we go then, you lead the way Miss Polly. I shouldn't call you that no more, you a married woman.' Her smile was warm. What Polly had always loved about the woman old enough to be her mother – and so completely unlike her mother – was her natural acceptance. She saw beneath the strata of society. If she liked a person then she was her honest, friendly self: if she didn't she had no time to waste on polite and meaningless conversation. Polly had always fallen into the first category.

The bassinet wheeled into the kitchen, Blanche lifted Bobby out and put him on the floor where he immediately darted on all fours towards the easy chair so that he could pull himself onto his feet and display his cleverness. His friend didn't fail him in her appreciation.

'Now you tell me all about yourself,' Blanche folded her plump arms and prepared to enjoy what she enjoyed most, 'a good chat'. 'I hear Mr Seagrove has gone off to foreign parts. That'll be why you and your Mr Carpenter tied the knot in such a rush? That's the line I've taken when folk have tried to give me a nudge and wink about the hurry of it all.'

'I like to do things in a rush,' Polly laughed. 'I never wanted the fuss of a big wedding. But I might not have got away with it if Pappy's trip to Italy hadn't come up so suddenly.'

'*I* know you can't abide to wait, but then that's because *I* know you, you and me got an understanding. Poor souls, just think, Miss Polly, what it must be like to have nothing better in your own life than to fill it poking your nose into other people's affairs. For all that, I'm glad they've got it wrong, I'm glad you're setting out on your wedded days brand new, so to speak.'

Polly laughed, it was just like 'sitting-in' on Bobby's erstwhile mealtimes. Blanche's straight approach to life delighted her.

'A fortnight ago, if you'd told me they would be watching me and speculating, then I would have said they were in for a disappointment.' Deep in her subconscious Polly must have known that this was one of the reasons for coming to Little Roost. In her memory she seemed to hear Harry's voice as they'd stood by the river's edge last night. 'Tomorrow it'll be four weeks since we were married,' he said, his arm around her shoulder. She'd heard the question in his words. 'I know.

191

Four weeks and I've been well all the time, is that what you mean?' For answer he'd drawn her into his arms. The moment had been precious; before it she had wondered, after it she was certain that already she was carrying their child. Something that was private and personal, known just to Harry and her, yet already she'd said too much to Blanche to leave it there. 'I've never been late – but I am this time. Two weeks late.'

'Don't start counting your chickens too soon, duckie, just married like you are, it might have thrown your insides out of step a bit. Ah, here comes Clara, I'm glad she's home in time to see you. She's been walking into town to the market. I would have gone and saved her the step, but she insisted; she's done the marketing regularly, looks on it as her job. A good girl is Clara, takes life in her stride. That's how it is she keeps so well if you ask me. You don't see animals lying around resting themselves. Chaw has seen her coming. Now look at that won't you, he's come right out to meet her and take her basket. One of nature's gentlemen is our Chaw.'

A quick glance in the mirror that hung on the wall by the side of the kitchen range reassured Polly. If Charles had gone down on bended knee to her she wouldn't have wanted him, what she *did* want – and would delight in its sweet revenge – was for him to want her knowing she was beyond his reach, to desire her without hope of ever having her.

'Hello, Clara,' she turned to smile as red-faced, perspiring Clara walked heavily into the kitchen, then as casually as if he'd been a farmhand, 'hello Chaw.' No longer was he Charles, her Gypsy King of the waterways; Chaw belonged to the farm, to Clara. Polly had greeted him coolly enough, but she'd avoided looking at him. But that was crazy, she told herself, if she was afraid to see him it was tantamount to keeping alive the ghost of the dream she'd created.

'Just look at you!' Clara got clumsily to her knees and held her arms out to Bobby. 'Come on then Bobby baby, one step, two steps, come to Clara.'

Bobby had no time to waste on one step, two steps, his quickest method of getting to her was on his hands and knees. He was the centre of her attention and Blanche's too, neither of them were conscious of the silent play between the others. Polly was honest enough to admit that as she'd changed her gown and topped her freshly brushed and dressed hair with the jaunty pancake straw that sat on the front of her head, her intention had been to bewitch and punish Charles. From his expression she knew she had succeeded. He'd never been more aware of her loveliness. His dark eyes sent her their message of appreciation, of longing, of hope. She met his look with casual disinterest, her heart singing with joy. He meant nothing to her, *nothing*. No, that wasn't quite true, he did stir an emotion: cold dislike. On the floor between them Clara knelt, trusting him, never doubting his faithfulness. Outside in the yard, not knowing that they had visitors, he had gone to meet her to carry her basket. Now, conscious that Polly was watching, he made no attempt to help as Clara struggled to her feet.

Polly wanted to be gone. The welcome Mrs Warwick and Clara always gave her made her ashamed. Her reason for coming had been to punish Charles – Chaw, she corrected herself – to let him see how happy she was without him and to make sure she still had the power to excite him. Even more degrading than that she'd meant to tell Mrs Warwick that she believed she was pregnant knowing that a word to her would soon be passed to Clara and from there to Clara's Chaw. And here was the part that more than any filled her with self-disgust, she had wanted him to be jealous of Harry that this lovely woman was his wife, carrying his child.

Clara pushed the bassinet through the yard as far as the gate to the lane so that Polly could walk carefully and not soil her shoes in the mud 'and worse', and could hold her skirt up to keep the hem clean.

'Nice you troubled to come and see us, Miss Sea – Mrs Carpenter. Ma has a special feeling for little Bobby, it's natural she should I suppose. I'm ever so glad to see you so happy. Ma and I would have come to St Peter's to throw some rice but we didn't hear about it till too late. But we do wish you and Mr Carpenter a real happy life together.'

'Thank you, Clara. I know that's what it will be.'

'Don't do to take anything for granted, you tap on this wooden gate for luck.'

Polly tapped. Doing as Clara said eased the shame she felt for her behaviour, it was as if the luck she wanted to ensure was for herself and for Clara too.

During the month that followed Polly didn't visit Little Roost again. There was a morning when, on her way to the boatyard, she came upon Clara walking to Reading to the mid-week market.

'Whoa, whoa there, Tubby,' she stopped the trap alongside Clara.

'I thought you meant *me*,' Clara laughed. 'I thought "Well, that's calling a spade a spade". Are you offering me a lift? That's nice, Miss Polly, I declare the road to town gets longer every time I go to market.'

'Chaw ought not to let you do it, not with the baby due so soon.'

'I've a few more market days ahead of me yet, I'm not due for another month. Ma tells me you're starting a family of your own. A playmate for your little Bobby, that's what it'll be in another year or two.'

'Once my father gets home Harry and I will move to a place of our own. But I hate the thought of leaving Bobby.'

'Not half as much as he'd hate you to be gone. Still, worry about that when it happens. Doesn't do a hap'orth of good going out to meet troubles. If you don't start looking for them they might pass you by. That's what Ma says.'

Lumpy, slovenly Clara, but scratch the surface and there was another Blanche, good natured, warm, so faithful in her affection that she wouldn't even suspect she was being cheated. Too good for Charles. From this distance Polly looked back on her infatuation and was sure of something she'd never considered at the time: roaming the waterways as he had, there would have been plenty of other women in his life beside her, women to dally with and take his pleasure, always secure in the knowledge that Clara was waiting for him. Poor Clara, she deserved better.

Taking off her bonnet – headgear that had fallen out of fashion with Polly quite five years – Clara used it as a fan, blowing out her cheeks.

'Cor, another scorcher today. I'd have been a grease spot before ever I got into town if you hadn't picked me up.'

'I'm not staying long at the yard, only seeing if there's anything important in the post and making sure things are all right. How long will you be in the market? I can pick you up there if you want a ride home.'

So it was arranged and Clara had no idea that the offer wasn't solely made out of kindness on her account. But would Polly have thought of it had she not been prompted by the image of the trap arriving in the farmyard. Elegant and unruffled she would sit holding the reins while Charles would help Clara and her loaded basket to the ground. She wouldn't be persuaded to go indoors, with a proud inclination of her head she would tell Tubby to 'walk on' knowing that Charles would have to close the gate after her and would watch her disappearing back down the lane, the steady clip-clop growing fainter until he was left with silence – and, she hoped, a sense of his own inadequacy that his wife had been glad of the help *she* had offered.

A week or so later, as dusk gave way to darkness, Polly and Harry were in the drawing room where Daisy had just lit the lamp. Horace had slipped in with Daisy, now he looked hopefully first at one and then the other. Lamplight was a bad sign, it indicated they weren't considering saying any of those magic words – 'out'; 'walk' or even 'quick run'.

Harry fondled the top of his head, and he quite enjoyed that, but he knew of a better way of spending the remaining minutes of fading daylight.

'You've not been to the boatyard once since Pappy went away, Harry,' Polly said. And knowing she wasn't talking to him, Horace sighed and lay down on the hearth rug in front of the empty grate.

'Nothing bothering you there, is there?' Harry asked.

'Of course not. But you used to be forever looking over my shoulder.'

Folding away his copy of the *Times* he held a hand towards her, then, when she took it, drew her to his lap where she lay back in her accustomed way, her head against his neck.

'And why do you suppose I was, as you put it, forever looking over your shoulder?'

'You couldn't be sure that I was up to the job. So what's so different? Marriage can't have given me an efficiency I didn't have before.'

He rubbed his chin against her head.

'Guess again. How else could I have found a way of being near my prickly Polly unless it was behind a ledger?'

She laughed, wriggling closer if that were possible.

'With so many irons in so many fires, I suppose Seagrove's is small fry.'

'Seagrove's is never small fry. But it's in safe hands with you. I'm always here if you want me, you know that. And by the way, I'm taking an associate of mine to see the Seagrove steam launch. If you're a good girl you can come with me, I think we shall be able to negotiate an order for something similar. Do your sums, Polly, get a rough estimate ready.'

'Tell me about it. Who is it we're going to see? Is it one of the fires you have an iron in? Isn't it wonderful, Harry, we don't keep our lives in separate compartments, we share everything.'

'Didn't I try and tell you, we're two sides of the same coin.'

She sat upright on his knee, stretching her arms high above her head.

'Tired?' he sounded anxious. 'Darling, you ought not to put in so many hours at the yard—'

'Bedtime,' she cut in, then leant towards him, her mouth teasing his as she added, 'who said anything about being tired?'

His response didn't fail her.

'You go on up, sweetheart. I'll take your hopeful friend as far as the river.'

Her hopeful friend was on his feet and ready to go.

Life was perfect. Every day she and Harry grew closer; every day she felt herself more in control of the work at the boatyard. As Harry turned down the lamp and plunged the room into late evening gloom, and Horace's tail swung out of control, despite the warm night she gave an involuntary shiver. 'I hope you and Mr Carpenter will be real happy,' came the echo of Clara's voice, and her own reply, 'We will, I know we will.'

Never take anything for granted, Clara had said, and to please her Polly had knocked on the wood of the farmyard gate. Perhaps now it was the shadowy gloom that gave her the sudden unreasonable premonition of trouble. She told herself she was being fanciful, but the foreboding wouldn't be ignored. Not that she was superstitious, but she rapped her knuckles on the rosewood occasional table just the same. There was no point in taking chances.

Chapter Ten

'Mind you sit still,' Polly told Bobby, crediting him with more understanding than any eighteen-month-old could be expected to have.

The previous summer she had often taken him on the river, once laid safely on his nest of cushions she had had no need to watch him. Now they were more than half way through August and this would be his first outing of the year. When Millie had tried to persuade her not to take him on her own she hadn't listened.

'He could sit on my knee, Mrs Carpenter, he'd be safe as houses and he'd see better too.'

'He'll be safe, I'll put a cushion by my feet where I can make sure he doesn't wriggle about. You have the afternoon to yourself, Millie, take a book out to the hammock or something.'

'I'll be worried ...'

'Then don't be.'

She'd known she ought to be grateful for Millie's concern but, instead, she was irritated. As if she couldn't be trusted to take care of Bobby! She didn't want an outsider, no matter how caring, on the river with them.

While Millie had been getting him ready Polly had prepared the canoe, taken it from the boathouse and tied it under the willow tree, then put one long cushion on the thwart where she would sit and a second on the floor for Bobby so that he would be by her feet where he was in easy reach.

As she clambered aboard, holding him firmly in her arms, her instruction was for him to sit still.

'Bo . . . ,' he pointed to the canoe, laughing with delight at its slight motion. 'bo . . . poh . . . bo.'

'That's right, Bobby. Boat,' she agreed, understanding his language as well as he did himself. 'Polly and Bobby on a boat.'

He planted a slobbery kiss on her cheek, although his expression clouded when she dumped him on the cushion that was to be his seat.

'Off we go! But Bobby must sit.' She negotiated the canoe from beneath the shelter of the willow, and that in itself was high adventure for him. He struggled to reach the leaves, grumbling to himself because he couldn't get to his feet without the help of a piece of furniture. She could read his thoughts and a restraining hand was on his shoulder before he could turn himself ready to crawl.

'If you're a good boy, a really good boy, I'll take you to the yard,' she told him, even though he had no idea what she was talking about. It was something she'd been looking forward to doing, but before they'd gone a quarter of the way she knew it was something she'd have to shelve until next year. No child of his age could be expected to sit still for so long. To start with he enjoyed the novelty of the motion of the canoe, he crowed with delight when a steam launch passed them leaving ripples in its wake. But after a quarter of an hour his goal was to get out of her reach and to explore the other end of the craft. He probably had in mind that there was another seat just like she was sitting on, if only he could get to it he could haul himself onto his feet.

It was as she decided she ought to get him home before his patience failed completely that she saw someone coming towards them on the towpath. Even at that distance she knew it must be Clara, a very weary Clara. Holding a straw basket in each hand she lumbered homeward from her weekly trek to market. Polly saw the way she dumped the baskets on the path and stood with her hands pressed to the small of her back, something she would never have allowed herself to do had she known she was being watched. Then she took up her load and forced herself on. Shaken by anger, Polly waved at her. They had a pony and trap at Little Roost – what in the world was Charles thinking about to let her walk to market? As if anything he could be doing on the farm was half as important as his wife – or at least as his wife *should be*. Sensing excitement was afoot Bobby forgot to fidget and looked around him expectantly.

'Let me give you a ride,' Polly shouted as she came nearer to Clara. 'Wait where you are, I can hold us steady by that tree.'

'I never saw it was you, Miss Polly. Fancy you nearly on top of me and I never noticed.'

Polly suspected she wouldn't have noticed if the Royal Barge had come down the river, with Victoria herself aboard, resplendent in her crown.

'You look weary.'

Sympathy found a chink in Clara's armour of brightness, her mouth trembled too quickly for her to hide behind a man's handkerchief and the pretence of wiping her perspiring face.

'Sit still Bobby,' Polly told him. Hardly likely he would even if he understood; but by now they were at the bank, it wasn't the water he was interested in, it was Clara. Moving to the bow, with one hand Polly grabbed the branch and with the other took the baskets and put them on the floor. That much was easy. Getting Clara aboard was more difficult.

'Grab my arm, that's it,' Polly encouraged her. 'I won't let the boat drift.'

'Got no spring in me,' Clara tried to laugh, 'reckon my spring's broken.' One foot was aboard, then eyes closed as if that way she had more courage, the second followed, tilting the canoe precariously and bringing shrieks of delight from Bobby. Thankful that at last she could sit, Clara lowered herself onto the hard wood of the uncushioned thwart.

'I'll get you my cushion,' Polly told her.

'Don't need to bother,' Clara panted, trying to put a smile into her voice, 'nature's given me plenty of cushion of my own. Lovely it is, just to sit down.' Again her mouth trembled and this time she was beyond caring. 'Can't 'elp it,' she sniffed. 'Good job Ma can't see me. All the babes she's had and she's worked right through till Pa's sent one of us to get Nurse Cox. There's me with another fortnight or more, and look at me. She'd be ashamed of me ... ashamed of myself.'

'If I manage half as well as you have I'll be proud not

199

ashaméd. Charles shouldn't let you do it. He should have gone with you to market, carried the bags, taken you in the trap and been there to carry the baskets. It's not right—'

'Marketing's not man's work. Nowt wrong with my Chaw. Any road, I never gave a hint how I been feeling. I told you, I'm not due for a fortnight and Ma says first ones are usually slow so it may be longer than that. As if I can give up my jobs yetawhile.' She put the large hanky into use again, mopping her perspiring face, drying her tears and finally blowing her nose as if that would pull down the curtain on her moment's weakness.

'When we get to Chaw's water meadow I'll leave you where you are and take Bobby, we'll go and get him to carry your baskets.'

'My back hurts the worst.' At home Clara would have suffered in silence, determined to show Chaw how naturally and easily she could have his children. 'The babe's quite still now, I been lying awake these last nights waiting for it to give me a kick but, no, not a movement from it. I've heard say that that happens right at the end. Just got this heavy – don't know how to put it, like as if I've got a sack of tatties sitting in there.'

'If that's what happens when it's ready to be born – and *you* know more about it than I do – then perhaps the backache is the beginning of labour and in a few more hours it'll be over. Just keep thinking *that*, Clara. Sit still, Bobby, don't wriggle.' Already Polly had the canoe away from the bank, turned and starting on its way back upstream.

'You were going the other way.' From one worry Clara jumped to the next, this afternoon her never-failing cheerfulness was lost to her. 'I never thought when I got in, Miss Polly picking me up's spoilt your afternoon.'

'No, Bobby,' Polly tried to grab him but he was too quick for her. In one movement he turned onto hands and knees then, heedless of the discomfort of crawling on the narrow wooden struts of the platform that covered the floor of the canoe, made off towards Clara.

'Careful Bobby baby.' She held her arms to him, but he was keen to show off his cleverness. As unexpectedly as his sudden turn onto all fours now, coming almost level with her, he took hold of the side of the punt and pulled himself to his feet.

'No!' she shrieked in terror, 'no, Bobby baby, you'll tumble in.' Forgetting everything but his danger, Clara struggled to her feet and blundered unsteadily towards him at the same second as Polly dropped her paddle and rushed to grab him.

A few moments ago when Clara had taken her final step from the bank the canoe had tilted, but then Bobby had been safely on his bottom. Now the sudden lurch was all it took for him to lose first his grip and then his precarious balance. Thrown forward with the tilt of the boat he toppled head first into the water. Polly's reaction was immediate, she didn't stop even to pull her hat from her head or kick off her soft leather shoes: she jumped straight into the water, into it and below it, as the canoe floated gently with the stream. Clara was forgotten, there was room in Polly's mind for nothing except Bobby, her precious Bobby, under the water, probably being pulled down by weeds. In fact, in that she was wrong. He'd sunk like a stone, Clara had seen him come to the surface and had stretched towards him with all her might in a futile attempt to reach him before he went down again.

On the bed of the river Polly grabbed him. Holding her breath she brought him to the surface, then swam with him to the bank.

'Save him, please, I beg, save him, don't let him be drowned. Help me to get the water out of him ...' Her prayers were automatic, even as she dug back into her mind to what, years ago, her father had taught her about life-saving, even as Bobby vomited, fought for breath, vomited again, and finally screamed in terror, still she prayed, 'Help me ... thank you ... he's breathing ... please help him ... help me ... he's so frightened ... but he's alive, thank You, thank You.' He'd been lying on the ground, she kneeling by his side as she worked on his tiny body. Now she picked him up, holding his dripping little form against hers, rocking him, weak with love for him.

Only then did she spare a thought for Clara. The boat! It was drifting ... empty except for two straw baskets. Standing up with Bobby wet, cold and unconsolable held tightly to her, she looked around frantically, helplessly. That's when she saw two hands clinging to the side of the canoe.

'Hang on, Clara, hang on. I'm coming, hang on.' But how could she come? Should she run far into the meadow with Bobby, put him down too far from the water for him to have time to crawl there? But supposing he did? He could move so fast. In a second she made her decision. Soaking wet, cold, frightened by what he couldn't understand, Bobby found himself dumped on the ground while Polly unceremoniously pulled up her skirt then stepped out of her petticoat. Her idea was to rip it into strips she could tie together, but when it wouldn't tear she did the only things she could: she put it over Bobby's head, the waist around his as yet unformed waist, then pulled the hem tightly around the trunk of the tree so that he sat with his back pressed close against it.

'It's all right, Bobby,' she talked even though he couldn't hear her above his shrill screams. If he'd been frightened before, being held fast against the hard tree trunk added to his frenzy. 'That'll keep you safe. I've got to get her out, she can't swim. Please God, don't let it have hurt her.' Then running to the water's edge, 'I'm coming Clara.'

As she waded back into the river she knew a moment's sick fear. The hands had lost their hold on the side of the canoe.

It had all happened within yards of the river bank, the whole incident had lasted only minutes, but to Polly time had lost all meaning as she swam beneath the murky water, surfacing for a gasp of air, then down again. Never swim where there are weeds, that had been the first rule she'd learnt. Supposing Clara was entwined in weeds ... help me, help me ... supposing they both got trapped, who would find Bobby? What would happen to Bobby? For a second she almost turned back. As she pushed her way into the weed bed she was shocked by the idea that sprang into her mind. If she turned back now, dropped the two straw baskets into the water, no one would know what had happened. And just as quickly as temptation came so she saw it for what it was – the Devil whispering to her 'Save yourself'. Forgive me ... help me to be strong ... help me to save her and please let her live ... please ...

Clara was caught in the weeds not far below the surface, once Polly saw her she got to her quickly, tearing off the slimy reeds then, holding the unconscious girl's head above the surface, she swam on her back the few yards to the bank. Dragging the inert form out of the water took more strength than she realized she had.

One blessing was that, seeing them, Bobby's yells quietened into an aftermath of hiccupping sobs until he thrust his thumb into his mouth for comfort. Then he watched, not understanding what Polly was doing to 'Clara gone to sleep'.

Stanley had been too happy-go-lucky for his own good in so many ways over the years, but never in his training of Polly. Until that afternoon she'd not had to put into practice the lessons he'd drilled into her in saving and resuscitating a drowning person. In truth more minutes went by while she worked on forcing water out of Clara's lungs, than the time the frightened girl had been clinging to the side of the boat before she could hold on no longer.

'You'll be all right,' Polly said over and over, to keep her own spirits up as much as to reassure Clara who wasn't sufficiently revived to be aware of anything but the cold that enveloped her and a battle to draw breath.

On Polly battled, confidence growing with the sound of Clara's whimpering. By the time she got her away from the edge of the river and propped next to Bobby the battle was won – and the boat was twenty yards downstream and right out in the middle of the river.

'I'll have to get the canoe. You two stay there. Clara, can you hear what I'm saying? You'll be all right while I swim for the canoe?'

Clara's answer was half belch and half moan; but she had come back through the veil.

Home for Clara was half a mile further upstream than Water's Edge and then a walk through the water meadows Charles rented, across a track and through another field before the farm buildings and house were reached. Polly still had the idea of tying up the canoe where Charles used to moor his barge then, leaving Clara there and carrying Bobby with her she'd go and fetch Charles. That's what she intended as she swam out to the boat, heaved herself aboard and paddled back to where the others waited.

'Want to be home ... home ...' Clara looked unseeingly ahead of her, 'help me get home.'

'I'll get you into the canoe first, then come back for Bobby.'

Obediently Clara let herself be helped to her feet then, standing quite still, she gripped Polly's arm, taking deep gasps

203

of breath. Thank God she's breathing properly, that was Polly's first thought. Then looking at Clara, she realized.

'The baby? You mean you're starting to have the baby?'

All her months of waiting Clara had lumbered about her daily tasks, she'd never complained, never so much as admitted to being tired. She'd grown up to look on having babies as natural. But there was nothing natural in the terror of clinging to a boat, feeling her fingers slipping, losing her hold, cold water on her chin, in her mouth, in her eyes, the weeds dragging her as she struggled. As Polly had fought to expel the water, force life into her, in her semi-conscious state Clara had believed the black wall of nothingness must be death. Now what had happened was clear to her, and even clearer was the searing pain that tore her. She had to get home. Ma would know what to do. Polly was in the canoe, holding out her hands. She had to get into it too. Supposing she fell. She could hear someone crying. Bobby was crying. And someone else. All she could hear was the sound of moaning, all she could feel was agony.

'I'll get you home, we'll send the trap for Nurse Cox, don't cry Clara, you're safe now, don't cry.'

Then Bobby was untied and carried to the canoe too, but this time, although holding him made it more difficult to use the paddle, Polly kept him on her lap where he snuggled against her seeking more comfort than her wet body could give him.

'We'll be home in no time,' Polly made an attempt to break into Clara's misery by speaking with more confidence than she felt, 'then Hume can take you on home. Millie will go with you if you like while I get Bobby warm.'

But by the time she eased the canoe to tie it under the willow tree and Millie came to meet them, it was clear that Clara couldn't journey any further.

'Takes me back to when it was the poor dear mistress,' Ida Hume muttered as she opened the damper on the range to let the fire burn brighter, then lifted off the lid so that the iron pan of water could be put right down on the coals for quickness.

Arthur had been sent to fetch Nurse Cox, Daisy had gone to Little Roost with a message, there was no one there to hear Ida but even so she voiced her thoughts aloud. 'If they'd listened to me,' she gave vent to her feelings by poking the fire, 'ah, *if*, then the girl would have been back in her own home pretty well by now. Babies don't come in five minutes. But when has young Polly ever listened to any opinion but her own? Not fit to go any further, that's what she said, expecting Clara Warwick – as she used to be – would drop her young at the first twinge. A bit of a kid like she is, what makes her think she knows so much? Half an hour they've been up there – and is there any sign of a baby? No, of course there isn't.'

Daisy was enjoying the drama. She ran all the way to Little Roost.

'Where's your Ma?' she panted to the children who were busy cleaning out the chicken run. 'Or – what's his name? Clara's husband, where's he?'

'Ma's in the dairy, Clara's Chaw is milking in the shed there. What's happened? Nothing wrong with our Clara?'

'She's having her baby, that's what's happened. She's back at our place, Water's Edge, Miss Polly said there wasn't time to bring her no further.'

The chicken run was forgotten.

'The baby's come,' ten-year-old Albert shouted as he charged into the cowshed. 'Hear that, Chaw. Our Clara, she's having it. Must'a got started on the way walking home from market. They just sent Daisy Dawkins over from Miss Polly's place – they got our Clara in the house there.'

Charles jumped up so suddenly that the milking stool fell with a clatter against the pail.

'Here young Albert, you finish off for me.'

In the yard the other children and Daisy were clustered around Blanche who'd come from the dairy to see what all the excitement was about.

'You better come back with me,' Daisy greeted him. 'That's what they told me at the house, to fetch Clara's husband. Better get a move on, she's probably had it by now. She was in a real bad way, I never seen Clara so upset. On account of the tumble they all had in the river, her and Miss Polly and Bobby. I was just telling Mrs Warwick.'

'How in the hell did they do that?' From Charles's glare,

Daisy might have been personally responsible. 'Enough to frighten her to death.'

'You can't come to Water's Edge dirty like you are,' Daisy told him, meaning to get her own back. Who did he think he was, talking to her like that! 'Go and scrub your hands after messing about with those stinking old cows. If you find the baby's been born you can't touch it with hands straight from the cowshed.' Surprised that this pint-sized child could give orders, and even more surprised that he obeyed them, Charles went indoors to wash his hands while Blanche followed him and Daisy settled down to enjoying being the centre of the young Warwicks' attention. There was a ring of pride in her voice as she told them, 'Fussy as anything they are at the house. 'Course, I'm used to it now. I dare say your Ma told you what it's like there, real lovely bits of china and brass and such, not just things you need every day for using, but extra, things put out for ornament. 'Course I'm getting used to it now, don't think nothing of it when Mrs Hume puts me to wash a bowl full of gimcracks and such. Mind you take care, she'll tell me, take a year's wages to pay for just one of those ornaments. Used to scare the wits out of me. But I got used to handling valuable things, I tell you it makes you feel real good, sort of ladyish.'

'What *you*, Daisy Dawkins?' At fourteen and tall for his age Fred Warwick scoffed at her, scrawny little Daisy Dawkins putting on airs and graces! 'You, ladyish?'

Daisy's mouth set in a firm line.

'At least I've learnt how to do things proper – proper*ly* – things like not taking mud into the house on your boots. Just a speck and off our boots have to come and get left in the lobby before we tread even into the scullery. I wonder they let your Clara inside the place this afternoon, dripping wet with slimy ol' weeds hanging from her bonnet. No good asking me how it all happened, I suppose our Miss Polly – Mrs Carpenter – had gone in to save your Clara's life. She swims like a fish so Mr Hume tells me.'

'What would our Clara have been doing in the river?'

Daisy felt her story had peaked and had nowhere to go but down just when she'd been enjoying herself. She shrugged, digging into her mind for something to impress her young audience.

'I've asked myself,' she shook her head sadly. 'Perhaps the pain was so dreadful she couldn't bear it, a watery grave tempted her. Or perhaps she fell unconscious and tumbled in. A bloomin' good job Mrs Carpenter was on hand.'

While Millie had been helping Clara to bed, Polly had stripped Bobby, rubbed him vigorously in a large towel, then sat him on her bed wrapped in the eiderdown while she tore off her own sodden garments and dropped them in a pile on the floor. His good humour was restored with some to spare as he watched the performance. Too young to analyse his emotions, he was aware of a warm feeling of companionship, it had to do with both of them having been wet, both of them having been frightened, both of them being stripped of all their clothes. He held his arms up to her hopefully. She couldn't resist him. He couldn't know what made her dance around the room holding him in such a bearlike hug, he was happy because he liked the feeling of his naked body pressed against her bare skin, he was happy because he sensed the moment was special; she was happy too, gloriously happy, his little body was warm again, she could hear him chuckling with delight, the afternoon might have ended so differently.

Poor Clara was having a horrid time, Polly made herself remember, but the sooner she got on with it the sooner it would be over and the feeling that she had a sack of potatoes inside her would be gone. Holding Bobby at arms' length she viewed herself in the pier glass. Even without the camouflage of clothes she hadn't started to look any different. And as the months went by she was going to stay beautiful. Undressed she would be proud for Harry to see her. (She imagined a scene in six or seven months' time, herself as naked as she was this moment, Harry gazing at her in wonder and adoration, telling her she had never looked more beautiful, he would kneel in front of her, rest his hand tenderly on her swollen body. Even imagining it made her feel weak with love and longing.) But dressed she would never let her standards slip, she would walk tall, wear heeled shoes just as she did now. She would do it for herself and for Harry too.

A tug on her still-wet hair reminded her that Bobby was awaiting attention. Soon she had both of them dressed again and carried him downstairs.

'I'm going to take Bobby out into the sunshine. Is Horace already out there?' she asked Mrs Hume as she carried Bobby into the kitchen.

'Talk about a dog's life,' Ida answered. 'That hound is better off than many a human if you ask me. Out there sprawled full length in the sunshine, not a care in the world.'

'Mention walk and he'll be awake,' Polly laughed. 'It smells as if you've been baking.'

'A batch of rock buns, sometimes I wonder if young Algie gets fed properly at home. Growing lad like he is, he needs good food. I make sure there's always a slab of cake of some sort to send out for his tea.'

'If you'll wrap a couple in a napkin I'll take them with us. Bobby will be getting hungry.'

'Don't you go spoiling his supper with cakes Miss Polly.'

'He can have his supper late this evening, it's not every day we have a baby being born.'

'And a good thing too, throwing our routine out like this. It's time Arthur set out for the station to meet Mr Carpenter's train – and where is he? Chasing around after that nurse. Been more to the point if you'd done as I said and let him give young Clara a ride home to her own bed. And where the rush is to bring her husband here I can't think.'

'Of course he'll want to be here, to know when the baby arrives. I hope he gets here soon though, once Nurse Cox takes over she'll probably turn him out of the room.'

'So I should think! A lying-in room is no place for a man. I've looked out plenty of linen and got pans of water hot. All very well for them at Little Roost, getting out of all the work and washing. If you'd listened to me she would have been home where she belongs before this.' Polly hadn't listened to her then – and neither did she listen now. 'Here's your buns, I've put an extra one in for *you*. The way things are going the evening will be at sixes and sevens for everyone.'

When Polly smiled at her like that even Ida Hume found it hard to resist.

'Off you go, Miss Polly. When Mr Carpenter gets here I suppose I'm to tell him you're down by the water?'

'Thank you Mrs Hume, you're a darling.'

'Get along with you. Time that young Daisy got back,

chattering away without a care for the work that's waiting for her. I suppose when the nurse turns Clara's man out of the room it'll mean an extra one out here with us for supper?'

'Yes, make sure he's looked after, won't you.'

Charles, handed over to Mrs Hume to be looked after in the kitchen ... Charles, her Gypsy King. Remembering how she used to watch for him, how seeing him, being with him, had been the high points of her existence, it was like looking back to another life. Today she meant to keep out of his way. Even as she thought it, she glanced down at the pale violet muslin gown she'd chosen to replace the sodden mess she'd discarded, the shoes that matched perfectly, and she imagined him looking out of the spare-room window and watching her. Of course it wouldn't really be like that, she wouldn't be in the garden, she would be in the water meadow, so how could he possibly see her? Later though she could walk on the lawn with Harry, yes, that's when she wanted Charles to look out on them, she wanted Harry to be there too.

If Charles were to come to her on bended knee she still wouldn't want him. No longer did she despise him, instead she felt nothing. Add to that that this of all days belonged to Clara. Yet she could not deny that while she dressed herself with such care she had meant him to notice her.

Hearing her step approaching across the terrace, Horace twitched one ear, raised his head hopefully and was instantly wide awake and ready to go, tail swinging as he led the way down the garden to the stile. Bobby jigged up and down in Polly's arms, taking his mood from Horace and finding the world a splendid place.

The afternoon had shaken Polly more than she'd realized. As one hurdle had been overcome so she had been faced with the next, there had been no time to give way to the fear that had driven her. Only now could she stand back from the events, stand back and be thankful. Perhaps it had been her own fault that any of it had happened: if she'd listened to Millie, Bobby would have been properly supervised, the accident wouldn't have happened. But be thankful it was over and no one any the worse. Carefully, almost gingerly, she climbed the stile, Bobby was heavy to hold but she mustn't let him feel insecure. He'd had one fright today, the last thing she wanted was for him to get another. Bringing him out to play in the sunshine had a purpose: it would help him forget. She could have kept him on the lawn at home; the grass was short and well cared for, easier for him to crawl on than the meadow. But, being Polly, the place to come to for solace had always been the river and it was important that for Bobby one bad experience shouldn't have a chance to grow into a fear of the water. Horace's role was important, and he played it to the full. Each time he brought his stick Polly hurled it for him, sometimes across the grass, more often into the water. Bobby shrieked with laughter at the dog's antics, the way his tail wagged above the surface of the water as he swam, the way he spattered them both as he shook himself.

'I couldn't believe what I was seeing, dripping from head to foot all three of them. And as for Clara Warwick – as was – it seemed the sudden ducking had started her baby coming.'

'You're sure Polly wasn't hurt?' Harry asked for the second time.

'Our Miss Polly, hurt by a tumble in the water? As much at home in the river as on the land, never known a girl like her, right from when she was a nipper and the master used to take her out on the boat.'

Arthur Hume enjoyed his trips to collect Harry from the train just as much as he'd always enjoyed bringing the master back from the yard. Old George Baker who tended the garden was as deaf as a post and had never been much of a talker at the best of times; young Algy was a bit of a kid still, no chance of a proper talk with him. Apart from that Arthur was surrounded by womenfolk, all of them good enough in their way – and he'd not harbour even a thought against his Ida and her sharp tongue, he knew when to turn a deaf ear – but a man needs a man's company sometimes.

Arthur was now in full spate, recounting the events as he had heard them from Ida.

'And Polly saved Clara?' Harry asked.

'Oh ah, she did that right enough. Tell you one thing, Mr Carpenter sir, young Clara'll remember this baby's birthday well enough even if she's like her ma and has another dozen or so to follow. Reckon we'll remember it, all the fuss and commotion there is back home.

'But Polly and Bobby, you're sure—'

'Sure as my name's Arthur Hume. Last Ida saw of her she'd got the both of them dry and dressed again and gone off with that hound of hers down to the meadow.'

Still Harry wasn't reassured. Suppose Polly had lost their own baby? As soon as this it could happen so easily and what else could they expect after all she'd gone through this afternoon? If that's what had happened she would have wanted to escape the house and all 'the fuss and commotion' going on around the birth of Clara's full-term child.

'Drive straight to the stable, I'll not bother to go into the house,' he told Hume. Then taking off his silk top hat, 'Drop that indoors for me, will you?'

From the stable yard he went through the gate into the kitchen garden, then took the path that brought him to a gap in the hedge near the stile. He dreaded what he would see, for one look at her and he would know.

Horace was the first to notice him and come bounding to meet him, then Polly turned, said something to Bobby, swooped him into her arms and came running towards the stile.

'Hume told me,' he crushed her against him, or as near to crushing her as he could with Bobby sitting astride her hip. 'You might have been drowned.'

'Me drowned? As if I would!' she laughed. 'I wasn't the one who might have been drowned.' As she remembered, she gave an involuntary shiver. 'Never been so frightened. We mustn't talk about it, not in front of him. Let's throw another stick for Horace.'

'Come on lad, you're getting too heavy for your big sister.' Taking Bobby – and Polly too – by surprise, he lifted the little boy from Polly and hoisted him over his head to sit astride his shoulders, holding him securely with both hands.

'This is nice,' Polly nuzzled her face against him as she walked by his side, 'good practice for you.' Then she ran ahead of him, picked up Horace's stick and hurled it so hard it almost reached the further bank.

It was a moment Harry would never forget: Polly so lovely, her chestnut hair shining in the light of the late afternoon sun;

the cattle making their leisurely way down to their drinking place; Horace with his tail telling its own story of pleasure as he retrieved the stick; the warm weight of Bobby on his shoulders; Polly who still played with all the enjoyment of a child and yet had a woman's understanding, a woman's passion, Polly, his beloved Polly ... If the afternoon had gone differently ... Dear God, even to think such a thing was like tempting Fate ... keep her safe, always keep her safe, I never imagined it were possible to feel as I do for her ...

Polly came back to meet them.

'You look very solemn for such a lovely afternoon,' she said, a teasing laugh in her voice.

'I had solemn thoughts.'

'Oh? Why? What's happened?' Immediately she supposed his thoughts were on his own day which had been spent with a business associate in Oxford.

'It's what might have happened,' he said softly. Bobby was busy ruffling his hair but he hardly noticed. 'Polly I want to go down on my knees and thank God that it didn't. If I lost you my life would be nothing.'

Her smile had gone. She raised her face and laid her mouth gently on his.

It was nearly an hour later when they strolled back across the lawn. Mrs Hume's buns had kept Bobby in good humour despite it being well past his usual bedtime.

Nurse Cox had expelled Charles from the bedroom although there was no sign of an imminent birth. If Ida Hume had her way even at this stage Clara could have been bundled into the carriage and taken back to where she belonged.

'No use you getting fidgety, young man,' she told Charles. 'You'll very likely still be waiting when morning comes. First babies don't come in a hurry. I told Miss Polly there was no need to keep Clara here, but would she listen? Not her. She'd made her mind up, even if Clara had argued it wouldn't have turned her from the idea.'

Was he listening to her? In her view it had been nonsense to send for him, men hanging about were no more than a nuisance at times like this. He stood staring out of the window as if he was full of hate, now what could he be thinking about to put that look on his handsome young face? He didn't notice as she moved nearer and followed his gaze.

And strangely Polly, who had dressed with care imagining him watching her as she walked in the garden on Harry's arm, by now had forgotten all about him. Her arm was around Harry's waist, his around hers; Bobby was lying on the grass kicking his feet in the air while Horace rolled by the side of him. It was a scene of domestic bliss.

'Come on now, lad,' Ida's voice cut into Charles's thoughts and he turned away from the window. 'I've poured you a nice strong cup of tea, that'll buck you up. She's a healthy girl, very like her mother and having babies has never given *her* any trouble. Another few hours and you'll be a proud father.'

She was wrong. The evening dragged on, Millie took Bobbie off to bed, Daisy served a meal in the dining room for Polly and Harry, Ida served one in the kitchen for the rest of them, while upstairs Nurse Cox wasn't happy with the way things were going. They heard her heavy tread on the back stairs and looked to the door expectantly. Was she bringing news? No, she went straight along the passage. A moment later the dining-room bell, one of a row high on the wall in the kitchen, jangled.

The nurse had asked that someone could be sent to fetch Dr Wright. And that 'someone' of course was Arthur, which only reinforced Ida's opinion about where the girl ought to be having this baby. Although she wouldn't admit to it, at the back of her mind was the memory of the night Bobby had been born: things hadn't gone right then, either, and look at the outcome of that night.

The day was over. The Humes, Daisy and Millie had all gone to bed. Blanche had arrived and, unlike Charles, she had been allowed into the bedroom while he waited in the kitchen with only Horace for company.

Whatever Clara was suffering now must lie ahead for Polly in another seven months. No wonder neither she nor Harry could forget the battle being fought out in the spare bedroom.

Through the evening midges were the accepted plague of riverside gardens, but even they disappeared as darkness deepened to night.

'Let's go outside for ten minutes,' Harry suggested.

It was almost midnight, a fact neither of them mentioned. Instead he lit a taper from the lamp, then drew on a cigar until its tip glowed red.

'Let's go through the conservatory – quietly so that Horace doesn't know he's missing anything.'

From the conservatory to the terrace then across the lawn to the wrought-iron seat. Out here, although they were right away from the house, it was natural to whisper – or even not to talk at all – the soft, still air of the night was like a caress.

'It won't be born today, hark, there's the church clock. Midnight,' Harry murmured after a few moments, then he put his cigar aside and drew her closer.

'Now it's another day.' She nuzzled her face against his neck. 'What will it bring, I wonder. A boy or a girl? She will be all right, won't she Harry. She won't be like Mother . . . ?'

'Look! Isn't that her mother on the landing?'

Polly followed his gaze. On these summer evenings the curtains were seldom closed across the long window at the end of the first-floor corridor, a place where the single lamp threw it into bright contrast against the background of night. She saw Blanche hurrying towards the back staircase, then before she even reached it she saw Charles push past her and go towards the bedroom.

'It must be over.' Mutely they looked at each other, instinctively they moved even closer. One day this would be Polly, the new life would be flesh of their flesh, a living proof of their love. His mouth covered hers, she clung to him, in that embrace they both knew a thankfulness deeper than any words.

'We'd better go in,' he said as he loosened his hold on her. 'If we're not there Mrs Warwick will think you've gone to bed and not bothered.'

'They won't want me upstairs, they won't be ready for outsiders yet. You go on up to bed if you want to, Harry, I'll wait in the drawing room and leave the door open so that they know I'm there.'

'I've one or two things to look at that came out of today's meeting. Tomorrow I'm back in Oxford. I want to get things clear in my mind.'

So when they went back into the house he went to the study

and closed the door, she to the drawing room and left it open. It was Blanche who came down, meaning to wait in the kitchen, but seeing the light streaming across the hall from the drawing room she came in search of Polly.

'Is it over, Mrs Warwick? Which is it?'

Blanche shook her head, making no effort to hide her tears.

'It's Clara! What's happened?' The night of Bobby's birth was alive in Polly's mind – just as it had been all the evening she realized now.

'My poor Clara, her first baby. Dead.'

'Clara? Oh no, she's been so strong, she—'

'Not Clara, thank God not Clara. The poor wee mite. Not a breath in his body. A fine boy, a shock of dark hair like Chaw's – not that that means a lot when they're newborn. Never seen Clara cry like it, not as a child even, no never. As for Chaw ... poor boy. I've said my good nights, I'm getting off back home now, break it to the others first thing in the morning. Don't want the poor girl to see me with my face all blotched with crying for her.' Blanche gave her nose an almighty blow, then scrubbed her reddened face with the rolled-up handkerchief. 'It's not fair, she's never done nothing but good in all her life. And looked forward to this baby as natural as any animal in God's kingdom. So what's He gone and done this for? Just tell me that.'

Anything Polly could say would be lost on her, and in any case she couldn't find any words to express her own sick disappointment. Selfishness played some part too, she knew it did and she wasn't proud, selfishness and fear. Her mother had died giving birth to Bobby, and was Clara's story any easier? All the excitement, stitching baby clothes, looking forward ... Polly came face to face with the scorn she'd felt for the hard-working girl, how she'd always – even this evening – made a point of making play of her own slim body, her own lovely and flattering gowns.

Coming out of the study, Harry said, 'You're not walking, Mrs Warwick. I shall get the trap ready and drive you home. What about your son-in-law?'

'Charles will want to be with Clara,' Polly told him.

'Charles!' Blanche attempted to smile, 'Charles, indeed, Only Miss Polly always calls him that Mr Carpenter, sir.

215

Chaw, that's what we call him. Always have, right since he was a little lad. It's kind of you to offer me a ride. I ought to say no, but to tell the truth I feel that done up if I walked by myself I think I'd sit right down there in the lane and blub all over again. Can't make it out, nor can Dr Wright. If ever a babe was lively it was that one, never still a second she used to say, turning and twisting every which way. Do you reckon an unborn baby can be drowned? I mean, going in the water like she did, that must have been what set it going wrong.' She was voicing her illogical thoughts aloud, she didn't look for an answer.

She was silent for most of the drive home, wrapped up in her own unhappiness. He opened the gate of the farmyard and it was as he climbed back onto the trap that she said, 'You take good care of Miss Polly, you've got a real treasure there. And, Mr Carpenter, sir, don't let her go worrying about what's happened tonight. She looks as fragile as fine porcelain but, bless her heart, she has a will like steel. Well, you don't need me telling you about your own wife. But I'll tell you this, if she'd listened to Dr Wright and that Nurse Cox, Bobby would-n't have lasted many hours longer than my poor Clara's little boy. It was as if she filled him with her own strength, *willed* him to hang on till we could get him taking nourishment.'

'She's a fighter, she never gives up.' And he should know, they were two of a kind.

'Hark at me, blathering on and keeping you from your bed. If the truth is told, it's because I dread going indoors, telling my Bert what's happened. Our first grandson – hair as dark as dark – no rhyme or reason in it. Babies get born every day to parents who don't want them. And this lad ... sometimes I wonder what the Almighty thinks He's up to.'

Harry helped her down from the trap just as Bert brought a lantern out to meet her.

And that must surely be the end of the day, he thought as he hung up Tubby's harness and started back to the house. The doctor's trap had gone, the nurse would still be here and, since he hadn't passed Chaw – Charles, Polly had always called him Charles – in the lane, he supposed he must be meaning to spend the night by his wife's bedside.

He closed the door quietly, so quietly that even Horace didn't hear him, and came along the passage to the hall. That's when he heard a man's voice, the tone of it warning him that something was wrong.

Then Polly. 'Charles, you're overwrought—'

'Don't you ever give up? Didn't go as you planned did it? No, you thought you'd get rid of them both, you and your bloody river ...' Harry moved as if to intervene but Charles's next words rooted him to the spot, the way they were spoken telling him they were meant as an echo of something Polly must have said. '"You can't marry *her*, it's *me* you love." I told you I wouldn't give her up. Why couldn't you understand?'

'I won't listen to you.'

'Did you ever listen? Even when she was pregnant you didn't give up. Lucky for you you had a tame lover ready to take you on.' His voice broke. 'Now you've done this! I suppose you couldn't bear the thought that I'd acknowledge *her* child as my own.'

'Go back to Clara.'

'Clara's asleep or I would. Tomorrow I shall fetch her. I'm going home when I've finished with you, *when* and not before.'

'You'll go now.' Harry stood in the doorway. The sight of him frightened Polly more than anything Charles could have said to her, more than anything the horror of the afternoon had thrown at her. His face was like a mask, he looked at her as though she were nothing, no light of affection in his eyes nor even any anger. In that moment from some obscure recess in her mind came the memory of the first time she'd seen him, Shylock, tall, not an ounce of spare flesh on him, the bone structure of his face warning her that he would never be a man to trifle with. Now his face was pale, almost grey, the skin looked tight.

'Ah, the lovely Polly's husband.' Charles was indeed more overwrought than he realized or he'd never have looked at them both with such scorn. 'I wish you joy of her. As good a tumble as any whore, but a whore plies her trade honestly.'

'I said – *out*.'

Thank God, his anger was against Charles, her moment's terror vanished. She wanted Charles gone, she wanted just to be with Harry, to feel his arms around her and to forget Charles's sordid outburst. She watched as he took the younger man by the back of his collar, marched him through the hall to the front door. Hurt and disappointment must have been driving Charles, still he ranted.

'Never thought she'd plant someone else's kid on you, did you?' she heard him say. 'Still, she might have married you anyway, money buys most things and I hear it's yours that props her old man up. Her sort would sell their soul for comfort. Played you along while she was—'

The front door slammed on him. Then Harry came back and one look at his face was all it needed for her world to fall apart.

Chapter Eleven

'Don't Harry ... don't look like that. Everything's different now. I heard what he said. Harry, it's not true.' Polly hardly knew what she was saying. At that moment she had only *one* object and that was to see Harry's expression change, to look at him and know that nothing Charles had said had come between them. 'Charles isn't important, I swear to you, on everything I love I swear to you – as God is my witness—' Surely now he must believe her, he must listen to her, 'I swear that he means nothing to me, less than nothing. Don't look at me like that. Harry, Harry, please ...'

He had closed the door and stood leaning against it. If she read his expression as anger, even disgust, then she over-simplified his emotion. He listened to Polly, he saw fright and pleading in her brown eyes. Pleading for him to accept their marriage? Pleading for him to accept Charles Dunton's child? He shut his eyes, the wood of the door against the palms of his hands his only hold on normality.

'Harry ...?' Don't let him look at me like that, make him open his eyes and let me know he's come back to me, please. Let him still love me. She felt herself willing him to look at her.

Certainly he opened his eyes, but they carried no message of love or trust, nor yet anger. Was it contempt she read there? He came towards her. Would he touch her? Would he hold her close? Then all the mistrust would be gone ... When he put his hands on her shoulders she raised her arms. Thank You, thank You, her thoughts flew ahead of her. But all her thankfulness was dashed. Instead of drawing her closer he held her at arms' length, compelling her eyes to meet his.

'Has Charles Dunton ever made love to you? For once I want honesty from you.'

She started as if he had hit her.

'That's not fair!'

'You haven't answered me.'

'It wasn't love. Harry, don't look at me like that.'

'So, he has. You once told me – God knows whether it was fact or another of your flights of fancy – you told me you could never marry me because there was someone else, a married man.' He gave her shoulders a slight shake as if to drive home what he was asking. 'Was that man Dunton?'

'I thought it was the truth, but Harry he means nothing to me, less than nothing.'

'So it *was* him.' He felt defeated, drained. 'The child – he says the child is his.'

'Of course it isn't *his*. I tell you there was no love in what happened. I knew straight away that all I'd felt for him had been a sort of childish dream.' Had he even heard her? His face was a mask, it told her nothing. She clutched his hand but there was no answering pressure on her fingers. Instead he turned away from her. 'We ought to be grateful to him,' she rushed on, voicing her thoughts as they came into her head, 'it was the way he made love – no, it wasn't love, it was hateful – but it was then that I knew so surely that you'd been right, I ought to have listened to you. We belong together Harry—'

'When?'

'Turn round and look at me, Harry, then I'll tell you, I'll tell you all of it.'

It would have been easier to talk to his back.

'Charles used to own a barge – it was his father's, he worked for his father – he used to moor it just up the river. I didn't know he really came to see Clara, I thought it was because of me. They weren't married then. That was the first time we made love – I was a child, Harry, I was infatuated. I took it for granted that we would marry. When I found out he was the Chaw Mrs Warwick used to talk about I thought he would give Clara up; even when he married her I thought it was because he didn't want to let her down. I wanted him to regret he'd chosen her instead of me – I went out of my way to let him see Clara and me together and know it was *me* he really wanted.

You can hate me for that, I *want* you to hate me for that, it's what I deserve. The next time it happened it was chance that he was in the meadow the night I was on the river. I hadn't expected to meet him.'

Harry took her chin in his hand and raised her face to his. 'Go on.'

'I thought it was *me* he wanted. I suppose I was excited to believe all his months with Clara he must have been wanting me. I did try to stop him. I told him to go home to her. But – it was horrible, he was like an animal, he *used* me. We were on my canoe, I just wanted to get away from him. I pushed him into the water and escaped. Harry, listen to me, believe me, please, please Harry. It was *then*, out there alone on the river, don't you remember what I told you when I found you in Brighton? I said I'd wanted to keep on paddling until I reached you. It was a sort of revelation – Harry, don't look at me like that—'

'So what he said is true.'

'Damn what he said, yes, damn it. It's what *I* said that matters. Harry, I came to you because I knew it was where I should be. Two of a kind, you'd said. Yes and something else: remember? "I'll love you until the day I die", you said that too.'

'Don't. Have you *ever* been honest with me, I wonder? Why couldn't you have told me the truth, told me this married man of yours might have given you his child? I think that's what I can't forgive, Polly. That you had so little trust in me.'

Had he really loved her so much that he would have married her knowing that she might already be pregnant with someone else's child? She tried to hold her mouth steady, but speaking was her undoing.

'Can't be his,' she blurted out, giving up the battle, her eyes burning with hot tears, 'with you and me it was different, I never knew anything so – so – perfect—'

'Don't!'

'It's *our* baby,' she tried to pull him towards her, to press herself close so that he would hold her. 'Ours, we made it because we love each other.'

He took her arms from around him and pushed her firmly away.

'Perhaps it's ours, perhaps it's yours and his. But that, my dear, is your problem.'

Only once had he used that tone to her, the 'my dear' holding scorn but no affection. Hearing it again now, that other occasion came back to her memory, the evening he'd come to Water's Edge knowing her father wouldn't be there, the evening he'd first kissed her. How could she liken that moment to this?

Now his back was towards her, without another word he was leaving her.

'Harry!'

But he'd gone. She heard his footsteps on the stairs and fresh hope sprang within her. Wiping the backs of her hands across her still tear-wet face she made to follow him, first turning out the lamp. In bed it would be different. Sleeping together would make quarrelling impossible. She daren't let herself imagine them making love; the lesser intimacies were what she craved. Lying together their feet would touch, she would move close to him so that she burrowed her face against his neck, he would rub his chin against her head.

A shaft of light showed under the door of the spare bedroom and as she passed by Polly could hear Nurse Cox moving about. Listen! Mrs Hume must have only just gone to bed too, she could hear someone walking overhead in the Humes' room. Then her mind jumped back to Clara, poor, uncomplaining Clara, worn out and sleeping now. Would she wake up knowing what had happened, or would consciousness return with its usual feeling of hope, only to be dashed as reality closed in on her? Help her, please help her not to be too miserable ... and help me too, me and Harry ... with that silent plea at the top of her mind she opened the door of their own room.

'What're you doing?' As if it wasn't obvious what he was doing. With a large leather grip open on the bed he was packing his personal things. His silver-backed hairbrushes had gone from the top of the chest of drawers, so had the case where he kept his studs, cufflinks and cravat pins. 'No, Harry!' She was across the room, forcing herself between him and the bed.

'No, Harry,' he mocked her. 'What game is it you want to

play now? Are we to pretend I'm still in happy ignorance of why you were suddenly so keen for me to marry you – a tame lover was the expression I believe – or do you want us to make-believe you were a virgin bride? Humph?'

Something in her snapped. With clenched fists she pounded his shoulders.

'Don't want to pretend anything. You weren't perfect before you married me so you needn't sound so – so – pompous. Pappy told me you heard about him from a mutual lady friend – a whore is what he meant.' She was unnerved and trembling, angry and terrified, out of control. Harry might have been made of stone, his expression didn't alter. It was as if neither her fists nor her words touched him. 'I suppose that's what you think I am, a whore.' With each word her voice became more shrill, she was crying and shouting, hearing herself from afar and hardly knowing what she said. 'Love me till you die! You don't know what love is. Clara would understand, if Charles told her she'd listen, she'd still go on loving him – but *you*, you don't understand anything except how to make money. Shylock, that's what I thought of you.'

'You'll wake the whole house.'

'Good. I don't care if I wake the dead. I don't care, I don't—' The sting of his hand on her cheek made her catch her breath. Wherever her wild and meaningless outburst had been taking her, she was pulled up short. 'Anyway,' she mumbled, 'you can't go anywhere tonight.'

'Hume will be waiting with the trap by now. I don't know what story you mean to put around, but in truth I intend to follow up a business proposition in America.'

'No,' she breathed. It was like living through a nightmare.

'I hadn't intended to go personally, but now I shall.'

'What about me?' Even now surely she could make him change his mind. 'What am I supposed to do? Harry, don't leave me.'

She saw the first crack in his steely control. His mouth trembled but only for a second before he tightened his jaw. Then he reached around her to the half-filled grip and snapped it closed.

'You are my responsibility, you need have no worries on that account.'

'Money? I don't mean money.' She dropped to her knees in front of him, clinging to him. 'If you loved me you wouldn't do this to me. Think of how it's been these last weeks – you've been happy, you know you have. We could be like that again. I'm no different now just because—' Because he didn't know if the baby was his. 'Harry, perhaps I could get rid of the baby, lots of women have miscarriages – we could start again – pretend none of that ever happened.' As he moved so she clung tightly to his legs.

'Get up, Polly,' Harry bent down to hold her under her arms and raise her. In an instant she let go of her hold on his legs and pressed her hands over his and forcing them to her breast. 'Get up,' he breathed.

'You don't even want to touch me,' she mumbled. But she knew it wasn't true and in that second she was on her feet, her arms around him. 'Don't go tonight, stay with me tonight, we can't part like this.' Against his will he was crushing her to him. 'If you don't want me any more, then go tomorrow. But not tonight.' That she had turned the situation around so that it was he who was deserting her, not she who had cheated him, didn't enter her head. In that moment all she knew was one thing: tomorrow was another day, between now and then were hours in the intimacy of their bed, hours that would put everything right between them.

She found her arms torn from around him as he pushed her with such force that she fell onto the bed. Then without a backward glance he was gone.

'I wish the master would get home,' Ida grumbled to Arthur. 'The place has gone to pot without him and that's something I never thought you'd hear me say. What sent Mr Carpenter off in such a rush I doubt if we'll ever know, but that's nearly a month ago and never a line from him for Miss Polly.'

'You can't say that for certain.' Then her loyal and understanding Arthur gave her a knowing smile to take away the sting of what he was about to say. 'Not for the want of trying, I dare say, but there must have been times aplenty when young Daisy has picked up the post from the mat, either her or Millie.'

'Millie I'm not so sure about, she plays things closer to her

224

chest. I'll come to that in a minute, something I want to tell you. But we were talking about a letter from Mr Carpenter: not a day goes by without young Daisy blabs out what the mailman has brought, or whether he's not come at all. She never voices her opinion – well, she'd know better than to try and chit-chat to me about the family – but I know she keeps an eye open for a letter as much as I do myself. And as for Miss Polly, even you can't pretend she doesn't look as miserable as sin lately.'

'Ah, that she does. It's not like her to be so down in the mouth.'

'Doesn't eat enough to keep a sparrow alive. But here, come up close, I don't want this to go further than just you and me—'

'Not likely to, unless Tubby here has learnt to talk the Queen's English.' Nevertheless, he put down the cloth he'd been using to polish the brass on the carriage lamps and came close to Ida, then cocked his ear ready to receive the latest gem of gossip.

'Two things. They're the reason I came out here to have a quiet talk. The first is fact, no guessing about it. That husband of Millie's has turned up. If I'd been the one to answer his knock he would have been left waiting on the doormat until I asked her if she wanted him to be let in. But not Daisy! Sometimes I don't think that girl has the brains she was born with. Marches him up to the nursery as bold as brass. I wondered who it was, what she was up to. So I went up the back stairs, quietly mind you, and there was Madam Daisy if you please, squatting down peeping through the keyhole, ears wide open too you may be sure.'

Arthur chuckled, picturing the scene.

'Wide open or not, I wager she got a flea in them when you got hold of her.'

'Not that Millie is family, but all the same she cherishes her privacy. Only right and proper I spoke sharpish to the girl, she's got to be made to learn. Subdued as anything she was for all of five minutes. But with so much inside her bursting to be told, soon she was prattling away as if I'd never spoken sharp at all. And listen to this, Arth, listen to what she said. I didn't let her repeat all they'd said to each other – well, I don't think she understood the half of it, after all she didn't know what it

was that had sent Millie off any more than we do ourselves –
but it seems he was kissing her. What do you make of that?
Kissing her and she seemed to like it.'

'And a good thing too, Ida, my dear. Nothing sadder than a
couple's hopes dashed to pieces by misunderstandings. We take
each other on for life, rough with the smooth.'

'That's so.' She nodded complacently, as if none of the
rough patches in their path had been of her making.

'That's what bothers me about our little Polly. Is she miserable because she misses him or is it something more? Business
mad some of them, put making money before everything. It's
not right for him to go chasing across the ocean to the New
World and leaving his bride behind. I'd say the same of any
couple, but it being Miss Polly, well I tell you it makes me
angry to see her used like it.'

'And not writing . . .' Ida threw in for good measure.

'Letters will take weeks. One of these mornings an envelope
will come and she'll be her old self again.'

'Don't be too sure. I was looking at her this morning,
watching her walking out to take the trap from you. You know
what *I* think – *I* think there's a baby on the way there.'

'You mean he went off without knowing?'

'I don't know what to think. But listen Arth, I said there
were two things – and that wasn't counting my suspicions
about the baby. Mid-day post brought another letter from the
master. Perhaps he'll be telling her when he's to be expected
home. All these weeks gallivanting out there with a widow
woman! The poor dear mistress would turn in her grave.'

The letter was waiting for Polly on the hall table, the handwriting unmistakably her father's. She carried it upstairs with her,
meaning to read it in her bedroom as soon as she'd taken off
her cape and hat.

'Mrs Carpenter, madam, could I have a word?'

'Hello, Millie,' Polly answered, ready to add, 'I'll be along
in a minute,' until a glance told her that the nursemaid must
have been watching for her. 'I'll come into the nursery before I
take my hat off. Is something wrong?'

'Oh, no, ma'm. Nothing's wrong at all. He came this afternoon, my Bruce did, I mean.'

'Here? How did he find you? Had you written to him?'

'No, ma'm, that's what's so grand. He'd had a hard job to find me. First he'd tried in Somerset where we met. All he learned there was that I had a brother working near Reading at your yard. That was enough to set him in this direction, but Hugh pretended he didn't know anything about me. When the men have their dinnertime break you know how they mostly go for their bread and cheese and an ale at the Red Cow, that's where he got talking to them, leading them on as cunning as anything so that they didn't know what he was ferreting for, talking about their families, asking casually as anything whether Hugh's sister kept house for him, him being a single man. Oh no, they said, Hugh was in lodgings in Reading, his sister looked after the Seagrove child. That was yesterday, he still had to find out where the Seagrove family home was, he couldn't tell them straight out what he was after. Don't know how he managed to get as much out of them as he did without them twigging they were being pumped. Cunning as a fox, he must have been.'

Millie said it with such pride. Polly felt an inexplicable pang of envy. In her joy that Bruce wanted her home, Millie had forgiven and forgotten all she'd run away from.

'I shall love you until the day I die ...' came the echo of Harry's voice, the words spoken like a vow. Yet he'd listened to Charles's taunts, had been ready to believe that she'd used him as her 'tame lover'. For her their time together had been perfect, she'd been sure it had for him too – but how could it have been when he'd been so ready to believe she was the sort of person who would marry for convenience not love. Convenience? The child wasn't Charles's, it musn't be, it couldn't be. Supposing – dark eyes, dark hair ...

'Anyway,' Polly pulled her thoughts back to Millie's tale, 'this morning he asked around and got the address and walked all the way out here, got here just as I was going to get Bobby up from his sleep and take him – and Horace – walking.'

'You look excited Millie. You were glad to see him?' As if it needed to be asked.

'Oh, you don't know how glad. Glad doesn't even start to say it. All this time I've been trying to pretend I've something in my life without him. But the truth is, Mrs Carpenter, I haven't, I never could have.'

'D'you think he's changed his ways? Be certain, Millie.'

'Don't expect he has. For a bit he will have, but a leopard of his age can't be expected to change his spots. You say, be certain. I'm certain of one thing, *any* sort of life with Bruce is better than all the comforts in the world without him.'

Polly felt the sting of hot tears. Any sort of life with *Harry* ... if only he'd write, if only he'd find he couldn't live without her, if only she'd never seen Charles Dunton passing on his barge and put him on a pedestal as her Gypsy King, if only ...

'... letting you down. And Bobby, it's going to mean an upset for Bobby having to get used to someone new. I've told Bruce I must wait here until you find someone you like – unless you can take him each day to Mrs Warwick like you used to before I ca—'

'No,' Polly cut her short. 'No, I shan't do that. I shall look after him myself, I've done that before and anyway ...' Something stopped her completing her sentence, telling Millie the reason why she would soon have to give up going each day to the yard. She longed for the comfort of knowing the first early changes in her body were evidence of the love she and Harry had known, longed for it yet was frightened to believe. That was partly why her sentence hung in the air, unfinished. There was something else, harder to define: it had to do with her mother's death and Clara's stillborn son; it had to do with her own confused emotions towards the embryo of that new life, frightened to love a child who was Harry's because of her revulsion towards one who was Charles's, frightened that she would be punished by losing Harry's child or be forced to have a constant reminder of Charles. 'When is he going back to Devon? Will you be in time to go with him?'

'No, I told him I couldn't do that. He took it like a lamb, m'am. He's going home by train this evening. I promised him I'd follow on just as soon as you could get suited with someone for Bobby.'

'If Hume took you in the trap would you be in time to catch him at the station?'

'Tonight you mean? His train doesn't go out until past bedtime, it's the night one, the one that carries the post right the way to Cornwall. You mean I can pack up and go now? I haven't even got Bobby to bed.'

'Pack your bag and I'll tell Hume to bring the trap round in half an hour.'

'Pol, Pol,' Bobby came staggering from the adjoining play-room, then went down on all fours for quickness, 'up me, Po'.'

She swooped down on him and lifted him high, suddenly feeling happier than she had for weeks. There was nothing complicated in her love for her small brother, nor in his for her.

Polly always enjoyed her father's letters. He wrote frequently and it was apparent that his holiday was in no way marred by Cecily's elderly uncle's fast-failing hold on life. He had never imagined anywhere could be as beautiful as the views from the window of the villa. Reading between the lines she knew that the lifestyle suited him perfectly; in an earlier letter he had told her about the local people, people who were lacking in worldly goods but not in good humour. Sunshine made people cheerful, he'd told her, and knowing how he responded to cheerfulness she liked to imagine him in his newfound Utopia.

Instead of reading today's letter in her bedroom she put it to one side until later. Her evening was to follow a new pattern. In his delight that Polly was giving him his supper and putting him to bed, Bobby hardly noticed Millie's absence. As for Polly, she was thankful for the responsibility that had come her way, it gave her a new purpose.

At last she sat down to her solitary meal and that's when she slit open the envelope and started to read.

My dearest Pol,

I know you like surprises, that is something you must have inherited from me. So I will tell you straight away: Cecily has consented to become my wife. On reflection, I wonder if my news will come as a surprise at all, even before we came out here you must have been aware of the happiness I found in her company. I am thankful to tell you that her feelings are the same as my own, we are certain the step we are taking is the right one.

As soon as I seal this letter to you I intend to write to Mr Buckeridge. Cecily is in perfect accord with my wishes. Indeed any assets I could bring to the partnership would be insignificant in comparison with her own wealth. You are aware I dare say that she inherited wealth and property from her first husband. It is her wish that I take control of her – 'our', her word, not my own – finances. I have talked to her about my own position and yours. Similarly Harry no doubt will look after your affairs and the fact that I have so little to hand over to you is of small importance now that you are his wife.

Our plan is that Cecily and I will be married quietly over here in Italy; and it is here that we shall make our home. Any monies that I have in the bank will be transferred to me out here, but so far as the business is concerned and Water's Edge I am arranging with Mr Buckeridge that assets and responsibilities will be passed to you. Indeed, as Harry will have told you, little by little I have handed the business over to him. You will see why I was so delighted at your marriage. It had worried me greatly as the Seagrove share dwindled, but Harry promised the name would always be kept and, indeed, he also asked me not to divulge to you just how great is his control. However, I comfort myself with the memory of his vow 'with my worldly goods I thee endow' and am thankful. As for Water's Edge, you and he may decide this is the time for you to move elsewhere; alternatively he may decide to repay the money I raised on the house.

Pol my dear, ever my very dear child, you and I have always been close, I know you will be glad for me that I am to start a new chapter in my book of life. As for me, I wake each morning eager for the day – and am thankful for the knowledge that you are with Harry and doubtless as full of joy as I admit to being myself.

I have made no mention of the child. You have cared for him from the first and I know you will continue to do so. I am saddened by the knowledge that the son your mother gave her life for has no inheritance from his father, but my faith in you is absolute, I know you will never fail him.

When you write to me next remember there will be a new Mrs Seagrove. She will be happy for you to call her by her first name, but for myself I shall always be

Your loving Pappy.

Polly read the letter twice. On the first reading her main emotion was relief for her father, relief but not surprise. Preparing for his trip he had been as excited as any young man hurtling willingly into love. That he should have decided to spend his future in Italy was a possibility she'd not considered. She read it through again, this time her focus on her own involvement. When had he raised money on Water's Edge? He had gone away knowing that the house was mortgaged and the business almost entirely Harry's. No wonder he'd been so keen for her to marry Harry.

'Are you ready for your pudding, ma'm?' Daisy's voice surprised her. 'Oh, sorry, you've hardly started your roast. I'll come back presently.' Then seeing the letter lying by the side of Polly's plate curiosity got the better of her. 'You've not had bad news from the master have you, Mrs Carpenter, ma'm?' Bad or good, the letter must have been important to put her off her lovely roast lamb! Daisy imagined herself carrying a gem of news back to the kitchen.

'No, just a long letter from my father. You may clear my things, Daisy.'

'You've let it go all cold. Never mind, I'll bring your pudding.'

'I'm not hungry—'

'You will be when you try it,' Daisy beamed. 'Mrs Hume's bread-and-butter pud is always good. I'll get it for you, shall I?' She didn't fit easily into the role of housemaid. She enjoyed cleaning and polishing, she worked hard and willingly, but a simple 'Yes, ma'm' or 'No, ma'm' was beyond her, she talked to Polly as she would to family – if she had such a thing beyond a father with unhealthy designs on her.

Polly had long since forgotten Daisy's lack of ability with Bobby. Even now the girl was hardly more than a child; and what a life for her with no one for company but Ida Hume.

A mortgage on Water's Edge, the thought pushed itself to the front of Polly's mind again, and what chance of repaying it when Seagrove's Boatyard belonged almost entirely to Harry? What Pappy has done won't just affect *me*, it will upset all of them, the Humes, old George Baker who'd worked in the garden more years than she'd lived, even Daisy and Algy. But how can I hope to repay a mortgage when the only money I shall have is what I get from the small share I'm left with in the business? And that thought led to the next, one that pushed everything else from her mind. Locked in the desk drawer in the study was a letter she'd received a fortnight ago from Cox, Crisp & Buller, a firm of London solicitors acting for Harry, setting out for her details of a banking account opened in her name – Harry had even given the bank a specimen of her signature.

Before leaving for America your husband instructed that each month a sum of £35 should be paid into your account, and I am to advise you that should this be insufficient for your needs you are to contact me ...

The letter remained unacknowledged. Of course even though he hadn't known that her father intended to stay in Italy he must have realized the financial difficulty there would be in meeting their debts. Thirty-five pounds was a generous allowance, thirty-five pounds and the offer of more if it were insufficient. Well, *she'd* show him! She'd not touch a penny of his money. Tonight she must think, she must plan her own future, hers and Bobby's. All this was going through her mind while she looked at Daisy's thin little face with its eyes bright with curiosity.

'You work hard, Daisy,' she mused, watching the little maid while her mind was leaping ahead of her. 'Do you like helping Mrs Hume run the house?'

'Me, helping run it?' Daisy giggled. 'Better not let Mrs Hume hear you say that, ma'm. The only running I do is at her beck and call. But her bark's worse than her bite, as long as she calls the tune she lets me dance to it with my own step, if you see what I mean. And, any road, I like making things look nice. You got some real lovely things, ma'm, all your bits of china and that. No wonder I like looking after them – and putting a shine to the furniture. I didn't make much of a fist of taking care of Bobby – I wonder you didn't give me my marching orders but I'm jolly glad you didn't. Hark at me and my chatter! Why didn't you stop me, ma'm? I'm off to get you your pudding.'

'I'm really not hungry.'

'You will be when you try it. And, any road, Mrs Hume made it specially because when you were little it was always your favourite, that's what she said. She worries because you've looked so miserable since Mr Carpenter had to go away. She reckons if you're pining the best she can do for you is feed you up. No news from him yet, you don't know when he'll be able to get home?' There now, she'd asked it! If you didn't ask you didn't get told, that was Daisy's motto. And imagine Mrs Hume's long face if she could go back to the kitchen and say – casual as anything she'd say it, just as if she and the missus were in the habit of having a good chat – 'Mrs Carpenter tells me her husband will be back by ...' and then whenever it was.

But the scene hardly had a chance to take shape in her imagination before Polly answered.

'I'm sorry not to want the bread and butter pudding, but tell Mrs Hume I had a good meal at lunch time. I have letters to write and one or two things to see to, I'll leave the study door open in case Bobby cries out.'

Disappointed, Daisy cleared away the half-eaten first course and went back to the kitchen.

Far into the night Polly lay awake. Determined not to let her sights turn backwards, not to give way to regrets or thoughts of what might have been. She tried to form some sort of a shape of the future. Tomorrow she would visit Mr Buckeridge. He knew more about her father's affairs than she did, even after today's letter. Until she talked to him she couldn't know exactly how her finances stood. Perhaps she could draw more from the business and repay what her father had borrowed on the house. That would depend on how much of a stake in the boatyard was still his. Whichever way she viewed the situation her thoughts always brought her to the same conclusion, one sentence in her father's letter telling her he was thankful she was with Harry.

The next morning, having no alternative but to take Bobbie with her, she visited Mr Buckeridge. He had known her father since they had both been young men. A junior in the firm of Hawkes & Hepworth, it had fallen to him to deal with the affairs of Stanley, the fun-loving and indolent brother of Fred who had already made Seagrove's a highly thought-of firm of boatbuilders. In truth Clive Buckeridge, a solemn and inexperienced solicitor, had envied Stanley his wayward habits. That was long ago, and while now Stanley was marrying a wealthy widow and making his home in Italy, steadfast and diligent Clive had risen to becoming the senior partner in the firm. It was for him to tell Polly exactly what was meant by taking over her father's assets and responsibilities. Thankfully his task was made easier knowing that Polly was married to this man Carpenter who had such a hold on her father's finances but, even so, he had never faced a task with less enthusiasm.

'I understand from your father's letter that he expects your husband will wish to clear the debt raised on the house? Perhaps if he could come to see me? Or arrange an appointment when it would be convenient for me to visit him at Water's Edge?'

'Neither at the moment, Mr Buckeridge. My husband is abroad, in America in fact. It will be up to me to deal with any arrangements – and in this case to carry on repaying the mortgage until a decision is made. Have you been handling it since my father went away?'

'Indeed, yes. Now, I fear, that arrangement must end. He is having his money transferred to him in Italy and his bank account closed.'

'You mean, I have to pay from the share in the business that is still in his name – the share that will be transferred to me.'

The poor man looked uneasier by the second. Sensing his discomfort Bobby took a comforting suck at his thumb and wriggled to get down from Polly's knee.

'Sit still, Bobby. You can't run about in here.'

'Down. Home, Pol.' He drummed his heels against her legs.

'Put the boy down, he can't come to any harm,' kindly Mr Buckeridge told her, glad of the brief respite before he had to say what must be said. 'I'm sorry your father hadn't thought it necessary to keep you informed. But, indeed, one can understand it. Where was the need, when you are Mr Carpenter's wife? It's not for you ladies to trouble yourself with matters of money.'

'Keep me informed . . .?'

'The remaining shares of Seagrove's yard were taken over by

your husband a day or so prior to your father leaving the country. I drew up the final Deed. They came here to sign and payment was paid into your father's account.'

She couldn't be hearing him right, Pappy would never have done a thing like that and not told her. Even in his letter he hadn't admitted that he'd sold out entirely.

'Mrs Carpenter, you're not well. Let me get you some brandy.' The solicitor had expected her to be disappointed that all her father was passing to her was a mortgaged home, but disappointment oughtn't to make her look so stunned. She seemed to be gasping for breath. Dear, dear, he mustn't let her faint, what with the child crawling all over the place and the poor young lady looking white as parchment ... He opened his desk drawer and took out a bottle of smelling salts. 'Here, take a good whiff of this and I'll pour you a little brandy.'

'No. No. I'm better. Just for a moment I felt swimmy. The mortgage. Mr Buckeridge, how much did he borrow on the house?'

She steeled herself for the worst. And that's what she heard. Mr Buckeridge had arranged the mortgage about six years ago, a client with money to invest had made the loan, the Deeds of Water's Edge had been handed over as security. Since then Stanley had paid interest on the loan, but nothing more.

Hardly aware of what she did, Polly picked Bobby up and held him close. He, who a minute before had fidgeted to be free, put his arms around her neck and planted a loud and wet kiss on her cheek. Bobby, he was all she had. The yard was gone, her home was gone ... Harry ... no, don't think about Harry.

In a voice devoid of emotion she took Mr Buckeridge into her confidence, extracting from him a promise not to tell her father that she and Harry had separated. And in that same matter-of-fact tone she enquired how soon she could sell her home. No wonder she hugged Bobby so close.

Closing the front door on Mr Wiseman, a partner in Wiseman & South, Auctioneers and Estate Agents, Polly walked back into the sitting room. She felt mercifully numb. She was selling Water's Edge – or, more accurately, she had asked the agent to find a buyer for Water's Edge. Her home, a place full of memories. Every ornament almost too familiar to be noticed, every room full of ghosts of yesterday, yesteryear. She opened the lid of the piano and played a few single notes, softly this time, not with her usual hammered precision.

'P'ay. And me p'ay.' Bobby drummed his fists on the ivories, laughing with delight at the noise.

She ought to want it to sell quickly. Indeed it must sell quickly, or what money she had would be eaten up. Anyway, she mustn't brood. As if to stress her determination, she squared her shoulders. Tomorrow was another day, a new start – yes, and she'd see to it that it was a successful one too, for her and for Bobby.

'Come, p'ay,' Bobby tugged at her skirt, 'H'ace and p'ay.'

'Soon, Bobby.' She picked him up and he obligingly put his arms around her neck. She looked up at the portrait of Elvira, surely the loveliest person she'd ever known. Oh, Mother, what would you make of it all? Pappy with another wife, me married but with no husband, and soon I'll have a baby – how am I going to manage? If you were here would I be able to talk to you? I never could, but would it be different now? Worse perhaps, you'd probably condemn me and who could blame you? A baby and I don't know who the father is, don't know whether I love it or am revolted by it. You wanted me to marry one of our friends – 'no fresh-faced youth could ever satisfy you' came the memory – and Harry was right, he opened the door of heaven for me. I want him, every day I want him more. Can you understand that, Mother? I want him for my friend, I want him for my lover, she hugged Bobby close, shaken by the aching longing that raged in her. You never felt like that about making love, did you? No, I know you didn't, you suffered it but you never knew the joy, the abandon. Perhaps you did in the beginning, before you were frightened of having more babies. Yet even suffering it as a duty you conceived Bobby. That hateful time with Charles, could that have done this to me? Oh Harry, I can't bear it without you. I want you, want you, want you—

'Tum on, let's p'ay.'

'Yes, we'll fetch Horace and go to the meadow.'

They did, and watching them go down the garden, Horace leaping ahead, Polly carrying Bobby for quickness, Mrs Hume nodded sagely. Something very wrong with that marriage ... hadn't she said to Arth only the other day she had her suspicions young Polly was pregnant, and there she was all alone with her husband making money thousands of miles away. What sort of marriage was that? And the master spending all this time with that Mrs Banks – no oil painting. Certainly it couldn't have been for her looks he trailed after her, not after the poor dear missus. Likely it was for her brass, they said she was worth a mint of money. Well, if he must take another wife it might as well be one with a bit of money to sprinkle, at least he'd get pleasure in helping her spend it. If that's what happened, best thing if they stayed out there in those foreign parts, she'd rather serve young Polly and her Mr Carpenter – *when* he condescended to come home and play the part of a good, decent husband. Now where was that Daisy? Out chattering in the garden most likely instead of being in here peeling the potatoes. Algie was staying for his supper this evening. That meant there would be four of them in the kitchen, plus Miss Polly in the dining room, not that she seemed to care these days whether they put a meal in front of her or not.

By the river Polly played with Bobby with all the verve he expected of her. Later, when he was in bed, she would marshal her thoughts, make her plans. But for the moment she made a supreme effort to hold all her troubles away where he couldn't guess they existed. Looking after Bobby was her lifeline and she clung to it with all her strength.

Chapter Twelve

The still air hung in a mist over the Thames and water meadows, even though overhead Polly could see stars peppering the moonless sky. Climbing to sit on the stile, she pulled her cloak around her but its warmth brought no comfort to the chill in her heart. As if he sensed she was troubled, Horace hovered nearby instead of making his usual wild dash into the darkness. When he stood on his hind legs with his front paws on the step she automatically put her hand on his head. She knew he was swinging his tail even though the knowledge didn't penetrate her confusion of thoughts.

'I had to do it,' she muttered, to be answered by a lick of understanding. 'There's no other way, Horace.'

It had always been her belief that if one was faced with something difficult it had to be grappled with, not put off until tomorrow but faced head on. Well, that's what she had done, not simply because it was the way she did things but because there had been no other course open to her. Now that she knew the yard was Seagrove's in name only, she wouldn't take a penny from it any more than she would draw on the thirty-five pounds Harry had arranged should be paid each month to the account he had opened for her. So what had she of her own? Fifty pounds left to her by her grandfather, that and anything she could raise from the sale of their old home after the debts were paid.

Mr Wiseman of Wiseman & South had been as good as his word. He had told her he expected Water's Edge to sell quickly – waterside properties were hard to come by. He had been even better than his word when it came to finding her somewhere else.

'I don't care how small it is, but I do care that it is by the river. I've always lived by the Thames ...'

She hadn't known how the expression on her lovely face had touched him.

'Large or small, they seldom come on the books. But I'll do my best for you, that I promise.'

He did better than his best. A buyer was soon found for Water's Edge and she was given details of a cottage on the bank of the Thames between Henley and Marlow. From the description she knew it was tiny, she knew most of the furniture from her old home would have to go.

'I don't want to see it,' she told Mr Wiseman. 'If you can make the arrangements for me I'll move out a few days before the new people arrive here.'

'But you ought to see it. It's not suitable for you, I only mentioned it because you were adamant you wanted to be by the water. I feel I should insist you see it before anything is signed.'

She forced a smile that must have looked more natural than it felt.

'You say it has been lived in by the blacksmith and his family. If they can make a home there, so can Bobby and I.'

So the arrangements went ahead, and the time had almost come to leave Water's Edge. It would be someone else's home, another portrait would hang in the drawing room (even if I am going to a tiny hovel and can't hang it, I shall take Mother's portrait), someone else's punt would be in the boathouse, someone else's pony in Tubby's stable.

Horace nuzzled closer and she stopped to rub her face against the top of his head as he stood tall on his hind legs.

'When did he start to borrow, Horace? Six years ago Mr Buckeridge said. All the time Mother and I were spending without a care he was borrowing, gambling in a vain hope that Lady Luck would change his fortune. And I always thought it was just Harry he owed money to. Oh Pappy, how could you go on believing you could gamble your way out of the mess. Or perhaps you have, perhaps Cecily is your Lady Luck after all. I hope so, truly I hope so. But what about me, what about Bobby – yes and the Humes and Daisy and old George Baker? And what about all this, have you forgotten the happy times before any of this happened?

If only Harry were here, the longing was there before she could stop it. Well, he's not and he won't be, she told herself brutally ... and it's no good your blaming everything onto Pappy. The mess you've got your own life into is no one's fault but your own. Don't think about that, you've got to plan the future. Precious little in the way of assets but a mountain of responsibilities.

When first she'd read her father's letter she had supposed that that, and the one he had written to his solicitor, would be sufficient for some sort of alteration to be made on the Deeds and then Water's Edge would be hers, mortgage and all. Her visit to Mr Buckeridge had opened her eyes. It would be weeks, perhaps months, before everything could be finalized; at the best the wheels of law turned slowly and she was left in no doubt that her situation was far from 'the best'. She thought back to her visit to his office, to the hollow feeling of misery as she'd heard herself telling him she and Harry had parted. Poor Mr Buckeridge, entrusted with a confidence that he couldn't pass to her father. If, thinking back to that afternoon, Polly could find one atom of cheer, it was her certainty that he would never break his word to her.

In the murky darkness she could see the black shape of the boathouse; looking up the sloping lawn towards the house she could detect eerie beams of light penetrating the mist. Home – taken for granted just as surely as the sight of her own face in the mirror – she knew the feeling of each tread on the staircase, the shape of each door handle, the smell of baking from Mrs Hume's kitchen, the sound of Arthur Hume whistling between his teeth as he polished Tubby's harness ... Her eyes stung with tears. She wanted to believe they were solely for the lost days of her childhood, but they were for so much more. Horace seemed to know it too, he buffeted her with his head as if to say so. She and Bobby – yes and you, too, Horace – would make a new home for themselves.

Would there be enough money? There could be no 'would there be enough?' There *had to* be enough. She would choose what furniture to keep and what to get rid of. Her mind jumped to her mother's room and to the wardrobe still full of clothes. When her father had asked her to sort them and do as she thought best with them she had emptied the drawers of underwear. In a rare moment of thrift she had kept some for herself, underwear that had never been worn, for Elvira's love for beautiful garments meant that even when she was pregnant she looked to the future; with far more interest than she had given to the baby's layette she had laid up a store of exquisite undergarments for after the birth. Mostly, though, Polly had taken the things to Mrs Warwick to share with her daughters. Despite her present pressing worries she smiled remembering Blanche Warwick's look of wonder when she'd taken the lid off the basket of silken garments. 'Oh, duckie!' Reverently she'd touched the fine material, 'I've never seen such lovely things. Seems a pity to have to hide them away underneath top clothes. Me and the girls, Emmie too of course, we'll keep them for real best. I'll see something is put by for later on for Clara.' Some of the garments had been essential to Elvira's last months, and Blanche had held a voluminous nightgown of fine silk against her. 'Cor, did you ever see the like ... my Bert'll think it's his birthday when I come to bed in this.'

Still smiling at the memory, Polly pulled her wandering mind back to the present. What unrecognized premonition could have made her keep her mother's gowns? The House of Duprés had always been a leader of fashion. It would be a long time before she could spare money for gowns, she was thankful for her mother's flair in dress. Resolved not to be beaten by her plight, she clung to the thought of the gowns, a bright spot in an unknown future.

On the first day of December, with Bobby on her knee, Polly sat by Hume's side as he drove the trap out through the gates of Water's Edge for the last time. With no idea of the enormity of the step they were taking, Bobby looked on the outing as an adventure. Being perched on Polly's lap and getting pulled along by Tubby was a great improvement on being pushed in a bassinet, but the real delight was having Horace sitting on the floor, his mouth wide open in what was almost a smile and his tail giving the occasional thump. For safety's sake, in case he might catch sight of a cat and his canine instinct prove irresistible, Polly had him attached to the leash she held firmly. Behind them was a wagon pulled by shire horses, a wagon so wide it took the whole of the drive.

Tubby led the procession, the trap followed closely by the two shire horses and the furniture wagon. They kept a steady pace, towards Reading, through the town where a few shopkeepers standing on their doorsteps in Broad Street turned to watch – probably their attention attracted more by Polly and her entourage than by the large wagon. Always smart, always taking care and interest in her appearance, today it was even more important than usual that she should look her best. Leaving behind the comfortable and well-run home she'd always known, going to a rented cottage further downstream, she was determined to accept the move as a challenge she would meet head-on and overcome. The first essential was her appearance, probably the one thing she had inherited from Elvira.

Leaving the town behind, they rattled eastward along the main road which until the coming of the railway had been the one used by the Bath to London stagecoach. The plan was that Hume should help Polly arrange the furniture, erect beds and hang the curtains. It couldn't be done in a day, even in a house so small, for Hume was determined he'd not leave her until everything was shipshape. Then they would find someone in the village who would take him back to Water's Edge where Ida was seeing the furniture collected for the saleroom and making sure the house was clean and ready for the new owners to take over at the end of the week.

From his perch on Polly's knee Bobby surveyed the passing scenery, his baby mind awed by so many new sights. Until now his life had been lived in the backwater of a few lanes around Water's Edge; now he was enthralled by the carriages and traps that passed them in the opposite direction. Despite his excitement at the adventure he shivered and thrust his thumb deep into his mouth for comfort.

'Take the rug off my knees, Miss Polly. I only brought it as an extra in case you or the lad felt the chill.'

Polly felt a rush of affection for Arthur Hume. All her life she had taken him for granted, accepting him as unthinkingly as she had the food on the table, the trimmed lamps always lit at dusk, the fires in the grates. Just as Bobby had, now it was she who shivered.

'Pull it up around you too, Miss Polly. There's a cruel bite in the air for so early in the season.'

But it wasn't the cold that made Polly shiver, it was a sudden, overwhelming panic for what lay ahead. To please Hume she pulled the blanket to encase both Bobby and herself, at the same time pulling her spirit back from the plunge it had threatened to take. She must hang onto the belief that, despite all that had happened, somewhere a guardian angel must be keeping an eye on her. Why else should Mr Wiseman have told her about the smithy?

'I'm only mentioning it because you said you wanted to find a place by the river,' he had said. 'I'm sure this couldn't possibly interest you but because of its position and the rarity of anything on the waterside I feel bound to tell you. The blacksmith died recently and the occupants, his wife and son, are moving to Reading. The son used to be with his father, but he didn't want to carry on and there's plenty of factory work in town. It's no more than a working man's cottage, that and the sheds where he had his forge. And for rent, not sale. Not at all suitable, I'm only telling you because riverside properties are hard to come by.'

'Where is it? Do I know it?'

'That's another reason I can't feel you'd be interested. It's too far away. Downstream of Henley – upstream of Marlow.'

She been to Henley at Regatta time, but never to Marlow. But if she had to make a new beginning, where better than in new surroundings. Another thing that tipped the scales in favour of the cottage was that he described it as situated upstream of Marlow, downstream of Henley. Had he told her the road-miles from either place, it could never have made such an impact on her imagination.

'It sounds just what I need. How many rooms?'

'It's not what you've been used to, Mrs Carpenter. The kitchen is smaller than the scullery here, everything is small. Two bedrooms – smaller than your attic rooms – and downstairs two more living rooms and the kitchen I mentioned. Outside sanitation.'

It had taken all her courage to keep the smile on her face and an expression of hope in her voice as she'd asked him to arrange the tenancy for her.

In less than a month it would be Christmas and still there had been no word from Harry. Just once Polly had been to the

243

yard. Now trundling towards her new home she remembered her conversation with Hugh Davies who had always been her friend.

'Are things going well, Mr Davies?'

'Plenty of work, Mrs Carpenter. We've missed seeing you here.'

'I had to stop coming. You can see why,' she laughed hoping to overcome his embarrassment. 'After the baby arrives I shall be free again.'

'And Mr Carpenter? He's gone overseas I hear? Is that the case?'

'Yes, he has. I don't know how soon he'll be able to get home. You all know that my father is making his home in Italy? Yes, of course he will have written to you.' (Would he? With a stab of conscience at her disloyalty, Polly doubted that it would have crossed his mind.) 'I've lived at Water's Edge all my life. Now that my father will be living abroad he has made the property over to me and I'm selling it. I want us to make a fresh start, somewhere of our own. But I don't want to be moving house when the baby's due, I want time to settle into a new neighbourhood before then. So I've gone ahead without waiting for Harry to get home. I've written my new address down for you just in case you need it. See, I'll pin it on the wall so that it won't get lost.'

So far she had acted well in her role of a happily married mother-to-be; the next part hadn't been so easy. 'Mr Davies, I don't know whether my father told you this himself – probably not, because as far as you or any of the men are concerned it will make absolutely no difference. Before he went away he sold out to Harry, knowing that we were marrying you see. They'd been partners here for some time and Harry is adamant the yard will continue to trade as Seagrove's.'

'I'm sorry the guv'nor won't be coming back, but we couldn't have a better one than your husband – and *you*, Miss Polly. I don't forget your kindness to Millie. Can't understand her, you know, the first crook of his finger and back she goes to that burley loud-mouth she's wed to.'

'She's done what she had to do. Any sort of life with him was better than all the comforts without him, that's what she said.'

'More fool her, that's all I can say,' Hugh grunted.

Now, recalling the conversation, Polly felt a sense of shame that she had deceived her old friend, that her real purpose in going to the yard had been to leave her new address, make sure that when Harry came back to England he would know where to find her – if he wanted to find her. She shivered in the raw December air. Any sort of life with him ... she understood so well how Millie had felt. But Harry couldn't be compared to a man like Bruce! What had happened had been all her own fault, each day she realized it more. She'd thought she was in love with Charles, but she'd understood *nothing*. A young girl, infatuated with secret and nocturnal meetings, infatuated with a handsome face, believing what she wanted to believe. In love with romance, and look what it had done to her life.

The bumps of the rutted road made the unborn child lively. It *must* be Harry's, she daren't even contemplate that something of Charles was growing inside her, taking possession of her, the thought filled her with revulsion. Sometimes lying in bed, half awake and half asleep as consciousness returned, she would rest her hands as if she caressed the new life, longing for its movement, a part of Harry, a blessed legacy of their love. Then she'd wake, even more clearly than Harry she would see Charles and would be filled with such loathing for him, for the baby too, that she would be frightened by the intensity of her blind, consuming hatred. She remembered Blanche Warwick holding Bobby to her breast, remembered seeing her weathered and kindly face contorted as she battled to fight back the tears that first morning when the mouth that had tugged at her hadn't been her own baby's. But she had come to love Bobby. In her imagination Polly would see a tiny baby, its eyes dark as coals, and its hair too. How would she bear to let it draw food and strength from her body?

On the December morning as she travelled the miles from her old life to her new, she refused to let anything puncture her determination.

Occasionally Hume gave her an uneasy sideways glance, trying to fathom what went on behind the façade of a happy woman who awaited the return of her husband from the other side of the world, awaited the birth of his child. It seemed to him a rum thing that anyone married to a man with the kind of money Harry Carpenter appeared to have should choose to leave a lovely home like Water's Edge to go to some old blacksmith's cottage. There was more to it than met the eye if anyone asked *him*.

They'd already left the main coaching road, now they turned onto a narrow lane, the following wagon lumbering after them. Coming down the hill they saw the first glint of water through a gap in the trees. They were almost there.

As the men started to unload the wagon, Polly carried Bobby to the water's edge. At least she had *this*. Bobby stumbled about getting in the way as the men put the furniture in place, until Hume called him to 'help' see to lighting the fires. The lamps were lit and hung from ceiling hooks for it was dark long before the corner cabinet – the last item to be unloaded – was brought to its position in the living room. Its gleaming rosewood looked out of place in its new surroundings, but so did everything else that Polly had saved from her old home. Perhaps it was because she was suddenly weary that her spirit sunk so low.

The empty wagon had trundled away. Hume was upstairs erecting her bed.

'Come on, Bobby, we have to put up your cot. You can help me. Upstairs.' The stairs were off the living room, the door leading to them left open. Bobby didn't need telling twice: climbing stairs was one of his favourite things. Polly followed, envying him his energy.

Upstairs, 'helped' by Bobby and with hands so cold she could hardly grasp the nuts and bolts, Polly erected his cot.

'Me told,' Bobby shivered, his energy and delight gone like the flame from a snuffed candle.

'Let's cuddle, that'll make you warm.' She held her arms to him wondering whether touching her might not make him even colder. Clearly love and imagination helped, for he wrapped his arms and legs around her as she knelt on the floor, all thoughts of chill forgotten. But Polly's spirit wasn't so easily restored: he was hardly more than a baby, he put all his trust in her, had she any right to bring him to the sort of existence he would have to get used to here? For *his* sake ought she not to have sunk her angry pride and drawn on that thirty-five pounds Harry paid into her account each month?

Usually she could fight off the demon doubt; tonight she fought a losing battle. With no leaves extending the dining table it was small and round, which was as well for nothing larger would have fitted into the room. She spread a cloth on it and set the meal for two people, herself and Hume; all Bobby needed was a spoon and a helping hand.

'I'll eat mine in the kitchen Miss Polly. It's not right all sitting to table together. There's a lot that's not right about you coming here. What the master would say I don't like to think. Or Mr Carpenter, come to that. Even if it's only for a few weeks it's not the thing at all for you to be here just with Bobby, no one to clean for you, no one to prepare your food, no one to do the wash or iron your things.'

'I haven't come here to idle my time away and be waited on. I have plans for what I mean to do, but I'm waiting until the money comes through for the sale of the house.'

'I don't like to think what Mr Carpenter will say when he sees this place. It's not like the home he left you in when he went off on his business journey.' Hume knew he was sailing on troubled waters but there was something very odd about the whole thing. Mr Carpenter had been coming to the house, but coming as a friend of the master's. Then suddenly, with none of them in the kitchen having any idea that they were sweet on each other, Miss Polly had married him; they'd been like love-birds, that's what his Ida called them; then, without a word of warning he was gone. No letters, no talk about when he was coming back.

'He may not be coming back, Hume.' There, she'd said it! That seemed to make it final, drop the curtain on her brief period of what had surely been perfect happiness. 'Something happened – I can't tell you what – it was all my own doing. I don't blame Harry for feeling as he did.' She squared her shoulders. 'But this isn't the end—'

'You mean you think later on he'll come round to your way of thinking? But Miss Polly, child, why couldn't you have bided your time where you were comfortable and cared for?'

'I mean that for *me*, leaving Water's Edge isn't the end, it's a new beginning. Houses by the river are hard to come by, houses by the river with sheds like the old foundry here are rarer still; but I found this one. It may not be a wonderful house, but we'll smarten it up. As for the sheds, I know exactly what I want them for.'

'Are you going to tell me, Miss Polly, or is it a secret?'

'I want the sheds for a boatyard.'

'But you can't do that, Miss Polly. You say you don't know if Mr Carpenter is coming back – boat work is men's work – and with the little lad here to care for and another one before another summer. Dear oh dear, I don't know what to say.' All he did know was that whatever he said Polly would go her own way.

'From tiny acorns come oak trees. I've learnt a lot about running a business, a boat business. And I shall have boats for hire. I wanted us to do that at Seagrove's, but Harry said people would get the wrong impression and think we were doing it because we weren't doing enough boatbuilding.'

'I just wish the master would come home ... or your Mr Carpenter. If he were with you I'd have no fears. But a woman on her own – worse than on her own, a woman with babies and a home to care for.'

Polly forced a laugh, then surprised herself to find that it wasn't as forced as she'd believed. Whatever she made of the future she would be captain of her own ship; if it sailed on stormy waters she would be a good captain and would keep it steady until she reached the calm.

'Come and see me in six months' time, Hume. No, give me longer than that, give me until the summer season is in full swing. You'll eat your words.'

It was as much as he could do to make himself eat the splendid stew his Ida had cooked yesterday and made them bring to warm up for their supper.

That night he slept on the sofa that looked larger in the small sitting room of the cottage than it ever had at Water's Edge. He told himself it was his cramped space that kept sleep at bay, but in truth it was anxiety and helplessness. The next morning he was up early to light the fires and boil water, then after a breakfast of cold ham and poached eggs – all sent by Ida – he spent his time chopping a good stock of wood while Polly and Bobby went to discover what the village had to offer.

It offered a general store where she brought the essentials for her larder, enough to fill two straw fish baskets.

'It's you who've taken the old smithy, I suppose?' Thomas Searle welcomed her, his rosy face aglow with pleasure at the sight of the new addition to the village community. 'Your hubby a blacksmith, is he? You'll soon settle in, you'll find this a friendly place.'

'I'm sure I shall. No, my husband isn't with me – and he's not a smithy. I intend to start a boatyard. If you know of any good carpenters and joiners, even if they've not been used to boats, I wish you'd tell me. Probably I'll only need one to start with.'

'You're young to be widowed – my goodness some folk do get knocks in their lives. And for this poor little lad too. Don't seem right.'

'I'm not a widow and Bobby is my brother not my son. My husband and I have parted, he's in America. But we were talking about my wanting to hire someone ready to work as soon as I get orders coming in. I know the boat trade.'

The grocer shook his head, lost for words.

'Anything more we can get you?' It was his wife, Jessie, a small woman with a sallow complexion and thin clawlike hands and a sharp voice. Polly had no welcome from her, but she was too busy concentrating on what she considered essential purchases to notice.

'Oh, and one thing more I wonder if you can help me with,' she said, as the jangle of the shop bell announced another customer and she waited while Jessie fitted the groceries into the two baskets. 'Is there someone in the village who runs a cab – any sort of transport, a trap, a hansom, anything? I have someone with me who needs to get home. It's about three miles the other side of Reading.'

The Searles looked at each other doubtfully. Clearly they did know someone and on his own Thomas would have told her but he wasn't ready to oppose Jessie and he could read her thoughts and knew what *she* made of the newcomer: a dressed-up beauty who had a ring on her finger and no husband to show for it, a boy she pretended was her brother and another on the way to fill that bassinet.

'There's Ben, he'd do it,' the other customer spoke to the Searles rather than to her.

249

'Oh ah, so he would,' Thomas beamed at the man who'd made the suggestion.

Polly turned to thank the man and her glance was met by a boyishly frank smile. It was the smile that deceived her into seeing him as younger than he was. It was unusual for a man to be out without a hat, just as unusual as it was for a man to announce that he'd been about to boil the potatoes when he'd found he was out of salt.

'There you are then, Tom my dear,' the hatchet-faced Jessie smiled at him as she put the block of salt on the counter. 'A nice job for one of the boys to rub it down for you. Nothing else you've forgotten?'

It seemed there was nothing else, so the man called Tom and Polly, with Bobby at her side and holding her skirt, turned to leave the shop together.

'Those are heavy, let me carry them outside for you. My bar of salt can sit on top.'

'That's kind. Thank you.' And with hands free she picked Bobby up. 'Can you put them in the bassinet, that's the easiest way of getting them home.' Then, once outside and the straw baskets safely stowed, 'You said you knew someone who might take Hume home? Ben, was it, you called him? Is he far away? Ought I to take this shopping back first and come out again?'

'You're at the smithy?' It seemed the whole village knew!

'Yes. Hume came with me yesterday to help get us settled, but the trap will be left here and I want to make sure I get him home today.'

'Leave Ben to me. What time do you want him to call?'

No wonder Polly gave him that warm smile in her relief to find someone willing to help her. His kindness had already restored her hope in tomorrow.

'Well? What sort of a place has she taken?' Ida hardly waited until Ben and his trap had left them before she asked.

'Not fit for her, not a bit what she's been used to. It's not right, a girl brought up carefully like she has been finding herself with fires to make, cleaning and cooking. Never in her life so much as boiled an egg, how's she going to fare?'

'She'll get help, once she settles in she'll get a daily woman.'

'The sort of place she's gone to you'd expect to find a daily woman living in it, not working there. I tell you, Ida, I don't like to see our little Polly so alone, I'm jiggered if I do.'

'Better off if she was alone, poor girl. But how she's to manage with Bobby so small and another one on the way I tremble to think. It's not often I'm mistaken about a person, but I tell you, Arth, I got taken in by that Harry Carpenter. What they quarrelled about we shall never know – and she always had a will of her own, there's no denying that – but quarrel or no, what sort of man swans off and leaves a new wife, and her already on the way to having his child? More interested in making brass than in looking after a family.'

'Ah,' Arthur agreed, dragging their portmanteau near the door to help the removal men who were collecting them the next day. 'If I were twenty years younger and got my hands on him I'd like to ring his neck for him. Well, lass, we're all set. They won't take long in the morning to collect up the furniture Miss Polly's let us have, then we'll be on our way. End of an era.'

'Good times we've had, Arth. Still, we're to be our own masters, that's one blessing. We don't have to get used to a new household. Give us a day to get straightened out and we'll be cosier than we've ever known, living there above our little shop.' Ida came as near to being excited as nature allowed as she imagined the future that waited for them. 'Always fancied selling groceries, having folk coming in and out to have a chat with. Nice home we shall make there.'

'That we shall. Young Polly's been generous with the furniture and extra bits. And think of Daisy. Frightened to death she'd be sent home to that father she used to make excuses rather than visit. But that was Miss Polly again, getting in touch with the Maidment family and getting the child a place with them. Can't have been easy for her having to write that she had to sell up her old home—'

'Not for us to say what it was she saw fit to tell them. The whole truth, half the truth or a yarn of her own making, that's *her* business and not for us to wonder about. No, Arth, not for us to go round spreading the tale that she's fallen on bad times. We never have talked the family's business around and we won't start now. Enough that Miss Polly and her husband have

251

left the district. But, back to what you say about the furniture she's given us – and all the other bits, curtains, rugs, linen, china enough and a few fancy knick-knacks. When I tried to say my thanks she didn't want to listen. And it's true what she said, if we'd not been living here all our married days, we should have been getting our own things around us all these years. So I suppose it was no more than fair to see we didn't lose out by giving loyal service.'

'Our dues or not, it's not every mistress would have thought that way. I'm bothered about her. Why couldn't she have found somewhere with an extra room, space enough that we could have helped her?'

'End of an era for her and for us too. She's got spunk enough to stand on her own two feet, just because she's never had to do it doesn't mean she isn't able.' To Arthur her words sounded uncaring, but Polly would have heard them as the compliment they were intended.

If there is one thing that spreads faster than a heath fire on a windy day, it's gossip in a small village. Before the week was out there wasn't anyone who didn't know that the new occupant of the smithy was a woman on her own, a woman with a wedding ring but no sign of a man.

'Must think we're stupid, as if we'd believe a yarn like she tells.'

'I'd stake my last sixpence that she's no more got a man than our Mad Monica.'

The women of the village were enjoying someone so unlike themselves to gossip about. Had Polly been widowed, shabby, showing the signs of thrift, that they could understand. Then they would have rallied round to help and not spoken a word against her.

The group was gathered at one side of the small green, where all of them had just come out from buying a few things at the Searles' shop and catching up on the latest news at the same time.

'I saw her sweeping out the old forge. Not that she gave me the time of day, thinks herself *somebody* if you ask me. The little lad was helping – or hindering according to how you look on it. A brother she says. A likely thing!'

An older, but no more benevolent, member of the group nodded her head sagely.

'We can do without that sort in the village. One hanging on to her skirt and one on the way – before many more months she'll be looking for a bit of home comfort. Have you seen the clothes she decks herself up in! Put two and two together and what do you get, eh?'

'Oh Mrs Blunt, you mean you think she's a – well, one of those sort?'

'If she'd got nothing to hide she would give us the time of day, tell us where she's come from. All I say is, wait till she's shed this load she's carrying and you'll find she feels the itch for someone to cuddle up to. Nothing more dangerous that a good-looking woman – and she's *that*, there's no denying – lonely for a man. They're all soft when it comes to a pretty woman giving them the old come-on look and a word or two of flattery to go with it.'

Feeling better for their talk they went their separate ways.

There was nothing Polly thrived on more than a challenge. Not that there was much pleasure in the things she had to do: washing clothes, hanging them out on the line with wet fingers that lost their feeling in the cold, raking the ashes and lighting the fire, filling the lamps, cooking ... it amazed her the eager way Bobby opened his mouth for the failures she mashed up for him! If she found their life a challenge, Bobby found it a joy. All day and every day he was with his favourite Pol, when she shook a rug he jumped with delight, when she set the wood and coal in the grate and lit the fire he squatted by her side, when she groomed Tubby so too did he.

Work she could cope with; each night she went to bed so tired that she collapsed into sleep. There was one thing she hadn't yet found the courage to face up to: her baby was due in April. Long before then she must have arrangements made with a lying-in nurse, someone who would stay at the smithy, look after the birth and take care of Bobby for the time she had to stay in bed. She was strong and healthy, she told herself, having a baby wouldn't be any problem. In her mind she said it over and over, each time refusing to give room to fears ... her mother – what would become of Bobby if she died as their mother had? ... Clara – she'd been strong and healthy too and remember what had happened to her. Would it be retribution that she would lose her life like her mother had and the baby would live, Charles's baby. Oh but it couldn't be his, it mustn't be his. Easier to pull her thoughts away from the whole thing and concentrate on making a home for Bobby and herself, and getting the sheds ready for the summer.

They'd been at the old smithy for a week when she and Bobby took the trap to the village ironmonger and brought home a large packet of whitewash, a bucket and two brushes, one large and one small. She meant to whiten the walls of the one-time blacksmith's shed. Time wasn't on her side, another month or so and she'd find everything more difficult.

Bobby knelt watching her as she dressed for the work ahead, with the agility of the young he squatted back so that, kneeling, his bottom was on the floor and his legs splayed out at the sides.

'What dat?' he asked, unfamiliar with the sight of Polly in a much too large pair of tweed knickerbockers of her father's, knickerbockers that should have come to just below the knee but reached almost to her ankles, the waist held in place with a leather belt. She would have slipped out of the Norfolk jacket if she had buttoned it so, instead, she fastened it around her with a large brooch (completely unsuitable but all she could find), then she pushed her hair inside the matching deerstalker cap.

'What d'you think?' she beamed at her attentive audience. 'I look as big as a barrel. Whatever would Mother say!'

'Ou 'ook man,' Bobby bounced up and down on his bottom, the whole thing was great fun.

Before she could set to work Polly mixed the chalky powder in a half-filled bucket of water then, needing all the light she could get, opened the wide doors leading to the lane.

'Here's a brush for Bobby,' she passed him the small one and he immediately set to work sweeping the floor with it. When he saw what she was doing she expected he would want to do the wall too, but wherever he brushed he could do no harm for she carried the half-full bucket of whitewash and set off up the ladder. There was something very satisfying about sploshing whitewash onto walls covered with the grime of years. In her enthusiasm she found herself sending drops of white all around her, even down the front of her father's jacket. The thought of him made her suddenly homesick for all that was lost, for a childhood when he'd been her hero. How he would have enjoyed doing this, she thought, it wouldn't have been work at all, for both of them it would have been a new experience, a way of having fun. But he was gone from her almost as surely as her mother – and Harry? She looked at the patch she'd whitened, then at the rest waiting to be done and in that moment there seemed no point in any of it.

'You shouldn't be doing that,' a voice surprised her.

'I forgot to bring my Aladdin's lamp,' she retorted none too politely, thumping her dripping brush against the wall and hearing the splash of whitewash on the brick floor.

'Let me be your genie.'

It was then that she recognized the voice and turned to see the cheerful smiling face of the man she'd met in the grocer's shop the previous week.

'It was you who arranged for Ben and his trap wasn't it? You were something of a genie on that occasion. I've a suspicion if you hadn't been there, poor Hume would have had to use his feet.'

'Now there's proof for you that I'm a servant of the lamp! Tell you what, I'll go and get my own brush and bucket then you can do the low bit and I'll mount the ladder.'

'I know it sounds silly – and truly I'm grateful – but if I give up right at the beginning I can't hope to make a success of what I'm going to do here.'

By this time her visitor had come into the shed and was standing by the ladder.

'It's just you and the lad? No one else living here?' he asked. Yet there was nothing inquisitive in the question. He didn't wait for an answer. 'Supposing – I'm not wanting to scare you, but you have a responsibility to the boy – supposing you slipped, got dizzy perhaps. All your determination wouldn't help. He'd be alone here, he wouldn't know what to do – and he'd be too young to do it even if he did. There's no one living close by—'

'I'm never dizzy,' she cut in.

'I doubt if you've ever worked from up a ladder before.'

She climbed down, glad to put her bucket on the ground.

'Let me help, why don't you? We're turning the world topsy-turvy, you doing a man's job here and me cooking and darning – I'm the world's worst darner, the boys would vouch for that – at home.'

'Boys?' Had he been left with brothers to look after, just as she did Bobby?

'My two sons. Herbert is eleven and Archie nine. My wife, Dulcie, died five years ago this month. Up till then I worked at the mill, but now I take on anything that's going and me and the boys get along. I've done so many jobs for folk – to tell you the truth I think they tried to give me work out of pity in the beginning. Taking help out of pity is a hard pill to swallow, but I had to do it because of keeping the home going for the boys.'

'If you do decorating jobs that makes me feel better about letting you help me with the sheds. What do you think it would cost me?'

'Genies don't take money,' he laughed. 'I wasn't looking for work, not paid work.'

'Then humour me. Tell me your rates and I'd love to have your help. But if you won't, then I shall go on doing it for myself.'

'Supposing you fall?'

Polly looked at Bobby, trying to pick up the spots of white and transfer them to the wall; she felt the movement of the new life inside her.

'Pride might be a sin, but it's one I'm stuck with. Please let me pay.' Looking at him with those pleading brown eyes, her solemn face topped by that silly hat, he relented. The price he quoted was low, but she wasn't to know that and her conscience was eased.

That was the beginning of friendship between Polly and Tom Pritchard. Her first impression of him had been as young, openly friendly with everyone, carefree. She soon came to know him better: not so young as she'd imagined, certainly friendly with everyone, but far from carefree. There was something in his cheerful disposition that wouldn't let worries get the better of him. She made up her mind that if *he* could overcome the knocks life had given him and not be cast down, then *she* most certainly wasn't going to be beaten. Her own past had been very different from his, but surely he must have faced a challenge akin to her own.

If she hadn't met Tom the winter would have been completely desolate for her in a village where the local women sensed her background was alien to their own and, more than that, suspected a husband was a figment of her imagination and her advancing pregnancy nothing but proof of the sort of creature who had moved into their midst.

'I can't put off the inevitable,' she said to Tom the week before Christmas. 'If there isn't a lying-in nurse to be found in the village I shall have to try in Henley or, better still, in Marlow.' Henley was probably too near her old home, Reading impossible.

'Have you asked Mrs Peatty? She attended Dulcie for both of ours. Didn't Dr Routh suggest her to you?'

'I've not seen a doctor. Why should I? There's nothing wrong with me except that I'm going to need someone to take care of a confinement. I'm never ill, I told you. But I must find someone to move in here by about mid-April in case it comes early. There's Bobby to be considered, I don't want him to be frightened. Whoever I find will have to be here beforehand and look after Bobby until I can do it myself again.'

'Have you enquired in the village? Jessie Searle knows all the goings on. She would know if Mrs Peatty is already booked to go somewhere out of the village around then.'

'I did ask her but she said she couldn't help.'

Tom looked thoughtful. Was Polly unaware of the gossip about her? Or was she unconcerned? Perhaps both.

'Find me a scrap of paper and I'll write down her address. It's just beyond the green, in the middle of Victoria Terrace. Why don't you slip along there now, while Bobby's having his nap, I'll be here if he wakes up.'

'Tom, what would I do without you?' In her gratitude, she said it spontaneously.

'Get along with you! While you're out I'll do a bit of digging out in the front. Whatever you mean to do with the garden, fruit bushes, veg, even flowers, the ground hasn't seen a spade for years. The soil needs turning and the weeds got out.'

She put out a hand as if she wanted to touch him, an action just as spontaneous as her words. Then convention – and something else she wasn't prepared to admit to – made her withdraw it, simply saying. 'When I get back I'll help.'

It was such an easy relationship with Tom. He was like a bridge between the life she'd been used to and the one she had to face.

Mrs Peatty had been as fast to surmise, put two and two together and make five, gossip and enjoy the interest of this fast young hussy who'd come to live in their midst, as the next one. But she'd been a midwife too many years to put that in front of a woman's call for help.

'I'll look in on you every two or three days once we get to April. Until the baby drops you won't need—'

'Drops?' Polly's eyes opened wide in horror, she recalled hearing Mrs Warwick talk about cows dropping their calves.

'Drops in your womb, gets itself in position ready. Once you get like that I'll bring my things along and stay in the house ready. Put me to share the little lad's room.'

Polly walked back round the green with the nearest nature would allow to a spring in her step. Her visit to the midwife had been noted from behind lace curtains in Victoria Terrace and before the morning was over news was on its way: if Mrs Peatty was seeing to the flighty young minx then they would soon get to know the whys and wherefores.

Outside the wooden fence that divided the old smithy's front garden and the lane Polly recognized a woman she had noticed once or twice in the village.

'Look at 'im,' she turned with a toothless grin as Polly approached. 'Good boy he is, dig, dig,' she laughed delightedly.

'Hello, Polly.' Tom looked up but didn't stop working. 'Can she do it?'

'Yes. I'm so relieved.' So she was, for with her confinement arranged she felt she was free to concentrate on the plan she had for turning the smithy into a boatyard.

'Aw, you'm a pretty lady,' the unknown woman stared at her, eyes and mouth both wide open as she nodded her head to emphasize what she'd said.

'This is Monica, Polly. No, Monica, not with your hands. You mustn't touch Mrs Carpenter.'

'She'm pretty.' Her none-too-clean hands stroked the heavy

velvet of Poly's hooded cape. 'Soft ... ah ...' She bent as if she were going to rub her face against the material. Polly recoiled and went past her to reach the gate, so with her back turned she didn't see the sudden change in Monica's expression, her smile giving way to a look of uncomprehending hurt.

'Time you got off home, Monica,' stabbing his spade in the ground Tom came out of the garden and put his arm around her, coaxing her to face towards the village. 'Your Smut will be wanting his dinner. What have you got for him, eh?'

Happiness was restored.

'See,' she opened the package she carried and showed him fish heads and scraps in a crumpled piece of brown paper.

'Good girl, he'll like that. Off you go and give it to him.'

'Smut'll like that,' she repeated, chuckling. 'He'll like that ... he like ...' She went out of earshot walking with purpose towards home.

'You mustn't mind poor old Monica, she wouldn't hurt a fly. Mad Monica, that's what she's known as. She'd been like it all her days. Lives in a tumbledown place up by the wood. She kept asking where the boy was, hoping he'd come out to see her.'

Chapter Thirteen

In the shed where the blacksmith had plied his trade, instead of a forge and anvil there was just one canoe; but where the walls and ceiling had been grimed by years of smithying, now, by the time Tom Pritchard had finished with them, they were clean and white. It wasn't the first time Polly had gone into the shed and, in her imagination, seen not just one canoe standing alone but the floorspace taken up with craft that waited for the days of summer.

That's where she went on a bright frosty morning just three weeks after she moved in, Horace coming to sit at her feet and gaze at her as if he shared her thoughts. Following them, Bobby dropped to his knees to crawl for speed, then pulled his hands up as if he'd been stung.

'Pol ... an' me, Pol.' He wanted to tell her how the brick path, looking funny and white this morning, had bitten his fingers but he hadn't the words.

'And you, Bobby.' She lifted him into her arms where he cupped her face with his soft, baby hands to illustrate what he hadn't known how to say. 'Poor fingers, so cold, put your arms round my neck and cuddle up.' Even better, he put his icy hands down the back of the neck of her gown, his smile back in place as he touched her warm skin.

Inside the shed they surveyed the waiting floorspace.

'Bo ...?' he enquired hopefully, 'Pol an' me, bo ...?'

'Not today, Bobby. It's too cold. Soon we shall have lots of boats.' She knew perfectly well he couldn't keep up with her conversation but she needed to speak aloud. 'I must have a landing pier built. I'll speak to Tom. He'll know who'll do it for me. D'you think we'll get our money from Mr Buckeridge before Christmas?'

He had no idea what she was talking about, but it was nice in this funny place, just him and Polly. He gave her a loud kiss on the cheek to express his feelings. He heard the sound of footsteps in the lane, yes, they were stopping, someone must be coming. He pulled himself as tall as he could in her arms so that he could see out of the high windows in the big doors that led onto it. Perhaps it would be those boys again, the boys who had come with the man with curly hair and a big smile Polly called Tom. He couldn't quite reach to see, but the footsteps had gone past.

Polly had been listening too, she knew just what it was passers-by stopped to look at.

'Shall we go and see the sign Tom made for us? Come on, let's go and read it again.'

He had no idea where they were off to, but wherever it was he had a warm, cosy feeling; there was nothing he liked better than when he and Polly did things together. Still holding him, she opened one of the heavy doors of the shed and stepped directly into the lane, followed by Horace who anticipated something more exciting than walking the few steps to the little wooden gate leading to the front garden. On it was a new wooden sign: Riversway. Tom had burnt the letters into the wood with a red-hot poker, letters that stood out bold and clear and caught the eye of every passer-by.

She was still admiring it when Bobby pointed to a red-clad figure coming from the direction of the green.

''Oo dat?' he wanted to know, certain that he only had to enquire and Polly would be sure to have an answer for him.

This time he wasn't disappointed.

'It's the postman – and he's coming to *us*, Bobby.' It was no use, try as she would to tell herself there was no hope, yet each time she saw that scarlet-coated figure she imagined an envelope bearing Harry's writing.

'Good day, ma'm. One for Mrs Carpenter.'

'That's me. Thank you.' She could feel the wild beating of her heart. Almost frightened to look at it, she took the letter.

Since she'd moved in, her only correspondent had been Mr Buckeridge. A straight transfer of the mortgage to her name wouldn't have entailed so much legal work as that and the sale of the house too. Legal wheels grind slowly and she was still awaiting anything due to her after the debt had been cleared. She told herself that today's letter would be something to do with the repayment – she even prepared herself to learn of some unanticipated hitch. By schooling herself to expect the worst, anything better came as a good surprise. But today her heart told her this letter was different. It wasn't in a long parchment envelope like the others had been.

Forgetting her momentary pride in the new nameplate she hurried up the brick path to the cottage. She wouldn't let herself so much as glance at it until she was indoors. Like a child savouring a sweetmeat, saving it until last, she put it on the table, face downwards and took off her heavy cloak. Then she helped Bobby out of his coat.

Let it be from him, let it be him and – and what? She was afraid to finish her silent plea, even in her mind she was frightened to ask. Was it excitement or fear that made her fingers feel like cotton wool as she turned the envelope over and looked down at the writing.

It wasn't from him. She was ashamed that she could feel such sick disappointment at the sight of her father's handwriting.

'Pol?' Bobby tugged at her skirt.

'We've got a letter, Bobby. A letter from Pappy.' This would be his reply to hearing that she was moving to Riversway, for even before she'd seen the old smithy that was what she had decided her new venture should be called.

'My dear Pol and Harry,' she read.

Had she been dreadfully wrong not to tell him the truth? She'd been careful not to tell him lies, only by inference had she left him to suppose that when she wrote that:

We are moving down the river to a waterside property beyond Henley. A long time ago before we were married I told Harry that I wanted us to branch out into hiring out rivercraft at Seagrove's. You know how each summer there are more pleasure boats on the river. He was adamant that putting another string to our bow would give the impression that the boatyard was on hard times. Of course I can see he was right. So Riversway will have no connection with the yard and I'm having a free hand, more or less. At least I shall have, once your grandchild is born!

What crime was there in letting him believe Harry was with her, in letting him imagine Riversway a property of the same standard as Water's Edge? He would know that Harry would go to nothing less. Telling him the truth would only mar his newfound paradise.

She read on.

You are wise to move, every married couple deserves somewhere that isn't full of memories of the past, especially memories that haven't been shared. As for the new venture, I'm sure it will be a great success, I too could see the future in it but there is no doubt of the truth in Harry's view. Time was when there would have been truth behind the opinion people would have had about such a venture; but, thankfully, those days are gone as far as the yard is concerned. You have been my salvation, Harry, I am humble enough to admit that without the hand you took in my business affairs my own life would have been poorer indeed. It was knowing that you were there to shoulder my burden and to care for my very dear Pol that made my present life possible. One day, perhaps when your child is settled with a capable and dependable Nanny, the two of you will make the trip out here to visit us. The beauty of the surroundings, the release from the pressure of business and the ever-present company of my dear Cecily must surely make me the happiest of men.

I await your letters with interest. As for the business side, I take it as read that you will prosper. *You* of all people Pol know my love for the river. Give a man a stout pole, a punt and the river, he is surely king of all he surveys.

Cecily and I are now going to don our walking boots and stride out for an hour to give ourselves an appetite for our meal.

Give my regards to Davies when you next visit the yard.

I remain, as ever, your devoted Pappy.

She was happy for him, of course she was, she told herself as she folded the pages and pushed them back into the envelope. She felt the touch of Horace's cold nose on her hand.

Bobby felt uncertain. Why did she sit, her eyes closed, and that funny sad look on her face?

'Pol? Up me, Pol.' She lifted Bobby onto her knee, rubbing her face against his. Pappy hadn't even mentioned him, he might have forgotten his existence ... poor little boy. It was easier to think that her feeling of loneliness was on Bobby's account.

She dreaded Christmas, Bobby too young to appreciate any effort to make the occasion special. As a child she had always gone to the village church with her parents on Christmas morning, feeling an aura of wonder all around her; perhaps it had been frosty, perhaps dull or even wet, but nothing had been able to take from her the illusion that on that one day the world was full of goodness, different from yesterday, different from tomorrow. She'd never shared Christmas with Harry – and for that she was almost grateful as the days of December built towards the festival.

It was Tom's eldest son, Herbert, calling at Riversway with his father to bring her some homegrown Brussels sprouts, who made the suggestion. He was kneeling on the floor with Bobby playing with a wooden train, something else fashioned by Tom.

'Why can't Mrs Carpenter and Bobby come to us for Christmas Day, Father?' In truth he had been ducking the thought of the day as much as Polly had herself. At eleven, he could remember back to when Christmas had been so different. His mother had cooked a goose, and he and his father and Archie had cheered with all their might when she'd brought in the plum pudding topped with a sprig of holly from the garden. It hurt to remember even, it gave him such a wobbly feeling in his tummy.

'She's probably got family coming, or perhaps she's being taken to visit her people.' But from the way he looked at her Polly heard what Tom said as an invitation.

'No, Bobby and I will be on our own this year. But talk about it to Archie too, all of you decide before you invite us.'

There was no need. It seemed that Archie had been the one to suggest it to Herbert.

'Then, as long as you let me help with the preparations – my cooking isn't up to much but I can make decorations, holly balls, stars, all that sort of thing. I always used to make them at home and gather holly to deck the pictures and ivy to twine through the banisters.'

'Will you do that to ours?' Herbert forgot that eleven was almost adult.

'We'll all go out on Sunday and gather the greenery,' Tom caught the spirit and, Bobby, without a clue what the sudden change of mood was about, bounced up and down on his bottom laughing uproariously. And hearing the magic word 'out', Horace misunderstood the arrangements and went hopefully towards the door.

So they got through their first lonely Christmas. Polly made her first appearance in the tiny village church (no doubt giving the locals plenty to gossip about) sitting with Tom and his boys, Bobby wriggling from her knee to Tom's in an attempt to get near Herbert and Archie. In her slightly off-key voice she sang, bidding 'Good Christian Men Rejoice'.

For the Pritchards it was the best Christmas they had had for four years and, for Polly, it helped to put her aching unhappiness temporarily to the back of her mind. There was an upright piano against the parlour wall and Tom, showing yet another talent, playing it almost as efficiently as Polly. Unlike her, he had no party piece with fireworks and a loud pedal (how the thought of it brought back the first night she had met Harry, the night Bobby had been born and their lives had changed), but he played carols while they all sang, even Bobby crowed with delight and Horace stretched luxuriantly as he lay on the hearthrug content that all was well with his world. Then Tom was persuaded to open a music book of ballads. His tenor voice wasn't strong, but it was in tune and easy to listen to.

'Play your squeezebox, Father, you haven't played it for ages. Let's get our things out. We know lots of tunes. Yes, let's do that!' Archie was beside himself with excitement.

'A good thing the neighbours are out,' Tom laughed as Herbert gave Bobby an upturned saucepan and a wooden spoon to bang it with.

Now it was Polly's turn to take her place at the piano. It

seemed Tom's talents knew no bounds as he took up his accordion, and what the boys lacked in expertise they made up for in enthusiasm while Bobby banged his upturned saucepan with all his might.

So passed the days she had dreaded, and soon the year was over and new one begun.

By mid-January Mr Buckeridge's letter arrived enclosing a statement of her finances resulting from the sale of Water's Edge, his own expenses being withheld. She wasted no time, that same morning she wrote thanking him for all his help and, perhaps out of interest and perhaps because she was uncertain whether what she planned would involve any legal work, she told him exactly what she meant to do. Then she wrote to two firms of boatbuilders, both of them well down the river and away from Seagrove's yard, telling them her requirements and asking for quotations.

It was a bright day and Tom was working outside. From her canoe he was sinking supports into the bed of the river ready for a landing stage.

'There's some hot soup – it may be awful, but at least it's warm,' she called to him.

He had done many odd jobs for Polly, jobs he'd undertaken of his own accord out of friendship. But what she wanted to talk to him about today was different.

Their meal consisted of homemade vegetable soup thickened with split peas and garnished with thyme to enhance the flavour. In fact Polly was beginning to enjoy cooking, there was something very satisfying about preparing food. As to cleaning grates, lighting fires and persuading them to burn, washing clothes, they were a necessity that had to be endured – at least they had to be endured until the day when Riversway Boat Hire would make enough for her to afford to have them taken off her hands.

Their meal was simple, crusty bread, a wedge of cheese and a bowl of soup.

'This is good, really good. What's that green stuff on it? I must do this for the boys.'

'It's thyme. Mrs Hume gave me lots of herbs she'd dried from the garden before we—'

She stopped short and he looked at her enquiringly. Pretending not to notice she helped Bobby keep his spoon the right way up and carry the mush of bread and soup to his mouth.

'Tom, I've written to boatbuilders to ask for estimates. Three skiffs, three punts and probably two fishing boats. I've asked for prices for building – and I shall know if they're fair prices—' Again he waited for an explanation which wasn't forthcoming. 'I've asked if they have, or know of, any good used boats instead of having them built purposely. If they ignore my question I shan't think much of them, I know very well that at a boatyard they usually know where something can be found. If I have to buy new, I do. But I want to be sure we have them on the water for the beginning of the season.'

'We?'

'I was coming to that. Tom, you've a living to earn. I can't have you spending hours doing friendship jobs for me. It's not fair to Herbert and Archie. And I'm not stupid, I know very well you underpriced yourself when you told me your charges. Riversway won't earn us a fortune in the beginning, I have a feeling the villagers aren't going to be queuing up to hire my boats.'

'You mustn't be upset by them, Polly. They're slow to accept new people, but get to know them and they're a good crowd. I know that's true. When Dulcie was ill I was smothered with kindness – and after she died, too. They surrounded the boys and me with loving kindness, yes, I mean that, *loving kindness*. Can I speak out to you? You won't let it spoil things between you two and me and the boys?'

'I'd be foolish and lonely if I did.'

'Well, the folk in the village are plain, simple sorts. You, a woman on your own, yet you keep a pony and trap. Not many of them have a trap, even those with a husband. When you walk down to the Searles you're always so smart, so elegant – there's never been anyone like you in the village, it sets you apart. Even the lady from High Court, the mansion a mile or so out, high on the hill, even she hasn't your sort of elegance. Not that she ever walks in the village. They can't make you out. That's the truth of it.'

'What do they want? My life history?' she replied tartly.

'No, Bobby, eat it properly.'

Bobby pouted at her sharp tone and stirred the mush in his bowl in retaliation.

'There!' Tom was working a piece of bread between his fingers, turning it into a doughy pellet without realizing what he was doing. 'You don't like what I said, that's what I was afraid of. I just wanted you to see that when they don't seem friendly it's most likely that they feel uncomfortable. You probably intimidate them. Just to hear the way you speak tells them that your life hasn't been like theirs. If they have daughters they go into service or, if they're clever with their sums, there might be a chance that they'd rise to serving behind a counter somewhere. They don't resent you for being different, they just don't know how to deal with it.'

'Tom, they can please themselves. I don't give a fig for what they think of me. I was just saying that if I'm looking for river trade I'll have to cast my net further afield.'

'Once they see you working with the boats their attitude may change, some of the men will want to take out your fishing boats.'

'Perhaps. But I can't keep a business going on the pence I can make from the villagers. And we're a long way out of town here. Harry said it would be no use trying to hire out boats if people had too far to come to get on the water.'

'Harry?'

She'd spoken without thinking. No, she admitted as she looked at Tom's questioning expression, she'd voiced Harry's views out of a despairing need to relate what she was doing now with what she had suggested that afternoon on the landing stage, a despairing need to say his name and remember the grip of his hands on her shoulders, his softly spoken words saying he loved her.

'I'd wish you'd talk to me,' Tom said helplessly. 'Don't you know I'm your friend? Won't you trust me?'

'I do trust you. But, Tom, what's the use of looking back? It's the future I have to think of.'

'As you will. But it might be easier to look to the future if you could lift the burden of the past.'

'Forget Harry, you mean? I'll never do that, I don't even want to. But I'll tell you.'

She did. Not everything, she had too much loyalty to her beloved Pappy to disclose how it was Harry had come into their lives.

'My father and Harry had been friends a long time, in fact Harry had had an interest in Seagrove's Boatyard. My mother died when Bobby was born. That was what changed so much at home. I married Harry and father sold out to him—'

'Wait! Sold out what?'

'The yard, of course, I just said he already had an interest. Before I married Harry I used to help Pap – my father – look after the bookwork, that's how I know about pricing. Anyway, after our wedding my father went abroad where he re-married.'

'What about Bobby?'

'You can see "what about Bobby". I'd always looked after him, he's better with me. My father doesn't know it's *just* me, I've never told him that Harry and I have parted. He's so happy – and he deserves to be, I'll not spoil anything for him.'

'Do you still love Harry?'

'That's a pointless question. I don't want to talk about it. But you deserved to be told about Seagrove's and how it is I've had some money from the sale of our old home.' No more than that, not a word about a mortgage having to be paid, not a word about her father having sold out the entire business to Harry without telling her – and not a word about the reason she and Harry had parted.

By the end of the week she had received estimates from the two boat-building firms. She had worked out her own estimate of costs and knew that both yards were making a fair bid. The scales were tipped in favour of Kennedy & Child because their letter contained something more than a quotation for building new craft or even details of secondhand ones that had come into their possession at the recent closure of a rival company.

The landing stage was taking shape, but of course it was over shallow water and for use with small craft. Even as she read the letter Polly's mind was racing ahead.

'Tom, read this.' She hurried to the water's edge, the letter in her hand and Bobby hard on her heels.

'Stop,' he repeated the warning he'd had constantly drilled into him, 'not go near water.'

Tom read. 'But Polly,' he said, 'you'd get no trade for a boat like that! Not here.'

'But it wouldn't be *just here*. Put your hammer away and come indoors, it's too cold to talk out here.'

Indoors she poked a blaze into the coals and spread the letter on the small dining table. Tom could see by the way she smoothed it flat that she meant business. Bobby sensed there was nothing for him here, so he trundled the wooden train Herbert had given him into the kitchen where the cold stone floor had been covered with a rug from his old nursery bedroom.

'It will be four or five months before the river's busy with pleasure traffic. I shall order two new boats to be built and I shall ask Kennedy & Child to do any necessary work on the used boats for me. As for the steamer, I shall expect them to make sure it's sound and the engine in good heart, but as to smartening it up, we can do that ourselves. We must have it here by May, that'll give us time to make it shipshape before Henley Regatta at the beginning of July. It's providential, don't you see? A firm closing just when I want to get started. And a steamer! I've driven one, you know. When we built one at the yard we gave it its trial when the engine was fitted. I took it upstream, learned how to turn it, then brought it back ...' Her voice trailed into silence ... Harry standing close behind her, his arms encircling her as she held the wheel, his hands covering hers and guiding her, his voice quietly encouraging her.

Tom watched her closely, knowing he'd lost her attention and, in part, guessing why.

'Why don't you write to him, Polly?' he said softly. 'Not for me to interfere, but pride isn't worth the heartache it can cause. One day it might be too late.'

She shook her head.

'It's not pride, Tom.' Then she braced herself to face the job on hand, gave him her usual bright smile and told him, 'Anyway Fate decides in the end. Why else do you think an opportunity like this has dropped in my lap.'

It had always been her nature to rush at what she wanted; Tom was more wary.

'You don't have your baby until April. That's going to take

270

your time and attention for months after that – and there's Bobby.'

'I know … I know … and I can't see how I'm going to manage any more than you can. But manage I will. Each day has to be taken as it comes, that's something I've learnt already – and I know you have – then, before you know it, you find a piece of the pattern has slotted into place and you're on to the next hurdle.' She spoke with such resolve that he knew she wouldn't give an inch to doubts. He envied her her hopefulness.

'Overcome one hurdle, then on to the next,' he repeated in a note of dejection she'd not heard from him before. 'Not much of an outlook is it.' It wasn't a question, it was a hopeless acceptance.

'Not the one we'd chose, but it's up to us to make something out of what we've got to work with.' She willed his eyes to meet hers. 'Right?'

'Right,' he put his smile back in place. 'Sorry, Polly. It's just that once in a while it hits me what an uphill road it is. So? Get it ready for Henley, you say. I'm your man.'

'There will be plenty of trade for the small craft at the Regatta.'

'But there's a yard there already. No one's going to hire a boat here to go to Henley. The races would be over for the day by the time they got there,' he added with a laugh that told her he was overcoming his rare attack of the blues. 'Polly, I don't want to put a damper on your hopes, but do think carefully. You're talking of investing an enormous amount of money. It's an awful gamble.'

'I can't live on capital and do nothing. What money I have has to be made to work for me. And as for people taking a boat down the river to Henley from here, give me credit for more sense than that! Don't you know what happens?' Henley Regatta had always been a social event for the Seagroves, a place of high fashion and elegance – and for Polly, all that plus the excitement of the races. Elvira had gloried in the admiring glances turned on her, Stanley had enjoyed the festive atmosphere, Polly had loved it all.

'You mean the racing?' Tom asked her. 'Of course I do, everyone knows. Walk up the lane here to the main road at

Regatta time and the place is alive with carriages. I've walked all the way to Henley to see the racing, many a year I used to do that when I was a lad. And, like you say, there must be a mint of money for the yard there, all the boats on the water.'

'And you shall go again this year, Tom, but you won't walk. We'll take Tubby and the trap. Or I suppose *you'll* take Tubby and the trap, and perhaps your boys. I'll have to be here, the baby will be too young to take out all day. Let me explain what happens.'

She had a wonderful effect on him, he felt more cheerful by the minute. He drew his chair nearer to the fire and prepared to listen.

'In June, about the middle of the month, there's an auction in Henley for renting riverside plots to boat hirers.'

'But you said you wanted the steamer to be ready? We can't go up and down Henry Reach giving people steamer rides.' Despite her certainty, he was still not convinced.

'No of course we can't, although I sometimes wonder why they aren't more strict about keeping all the small craft further back from the course, there's a positive flotilla of small craft on the water. That's why we simply must get all our boats there – but not the steamer. And we'll make a large placard saying who we are, the newest hire business in the area and – now, listen for it! – we'll set out on the placard exactly what services we have to offer for the steamer. We can't compete with the bigger boats, they cover the river from Oxford to London, they're on the water for days at a time. We don't want that, do we?' She didn't expect an answer, they both knew that being away from home was impossible. 'Anyway the *Victoria* will be different from all the others. She'll be for private hire – not for people to drive themselves, of course.'

Still he was unconvinced.

'How many people are there around these parts who'll want to hire a steamer? None, Polly, that's the truth. You'll be throwing away a mint of money.'

She tossed her head, he recognized the danger sign.

'Faint heart never won fair lady. There are plenty of people downstream, yes and upstream too, perhaps in Henley, certainly in Reading, who could be persuaded that a party on the river is much more exciting than a party at home or in a hotel. Think how splendid a Wedding Breakfast would be, or how romantic a twenty-first birthday party? Children's birthday treats would be much more thrilling than playing hunt the thimble or musical chairs at home. We'd take the boat wherever they wanted to board – Marlow, Maidenhead, Reading, Henley and all stages between or beyond. It's just an embryo of an idea, but just you wait until we have the *Victoria* here to be prettied up, you'll see how right I am.'

'I hope so, Polly. You're putting a lot of money into it. If it falls flat, what have you got to live on? Two children to bring up. Dreams don't feed them. Believe me, I know. I must get back to my work, you don't pay me to sit here by the fire talking.' Friend and employee, his boyish grin was as friendly as ever as he stood up and pushed the chair back tidily under the table.

'We'll need to hire a wagon to take the boats to Henley, and it'll take two men to load and unload. Think of someone if you can, Tom. The boys might like to earn a few shillings going along with you and helping you there.'

He looked at her affectionately. There she stood, a deserted wife, soon to be a mother, with stars in her eyes at the thought of turning her hand to something of her own and making a success of it. He'd never heard her give way to self-pity, she seemed to defy Fate to deal her another blow.

The boats arrived, three skiffs, three punts and two rowing boats for fishing, with oars, poles, paddles. Once they were unloaded from the wagon and brought into the erstwhile smithy she realized there would be very little room for taking in repair work. Looking proudly at her very own flotilla of boats, even one so small, she was prepared to brush that aside as irrelevant. This was only the beginning, the half of her that bubbled with excitement at what she was embarking on raised her spirit with hope; while the other half of her wasn't brave enough to look ahead and face what a sham it was to pretend that creating a business could ever fill the void in her life.

The wagon which had brought the boats had left. The landing stage finished, Tom had gone back to his work driving piles into the riverbed to support a short pier for boarding the steamer, which would be brought down the river as soon as they were ready. The afternoon was bright and, the better to admire the arrivals, she had left open the double doors leading onto the lane. That was why she was carrying Bobby who had reached the age when he liked to explore.

To anyone else, probably with the exception of Tom and his boys, Bobby's excited ''ook bo's, lo's bo's' would have been unintelligible, but Polly heard it clearly as 'Look! Boats! Lots of boats.'

'Ours, Bobby. Yours and mine.'

'Me down, me in boat.'

He'd be safe in there, and each day she found it more tiring carrying him. As she stooped to lower him into a rowing boat, a shadow fell across them from someone standing in the doorway. Bobby was facing that way, he was quick to recognize their visitor and from his delight it was apparent it was no stranger. Until she stood straight and turned she imagined it must be one of Tom's boys; who else could put that look on Bobby's face?

'Many boats,' Mad Monica was gazing in wonder at the shed she'd always known to contain the forge. 'They're for the water, you should put them out on the water,' she nodded sagely having imparted such wise advice to Polly.

'We shall soon, when the weather gets warmer.'

Whether Monica took in what she said she doubted for the vacant stare was back in her round blue eyes. The walls were the next thing to attract attention, she smiled as she ran her hands along the whitened brickwork. 'Dirt's all gone,' she nodded her approval.

'Tom did it,' Polly tried to coax her towards the door as she added, 'And here, see how nice he's made the doors look.'

'Tom?' Monica had forgotten her newly decorated surroundings at the mention of a name she knew. 'Tom here?'

To say that he was working on the river would have been like an open invitation. Although over the weeks since she'd first encountered the strange creature she had come to realize that Tom was right when he said she was harmless, this afternoon she wanted her gone. But apparently Bobby didn't.

'Tum i' bo'' he suggested, hopefully. Polly understood of course but, sure that the invitation would have been beyond Monica's comprehension, had another attempt to urge her to the door – to it and out of it.

Go, just *go*, she pleaded silently. I feel awful, I shouldn't have helped with the boats. It's my own fault, Tom told me not to. Please make the pain stop. Please make the wretched woman go away. Even as she thought it she was smitten with shame. Monica was as innocent and harmless as a child.

Thank you, the pain's going a bit. Oh, what's she doing now?

Monica was making to climb into the punt with Bobby. Easier to put the floor slats in than argue with her, with both of them in the boat Bobby would stay where he was.

'Wait while I put this in, then you can take Bobby on the boat.'

Monica's mouth opened wide in a smile that was evidence that her intellect was on a par with Bobby's. Hurrying to get the slats in before Monica put her full weight on the unprotected hull, Polly felt the world spin, she was overcome with a feeling of nausea. She must get to the air, to that dreadful outside closet she had never been able to get used to.

When Tom saw her blunder across the garden and into the shed-like place without waiting even to close the door, he knew something was wrong. He threw his mallet into the punt and took up the paddles, but by the time he'd tied it up and run to her she was outside in the air, leaning against the side of the wooden building.

'You're not well. Polly, you shouldn't have helped with the boats, I said you shouldn't. I ought to have made you go indoors—'

'*Made me*?' Her white face twitched into the semblance of a smile. Then she clamped her bottom lip tight between her teeth. 'Can it be the baby? It's too soon.' Please God help me, it was too soon with Mother too. Don't let me die, please don't let me die. Harry, oh Harry, if only you were here. In some blind, unreasonable way she was sure that if Harry were with her everything would be right. She gripped Tom's hands, her nails cutting into his palms. He saw beads of sweat on her white brow. 'Is it just ... because ...' she panted 'I was so sick ... oh, oh,' she was trapped in pain that blinded her to everything else.

'I'll take Bobby and get Mrs Peatty. First you must get indoors.'

275

'Bobby's in boat, Mon—,' she buried her head against his shoulder and felt his arms strong around her.

As the pain receded he took her indoors. Out of its grip, if only for moments, she watched as, with Bobby in his arms, he guided Monica out of the boatyard, as only hours ago she had rather grandly christened it. She saw him carefully shut the doors behind them then, with a final word to the simple soul, unheard by Polly but clearly enough to send Monica happily toward the poor hovel where she lived, he raised Bobby to sit astride his shoulders and set off at something between a walk and a run to fetch the midwife.

It was only midway through March. Polly's tortured mind was frantically doing sums: if the baby were Harry's it couldn't be born for three weeks, probably a month; if Charles had made her pregnant it was still too soon. But its father was more likely to be Charles than Harry. Fear rather than logic was behind her thinking. Black hair, eyes like coals – no, no, please no. When had she started to cry? I want to love it, I can't, oh don't let it be his. I was wrong, I was stupid, but how much more have I got to be punished? Isn't it enough for You that You've let me know what love is, real love, then taken Harry away? Are You going to punish me for the rest of my life so that every time I look at it I'll remember what I did? You're supposed to be a god of love, but if You do that you'll be a god of vengeance. 'Vengeance is Mine, saith the Lord.' Mrs Hume used to have that on the wall in the kitchen, worked in crossstitch, something she'd made when she was a child. 'Vengeance is Mine.' Here's the pain, it's coming again. Suppose Mrs Peatty doesn't get here in time, suppose she's out. Help me, help me. Forgive me for what I was thinking, don't make it worse because I couldn't trust You. Help me, there's no one else. Harry ...

Just as he had through the months she'd been at Riversway, Tom took charge of the situation, taking Bobby home with him to share Archie's bed. He'd looked after his sons since Herbert had been six and Archie four, but pinning a napkin on a child at night was a new experience for him. Bobby seemed to think the performance great fun and added to the sport by playing hard to catch, egged on by the boys. In fact, he thought the whole thing a surprise treat, actually to share a bed with Archie, to be 'one of the boys' with his friends.

Polly gave birth to a son that same evening, premature, a scrap of humanity no bigger than Bobby had been, bald and as blue eyed as all newborn babies. Holding him in her arms her whole being ached with an emotion that had no name: love, fear of loving, loneliness for the person she wanted and couldn't have, all that besides physical weariness.

Two days later Tom brought Bobby to make the acquaintance of his tiny nephew.

'He belongs to you and me,' Polly told him. 'We have to be very careful with him because he's so tiny.'

'Baby. Why 'ou bed?'

'The baby grew big in my tummy, that's how babies come.' Polly could see Mrs Peatty's tight-lipped disgust. Babies were either brought by a stalk and delivered down the chimney or found in the garden under the gooseberry bush in her experience, and quite right too! The idea of talking like that to a child! 'That's why I'm in bed, just for a few days.'

'See 'ou's tum.' She made no attempt to stop him when he pulled back the blankets, instead she bent down and hugged him.

Mrs Peatty opened her mouth to protest at the next move, only the quick shake of Polly's head stopped her.

'Up me,' Bobby held his arms and Polly lifted him onto the bed. 'Me bed too.'

'Boots off first,' she unbuttoned his boots then let him slide down between the sheets with her. 'Oh, I've missed you Bobby.'

'Kiss poor tum.'

Really that was the last word! Mrs Peatty picked up the linen bag and made for the door. Mrs (Mrs? Perhaps she was and perhaps she wasn't) Carpenter might dress herself in her silks and satins, but there was nothing of a *lady* about her, carrying on like that with a child – and a little boy at that! It wasn't her custom to discuss the mothers she went to care for with her friends in the village, but she owed no loyalty to madam upstairs. In bed with his clothes on, indeed, and pulling up her nightgown so that he could kiss her stomach, whatever was the world coming to!

A week later Polly took the law into her own hands and demanded hot water in her basin, she meant to wash, dress and feel like herself again. She couldn't wait to see if she could get into her proper clothes instead of wearing those her mother had had made when she was expecting Bobby. She couldn't. Disappointed, she turned to second best, thankful that she'd kept so much from Elvira's wardrobe. She pulled the lacing of her stays so tight she could hardly breathe and slipped a soft green velvet gown over her head. Let it fit, bad enough not getting into my own things, please don't let Mother's be too tight. Her prayer was answered. No wonder the corners of her mouth turned up to smile as she surveyed herself. Stepping into the matching silk-damask heeled slippers, she was ready to go downstairs.

First she peeped into the crib where Oliver slept, making snorting baby noises. Forget Charles, try even to forget Harry, think of Oliver as your own, yours and Bobby's. Poor little man. Bobby had a father who wasn't interested, but Bobby always had *me*. You don't look a scrap like either of them – please make him start to look like Harry. Today she wouldn't let herself dwell on Harry, today she must think of herself, of the future she would make for the three of them, herself, Bobby and Oliver.

She returned to her own appearance, so important on what she thought of as her re-entry into the world. It was mid-morning, Oliver wouldn't need feeding for more than two hours, she was free.

That afternoon when Tom brought Bobby to see her she said she was ready for him to come home.

Still dressed in winter clothes Bobby had been allowed to play on the grass in front of the cottage. The gate was firmly shut and, even if he had known how to unlatch it, he wasn't tall enough to try. It was nearly the end of April but on this bright morning there was a chill wind so Oliver was left in the living room where a fire burned in the grate and the fireguard was adorned with clothes airing. He had nothing as elaborate as a Moses basket to lie in downstairs. Instead Polly had taken a drawer from the chest in Bobby's room, laid a pillow in the base, then cut up a blanket to line the whole thing, inside and out. That might have sufficed for some young mothers, but not her. She took the scissors to a pale-blue maternity gown, yards of material, frills from the bustle. She found herself enjoying the challenge of making a beautiful nest for her fledgling. Indeed, it was so lovely it looked out of place in its humble surroundings.

Mrs Peatty was no longer with them so Polly now had her freedom back – coupled with the normal domestic tasks, a daily mountain of linen to boil, and the three-hourly demand from her hungry young son.

Even so she found time to help Tom varnishing the wood-work on the *Victoria*, the steamer that had been delivered to them the previous week. He had recruited the services of Herbert and Archie to help him finish the landing jetty. What they lacked in strength they made up for in keenness.

'They're both all right,' Polly told him as she stepped aboard, 'Oliver is fast asleep and Bobby's digging as if his life depended on it. I'll have to teach him that digging has to stop when the seedlings go in next month.' As she spoke she'd taken up her brush and continued with her task where she'd left it when she'd gone to do her ten-minutely check.

'I never thought you'd be able to cope with all of it, most women couldn't. Even women brought up to it would find looking after a home and two babies enough, without finding time to work with the boats—' He stopped speaking, yet she felt he had meant to say more.

'Don't stop,' she laughed, 'I was just enjoying listening to you sing my praises. Am I putting this on too thick do you think?'

He took her brush from her and led her to sit on one of the seats along the side of the cabin.

'Polly, I've got no right to say this, I'm a paid employee.'

'Tosh! We're friends, I don't know how I would have managed here without you and the boys. What's the matter, Tom?'

'The matter's something I never expected to happen, not after losing Dulcie. And it's not right that I should even talk about it.'

She was at a loss. He was her very dear friend and clearly he was in some sort of trouble.

'It's not something wrong with one of the boys?'

'What?' He looked mystified at the suggestion. 'The boys are fine – they come in and out here as if it's almost a second home to them. And Bobby, Bobby looks for them.'

'They're lovely with him – making a man of him already.'

'It's as if they're one family to see them together.' His courage was mounting, he told himself Polly's thoughts were moving in tune with his. 'We could make them one family ...'

More than his words, it was his sudden grasp of her hand that brought home to her what he was working towards.

'Tom, I have a husband.'

Tom hesitated, to say too much could so easily drive a unsurmountable barrier between them, yet what he was suggesting was too important to let him accept her answer as a final refusal. Very gently he took her other hand in his, turning to her and willing her to meet his eyes.

'You've told me as much as you wanted to about your marriage but, Polly, you've got to face up to it being finished. He left you when you were expecting his child. If he had any affection, any interest even, can you honestly make yourself believe that before this he wouldn't have wanted to know about the birth? Supposing you'd lost your life – and many a woman does – what sort of a man is it who would turn his back on a helpless baby? Forget him.'

'Nothing alters my being a married woman. He went to America, I don't even know where he is.'

'He could be traced. He's a businessman, you told me that yourself. Someone must know how to contact him. Do you know his solicitor?'

In a moment's weakness she indulged in the luxury of having someone caring enough about her to try to shape her future.

'My own solicitor has heard from him, he must have the address. But even if I agreed, I've no grounds to divorce Harry. *He's* not broken our marriage vows.'

'What sort of a husband is he? And what sort of a father? I know I've nothing to offer – except that I love you. I never expected to say that to another woman after Dulcie, I thought that if you loved once it could never happen again.'

Her silence dented his confidence more than her protestations that she wasn't free.

'Perhaps I shouldn't have said anything, I didn't mean to, like this,' he looked at their surroundings of wet varnish, half dry paint, the air heavy with the smell of turpentine.

'This is the way we usually are,' she tried to laugh, 'the time we've shared hasn't been a bed of roses – and if we spent the rest of our lives together, this is pretty much the way it would be.'

'You mean you—?' She heard the hope in his voice. Dear Tom, faithful, loyal, caring for her and for Bobby and the baby too. With Tom and the boys they could be one family ...

'You're rushing ahead too fast.' If Harry cared ('I'll love you until the day I die' ... and she'd believed him. How could she have been such a gullible fool?) then Tom was right, of course he would have made enquiries, wanted to know about the baby. Or would he? Tom had said, 'What sort of a father is he?', perhaps not a father at all. Oliver didn't look a bit like Charles, but then so far he didn't look a bit like anyone except himself.

'I must go and check the children.' She needed space, she couldn't even think straight while Tom looked at her like that.

'Stay here, I'll go. If you could never love me, Polly, then I understand and I promise I'll never mention it again. Is that what you're frightened of telling me?'

'No ... yes ... no, I don't think it's that. Tom you're very dear to me, and so are the boys. For their sake – your boys and mine – we would be doing the right thing, we would make a fine family. We'd work hard with the boats, we'd build a good business ... I've no grounds to divorce Harry even if I wanted to.'

'It's much more simple for a man to divorce his wife. You could all move in with the boys and me, my house is bigger than this. We could let his solicitor be told that you're living with me, I could be cited as correspondent. We only get one life, Polly, don't let's waste it in loneliness.'

She knew how difficult it must have been for Tom to make such a scandalous proposition.

'Are you going to listen for Oliver or shall I? And I expect Bobby's covered with garden dirt.'

'I'll go, you sit and think.'

He was gone longer than she expected. When he came back,

it was to find Polly busy varnishing the surrounds of the entrance to the cabin.

'I was a long time because I was talking.'

'To Bobby?'

He laughed. 'To Bobby and his friend. No wonder he's so quiet, Monica's there with him. They're busy making mud castles with the water from the butt, using an old paint tin to shape them. Nothing happier than a muddy child – or in their case muddy children, for that's what poor Monica is at heart. I thought you would be thinking, not varnishing.'

'I think better when I'm busy. Tom, I'm so fond of you – but while you've been getting used to what you're suggesting, I've always thought of you as a friend, someone who shares my interest in the business we're going to run. I need time to get used to seeing us all in a different light.'

She hadn't needed any time to decide that she was in love with Harry: she had known in a blinding flash the night she'd tipped Charles off her punt and into the river. Tom was like no one she'd known, father and mother too to his sons, he was big-hearted enough to be father to Bobby and Oliver. Honest and hard working, he wasn't a man to make speeches – flowery and empty speeches – 'I'll love you until the day I die'. Would she never be able to forget? In that moment, she believed she hated Harry.

Chapter Fourteen

It seemed that Tom could be relied on always to know 'just the man'. That was how he'd described Ernest Glover when Polly had said they would need a covered wagon to transport the boats to Henley, somewhere where Tom and the wagon owner could sleep and keep guard over the craft tied up at the water's edge in Mill Meadows.

'Is he from the village? Are you sure you know the sort of wagon I mean?' Polly queried. She'd certainly seen no sign of anything as roomy as she would need since the day her own furniture had been transported.

'He's only a few miles off, I'll walk over and see him, leave a note for him if he's out doing a job. You can trust Ernest. He does a bit of removal work – just from working cottages, not the sort of furniture you brought with you, but his wagon's plenty big enough for our needs. In fact, unless he's tied up already he's tailor-made for us. I've written a letter to the school, telling them I want to keep the boys off lessons at the beginning of next month so that they can come along with me.'

'Do you think they'll give permission?'

'For the Regatta? No one would stop them taking time out to work at the Regatta. I'll go and see Ernest tomorrow, just so long as the boys can come here to you if I'm late getting home.'

'Do you have to ask? I thought we'd established that this was their second home?'

The sentence hung between them. She wished she'd chosen her words more carefully.

In the weeks since that spring day when Tom had told her

his dreams of making their families one, neither of them had referred to it. If it was time she wanted then he would give it to her. But how long was he supposed to be patient? How long before she faced the truth that her husband wasn't worth remembering? Was that why she hesitated, did she imagine herself still in love with him? Surely a woman with Polly's strength of character couldn't be fooled by a man who could desert her when she needed him most and not even enquire after his child? If only she'd give him the chance, Tom swore he could prove to her that love and loyalty went hand in hand; they would share the interest of the business, they'd share the pride of seeing the four boys grow, they'd be one united family.

They both knew what was uppermost in each other's mind.

'Have you thought about it, Polly? I said I wouldn't push you, and I won't. It's just that I'm so sure I could make you happy. We're friends – above all else we're friends – but I want the chance for us to be more than that.'

'I think I love you, Tom. No, I don't *think* it, I'm *sure* I love you. And the boys too.' So why were her brown eyes so full of trouble as she looked at him.

'We've both loved before. Is that what stops you? Is it the thought that you would be second best to Dulcie?' His words took her by surprise, for that she could be second best was one aspect she'd not even considered! 'Nothing can be the same as the first time, Dulcie was the only girl I'd had eyes for even when I was just a lad. We have to take what life offers – and for you and me it's offering a second chance. We could make it work well for all of us. Put him out of your mind, Polly, out of your life. I swear I'll never give you cause to regret it.' He looked at her, but her face betrayed nothing but a sort of mute sadness. 'Write to your solicitor, tell him you're prepared to give Harry grounds to divorce you. Marry me, for my sake, for the boys' sake and I vow on everything I believe I'll see to it that it's for your own sake too.' She nodded. She imagined them in the future, a scene of domestic bliss. 'It's as if it was ordained for us to be together,' he told her, his hands firm on her shoulders.

She bit her lip, fighting to push away memories of those other hands. Tom was right, if ever marriages are made in heaven surely theirs would be, why else had Fate sent her to the old smithy, why else had Tom come upon her in the Searles' shop on her first morning here? They enjoyed everything they did together, Bobby adored him and the boys too, Oliver would grow up to look on him as a father – and no child could have a better one. She raised her arms to draw his face towards hers, his mouth to hers.

There was something akin to reverence in the way he kissed her ... Harry, what am I doing? I've closed the door on the past. And so I must, I mustn't remember any of it; this way will be a fresh start. I love Tom dearly, he's a truly good man – a better man than you are Harry Carpenter.

'I'll write to Mr Buckeridge,' she said, seeming to stand back and listen to her own words. There! It was done! And this time when he covered her mouth with his she knew there was more than reverence in his desire for her.

'We won't say anything to the boys yet,' he told her a minute or two later. 'We can't tell them anything as monumental as this and expect them to keep it a secret. It'll be a while before you're free to marry. Time enough then.'

'I thought I was going to live with you? We need grounds for me to be divorced.'

'That's just for you to tell your solicitor.' He held her close in his arms, she could feel the warmth of his face as he moved it against hers.

'Don't you want us to make love?' Sharply he pulled away as if her words stung him, she imagined she saw shock in his expression. 'Well? Don't you?'

'Of course I do. But we can't. It might be months, longer than that even, before I can make you my wife. We'd live in constant fear that you might get pregnant. Do you think I'd let you be the target of every gossipmonger in the region? I won't give any of them the chance to point a finger at you and, when you're finally free for me to marry you, to think it's out of necessity.'

Back flooded the memories ... would Harry have been prepared to wait? No, came the answer, no, and neither would she. They had been driven by something strong beyond themselves. Then another image: what if instead of Tom – dear Tom – it were Harry she meant to name as her lover? Would he care about the villagers' whispered innuendos? No, and neither would she. She rested her head against Tom's shoulder, she felt his fingers caressing the nape of her neck.

Fate, a guardian angel, God, call it by any name, it was giving her a second chance.

That's how Bobby found them as he came in from the garden followed by faithful Horace.

'And me,' he ran towards them, hugging their legs to try and include himself in the embrace. 'Me 'queeze too,' he laughed excitedly. Then he remembered the reason he'd come in. 'Holli c'ying,' he announced.

'Thanks Bobby. Let's go and get him, shall we?' Polly extricated herself from Tom's hold.

'Me wiv *him*,' indicating his intention to stay with Tom.

'Come on then my son, we've work to do. Find a polishing cloth for him Polly and he can rub the seats.'

Lifting Oliver from the bassinet, Polly watched them walk out across the jetty and onto the *Victoria*, Bobby riding astride Tom's shoulders, Horace close behind, his tail flailing. The river flowing gently where a swan glided silently by, the cottage garden with peas almost ready for picking (peas Tom had put in for them, plants grown from his own seeds), all around her the scents and sounds of summer, the baby in her arms, Tom and Bobby talking as they embarked on their work ... what could be more idyllic?

Polly's eyes stung with tears she refused to shed.

The previous day Tom had taken Tubby and the trap to Henley to the auction for moorings. Compared with the requirements of most boat-hire companies his needs were insignificant, space for nine small craft – and that included Polly's own canoe and the two rowing boats intended for fishing. He came back triumphant, their plans were falling into shape. So, the day after Polly had promised to write to Mr Buckeridge he went off on his second mission, this time to hire Ernest Glover and his wagon. And that same morning Polly dropped her letter to Mr Buckeridge into the pillarbox.

The day was oppressively warm, there wasn't a breath of wind and the leaden sky hung low overhead. The die was cast. No longer could she hide from writing to tell her father the truth – or part of the truth. Indoors the kitchen range made it unbearably warm, even with the windows flung wide there was no air. Leaving the mundane jobs she disliked, she went outside to trim the front hedge.

'Me do some,' Bobby's suggested hopefully.

Soon he was wielding a broom, scattering the fallen cuttings and imagining he was playing a useful part in the project. The day seemed empty without Tom.

'Ssh,' Bobby whispered, holding his finger to his lips. 'Dat Holli. We get?'

Oliver was thriving just as tiny, premature Bobby had. Now when she bent to take him from where he lay in his bassinet he opened his mouth in a gummy smile of recognition. At three months old what little hair he had was showing promise of being the auburny chestnut of her own and her father's; as for his eyes, they were a startling pale shade of blue, already fringed with dark, curling lashes. But what did that prove? Remember her mother's lovely blue eyes. Now, as she lifted him, Oliver thrust his tiny fist to his mouth and sucked furiously.

'We do Holli?' Bobby considered it to be a shared job.

A dull day, probably with a storm brewing, it was hardly the time to sit out of doors, but with such heavy cloud the cottage was gloomy, so she dragged a dining chair out to the brick path, then sat facing the river with her back to the lane. While she unfastened the buttons in the bodice and Oliver snorted and waved his arms in anticipation, Bobby waited by her side. Usually they went up to the bedroom and he 'helped' while she sat in the low nursing chair to feed their baby, but if he considered this a break with routine he took it in his stride and decided to roll on the tiny patch of grass with Horace instead.

Homing in on his goal Oliver sucked with all his might. Polly closed her eyes and clenched her teeth tightly together, as if that way she might escape the joy and agony that was almost unbearable and yet too wonderful to understand. Every nerve in her was alive with longing. She forced herself to open her eyes, to breathe deeply and evenly. And she forced herself to listen to the silent argument that filled her mind. Perhaps every woman feels this craving, or is it just me? Is it because I'm so starved – yes, that's how I feel, starved. Her hand gently touched the tiny head at her breast. Oliver fixed her with a solemn stare, she felt he was part of her aching void, a legacy of a joy she had believed would be hers for ever. If Tom were here, they would talk, they would laugh, they would work; she would be strong enough to ignore the ghosts.

Faced with a difficult task Polly had only one way of dealing with it: head on. Before the red-coated postman emptied the collection box in the wall by Mrs Peatty's cottage, she dropped a second letter through the slot, this one addressed to a villa in Italy. Now she had told Pappy there could be no turning back. Not that she wanted to, she added quickly.

That was in the middle of June, two and a half weeks before the Regatta. That evening the dry weather broke in a way all too familiar in the midst of an English summer. Thunderstorms heralded gales that tore at the trees and tore up the poles Tom had put in for runner beans, then hail that danced on the brick paths and rain that lasted for days. The first flush of roses gave up the battle.

Holding Bobby under her waterproof cape Polly came into the shelter of the shed where Tom and his boys were busy sorting out essential accessories ready for loading into the wagon with the boats in two days' time.

'If it goes on like this it'll be throwing good money away to take the boats to Henley at all,' she heard Tom say as the boys busied themselves checking rowlocks, poles, paddles, oars, piling everything ready.

'Where's your faith?' She heard her laugh as forced. 'By Monday there'll be sunshine. Whoever heard of Henley being rained off!'

Her optimism was far from in keeping with her own fears. This was to have been their début, five days with full trade for the small boats, a chance to advertise the *Victoria*. Not that she was relying on the Regatta crowds alone, she had written out a notice and paid good money to have it printed in local papers from Reading to Marlow. Faith, think positively, she told herself repeatedly; and to keep her spirits high she pictured Monday afternoon in Henley, still two days to go before the official start of the regatta, but even by then the town would be full, the air filled with a feeling of expectation. She knew, she'd been part of it! Her mother never attended until the second or third day of the four-day event, but she and her father had enjoyed the early heats, the atmosphere of festival. By the time Ernest's wagon trundled over Henley Bridge on Monday afternoon the sun would be shining, she'd not let herself consider anything less.

As if to reward her for her trust, on Monday she woke to feel early morning sunshine already warm on her face. There! Didn't I know it would be good? She felt she was entitled to personal credit. And as by mid-morning she and Bobby stood at the gate to wave the wagonload of hope on its way, she had only one regret – that she wasn't going too.

Henley town bustled with activity, gentlemen's attire taking on a sporty appearance seen nowhere else, for where else would they have donned cream flannel trousers and boater hats? At Henley the emphasis was on the term 'gentlemen', for those who rowed were all amateurs and the enclosure was filled with the well-to-do and elegant. Here was a gathering of the elite, gentlemen and their ladies, a social high point of the season. Even the less well-off who crowded the bordering meadows near the start of the course – as Tom had when he'd been a boy – or even jostled for a free viewing point in the position known locally as 'Pauper's Gallery' on the northern bank of the river at the bottom of New Street, there wasn't one who didn't willingly get caught up in the atmosphere. The townswomen wore their Sunday best, any menfolk who could spare time from work gave their boots an extra polish.

A quarter of a mile or so upstream the bank was thick with small craft waiting to be hired. Tom was pleased with his allotted patch, as near as any to the railway station.

'Hire a boat, sir?' Herbert accosted what he considered a likely customer as the passengers from the first train of the day spilled out onto the platform. 'No distance to walk. See where that large placard is, no one is better placed. Punts, skiffs, row boats ...'

He wasn't alone in canvassing for custom, every boatyard was represented, some with men looked for by their 'regulars' from other years. He and Archie were the youngest – and the most appealing.

'Hire a boat, sir?' Feeling surer of himself with each customer caught in his net, he smiled hopefully at the party coming towards him. There were four of them, a portly woman who hung heavily on her husband's arm, and following them a younger couple. 'You'll need a skiff, sir? Just down there, by that big sign. No distance, lady.'

'Let's take this boy's boat,' Muriel Maidment puffed, giving the young hopeful a smile which belied the discomfort of the tight lacing of the corset that battled to control her overweight form. 'See, we shan't have to walk too far.'

Herbert raised both hands, palms facing forwards, his signal to his father that this party needed a skiff. In acknowledgement Tom waved his hand in a wide sweep, telling his sons that this was the last boat taken, they could come back to the water.

'You're just lucky, sir, that's our last boat for hire. We're a small firm yet, you see, this is the first time we've had a patch at Henley.'

'Indeed,' Cuthbert Maidment answered, not altogether pleased that a child his age – a child of his sort – should allow himself to make conversation with his betters.

Muriel liked the ready smile, and the way the smaller boy took his lead from the elder.

'Not many small boats,' the younger one put in now, his voice surprisingly gruff for his size, 'but we've a proper steamer. Well, *we* haven't 'xactly, all the boats belong to Mrs Carpenter.'

'You can read all about it on the board there. *And* she's put notices in the newspapers, if you come from around these parts,' big brother added.

Some people might consider it spoke well for the way Tom was raising his sons that they had so much self-confidence; some, like Cuthbert Maidment, might think that they should be taught to mind their manners. Violet Maidment, following her in-laws with her hand through the puny arm of her husband Victor, wasn't interested in the boys themselves, only on what they had just said.

'Carpenter,' she whispered to Victor, 'do you think it could be the same? Remember what I told you Daisy said?'

Determined that there must be more to life than being at the beck and call of Mrs Hume, or her equivalent, Daisy had gone out of her way to catch the attention of the young Mrs Maidment and had been rewarded by being offered what she liked to think of as the post of lady's maid, moving with the Maidment Juniors to their newly built house in Pangbourne. It had been while she helped Violet dress for a dinner party at her in-laws' home that she had passed on a piece of gossip she'd recently heard: Polly Seagrove, or rather Polly Carpenter as she was now, was running a small boatyard the other side of Henley.

Violet enjoyed her chats with Daisy. Perhaps it might be frowned on if her family (or Victor's) could hear their girlish gossip and laughter, but behind her closed bedroom door there was no one to listen.

'It must be wrong,' she said in answer to Daisy's latest piece of gossip. 'Polly Seagrove married Harry Carpenter, you know she did, and he's a real live wire in the business world from what I've heard. What would he want with a small boatyard?'

'Well, I'm only repeating what I've been told, but I reckon it's right enough, I got it from a friend whose father works at Seagrove's yard. Miss Polly's husband was nowhere to be seen when she sold Water's Edge, gone off to America on business. Right off to America! Well, I know that's true, I was still at Water's Edge when he went. And, come to think of it – easy to be clever afterwards – but we never heard a word in the kitchen that he was planning to go, only that he'd gone.

'Anyway, I was telling you – stand up straight while I lace up your stays – I was telling you, Miss Polly went into the yard before she left the old house and gave them her new address. I asked where she'd gone, but it seems she pinned it to the wall and someone must have knocked it down so my friend couldn't find out. But one thing I do know and this is right enough, the yard doesn't belong to the Seagroves any more, it's really *his*, her Mr Carpenter's. But he's not been seen there since before he went off to America. What d'you make of that? Perhaps he's come back, perhaps he hasn't. But you'd think he would, it's a funny thing if he's stayed out there and left her to have a baby all on her own. Now your petticoat, let me pop it over your head.'

Walking down the path to the river, Violet thought of the conversation. At the time she'd assumed someone was adding two and two to make five, but now she began to wonder. And if she'd needed further evidence she got it when the nice-looking man who was hiring out the boats pushed them off from the bank.

'We're done now,' the younger of the boys hadn't mastered the art of modulating his gruff voice, 'that didn't take long did it. Won't Polly be bucked when she knows how well we've done.'

'You ought to call her Mrs Carpenter,' Herbert told him.

'Bobby doesn't, so it's silly for us to.'

A silent glance passed between Victor and his wife.

Henley Regatta saw Riversway Boat Hire well and truly launched. The small boats mixed shoulder to shoulder – or bow to stern – with the others on the Reach, crowding in on the racing craft until it was a wonder the oarsmen managed to keep a straight course. Better even than that, Tom had three enquiries for functions on the steamer, one of which turned into a firm booking for the Wednesday of the following week. It was a twenty-first birthday party, the food would be carried aboard by the household staff at Sonning at six in the evening, the guests would embark at seven. Sounding more confident than he felt, he made the arrangements. He had an enquiring mind and had learnt the rudiments of a steam engine. Twice he and Polly had bundled all the boys and Horace into the cabin and had taken the boat up and down the river. Between them they had handled it safely if not expertly. Once he was home from Henley he would have less than a week to become proficient enough to take it upstream to Sonning, negotiating locks, aligning it with the landing stage so that the caterers and, later, the partygoers could board ... less than a week ...

On the Saturday as soon as the last race was rowed and the last boat returned, he and Ernest Glover loaded them onto the wagon while the boys were in charge of the rest of the impedimenta, and they set out for home. The next day, come sun or storm, he was resolved to learn to handle his new craft. The prospect was exciting; the steamer played an important role in the future he and Polly planned.

Tom was a perfectionist, Polly had seen that in everything he did, whether it was planting out a row of peas (set perfectly straight, distanced evenly apart), whitewashing a ceiling (never a spot of whitewash left where it shouldn't be), making a

292

wooden toy or even cooking a meal. When it came to handling the steamer, he was nothing less. So, through that summer, the steamer trade grew, much of it having roots in that first party. But the days were growing shorter, *al fresco* suppers on *Victoria*'s deck hadn't the same appeal as a summer evening on the water.

'We need music,' Polly decided, determined not to let the season end without a battle. 'No one's going to want to chug up and down the river in the dark unless they're there for a purpose.'

'I could get Ernest to give me a hand carting my little piano aboard. Would people come if there was a singsong do you think?' Unlike Polly's full-size upright, Tom's had only five octaves. Fate again? she asked herself. It was a notice in Mr Searle's shop window that gave her the idea she sought. The Operatic Society were performing in the Town Hall at Henley: 'An Evening of Gilbert and Sullivan'.

'You'd have to pay them,' Tom could see she was fired with enthusiasm, riding so high that she must surely fall. 'Perhaps no one will want to come on the water so late in the season, it may be expense for nothing.'

'Rubbish! Of course people would want to come. We'll hang lanterns, we could colour the glass. Just think what interest it would create. The sound of the singing would be carried along the water, and think how our coloured lights would reflect. Tom, it's a brilliant idea, better even than the summer parties.' How pretty she was, her eyes shining with eagerness. By nature Tom was cautious, circumstances had taught him not to take chances, but it was impossible not to be carried along on the tide of her enthusiasm. 'We'll do some posters, Tom' (she was pleased with her efforts at sign-writing), 'you can take a day putting them up, go with the trap and see how far afield you can spread the word. Alehouses would be the best places, but anywhere you think they'd catch the eye. Our summer's been short this year, we don't want to put the steamer to bed yet.' That was the business woman in her. 'Anyway, think what fun it will be. If we can get one or two from the Operatic Company to lead the singing, you can play the piano – everyone knows the words of lots of Gilbert and Sullivan songs. It'll be the talk of the Thames ...' And that was the woman who loved fun, the woman who had learnt to love it as a child as she and her darling Pappy had gone from one adventure to the next.

That morning she had received his reply to her letter, something she had dreaded and yet now that she'd read it she felt a new certainty in what she was doing.

'Pol my dear,' he had written.

I have read and re-read your letter. What went wrong between you and Carpenter I have no idea. I know only one thing: no man who could leave you as he has is worth a second thought. What was it you used to call him? Shylock. Forget him, my dear, think of yourself and be happy. We only get one life and we have to grasp every chance it gives us of happiness.

When your mother was taken from me I thought that was the end, I'd never have a partner to run in harness with. I had you and I knew I was blessed in that. But Fate, Providence, call it by any name, it had my road mapped out and there was a new and different happiness from anything I had known before.

And so may it be for you, my very dear child. You have too much spirit to let Carpenter's treatment of you cast you down and keep you down – you have too much of me in you for that. So you have cut your losses and made a new beginning – and I may be sure it would have been with boats and your beloved river! This man, Tom, I know what he must have suffered in losing his partner but for him too there is a new dawn. Grasp your opportunities, follow your instinct. You say you are like one family, yours and his. If you needed more evidence of the rightness of what you mean to do, then look no further than Bobby. In a family of 'parts' as yours will be, he will fit comfortably. It has worried me that at some stage Carpenter might have said he ought to come out here to me, his rightful father. It wouldn't have worked, not for him, not for me – and, I believe, not for you either. Now I can put that threat out of my mind.

One thing more my dear. You tell me you are asking Harry to divorce you. He is a stubborn man, I'm sure you don't need me to tell you that. If he refuses to co-operate, then

Pol, put your own happiness above all else. Tell Tom to buy you a ring, go away for a day or two if you care what tittle-tattle your action would otherwise cause, let it be thought that you have been married, be known as Mrs ... you didn't tell me his name.

Remember my dear child you are lucky to have a second chance, grasp it with both hands.

Cecily joins with me in sending her good wishes to you and joins with me in what I say – take your happiness *now,* we none of us know what the next bend in the road may bring.

As always I am your loving – and loved, I am sure of that – Pappy.

The letter had erased a shadow from her mind, it was a blessing on her future from a past that was a cloudless and carefree memory.

The musical evenings went from strength to strength, or truer to say the foundation for what they would be in future years was laid firm and strong. Polly only had one regret; she was never one of the party. Oliver was barely six months old and Bobby little more than a baby – not that she would say so within his hearing, for he bracketed himself with Herbert and Archie and believed himself every bit as much a man. Despite Tom's friendship with her he was still universally popular in the village, so it was he who called in Ben Watt's services. It had been Ben who had taken Hume back to Water's Edge the day after Polly had moved. Always prepared to try his hand at anything, he was keen to learn to take control of the steamer while Tom was busy on the keyboard. There followed afternoons of instruction, but he wasn't a man to be beaten. Sensing their custom would be more likely to come from a larger town, Polly had sent Tom and his notices to distribute around the inns and factories in Reading. She knew that Wednesday was early closing day for the shops there, so she advertised evenings of 'Water Music' each Wednesday and Saturday until further notice. Word soon spread; the *Victoria* chugged a merry load on its watery way, upstream to Mapledurham Lock or sometimes downstream to Sonning or Shiplake. The end of summer had little to offer those whose long working days kept them indoors until the sun had disappeared, but light or dark there was a quality of magic about cruising along the river, seeing the water shimmering blue, green, orange, pink, from the light thrown out by the lanterns. Many a young man lost his heart to a girl made beautiful by the soft glow.

After the first two weeks the tenor and soprano, both leading soloists from the Operatic Society and both costing Riversway the price of their fees, decided the night air wasn't good for their voices. Sophie Brown, a rosy-faced young – or youngish – woman brought the message to Tom as the passengers were loading.

'You may not want me,' she offered timidly, 'but I could try and help. I don't need paying,' she added in a rush of confusion, 'I wouldn't have the cheek to ask, I've never been more than one of the chorus. Fact is, nothing I love more than to sing, and to get other people going. I came up the river with you last Wednesday, never had such a good evening. Like I said I wouldn't take money – just let me on board without a fare. What do you say?' He said 'yes'. Let down at the last minute he had no alternative, although he hadn't noticed her amongst the passengers, so didn't expect her voice to be much help.

The repertoire moved to take on well-known ballads of the day, in some ways everyone enjoyed themselves more without the presence of the two singers who considered themselves in a different category from the rest. Tom and Sophie attacked the lesser known verses, bringing the lusty voices of the passengers in for the choruses. Gladly Polly saved on the charges of the original singers and a week after Sophie had replaced them the boys persuaded their father to let them add to the merriment. Instead of Tom's piano being the solitary instrument the boys added charm, verve and fairly accurate melody, Herbert on a banjo and Archie a tin whistle.

But nothing could last for ever, not Indian summer nor even the still autumn evenings. It was time to lay the *Victoria* up for the winter which, in fact, was a rather grand way of saying they must off-load the piano, carry the assortment of lanterns into the shed and climb up to the loft to store the seat cushions.

'I reckon people would come this evening if we took her just one more time,' Archie pleaded on a Saturday afternoon when November was trying to fool them into believing it was April.

'Not a chance, lad,' Tom told him. 'Ben's coming to help us take the piano home. There's work for both you boys to do, putting the boat to bed for the winter.'

'And Bobby?' Again it was Archie, looking hopefully from his father to Polly.

'Just the man for shifting pianos,' she laughed. 'I can't come, it won't be warm enough to have Oliver on the water.'

'Bobby will be safe enough,' Herbert told her, then seeing Bobby's uncertain expression as he realized he was under discussion, 'and he'll be a help.' Ah, now there was something the little boy understood, so he nodded his head vigorously to show his approval.

'What d'you say, Tom?' Polly was less certain.

'Yes, he can help with the seat cushions, the boys will keep him busy.'

She watched them set out, Herbert hanging on to Bobby as they walked along the jetty and onto the boat. Such a look of pride on his face, it seemed to say that home was for women and babies, boats and work were for the men! From the landing stage she waved, making sure her smile was just as they expected. Then she turned back indoors. This afternoon she would do some bookkeeping, there was nothing like a column of figures to clear one's mind. A column of figures ... an afternoon in the little office at the yard ... Harry's finger running down the column ... Harry's voice telling her she had forgotten to carry from one line to the next.

This morning she had had another letter from Mr Buckeridge. Despite his efforts to obtain information of Harry's whereabouts from his solicitor, all that he had been able to ascertain was that 'his client had been informed that you are asking him to release you from your marriage in order that you may legalize your relationship with the co-respondent. Unfortunately to date he has received no reply and I have therefore requested that he press for action.'

Before she went indoors and forced herself to concentrate on her end-of-season figures, she crossed the grass to peep at Oliver who was sleeping in his bassinet in a patch of pale sunlight. From the *Victoria* she could hear the sound of voices but nothing of what was being said. She shivered, suddenly alone. What was the use of pretending all that was needed was for her to be on the boat with the others, one with them in their efforts? There was no logic in the way she felt. Harry hadn't replied, but what had she expected? A stubborn man, hadn't Pappy said that's what he was? Not to answer at all. Perhaps something was wrong with him ... perhaps he was ill ... perhaps he wanted to punish her ... perhaps—

Going back into the cottage she closed the door firmly and made herself take up her account book and pen. No, pencil first, she'd ink it in when she was sure figures tallied.

About twenty minutes later she heard the rumble of the small piano being pushed on its castors along the brick path under her window. Glancing out she saw the procession set off towards the village and Tom's house, he pushing from behind, Ben on one side, the three boys on the other. Despite her unusual mood of depression she smiled at the sight, then went back to her work with new determination to make the two columns arrive at the same answer.

Success! She dipped her pen, inked over the pencilled figures and underlined the totals. This year her expenses had been high, but she had made a start. Next season, starting with a clean sheet, the books would show a profit. Next year ... the year after ... the one after that ... a feeling of hopelessness stripped her of the pride she strived after. She thrust it away and closed the book. When Tom had finished 'putting *Victoria* to bed' she would show it to him, the pride and pleasure that eluded her now would surely be there when they shared the success.

I'll see if Oliver's awake – or perhaps I'll push him into the village to meet the others. She was lucky, she told herself, she had been blessed with a second chance. And I'll make sure I don't mess things up, she vowed. I truly love Tom, he is the kindest, *best* person I know, I'm lucky, so will Oliver be to have him for a father – and Bobby. If only they could jump ahead, beyond the scandal of a divorce, miss the next few years and start from a point in the future where they were settled, the business growing. At the thought, her mind was side-tracked: yes, it *would* grow, of that she was determined, it would give the other boat hirers something to worry about!

Who was that? At the sound of wooden wheels on the unmade lane, she glanced out of the window, surprised to see a carriage drawing up outside her gate. The cabby jumped down to open the door, she imagined she heard voices, the pounding of her heart seemed to deafen her. And then she saw him. Reason deserted her.

Chapter Fifteen

Harry had come to find her!

Rational thought lost, she ran to fling the front door wide as he walked up the brick path. What did she expect? That he would rush towards her, pull her into her arms? One look at his face and reason returned, her instinctive joy died as suddenly as it had been born. He'd come so that they could discuss divorce; soon she would be free to marry Tom.

Pride came to her rescue wiping warmth from her voice.

'You've come instead of answering the letter.' So controlled, her tone didn't even register surprise at seeing him. 'There was no need, Mr Buckeridge has the details.'

Was Harry rebuffed by her greeting – or did she imagine it? Just as she remembered the first moment her father had ushered him into the drawing room at Water's Edge, so she knew the sight of him now would remain with her always. His thin face, the tight look to his skin as if the flesh covering his high cheekbones and strong jaw was stretched too tightly, his eyes looking into her and through her.

'I heard from him only this morning,' she gushed unnaturally as if he were a mere acquaintance, 'he said you'd not replied.'

'We have to talk. Before I go and see my solicitor—'

'You've been to the yard? Hugh Davies told you where you'd find me?'

Still they stood just outside the door, the pale November sun disappearing behind the trees, the garden full of the decaying smell of autumn. Dark winter ahead, bright summer lost … Like us, like Harry and me, everything that was good – no don't think about it, look straight at him and don't be a fool.

'I shall go to the yard on Monday, I only docked yesterday. It was late last night when I arrived in Reading and booked in.'

'At the George like you used to?' What a pointless thing to say, no wonder he ignored it.

'This morning I went to Water's Edge. I had no idea you'd sold it. Only,' if his expression had told her nothing before, she saw it as scathing now, 'only that you have a lover, Thomas Pritchard, and want me to start divorce proceedings citing him.'

'Tom. He has been my friend since my first day here. He's the *best* person I know.'

'Then you're a lucky woman to have fallen in love with such a paragon.'

'What have you come here for?' She wished he'd go – no, she didn't! No, wait! Involuntarily she took a step to follow him as he turned towards the waiting carriage. As she heard what he said to the cabby relief surged through her.

'Find somewhere to turn the carriage and go back to wait for me at the top of the lane. I'll walk back there when I'm ready.' He waited until the cabby was too far away to overhear them, then he asked her: 'And you *are* in love with him, of course?'

'I told you. Tom's a widower, he has two sons, they're like brothers to Bobby – and to Oliver.'

'Oliver. So you had a son.'

This time she raised her chin and met his eyes with a look that defied argument or sympathy.

'I have a son – your son – but he has had no father. He's not lost anything by it though, he's had Tom. Tom will be a better father to him than one who didn't even bother to enquire if he'd been born.' Careful, careful, keep your voice steady. Don't get angry, anger is too akin to misery. Say something else, quickly, something polite, safe. 'So if you haven't been to the yard, how *did* you know where to find me? I can't believe Mr Buckeridge would have broken a confidence.'

'I intended to persuade him to, I was on my way to call at his offices this morning when I was stopped by a young man who appeared to know me although I can't say I had any recollection of him. One of your young swains, Polly my dear,' (oh, why does he have to say it with that sneer in his voice?)

301

'Maidment he said his name was, a very talkative young man. I had the impression he was leading me to tell him more about you than he knew but he wasn't quite bright enough to manage it. He told me how he'd come to hear that *we*' – she knew he emphasized the word only to stress Victor Maidment's stupidity – 'were running a boat-hire business, by chance he and his family had hired a boat from Riversway at the Regatta. From there it didn't take too much initiative to trace you, instead of calling on your solicitor I went to Henley, to the auctioneers who handle the licences for moorings and enquired where Riversway was based.'

'We did well at Henley,' she told him, partly to impress him and partly to reassure herself.

'Polly, must we talk out here? Aren't you going to ask me in?'

She stepped back and opened the door wider, then he followed her into the small living room. The afternoon light fell across the table where such a short time ago she'd been working, Horace stood up from his afternoon doze by the fire and came to lick Harry's hand in friendly recognition.

'Hello, old fellow.' The familiar way he greeted Horace almost destroyed her veneer of calm. 'I've no right to do anything but what you ask,' Harry told her softly. Perhaps Horace's acceptance of him had unnerved him too. 'None of this need have happened, I should have trusted you.'

'That's not fair,' she found herself defending his actions. 'I ought to have told you about Charles instead of expecting it could be buried just because I'd woken up from a stupid, hot-headed infatuation, and it was over before I came to find you in Brighton. Until that night when Clara lost her baby, I never even considered that mine couldn't be *yours*. Afterwards I could think of nothing else. Fine for you, sailing off to the New World, you didn't have to face it, day after day, night after night—'

'Oh yes, I did, Polly—'

'Not like I did. Every day the baby grew, I didn't know if it was ours or if it was going to be a reminder of what I'd done.'

'I should have been man enough to share that with you. I wasn't. I was too jealous, too hurt, too proud. But Polly never think I walked away and forgot. I wanted to, God knows I tried to.'

'Harry . . .' She moved towards him, she raised her face.

'No! What about the saintly Thomas? Is he to be cast aside when you think you have no use for him?'

If he'd hit her she couldn't have been more stunned.

'I'm not using him,' she said defiantly, 'I love him. That's God's honest truth.'

'And me? What's God's honest truth about me, about us, Polly?'

'You once said to me that you'd love me until the day you died. I didn't see much evidence of it.'

'*Didn't* you? The truth, Polly, God's honest truth, the same truth as I told you then.'

'Yes, I love you, Harry. That's the truth and I wish it wasn't. But I'm not going to hurt Tom, not even for *you*, for *us*. He's the best friend I've ever known, he's loyal, sincere. He lost his wife. He's been bringing up their boys on his own. Now we are like one family.' Her sentences were short, she couldn't trust herself for anything more.

'He sounds more like a brother than a lover.'

'He isn't my lover, he's never made love to me if that's what you mean. I wanted him to, I told him so. Tom believes in marriage.'

'There's only one real basis for a union,' with his hand under her chin he stopped her looking away. 'And we had it.'

'Don't, Harry. If you make me weaken I'd come to hate myself – hate you too. I love Tom, when I'm free I'm going to marry him.'

He dropped his hands to his side, the action distancing them from each other.

'Are you going to let me see Oliver?'

She led him out through the kitchen door to the garden. That was another moment that would live with her always, Harry gently moving back the blanket and gazing at his sleeping son. Harry standing straight again, not quite looking at her as he told her to go back indoors before she got cold.

'If you want your freedom, you shall have it. But not the way you suggested. *I* shall send evidence of adultery.'

When Tom and the boys came back they went straight to the *Victoria*, the work wasn't finished yet. Only later as Archie and Herbert jostled for position to toast teatime crumpets by the bars of the range and Bobby chattered to Oliver, imagining he was telling him about the adventures of the afternoon, did Tom come in from the shed.

'Everything done, except the cushions. It's too dark to put them in the loft tonight, I'll do that tomorrow.'

Wrapped up in their own affairs none of the children had noticed her swollen, reddened eyelids. Now Tom looked at her enquiringly.

'I had a visitor while you were out,' she made sure she said it casually, 'Harry is back from America. He's staying the weekend in Reading.'

The pause was so long she didn't think he was going to comment.

'With friends?' A casual enquiry. As if it mattered where Harry was staying, but she didn't appear to consider it an odd question.

'At the George, that's where he always used to stay. He's promised to be the one to give grounds. Now that he's home it might not take long.'

'Is that the way you want it?'

She forced a laugh. 'Him to be the guilty partner? For myself I wouldn't care one way or another – and it does seem a shame to spoil the village's fun, I suppose, but he insists that's the way it's to be.'

That wasn't what Tom meant.

Next morning he asked her to lend him Tubby and the trap and to give the boys their Sunday dinner if he wasn't back.

'Sophie wouldn't take payment. I know she enjoyed her evenings on the boat, but having her there to get everyone singing made such a difference. I thought we ought to drop something over to her. I've cut the last remaining chrysanths to take to Reading.'

'You know where she lives? That's a good idea. We don't want to lose her, Tom, perhaps she'll come again next season. But if she does we must insist on paying her properly, we don't want favours.'

What was so different about Sunday morning from any other? Polly and her parents had never been great churchgoers,

Christmas, Easter, Whit Sunday and sometimes Harvest Festival, the ceremonial occasions which, for them, had more to do with atmosphere than devoutness. Riversway was just outside the village, the lane was usually quiet, so it couldn't have been that that gave Sunday morning its special quality; without her realizing it, the distant peal of the bells may have had something to do with Polly's feeling that the silence was deeper, the stillness touched with calm, even weekends of lowering skies and rain couldn't turn Sunday into a day the same as any other.

In the stable next to the boatshed the boys were helping Tom get Tubby and the trap ready for his trip to Reading.

'Can't we come too? We could all get in if we squeezed up.' Archie was quick to sense his father's mood, and something told him this was more of an 'outing' than an 'errand'.

'An' me,' Bobby threw in, not knowing what was being suggested.

'No, I want you to get on cleaning up the paraphernalia we brought off the boat. Especially the lamps – it doesn't matter if you leave colour on the glass as long as it's clean colour. Help Polly with anything she wants.'

There were times when it was worth trying to persuade him, but they knew this morning wasn't to be one of them. So, feeling hard done by, they returned to the boatshed and started their jobs – with Bobby's help!

Indoors Polly donned a large apron and started to prepare lunch. Once or twice she looked out to be sure that there was no rocking movement from the bassinet, but its stillness reassured her that Oliver was sleeping soundly. An hour or so went by, the boys had spent as long as could be expected inside the shed and went out to kick a ball on the grass.

'Careful of Oliver,' she called.

Archie looked into the bassinet and fell about laughing.

'Silly Polly,' he shrieked, kicking the ball high and looking for her to share the joke when it landed fair and square where she had laid the baby.

'Stop that!' She was out of the door and across the grass like an avenging angel, while the boys stood still, looking more puzzled than apologetic. 'Why doesn't he cry? What have you done to him?'

'Nothing,' the more serious Herbert answered, embarrassed for Polly. 'He's indoors, don't you remember? You must have put him in his crib ...' That's what he meant to say, but his words faded to nothingness as he watched her.

Oliver was gone! But it was impossible! Upstairs in his crib, Herbert had said ... was her mind going? No, she remembered laying him down, she remembered bending over him ...

'Someone's taken him.' They were frightened by the way she looked around her as if she expected him to appear from the treetops. 'Go to the village, boys, ask everyone you see if there's been anyone about – a stranger ...' Harry! No, but it couldn't be Harry, he *couldn't* do this to her. 'I'll go the other way, I'll look in the water meadows.'

'But he can't be there, Polly, he can't even walk,' Archie pointed out, her look of helplessness making him frighteningly aware that it was up to *them* to do the thinking.

'Someone's stolen him. He didn't even cry.' Perhaps it was a murderer, someone who had crept in and held his pillow to his face to muffle the sound ... perhaps he was lying dead ... but why? Where?

'We'll take Bobby,' Herbert put himself in charge. Frightened by what he couldn't understand and by the atmosphere, already Bobby's lip was trembling ominously.

'Heave ho!' Herbert swooped on the nearing-three-year-old and lifted him into the baby's bassinet. 'How about a ride? We can run, you'll like that.'

Bobby's mind was diverted, laughing in excitement he was bumped onto the path, then out to the lane. The sound of their pounding feet grew distant as they hared towards the village just as the faithful were coming out of church.

'Someone's stolen Oliver, the baby, Mrs Carpenter's baby,' Herbert panted. 'Have you seen anyone suspicious?'

'Hardly likely, not where we've just come from. What d'you mean, someone's taken the baby? What would anyone want with a baby?' Mrs Searle was tempted to add 'especially a baby with a pedigree like that one!' but resisted.

'That gypsy woman was around the doors with her heather yesterday,' someone suggested. 'You never know with those people. They'd sell anything given the chance – even babies I wouldn't wonder.'

'Nonsense, the girl with the heather wouldn't hurt a fly.'

'They're the worst, the sort that looks like butter wouldn't melt in their mouths.'

'More likely the knife-grinder man. He's due any day, we've had the shears ready for him best part of a week. Makes you blood run cold, what a man could do with a sharp blade.'

'Children, children,' the elderly vicar looked despairingly at his flock. 'We mustn't think ill when we know nothing against these people.'

'Well,' Herbert couldn't waste time listening to suggestions – suggestions that were too dreadful to imagine – 'if you don't know anything we must go. Someone must have seen something.'

'Wait, my son, come with me and ask the Lord's help.' Kindly Reverend Sherfield cast his net.

'Thank you, sir, but we won't wait. If you could ask Him for us ...' No opportunity must be lost and, anyway, Archie reasoned, the vicar ought to have a better chance of being listened to. *Someone* in the village might have seen something strange, they mustn't waste time.

Minutes or hours, Polly lost all track of time as with a stick she parted the reeds that grew at the river's edge, scrambled under the branches of overhanging willows, hunted in the hedge that separated one meadow from the next, dreading what she'd see. But no one could have done that to him, an innocent babe, please, please, help me to find him. I'll go home again, yes that's what I'll do, perhaps whoever took him might have realized what a dreadful thing they'd done, he'll have been brought back. The bassinet's gone, but they might have left him in the porch ... No. The shed? No. Indoors ... room by room ... she was beyond reason, almost beyond sanity. Still wearing her apron, her hair that had been caught by branches of riverside trees hanging in loose strands, she set out on her next wild hunt. But where? Where? Help me ... help me ... show me where to look. Coming out of the gate she saw Herbert hurtling towards her and behind, struggling with the bassinet, came Archie.

'Has anyone seen him?' she yelled.

'Not a sign. They say the gypsies were in the village yesterday – if we could find where their caravans are—'

307

'Why should they do it?'

Reaching her Herbert laid a hand on her arm. What a moment for her to see how, even though he was just a boy, already he was so like his father. 'Polly,' he tried to comfort her, 'they say the girl who came round selling heather is kind, she wouldn't let anyone hurt him. They can't be far away, we must find where they've got their caravans. Lots of people are looking. Polly, don't cry like that.'

How long had she been crying? She didn't know, she didn't care.

'You two stay here – all three of you.'

'Pol, Pol cry—' and at the sight of her so, too, did Bobby.

'Stay here in case anyone brings him home. Don't take your eyes off Bobby. Promise me. Promise.'

'Of course we promise.'

Despite himself Archie's nostrils twitched at the smell of roast dinner. His tummy kept rumbling even though he tried to hold it tight so that it wouldn't, but he was man enough not to suggest that if they were left in the cottage they might just as well have something to eat while they waited.

Still carrying her stick, still without hat or coat, Polly sped up the lane in the direction of its junction with the old coaching road. Once she reached the stile she would skirt the field then up the sloping grazing land to the wood. Far up the lane she saw a trap coming towards her. Hope must have suggested to her that it looked like hers, it looked like Tubby; reason told her it couldn't be, there were two people in the trap. She seemed to have lost the power in her legs; she stood rooted to the spot. Her mind must be cracking! Tom and Harry had never even met, they couldn't possibly be sitting side by side in her trap. Could they? It *must* be him, please it *must* be him.

'Speed her up, that's Polly,' Harry peered ahead of them down the lane.

'Can't possibly be. Polly wouldn't come out like—'

'It's Polly, I tell you. Something's wrong!'

By then Tom could recognize her too, and something must be very wrong to send her running up the lane in an apron. He put Tubby into a fast trot, only slowing as they almost reached her. Before they came to a stop Harry sprang to the ground and would have been thrown off his feet had he not kept running in unison with the moving trap.

Then Polly was in his arms, clinging to him, crying, talking.

'Harry – thank God,' she sobbed. 'Someone must have taken him. We'll find him won't we? We will, won't we?'

'Darling, darling, don't cry so. Tell me. Yes, we'll find him.' Who? Oliver? Bobby? One of Tom's boys? Horace?

Nothing was any better than it had been five minutes before, but her panic was lifting. Harry was here, Harry had said 'Yes, we'll find him'. She took the large handkerchief he passed to her and wiped her face. Of course she'd known Tom was there, but only now did his presence really register.

'The boys are at home. I told them to wait unless someone brought Oliver back. He was in the garden asleep – then he'd gone. The bassinet was empty.' Again she was crying, but the frenzy had gone.

'Where have you looked?' Harry asked her, taking off his short overcoat and draping it around her shoulders. She felt the comforting warmth of it, anguish was tempered with relief. Their baby, hers and Harry's ... now he was with her the nightmare would be over.

'I'll enquire around the village,' Tom told them.

'The boys have. The gypsies were here, that's who must have taken him. I'm going to the clearing in the wood, I've seen their caravans there before.' Still she gulped and sniffed, but now there was logic in her thinking.

'We'll go together,' Harry kept his arm around her shoulder as they turned towards the stile.

Neither of them gave a thought to Tom as he watched them go.

Having skirted the edge of the ploughed field they climbed a second stile and started up the hill.

'A clearing in the wood, you say. How do they get their caravans there?' His words seemed to be warning her not to let her hopes ride too high.

'They come in from the next lane. There's a track from there to the clearing. I've seen them there when I've been out with Horace.'

'Horace! Where was Horace? Surely he would have barked.'

'I don't know, I hadn't been noticing him. In front of the fire asleep I expect. He didn't bark when you came in yesterday.'

His arm tightened

'He usen't to bark when I came home to Water's Edge either,' he reminded her.

'If he'd been in the shed with the boys he wouldn't have heard whoever it was. I didn't hear and I was only just inside, I wasn't making any noise. Why didn't he cry? Supposing some madman held the pillow over his face, poor little boy ... Can I borrow your hanky again.' He knew just what an effort she was making to stem the tears.

When they came to the clearing there were no brightly painted caravans, no traces of recent fires.

'They must be somewhere else. It's got to be them. There haven't been any other hawkers.'

On they went, the only sound the crush of fallen leaves under their feet, the first of this year's added to the pile of rotted leaf-mould already there. Sometimes they could walk side by side, his arm around her, sometimes there was room enough for only one so he walked behind her, the pressure of his hands on her shoulder giving her the courage she lacked.

'Hark!' He stopped walking, pulling her back towards him, 'Hark!' he whispered again. Rustling amongst the leaves, not a heavy tread, but something coming fast in their direction. How was it Polly was sure who it was?

'Horace!' she called, if a loud whisper can be termed a call. He bounded through trees and undergrowth towards them, his tail trembling in his eagerness, but when he reached them he spent no time greeting them with his usual licks and leaps; instead he stopped a few feet away then turned and rushed back the way he'd come.

'He's telling us something,' Polly turned to Harry. 'He's trying to lead us.'

Following wasn't that easy even though Horace rushed back and forth making sure they weren't going off course. Still surrounded by trees, in a place that looked no different from that which they'd been beating a track through, he stopped. He even gave a sharp bark, telling them as clearly as any words that they'd reached their intended goal.

'But Harry, he's not here. There's nothing.'

But there was. From behind the trunk of a tall beech a face

appeared, its inane smile one of pleasure in everything in general and nothing in particular.

'Monica,' Polly breathed. 'Mad Monica they call her. Harry, what's she done?'

'Monica,' Harry moved towards the simple woman. 'We've lost our baby. Do you know where we can find him.'

'He'm a beauty boy. Sleep, he'm sleeping.'

'Oh, no,' Polly felt the world reeling around her. Sleeping ... what did the imbecile mean? Sleeping? What's she done to him! It was as if a spring in her snapped. She rushed at Monica before Harry could stop her, shaking the poor child-like creature as if she'd dislodge her head from her shoulders. 'My baby, where is he? You wicked, wicked woman, what have you done to him?'

Harry hauled her off, holding her so tightly against him she could scarcely breathe while he looked over her head to Monica who stood in front of them crying like a child.

'Don't cry, Monica.' His gentle voice didn't stem her tears but she looked at him without fear. 'Just tell us where you've put him.'

'He'm here,' she pointed, 'made the babe a bed, I did. He'm had his dinner,' she turned to fetch a dirty tin plate on which was the remains of some mess that might have been bread and gravy except that it was hard to imagine Monica having the wherewithal to produce anything so nourishing. 'I never hurt him, mu'm,' she turned beseechingly to Polly, 'he'ms a beauty babe. Smiled at me, smiled at Monny.'

True enough Oliver was just as she said, asleep on a bed of leaves, Monica's worn and dirty cloak keeping him warm and Horace sitting by his side keeping guard. Monica's fright was forgotten already, she seemed set for a friendly chat.

'Nice doggy,' she stroked Horace who had the courtesy to lick her hand. 'Them were waiting for me. In the garden, pleased to see Mon. Smiled, 'e did. He'm beauty boy.'

'You shouldn't have taken them Monica. You should have stayed in the garden with them so that we knew where they were.'

'You won't tell no one? You won't get me into trouble? Them's got bars on the window, you won't let them send me where there's bars on the window?' she whispered. 'I never hurt 'im, doggy'll tell you, I never did him no harm.'

'You must never, never do anything like that again Monica,' Polly told her, in her relief she even added: 'I shouldn't have shaken you like I did. I was so frightened because we couldn't find him.'

'Monny didn't mean no harm.'

'All right, Monica,' Harry said, wrapping the cloak round the frightened woman as Polly lifted Oliver from the ground. 'You took good care of him, we'll say no more about it. But *never* do it again.'

'No, sir. I never meant no wrong, sir. Oh but it were won'erful,' the present seemed to be overtaken by memory, 'up the hill we came, Monny and the babe, doggy too. All—' She was lost for words how to express the joy of not being by herself: her, a baby and a dog and her world had been complete.

'Promise that if you want to see the baby you'll ask at the house.'

Monica nodded furiously.

'Tom, he'm weren't there. Would have asked Tom, but he'm gone out, watched him go. Tom a good man.' Until then Tom had been forgotten, now her words brought him close again.

When they started back through the wood Monica didn't attempt to come with them, she turned in the other direction the incident apparently forgotten. Making their way between the trees, careful to protect Oliver from straggling prickly brambles, was no place to talk. It was as they came out into open pastureland, Polly in front of Harry, that she stopped and turned to him.

'Time you held your son,' ordinary words but with a rare depth of meaning.

He took the tiny bundle in his arms. Yesterday he'd seen the baby asleep, now Oliver gazed up at him with eyes of that same light blue as his own. Very gently he touched the small head. 'He's going to have hair like yours. Two redheads to cope with! Do you think I'll manage?'

There was an unreal atmosphere in the cottage, even the boys were aware of it, although they supposed it was simply because Oliver had been brought home unharmed. Harry was conscious of what Polly had told him about the two families being as one: the boys carried the small zinc bath to the rug in front of the kitchen range, she lifted down a kettle of hot water, Herbert filled a jug with cold to add to it, Bobby squatted in his place of importance by the side so that he could dabble his hands. And so Oliver was bathed, put into warm clean clothes and a line drawn under his adventure.

The Sunday dinner had been well-nigh cremated, but there was a feeling of festivity about a meal of toast, spread thickly with butter, then eaten either with strawberry jam or cheese – or in Archie's case a combination of the two.

'It's been quite a day, the boys and I ought to get home,' Tom said, then with a teasing glance in Archie's direction, 'Oliver wasn't the only one looking as though he could do with a scrub.'

Polly's mind was on a plane of its own, if she noticed the meaningful glance that passed between the two men she didn't surface long enough to think about it. She immersed herself in the moment, yet she had no fear that time would carry it away. Like poor Mad Monica, she homed in on what she wanted, drawing every joy from it and seeing no further.

'I've not seen the boatshed,' Harry said. 'Before you go why don't you boys show it to me?'

'An' me. Me come,' Bobby wasn't going to be left out. As if to prove he was a man already he ignored Harry's outstretched hand and followed the others out into the dark. Harry came behind with the lantern.

'Polly, I want you to listen to me.' As she started to clear the used plates Tom pushed her gently back into her chair. 'I love you very dearly. First of all I want to say that. Secondly I know you feel exactly the same. A second chance, isn't that what we said.'

'Tom—' she started, with no idea what she meant to say.

'No, just listen. A second chance isn't like the first, not for either of us. Your Harry isn't the man I expected. What went wrong for you I don't know – no, don't say anything, I don't want to know. One thing is certain, no, two things are certain. One is that you don't need a second chance, your first is still with you. Make sure you never lose it, Polly. Unless it has to be, like I had to lose Dulcie.'

'Tom, I didn't mean to use you. Truly I do love you—'

'I know, I know. And I hope you love me enough to know that I don't want to be second best in your life. Now I come to the other thing. If Dulcie could walk through that door at this minute she is all I would see. And you're worth more than that.'

Her fingers entwined themselves in his. Dear, dear Tom. She ached with sympathy for him.

'You and Harry arrived together?' He heard the question in her voice.

'I knew last night. It couldn't have worked for you and me, Polly. The George, I knew I'd find him there ...'

In the silence, she knew that was all he would tell her.

Epilogue

'One of these days Cecily and I will come home for a visit,' he'd written often enough. In the seven years Stanley had lived in Italy, Polly and Harry had taken the children twice to see him and on each occasion when the time had come for them to leave he'd said the same thing: 'One of these days it'll be we who do the journey.' It had been said so often Polly had ceased to expect it ever to happen. Then had come a cablegram:

Roll out red carpet. Expect us on 12th July. Pappy.

Their house on the seafront at Hove bustled in anticipation, 'We must show Pappy ...' this, 'we must take Pappy ...' there. Until she knew he was coming, she'd forgotten just how much she had missed him through the years. Once the visitors arrived the old magic of his presence was the same as it always had been – and there was something else she saw too: all the children enjoyed him, but between him and his eldest grand-daughter was an immediate bond. Henrietta was five, red-headed, fun-loving, mischievous, just waiting to swim into his net as her mother had done before her.

'What a boy he still is,' Cecily laughed indulgently, delighting in Stanley's obvious pleasure as he let Henrietta teach him the skills of a diabolo.

Fate had given him a second chance, one where he probably found more carefree enjoyment than he'd ever known. Sitting on the balcony, while she talked idly to Cecily, Polly watched those who'd gone across the road and down the shingle beach to the wet sand: her father and Henrietta engrossed in the magic of the diabolo, she could hear their shouts of laughter; then further towards the water's edge, the boys. Bobby was nine and Oliver's hero and mentor. With the white trousers of their sailor suits rolled up to their knees, they were rushing to fill their buckets in the hope of giving their castle a moat. A shout of triumph from Stanley! Applause from his little grand-daughter. How strange that at that moment, as if out of nowhere, she should think of Elvira and feel a sudden rush of love for her, her gentle, lovely mother whom she'd so seldom given herself time to come near to.

Harry came onto the balcony, a letter in his hand.

'From Tom,' he said, handing it to Polly. 'Seagrove's are delivering the second steamer on the twentieth. They've not fallen down on their date. A big day for Riversway. How would it be if we all went up, made something of the occasion?'

They'd been to Riversway many times since she had left Tom to run the business. There had been his wedding to Sophie, and after the ceremony a party aboard the *Victoria* where the bridal pair made music just as they had on many a summer evening river trip; there had been the baptism of their daughter to whom Polly and Harry were godparents; and Herbert's fifteenth birthday which saw him a fully fledged working member of the team.

'Yes let's, I want Pappy to see it all. And he'll want to go to Seagrove's too.' But would he? She suspected he'd firmly closed the book on that part of his life. Was it like that for Tom too? Had his second chance given him enough happiness that he had learnt to let go of his hold on the past? How could one ever let go of it?

She shivered, she didn't want even to imagine. For no reason except a need to touch him, she gripped Harry's hand.